About the Author

Carol Marinelli recently filled in a form asking for her job title. Thrilled to be able to put down her answer, she put writer. Then it asked what Carol did for relaxation, and she put down the truth – writing. The third question asked about her hobbies. Well, not wanting to look obsessed, she crossed her fingers and answered swimming, but given that the chlorine in the pool does terrible things to her highlights – I'm sure you can guess the real answer.

New York Times and *USA Today* bestselling author **Heather Graham** has written more than a hundred novels. She's a winner of the RWA's Lifetime Achievement Award and the Thriller Writers' Silver Bullet. She is an active member of International Thriller Writers and Mystery Writers of America. For more information, check out her website, theoriginalheathergraham.com, or find Heather on Facebook and X, @heathergraham

The Sinful Sleuths Club

December 2025
A Date with Death

January 2026
A Trap for Two

February 2026
A Reunion on the Run

March 2026
A Midnight Mystery

A MIDNIGHT MYSTERY:
The Sinful Sleuths Club

CAROL MARINELLI

HEATHER GRAHAM

MILLS & BOON

All rights reserved including the right of reproduction in whole or in part in any form. This edition is published by arrangement with Harlequin Enterprises ULC.

This is a work of fiction. Names, characters, places, locations and incidents are purely fictional and bear no relationship to any real life individuals, living or dead, or to any actual places, business establishments, locations, events or incidents. Any resemblance is entirely coincidental.

Without limiting the exclusive rights of any author, contributor or the publisher of this publication, any unauthorised use of this publication to train generative artificial intelligence (AI) technologies is expressly prohibited. HarperCollins also exercise their rights under Article 4(3) of the Digital Single Market Directive 2019/790 and expressly reserve this publication from the text and data mining exception.

® and ™ are trademarks owned and used by the trademark owner and/or its licensee. Trademarks marked with ® are registered with the United Kingdom Patent Office and/or the Office for Harmonisation in the Internal Market and in other countries.

First Published in Great Britain 2026
by Mills & Boon, an imprint of HarperCollins*Publishers* Ltd
1 London Bridge Street, London, SE1 9GF

www.harpercollins.co.uk

HarperCollins*Publishers*
Macken House, 39/40 Mayor Street Upper,
Dublin 1, D01 C9W8, Ireland

A Midnight Mystery: The Sinful Sleuths Club © 2026 Harlequin Enterprises ULC.

Taken for His Pleasure © 2006 Carol Marinelli
Undercover Connection © 2018 Heather Graham Pozzessere

ISBN: 978-0-263-42113-2

Printed and Bound in the UK using 100% Renewable Electricity
at CPI Group (UK) Ltd, Croydon, CR0 4YY

TAKEN FOR HIS PLEASURE

CAROL MARINELLI

CHAPTER ONE

'LUCKY YOU!' Maria shouted, holding the punch bag as Lydia boxed away, repeating the words like some kind of chant as Lydia thumped ever harder.

Lydia's red curls had long since worked their way out of her hair tie, and moved in time as she pounded the punch bag, her pale, slender arms delivering surprisingly strong blows. The rhythmic, vigorous exercise was wonderfully cathartic as, egged on by Maria, Lydia vented some of her anger and frustration.

'Lucky, lucky you! Come on, Lydia. Hit harder!'

'I'm done!' Lydia breathed, shaking her head and resting her gloved hands on her knees. 'And *lucky* certainly isn't how I'd describe myself, being stuck here for the next few nights—I haven't had a day off for weeks!'

Even though the place was deserted, mindful that someone could be listening, Lydia spoke in low tones as she pulled off her gloves and turned the sink taps on full blast to distort their conversation. She needlessly refilled her water bottle and took a few moments to splash her face.

'What are you moaning about? Being joined at the hip with Anton Santini is my idea of an absolute dream job. Imagine how I feel!' Maria grinned, offering Lydia her own water bottle to fill. 'Being lumbered playing assistant to his female PA! Why couldn't they have given *me* Anton Santini to guard?'

Lydia held up a long strand of red curls in answer and gave a wry smile. 'I don't somehow think I'd make a very good undercover Italian PA, when the only Italian words I know are the names of pasta!'

'I'd go ginger in a moment if it meant sharing a bedroom with Anton Santini.' Maria giggled. 'I still can't believe they chose *you* to pass off as his girlfriend!'

If it had been anyone other than Maria saying it Lydia would have thought the comment sounded catty, but Maria was simply speaking the truth—it *was* unbelievable that she'd been considered the most suitable person to serve as Anton Santini's girlfriend during his whirlwind visit to Australia.

Anton Santini liked his women petite, stylishly groomed and demure.

Lydia was painfully aware that she failed on all three.

Although her body was slender and toned, she stood five feet eight without heels—five feet ten if her mass of red curls was running particularly wild! Lydia wore jeans and T-shirts like a second skin, and as for demure—well, it wasn't exactly a prerequisite for a detective. Sure, she refused to buy into the beer-swilling, coarse language world of some of her colleagues, but she wasn't exactly afraid of expressing an opinion…

'Smile, Lydia! You're a real misery this morning,' Maria observed. 'This is one of the top hotels in Melbourne, we've been given full access to everything, and here you are moaning…' Catching Lydia's frown,

Maria looked around and, seeing a yawning man staggering into the massive pool area outside the gymnasium, abruptly ended the conversation.

'Fancy a sauna?' Maria asked, and Lydia was about to shake her head—a sauna was the absolute last thing she *fancied* at this hour of the morning—but she knew it was the one room in the place where it had been agreed detectives could meet and talk unhindered.

After rolling her eyes in protest, Lydia gave a very sweet, very false smile. 'What a great idea!'

'How's Angelina?' Lydia asked, once they were wrapped in white towels with the door safely closed.

'Efficient.' Maria rolled her eyes. 'And extremely talkative! I can't believe his entire team travels ahead of him to ensure that everything is to his liking!'

'It's just as well that they do,' Lydia pointed out. 'It's thanks to Angelina's efficiency that we're even aware of the security threat.'

'Yeah, but it's not much to go on though,' Maria mused. 'A bunch of flowers sent to his hotel room before his arrival—they could just be from an old girlfriend—'

'I doubt it,' Lydia interrupted. 'Given that on the two previous occasions Santini was sent flowers he was involved in potentially life-threatening incidents! It's a bit of a coincidence, don't you think? Not forgetting all the abusive phone calls Angelina's been fielding. It's right the Feds are taking this seriously. Can you just imagine the negative publicity if something happens to him?'

'I guess.' Maria shrugged. 'It just seems a bit over the top—senior detectives acting as bodyguards. They've even got Kevin behind the bar fixing drinks—it just seems so extreme.'

'If this deal Santini's looking to sign up goes ahead, then it's going to be such a massive boost for tourism. I'm not surprised that all the stops are being pulled out to protect him!'

Cheerfully ladling water onto the coals and upping the already stifling temperature several degrees, Maria, unlike Lydia, was only too happy to veer off the subject of work. 'I love it here,' she rattled on happily. 'We're going to look fabulous by the time this assignment's over—can you feel your pores unclogging?'

'I can feel my hair frizzing,' Lydia replied, sitting down on the bench. Tears were appallingly close, and she wished she could snap out of her morose mood, surprised at how much Maria's 'misery' comment had stung.

Burying her face in the towel for a moment, Lydia closed her eyes and dragged in the stifling air. 'I really wanted the next couple of nights off,' she carefully elaborated. 'I had things to do.'

'What could you possibly have to do?' Maria smiled, her words laced with friendly sarcasm. 'You know that a detective's not supposed to have a life.'

'I just wanted a couple of days to myself.' Lydia gave a defeated shrug. 'You know—listening to music, eating chocolate, feeling sorry for myself…'

Seeing her friend and colleague, usually so assured, so driven and focussed, slumped on a bench with her face hidden by a towel, Maria faded out the wisecracks, and sat down next to her, her voice gentle. 'What's going on, Lydia? Is it you and Graham?'

'We broke up.' Lydia nodded, finally peeking out from the towel and seeing Maria's shocked expression.

'But you two seemed so happy!'

'We were.' Lydia shrugged. 'So long as I didn't mention work.' She took a deep breath and, closing her eyes, shook her head. 'And with a job like ours it doesn't exactly leave much else to talk about. I thought Graham was different; I thought the fact we were both detectives meant that he'd understand that I wouldn't be greeting him at the door at the end of a long day all scented and oiled in a strappy little number…'

'Graham didn't want that from you.' Maria gave a shocked laugh. 'Lydia, he adored you—jeans and all!'

'I thought he did.' Lydia swallowed. 'But over the last few weeks he's been acting weird. When I was on that drug stake-out he kept ringing me up about the most ridiculous things—'

'He was worried,' Maria broke in. 'That was one hell of a dangerous job, Lydia. I was worried about you too!'

'But you didn't phone me on the hour every hour,' Lydia pointed out. 'You didn't ring me at two in the morning to ask if I needed someone to feed my goldfish.'

'Your goldfish died last year!'

'Exactly,' Lydia said dryly. 'And then we were going to his mum's for dinner one night and he asked me to dress up a bit…'

'Dress up?'

'It wasn't as if I was in jeans or a tracksuit for heaven's sake. I was wearing a black suit! And then he asked if maybe while we were at his mum's I could try to refrain from mentioning work…' Lydia paused as Maria's lips tightened, watching as her friend struggled to give an objective answer.

'Lydia, it *is* a dangerous job, and we do see a lot of the more seamy side of life—it must be hard for any man to put up with, let alone someone who knows the full truth about what we do. I know my father and brothers *hate* my job, and they don't know the half of it! I'm the family shame.' Maria nudged Lydia until finally she managed a glimmer of a smile. 'So, who finally finished it?'

'Me,' Lydia said, chewing on her bottom lip for a moment, not sure whether to reveal her secret—the supposedly good news that had finally brought things between her and Graham to a head. 'I'm being considered for a promotion.'

Maria's eyes widened and a smile broke out on her face. Because they really were good friends, as well as colleagues, and because they both knew how tough it could be to climb the ladder in what was still very much a man's profession, Maria's smile was completely genuine and her embrace was warm as she hugged her friend. 'Inspector Lydia Holmes.'

'It's not definite,' Lydia quickly pointed out. 'But Graham found out, and suddenly all the little niggles, all the little problems we'd been having lately, seemed to magnify.'

'Is he jealous?' Maria asked, and Lydia gave a soft, mirthless laugh.

'Apparently not! He insists that he's just worried about me. He says that he's not sure if it's the sort of job he wants his wife doing. He doesn't think—'

'Back up a second.' Maria was way too sharp to miss a snippet of conversation as juicy as this! 'So you've had an offer of promotion and a proposal?'

'An offer of promotion *or* a proposal,' Lydia corrected. 'It would seem I can't have both.'

'Oh, Lydia.' Maria's groan was sympathetic. The problem was all too usual—one that had been pondered by female detectives the world over. As attractive and as sexy as a kick butt detective might sound to a potential lover, the cruel reality was that she didn't make promising wife material. This didn't matter a scrap, of course—until you met someone you really cared about. 'What are you going to do?'

'I've already done it!' Lydia gave a firm nod as Maria winced. 'We really are finished.'

'Then let's just hope it was worth it. I mean with the promotion coming up and everything—let's just hope you get it.'

'It doesn't matter if I get it or not,' Lydia said firmly. 'It would be nice, but it just wasn't working out between me and Graham. If he can't take me as I am, then it wasn't meant to be.'

'Well, at least you get to lick your wounds in style!' Maria said. 'Full access to the beauty salon *and* you've been placed with Anton Santini—you're a single girl now, Lydia. Who better to have a rebound relationship with?'

'Anton Santini doesn't *do* relationships,' Lydia said, a smile finally wobbling on her face. She felt so much better for having opened up to her friend. She gave a tiny shocked laugh. 'You haven't read what I read last night— his bio's unbelievable! He's always been a bit of a rake, but this last year I swear the man's been on a mission! His list of ex-girlfriends reads like the top one hundred most beautiful people in the world: actresses, European royalty, supermodels, soccer-players' wives…'

'Who?' Maria asked, agog. 'Anyone I know?'

'Yep.' Lydia nodded, but didn't elaborate. 'And every last one has ended in tears—for the woman at least.'

'Is he really that bad?'

'Worse!' Lydia nodded. 'And I'm supposed to be guarding him. God, I hope he behaves himself.'

'Well, if he doesn't you can always pass him over to me—I'll entertain him for you!'

'You'd be so much better at this than me,' Lydia happily conceded. 'You're way more suited to Anton Santini.'

'I'm not sure if that's a compliment.' Maria feigned a hurt expression. 'If you're implying that just because I once had Botox…'

'I'm implying that you're a born flirt.' Lydia laughed. 'I'm implying that you're so gorgeous no one would turn a hair if *you* were draped over Santini's arm. Whereas I'm going to look so awkward and out of place tagging along beside him…'

'You'll be wonderful,' Maria wailed. 'You'll look fabulous and you're going to have an absolute ball. Unlike me. Angelina's well over sixty, a confirmed spinster, and tops the scales at one hundred kilos. You'd think someone as divine as Anton would hire a gorgeous assistant. I guess this one must help him keep his mind strictly on business…'

'You're shocking.' Lydia laughed again. 'This is supposed to be work, remember?'

'I know.' Maria managed a tiny groan, but it changed into a giggle as she stared down at the very new, very false nails she'd had applied the moment they'd checked into the hotel yesterday. 'Right, I'm really cooked now.' Maria stood up. 'And if we're going to pull this off, I suppose we ought to hit the beauty parlour. I've got to start looking like a chic Italian businesswoman, while you, Lydia Holmes…' Maria's voice trailed off as Lydia groaned. 'It will be fun,' Maria insisted. 'It's going to be like one of those makeovers on the television—watching you turn from a dark-suited detective to a fabulously rich jewellery designer.'

'A fabulously rich *exclusive* jewellery designer,' Lydia corrected with a wry grin. 'Here in Melbourne to sell my wares!'

'Well, whatever you are and wherever you're from, Graham's going to be kicking himself when he sees what a stunner you are underneath it all!'

'Underneath what?' Lydia frowned, but Maria wasn't going to elaborate.

Glancing at her watch, she grimaced. 'I'd better get over to the salon—and you'd better get ready to head to the airport. Santini's plane is just about due in.'

Lydia shook her head. 'I don't have to head to the airport—Graham and John are going to pull him out at Customs, to warn him about the security situation and escort him back to the hotel.'

'So when do you get to meet him?'

'In the restaurant. They want the initial contact to look completely accidental—I'm accidentally going to spill my drink on him. You'd think they could have come up with a better pick-up move than that! I'm supposed to be about to check out of the hotel, and he's apparently going to be so bowled over by me that he moves me straight up to his suite…' She could see Maria's lips twitching as she tried not to smile. 'That's the sort of thing he does, apparently. I'm going to look a right fool.'

'A gorgeous fool, though. I can't wait to see what you look like.' Maria rubbed her hands in delighted glee.

'Right, I'm going to have a quick shower, and then off to the parlour—are you coming?'

Lydia shook her head. 'You go ahead. I think I'll have a swim first, and try to wind down a bit.'

'Will you be okay?' asked Maria.

'I'll be fine.' Lydia smiled, and the smile stayed in place until Maria had closed the sauna door behind her.

Finally alone, Lydia allowed herself an indulgent moment. Raking her fingers through her damp hair, she rested her head in her hands, bracing herself for the huge task that lay ahead over the next few days—guarding a VIP with a security threat *in situ*. She had to push aside her own problems—or lack of them, now that it was over with Graham.

God, it was hot!

Lydia stepped outside the sauna, visibly blanching at the sight of the cool plunge pool and opting instead for the hopefully warmer lap pool.

Popping into a cubicle she pulled on the rather boring navy bathers she used for her daily swim, knowing that if she was going to carry off the part of Anton Santini's latest girlfriend she'd better head over to the boutique and buy a decent bikini. Folding her clothes and placing them in her bag, she padded out to the pool area, glad to see that it was deserted again, and glad for a few moments of solitude before the rigours of the next few days began.

A wealthy financier, Anton Santini part-owned a vast string of international hotels. According to the detailed brief Lydia had been given, his hotel chain was considering adding this luxury Melbourne hotel to its impressive list of residences. More importantly, down the track he was considering building a vast, brand-new hotel complex in Darwin, which would not only mean more tourists, but would also provide many vital jobs for the locals in the Northern Territory.

Everyone wanted his whirlwind visit to Melbourne to go well—hence the panic that had ensued when a potential security threat towards Anton Santini had been revealed. There had been no time to reschedule the gathering—he was already on his plane and heading for Australia—so instead red panic buttons had been pushed and a massive security operation had been hastily put in place—with no expense spared! And though professionally Lydia relished the opportunity, she was cringing at the prospect of playing the part of Santini's girlfriend. She knew that no amount of buffing and coiffing was going to bring her up to his exacting standards—she could still hear the sniggers from her colleagues when she had been chosen—but, worse, she could almost see the scorn and incredulity that would surely be visible in Santini's eyes when they were finally introduced.

Swimming always calmed her, and a half-hour of concentrating on her breathing, focusing on nothing more than reaching the cool marble at the other side of the pool, was exactly what she needed now. Dipping her toe in the inviting-looking pool, Lydia found it pleasantly warm, the deep blue water seemingly calling her to dive in and forget for a moment the pressures of modern living. Diving in gracefully, she closed her eyes as she hit the water, and felt the tension that had held her together disperse as she slid beneath the surface, propelling her body along the floor of the pool, her breath bursting in her lungs as she held it in.

* * *

It was good to be alone. Punching his desired level, Anton glanced at his expensive heavy watch as the lift descended from the Presidential Suite to the lower ground floor and realised that had he caught his scheduled flight then his plane would only just be landing now. He was infinitely grateful to the unknown first-class passenger on the packed flight that had preceded his who had cancelled, allowing Anton the luxury of five hours' sleep in a hotel bed before he faced his horrendous schedule.

Sitting in the luxurious surrounds of the first-class lounge, sipping on a brandy as he'd waited to board the earlier plane, in a reflex action he'd reached for his mobile to call his PA and tell her about the change. But then, almost defiantly, he had clicked his phone off, filled with an urge to have a few hours in his life that were, for once, unaccountable.

Feeling as if he was playing hooky, Anton had boarded the plane and, in a move that was so unusual for him it bordered on the bizarre, he'd handed over his laptop to the flight attendant and refused the latest copies of overseas newspapers. Shaking his head at the endless delicacies that were offered as the plane hit altitude he'd chosen instead to pull on a pair of headphones and gaze unseeing at the international news, his eyes growing heavy as it morphed into a film…

As the lift doors slid open, Anton Santini, automatically polite, pressed the button to hold it open for a dark-haired woman wrapped in a white robe. Her flushed faced indicated that she had just come from the gym area where he was heading. She did a double take when she saw him, but Anton didn't give it a thought.

He was more than used to women giving him a second look. His six-foot-three frame and dark Latin looks merited that alone, and given that these days there was barely a newspaper or magazine published that didn't contain a photo of him, it wasn't just women who looked twice.

It certainly didn't cross his mind that the dark-haired woman might be an undercover detective who didn't expect him to be in the country just yet! And it never entered his head that Maria was battling with a surge of panic because an unsuspecting Lydia was swimming in the pool—where, judging from the towel draped around his shoulders, Anton was clearly heading!

With a brief nod he stepped out, following the signs for the hotel pool and gym, noting with a wry smile that despite the fact he was in Australia, literally on the other side of the world, he might just as well be in Rome, or London, or Paris, or wherever his hectic schedule took him. No matter how much the hotels fought to be different, to stamp their originality in the minds of affluent businessmen, each and every one was pretty much the same.

Still, at least he had the place to himself.

Even as he processed the thought Anton retrieved and corrected it. As he had turned the corner he hadn't acknowledged the massive marble pool—he was used to extravagant surroundings, and the marble floor and glittering blue water had barely merited a glance. All he *had* noticed was the still surface of the water, the thick scent of chlorine, the silence of an empty room. But now, in a beat, his eyes were drawn to the long dark shadow beneath the water, to a hand breaking the surface tension, followed by a slender, pale arm arching a perfect stroke. As he went to walk on, to deposit his towel and robe on the bench, something held him back. In another beat, after another moment's hesitation, his eyes were drawn to the figure in the water. Her pale length was effortlessly gliding the length of the pool, titian hair dragging behind her, eyes closed as she rhythmically swam towards the edge, then executed a perfect tumble-turn before disappearing beneath the surface again for an impressive length of time.

Anton found himself drawn to the willowy figure. There was something about the effortless way her body moved, a natural litheness that held his attention—something different about this woman. He took a moment to fathom what it was: she was actually enjoying herself! Unlike most early morning swimmers in a hotel pool, she didn't appear to be working on toning her thighs or extending her endurance. Instead she seemed to be taking a moment, an indulgent moment, oblivious to her surrounds, and inexplicably he didn't want to disturb her, didn't want to invade this woman's privacy, didn't want to break her delicate stride.

But it was a hotel pool, Anton reminded himself with a brisk shake of his head. It wasn't as if he'd climbed a fence and stood in voyeuristic silence as the lady of the house swum in her back garden. Almost defiantly he pulled off his robe. Unlike Lydia, he didn't test the water for warmth, didn't gingerly dip in his toe—ice could have been floating on the surface and Anton would have merely dived straight in—and as Lydia neared the far end of the pool he slid into the water.

* * *

She felt his presence.

She couldn't really explain how she knew the presence was male, but as she felt the wedge of water buffet her slightly Lydia knew quite simply that it was, and, snapping out of her almost hypnotic trance she shifted back to an alert, edgy state. The effortless strokes she had been executing were more cumbersome now. Her breath was no longer coming regularly, her strokes were no longer deep and rhythmic, and she grasped the marble beneath her fingers, turned around and held onto the edge to catch her breath a moment.

Her eyes gazed the length of the pool, idly focusing on the man coming towards her, and suddenly, despite the width, it was as if the pool had shrunk. Maybe she was too used to the routine of her usual gym—the lanes neatly divided by a row of yellow buoys, swimmers keeping strictly their lanes—but he was heading straight for her, every stroke drawing him closer, long, muscled arms stroking their way nearer. Inexplicably she didn't move, just held onto the edge as he came in too soon, too fast.

'*Scusi.*' Even though it was the shallow end the water was still deep, but he stood his ground, didn't need to clutch the edge as Lydia did, shaking his black hair, blinking his eyes and facing hers. 'I thought it was bigger…'

'Me too.' She gave a small shrug, understanding instantly what he meant—the regular length of a pool like this was twenty-five metres, but this one fell a couple short, and if you were used to swimming—as this man clearly was—used to pacing yourself, it was an easy mistake to make. 'You soon get used to it.'

'Sorry!' He said it again, only in English this time. Lydia actually preferred the more spontaneous response he had used earlier, but there were other things on her mind now. Her shrewd amber eyes focussed, and there was a nervous swallow in her throat as she realised that, way before schedule, the man she would be spending the next few days with, the man she should be 'accidentally' meeting in a few short hours, was actually here.

Her mind raced for an explanation and her helpless eyes darted around. She was half expecting to see her colleagues Graham and John appear at the doorway, or for Anton Santini to formally introduce himself, explain that there had been a mix-up in the schedule and that *this* in fact, was their accidental meeting.

That would explain it, Lydia decided in a split second. That would explain why he had swum so directly towards her—would explain why she had been so acutely aware of his presence, why his eyes were boring into her as if he knew her—he *knew* who she was!

But, far from introducing himself, he gave her a small nod before pushing away from the edge and swimming off, leaving her standing there clinging to the edge, her heart racing, her breath coming in small shallow gasps. Only it had little to do with the exercise and everything to do with the man who shared the pool. Her skin stung from the brief touch of him, and goose bumps appeared on her arms as she recalled the feel of his strong legs brushing against hers. Her mind raced to calm itself, to turn off the energy he had released, to switch off the adrenaline that was pumping through her veins right now. She didn't know what to do, unsure now if Anton actually did know who she was, if her lack of response when he had tried to approach her had confused him.

Taking a deep breath, even though her body was tired now, Lydia knew that she had to swim on, to give Anton another chance to talk with her, mindful that if Anton was here then anyone could be watching. Her eyes glanced up to the security cameras. Even though it was only the two of them in the pool this meeting had to look accidental; the biggest threat to Anton Santini's safety was the fact that no one yet knew who the enemy was— no one knew how sophisticated the plans that were intended to bring him down might be.

Swimming a couple more lengths should have been easy, but her effortless stride eluded her now, and Lydia tried to fathom why she couldn't resume the simple strokes. She decided that the work-out, the swim, and then the surge of energy when she had realised that Anton was in the pool had left her depleted. Her body was heavy and leaden as she dragged it through the water, and her mind was spinning like a stuck CD— whirring furiously for a moment before playing aloud the single track she didn't want to hear…

He'd aroused her.

It had nothing to do with the fact it was Anton Santini—the man she was engaged to protect for the next few days—in the water with her. Instead it had everything to do with the man who had dived in just a few moments ago—a man she had been attracted to even before she had realised his identity. It was that thought that panicked Lydia, made every supposedly natural movement a chore, made this *chance* meeting all the more difficult.

'You must swim a lot?'

He was waiting for her at the other end, as she had known he would be, and his voice was deep, husky and heavily accented when he spoke. Heart hammering in her mouth, Lydia nodded.

'Most days,' she breathed. 'Though I think I've done too much this morning. I was working out before, and then I had a sauna…'

Lifting her hand, she gestured to the gym behind them, but Anton's gaze didn't follow where she was pointing. Instead she felt his dark navy eyes drag the entire length of her slender arm, scorching her pale flesh from her fingertips to her creamy clavicle. He took in every facet of the subtle muscle definition, of the pale tea-coloured freckles, then slowly worked his way up her long slender neck, searing her with his eyes. The flicker of her pulse in her neck, his nervous swallow, every tiny movement was accentuated until finally he looked directly at her. But there was no relief, only recognition—a jolting recognition, not of familiarity but of attraction. It was a powerful, faint-making emotion, terrifying exhilarating, and Lydia felt her panic multiply. She struggled to retract what her eyes had just stated, to tell this man that this was strictly business—that she was only here because it was her job. She was supposed to be meeting him in the hotel lounge in two hours, as she pretended to check out of the packed hotel—was supposed to spill a glass of water over him. Their attraction was meant to be mutual—so much so that Anton Santini would overcome the problem of a full hotel, would fall so much in lust with this stranger that he would, within a matter of a few hours, install her into his bedroom. That was the plan.

At this very moment Anton Santini was supposed to be being pulled over by customs officers, and John and Graham would deliver those very instructions.

What had happened?

Lydia didn't have time to guess—didn't have time to go through the hows and whys. She had to swing her mind away from the delicious distraction of his eyes and force herself to operate—not as a woman, but as a detective. If the plans had changed then so must her approach—there wasn't exactly a glass of water handy to spill over him right now!

'I'm Lydia,' she managed, forcing a small smile to lips that didn't seem to want to obey. 'You are...?'

He didn't answer, just gave her a small, slightly superior smile, his full mouth twisting upwards slightly, his dark eyes still shamelessly staring. Lydia knew that he didn't want to play along, and considered introductions completely unnecessary when they both knew who they were dealing with—but *anyone* could be watching, Lydia reminded herself. They *had* to act as if they were strangers meeting, had to keep appearances up at all times. She would reiterate that fact to Anton later, when they were alone.

Alone.

Her stomach tightened at the mere thought. A knot of anticipation gripped deep within, a blush spread over her chest as a thousand inappropriate thoughts played in her mind. She understood now how it happened—understood how so many powerful, beautiful women had fallen for him so completely and utterly—how they had ignored his appalling reputation and thrown caution to the wind. The sheer, raw sensuality of the man was devastating, his presence overwhelming, blocking out reason, dimming rationality with the power and force of a solar eclipse. And right now, even if it was all engineered, that energy was focussed entirely on *her*.

Lydia struggled to reflect it. She struggled to keep a level head as her body begged a more primitive response. Angrier with herself than at him, her voice was more demanding, her eyes holding his boldly, as she insisted that he introduced himself. 'You are…?'

'I am…' His smile bordered on the cruel now, like a predator eyeing his victim. His gaze was inescapable as the massive room suddenly closed in around them, as the steamy warm air seemed set to suffocate her, the atmosphere so throbbingly sensual Lydia could almost hear the hiss of the temperature rising as he moved in closer '…going to kiss you…'

She didn't know what to do. Her head was telling her to pull back, reminding her that this level of intimacy wasn't in her job description. But instead she stared up at this stunningly beautiful man, her eyes wide, her body rigid with a curious dizzy expectation as his face moved towards her, sheer unadulterated lust drenching her far more than the water.

The morning shadow on his chin was almost as navy as his heavy-lidded eyes, his cheekbones exquisitely sculptured in his haughty face. Truly, Lydia decided, he was the most beautiful man she had ever borne witness to—such strength, such arrogance, even, etched in every feature. Yet his eyes were gentle as they held hers, soothing her terror and multiplying it at the same time. She didn't want to move, didn't want to back away from the pleasure that was surely to follow. Even if it was orchestrated, even if it was just for show, a tiny voice was telling her to go with it—a tiny, dangerous voice she'd never heard before was telling her that she didn't want to miss the feel of this beautiful man close to her, that never again in her lifetime was she likely to be kissed, to be held, by someone as supremely divine as Anton Santini.

Her eyes closed in giddy expectation as painfully slowly he moved in… But in a curious move his lips didn't meet hers. Instead he dusted his cheek against hers, the warmth of his breath tickling her face, and even if the kiss that was surely about to ensue was only for the cameras, for the sake of the hidden audience that might be watching, before his lips even met hers Lydia knew it would be one she would remember for ever.

His chin was scratching, dragging slowly along her pale, alert flesh, so slow it was almost painful. Yet it had the desired effect. His decadent stealth banished her fear and skilfully replaced it with need—a need that was physical, a need that was palpable. Her lips twitched with desire, her body flaming in its treacherous response to his touch, and lingering misgivings were gone completely. His touch had her moving her lips to his, and so magnetic was his force that reason and doubt were erased, and it was Lydia moving things along, Lydia's mouth searching for his, and finally, deliciously, finding it.

She relished in the bruising weight of his mouth against hers, the cool of his tongue as it parted her willing lips, the soldering feel of his hand in the small of her back as he pulled her a fraction closer, fanning the flames of desire. Her insides literally melting, she felt her fingers let go of the edge, but the bottom of the pool was too deep for her to stand. He supported her easily, her body weightless in the water, his arms holding her as his mouth ravished her, warm, muscular thighs tipping her further into heady oblivion.

Her swollen nipples were straining against Lycra, and heat was flaring between her legs. The need that imbued her was still not satisfied, the taste of such pleasure making Lydia greedier now, hungry for more. And Anton reciprocated. The nudge of his erection against her taut stomach was faint-making as she pressed provocatively against it, fuelling a primitive desire Lydia had never, not even in her most intimate moments, fully experienced—a total and utter abandonment, a complete, delicious loss of control.

He made her bold, made her wanton, provocative, immersed her in passion.

Her mind was completely focussed now on her own desires, on the pulse flickering between her legs. Her clitoris was engorged, twitching with want, and only this man could satisfy it. Still he kissed her, ravished her, but his mouth was moving now, tracing her neck, kissing the hollows. He buried his face in her dripping hair, and her fingers dug into his shoulders, and in a movement that was as provocative as it was instinctive she raised her hips several decadent inches. His fingers pressed into the warm flesh of her taut buttocks and the deep, languorous, throaty kiss was abandoned as she glided her swollen, most intimate lips along the endless, solid length of his manhood.

His breath was hot on the shell of her ear as she nestled the heat of her centre on the tip of his. She wanted him to take her, to part the tiny inch of fabric that covered her most private place. Wanted him to fill her, to calm the frenzy of her body beneath the still surface of the water. Her stomach tightened in rhythmic contraction and her legs wrapped around him as he pressed his velvet steel harder against her. Heady, drunken, faint, Lydia rested her head on a damp shoulder, nibbling at the salty flesh of his skin, willing him to take her, sure that the strength of his erection alone could part the fabric that covered her. She could feel the pulse of her orgasm aligning, the heavy pit in her stomach an abyss that needed to be filled. And, from the short, rapid breaths in her ear, the tension in every muscle beneath her fingers, Lydia knew he was as close as dammit too.

His hand moved from her, pulling impatiently at his bathers, the motion causing his knuckles to dig into the flesh of her inner thigh. The pain only intensified the experience, abandonment drenching her as she imagined him spilling his salty kiss inside her, visualised the decadence of Anton Santini making love to her…

Anton Santini!

The two words were a brutal slap to her flushed cheeks—a stab of self-preservation mercifully holding her back at the eleventh hour. The world suddenly came into sharp, unwelcome focus and she pulled back, struggled to catch her breath—appalled at what had taken place. She quivered with unsated desire as her mind fought for control and she stared at his questioning eyes.

This was work. This was her livelihood. But it wasn't just that that had stopped her. It was the knowledge, the realisation, that a man as suave, as sophisticated, as merciless as Anton Santini could reduce her in a matter of minutes to this squirming ball of desire. If she lost her head she'd go under; he would crush her in the palm of his hand and barely even notice.

'Lydia?' he murmured, clearly confused by the change in her.

'I have to pack...' She shook her head as if to clear it. 'I've got an appointment at the hairdresser...'

And he should have understood, should have been versed by Detective John Miller about the plan. But he just stared back at her. Lydia thought she understood his confusion—John would have told him that he wasn't to be left alone!

Her mind raced for a solution and almost instantaneously found one. 'We could go up to my room,' she said, suddenly desperate to get away from the pool, to find out just what the hell was going on and—perhaps more importantly—face this man dressed!

But she stopped talking abruptly as she heard loud chattering in the corridor outside. Aware of the potential precariousness of the situation she moved quickly, putting herself between Anton and the doorway.

'What are you doing?' He sounded irritated, confused by the change in her, but there was no time for explanation as Maria and another woman appeared. Although Maria was still dressed in her white robe a towel was rolled up under her arm, and Lydia knew that she was now armed.

'Signor Santini, che cosa fa qui?'

A large, irate woman Lydia could only assume was Angelina gesticulated wildly as she addressed her boss.

'Sto nuotando!' came Anton's curt reply.

Lydia bobbed under the water and swam towards the edge, her hands gratefully reaching the silver of the rail, dragging herself up the steps. It was as if the marrow had seeped out of her bones, and her legs were weak as she pulled herself out of the water and located her robe.

'I ask him what he is doing here so soon,' Angelina's exasperated voice greeted Lydia as she made her way over. 'And he say swimming—I had no idea he was coming!'

'Well, he's here,' Maria said, with a distinctly dry edge to her voice, frowning as she watched Lydia who, her fingers shaking, pale and wrinkled from her time in the water, was knotting her belt. 'Is everything okay?'

'Everything's fine,' Lydia said, hardly trusting herself to speak, still brutally shaken from her first encounter with Anton.

'Go up and shower quickly,' Maria said in low, urgent tones. 'Then get over to the salon. I'll cover him till you're dressed and ready—we'll get him upstairs and brief him.'

'Brief him?' Lydia blinked at Maria. Surely she had misheard? Or perhaps Maria didn't know that Anton had already been versed in the situation? That *had* to be the case, Lydia begged mentally. Because otherwise...

Panic rose in her as she attempted to confront the other appalling possibility—that Anton Santini really hadn't been briefed—that he had no idea who she was—that he had merely been attracted to her, had approached her, just as his bio suggested he would, with the supreme confidence that she would respond.

And she had!

'Where are John and Graham?' Lydia asked, trying to keep her voice even as Anton climbed out of the pool, her eyes darting away as she tried and failed not to notice the superb body that only moments ago had been pressed against hers.

'On their way back from the airport,' Maria answered, and Lydia's last vestige of hope disappeared—Anton really had no idea who she was. 'I rang them and told them what was happening.'

Cheeks flaming, she avoided even looking at him. Somehow she picked up her gym bag, and somehow she made her way out to the lifts, her heart hammering in her chest, only remembering to breathe when she was finally alone.

He would have made love to her if she'd let him, and—Lydia gulped as horrible truth flooded in—she almost had. She had almost let a virtual stranger in, let down her cool façade in an appalling unguarded moment. Anton hadn't just seen a different side to her character today, it was as if a complete *alter ego* had emerged—a wanton, sensual woman that knew her needs.

Oh, there *had* been a blistering attraction—that much she understood, that much she could accept. She could almost console herself that they had chosen to mix business with pleasure, had been caught up in the thrill of the moment, safe in the knowledge that they were making themselves look convincing to anyone watching… But if Maria was right, if he hadn't even known that she was a detective, that they were *supposed* to be meeting, then she wasn't just out of her depth with Anton Santini she had already been pulled under!

What sort of man had the confidence, the supreme arrogance, to approach a stranger and kiss them so blatantly, so fully, to arouse them to the point of oblivion and know, just know, that she would reciprocate—know that with one touch he would win?

On autopilot she headed for her room, showered and dressed quickly. She closed her eyes, her mind tightened in disbelief, a stinging flood of shame coursing through her body as another question exploded in her mind.

What must Anton think of her?

CHAPTER TWO

THE PRESSURE of the hairdresser's fingertips on her scalp as she massaged conditioner deep into her hair didn't even provide a vague distraction—Lydia's mind was working overtime, trying to fathom how she was supposed to face Anton Santini now. How on earth could she manage detachment, professionalism, after what had transpired in the pool? Hell, right now she'd settle for being able to look him in the eye.

But she had to remain in control—not only did her career depend on it, but Anton's life was in her hands. And, given she was signed up as his protector, her life too could be on the line. This was no time to be acting like a gauche teenager—she had to somehow regain control of this appalling situation, had to wrestle back her dignity. But for the first time in her life she was completely at a loss to come up with a plan. How could she deny her part in what had taken place? How could she deny the blatant, overwhelming passion that had engulfed her? The sensual, debauched *alter ego* that had emerged the second he had touched her?

'So, you're booked for nails, full make-up and a blow-dry?' Karen, the therapist questioned her as a warm towel was wrapped around Lydia's head and she was guided to the make-up room.

'Please.' Lydia nodded, lowering herself into the chair and trying to sound blasé, as if she did this type of thing every day. 'Though I'm not sure if there will be time to do my nails. I've got an appointment scheduled—'

'That's no problem,' Karen interrupted, clearly used to dealing with busy clients. 'Cindy can do your nails while I do your make up—let's have a look at you.' Pulling off the towel, she ran her fingers through Lydia's long red curls.

'Is it business or pleasure?' When Lydia blinked back, Karen elaborated. 'Your appointment? I'm just trying to get a feel for how you want to look.'

'It's business,' Lydia answered firmly. 'And I want to look fabulous!'

'Oh, you will.' Karen winked, tipping the chair backwards and setting to work.

Lydia closed her eyes as a few stray hairs around her eyebrows were deftly tidied and a thick layer of scented cream gently rubbed into her face, chatting amicably to Karen about jewellery and the one-off pieces she supposedly designed, practising the alias she would be adopting over the next few days.

'How long are you staying at the hotel?'

'I have to check out this morning.' Lydia gave a regretful shrug. 'When I checked in I was hoping to stay for four nights but apparently the hotel's been booked up for weeks—some VIPs are arriving this morning. The bellboy's bringing my luggage down now, and while I'm having breakfast the concierges are ringing around to find me alternative accommodation.'

'That'd be right,' the therapist muttered. 'Kick out the paying guests…' Her voice trailed off as she realised she'd probably overstepped the mark, but Lydia pushed on, more than happy to fish a little, giving a tiny swallow as she tried to sound like the rich little madam she was hoping to portray.

'Well, I'm far from happy with the situation,' Lydia bristled. 'And I sincerely hope that a concierge can find me somewhere suitable—somewhere with a decent salon at the very least. What sort of VIPs are they anyway?'

'The worst sort,' the therapist answered in a theatrical whisper. 'There's going to be a take-over of the hotel and some of the bigwigs from a massive European chain are coming. We're all supposed to be on our best behaviour—why don't we try grey?'

'Sorry?' Opening her eyes, Lydia blinked back at the woman.

'On your eyes. I know you said you prefer neutral, but a deep smoky grey will really bring out the amazing colour of your eyes—they're more gold than hazel—'

'I don't want anything too heavy,' Lydia broke in. 'I really prefer a more natural look.'

'Trust me,' Karen insisted, a long red nail hovering over an array of tiny pots, her eyes narrowing as she stared closely at Lydia's face. 'You're going to look stunning. One wave of my magic wand and I can create an entire new you.'

A 'new you' was exactly what was needed, Lydia thought ruefully, if she was ever going to face Anton. A tiny glimmer of a plan started to emerge. 'Can you do anything to tone down my complexion?'

'You're as white as paper,' Karen tutted.

'But I blush terribly.' Lydia gave a dismissive shrug. 'And, like I said, I've got an important meeting this morning—I don't want to give myself away when we discuss prices.'

'You need a green base.' Karen nodded knowingly. 'Nothing like what you're thinking.' She grinned at Lydia's rather startled expression. 'I've got this fabulous mineral powder; we have it flown in from New York. Wearing that you can double your prices—triple them, even—and you'll be as pale and as cool as porcelain.'

'Really?' Lydia gave a dubious frown.

'Really!' Karen winked. 'We'll have to pay extra attention to your *décolletage*—that's a real give away when you're blushing.'

And she *would* blush!

Just the thought of facing Anton had her pulse pounding in her temples and a scorching, shameful warmth flooding her. But as Karen worked on slowly the horror receded, and Lydia gave in to the pleasure of the moment, knowing that in a few short days she'd be back to a few dabs of sunblock and slick of mascara if she was lucky.

Lydia let Karen transform her as Cindy worked on her nails. She didn't even glance in the mirror when she sat upright for her hair to be dried—she focussed on a magazine as her curls were dragged beyond her shoulders.

For the first time in ages Lydia didn't turn automatically to the health section, didn't read how she could increase her stamina or detox her entire system in a mere weekend. She even bypassed an in-depth article on a recent high-profile court case. Instead, with a flutter of excitement, she flicked to the social pages. She gazed at photos of the rich and famous, at their smooth botoxed faces belying their age, their divine dresses and long, smooth legs that ended in jewel-encrusted shoes. She could almost smell the expensive perfume wafting from their silicone-enhanced bosoms. She looked at the Russian-red lips smiling for the cameras, and for the first time since she'd checked in Lydia smiled back.

The diversity of her career hit home: only this time last week she had been on a stake-out, dressed in a navy tracksuit, a world away from the glamour she was *forced* to sample now, boxed up in a supposedly abandoned van for forty-eight hours. She had watched pimps and drug dealers infesting the vulnerable with their wares, staring through the bolt holes fitted with telescopes as weary prostitutes willed the morning to come, drinking endless cups of coffee to stay awake as she made small talk and tried to cheer up Kevin Bates—an inspector on the force she regularly worked alongside, a man she both liked and admired.

Forty-eight hours confined in his company, listening to him fret about his eldest child who was having his tonsils out that week, was a world away from what she was experiencing now! A freshly squeezed orange and guava juice was the order of the day, instead of her usual flask of coffee. Now, massive marble bathrooms replaced the rudimentary portaloo in the corner of the van that she'd had to endure so they didn't blow their cover by stepping outside.

It wasn't just a world away, Lydia corrected herself, but an entire universe from where she was now. And for a slice of time this opulent world was the one in which she was supposed to belong, with which she had been ordered to blend in. Lydia made a vow to revel in it the same way Maria was—to live the fantasy of being obscenely rich. She'd taken the bad over and over again. For the next few days she'd enjoy the good.

'You're done!' Karen's voice was triumphant as she pulled off the towel and gown and smoothed Lydia's hair over her shoulders. 'I'll get a mirror so you can see the back and sides.'

Normally for Lydia the mirror bit of a salon visit was an uncomfortable, painful experience—a mumbled *thanks* as she wondered how on earth she could correct the appalling creation, grappling in her purse to give a very undeserved tip as she blinked away tears. This time, however, she was trying hard to keep herself from smiling, desperately trying to remember that she was supposed to be used to this, that she was always *supposed* to look groomed and divine.

Staring at her profile from every angle, Lydia barely recognised herself. Her curls were a distant memory. Instead her hair shimmered in a straight silk curtain. But it wasn't just her hair that had her mesmerised—it was the entire package! The sparkling gold of her eyes as they peered out from underneath smoky grey lids was deliciously framed by her newly darkened lashes, and even her skin seemed to glow with healthy delight, a cheeky dot of colour on the apple of each cheek drawing her gaze to the dark, sexy red of her lips.

'Try it now.' Karen giggled.

'Try what?' Lydia asked, still mesmerised by her reflection.

'Think of your deepest, darkest secret, something that will make your toes curl with shame, and watch that make-up do its magic.'

So she did…

She relived in her mind the sheer abandonment that had doused her this morning. The stinging sensation of Anton's kiss, the cool of his mouth, the nibble of his teeth against the wedge of her tongue. She could almost feel the steel of his erection nudging her most private place. She could almost feel herself willingly overstepping boundaries that until today had always been firmly entrenched. Staring at her reflection, Lydia envisaged what had just a short while ago seemed impossible—facing Anton Santini, confronting the man she had revealed so much of herself to, staring deep into those cruel, sensuous eyes and somehow appearing in control, portraying the cool, detached detective that she was supposed to be, somehow pretending that he hadn't touched her so.

'Cool as a cucumber,' Karen enthused, and Lydia blinked back at her reflection, amazed that the therapist was right—her face was pale, not a hint of a blush darkened her cheeks. Her shoulders were creamy white against the flame of her dress and Lydia was infused with possibility…

Maybe she could pull it off.

Stare at Anton and tell him that he didn't move her.

Tell him that the scorching intimacy they had shared hadn't been pleasure but merely a duty—a cross she'd had to bear.

She would get through this!

And because she was supposedly rich, a mere detail like payment shouldn't even enter her head—with a swish of her fragranced hair Lydia should stalk out. But, rummaging in her bag, she peeled off a note and pressed it into Karen's hand. She shared a tiny smile as the woman's fingers gleefully closed around the crumpled paper before heading out into the massive foyer, staring at her luggage being wheeled through the foyer by the bellboy. A concierge was juggling a telephone call and two rather irate Americans and attempting to catch her eye—no doubt wanting to inform her of the reservation he'd made on her behalf. But Lydia deliberately ignored him, heading over to the restaurant instead, ready to face Anton again. But on her terms this time—not as the woman he had witnessed earlier, but as the detective she was.

CHAPTER THREE

'SHE OVERREACTS!' Anton's words were like pistol shots shooting across the Presidential Suite. Showered and dressed now, he wanted to get on with his day, wanted to end this ridiculous conversation and get on with his work. 'Angelina had no business calling the police without consulting me.'

'She tried to contact you, sir, but your telephone was turned off.'

Kevin Bates faced Anton and tried to bring the situation under control—Maria's attempts to explain things had been greeted with scorn, but it was hoped the more authoritative air of an inspector might calm things down. 'Sir, you don't seem to understand the seriousness of the situation. As Maria has tried to explain to you, we have serious concerns about your safety… We have reason to believe that there is going to be an attempt on your life—'

'Because of some flowers?' Anton snapped.

'Because of this.' Kevin handed him a neat typewritten card.

'It says "Welcome, Mr Santini." What has that to do with anything?'

'You have an excellent PA, Mr Santini. In fact, the reason we've been able to rule her out as a suspect is because it's her attention to detail that has enabled us to recognise the threat. The hotel usually provides a display of native Australian flowers for the Presidential Suite…'

'So?'

'These flowers were delivered to the hotel last night. They were ordered from a florist down the road and paid for in cash. The card was already typed up.'

'By who?'

'The florist can't remember—after all it wasn't a particularly unusual request. What is unusual, Mr Santini, is that an identical card and lilies were delivered to the hotel you were staying at in Spain six months ago, when you were shot at.'

'I was *not* shot at,' Anton countered. 'The police decided at the time it was a gangland fight I was caught up in. I was merely in the wrong place at the wrong time. It was just bad luck.'

'At the time, it appeared so.' Kevin nodded. 'However, Angelina gave a very detailed statement to the Spanish police—at the time of the shooting she was in her room, attending to correspondence. She should have been with you. Flowers had been delivered and she couldn't work out who they had come from—a seemingly insignificant detail, so insignificant that when flowers were delivered to your hotel room in New York still it didn't seem relevant…'

'I was nearly run over in New York…' Realisation was starting to hit, and his hand raked through his hair as he recalled the details. 'A car came straight at me, accelerating as it did so. I jumped just in time. My shoulder was dislocated but I knew I'd been lucky—the police said…'

'Wrong place, wrong time?' Kevin offered, and Anton nodded.

'These flowers are a calling card, Mr Santini. A warning that we have to take seriously. You've also been getting some nuisance calls, I believe?'

'A few.' Anton shrugged, but Kevin shook his head.

'Not according to your PA. During the last twelve months or so you've received numerous calls—so many, in fact, that not only the telephone company but the police in Rome are investigating. Am I right that in recent weeks they've become more frequent?'

Finally Anton conceded with a brief nod of his head. 'Who?' he asked. 'Who wants to harm me?'

'That we don't know,' Kevin admitted. 'Believe me, we intend to find out. However, our primary concern is your protection while you're here in Australia. Now, you're not to discuss this security operation—not even with your own staff.'

'Why not?'

'Because right now they're all suspects in this investigation.' As Anton opened his mouth to argue, Kevin overrode him. 'It's a possibility that we have to consider—for that reason your PA is the only one who is to know about the undercover operation in place. Maria will stay with Angelina, given that she has direct access to you, and we'll have other detectives in place in the hotel. Naturally we'll have a detective with you at all times. '

'How do you expect me to explain to my staff why a police officer is by my side? With all due respect, you do *look* like a police officer,' Anton said, impatience evident in his every gesture as his heavily accented voice filled the room.

'We're not that stupid, Mr Santini.' Kevin gave a wry smile. 'I can assure you that the detective shadowing you is going to blend in.'

'How?' Anton asked, more intrigued than annoyed now. 'I can see that we could pass off Maria's presence by explaining that Angelina needed some assistance, but…'

'Do you remember the woman in the pool this morning?' Maria asked, watching as Anton frowned. 'She was there when Angelina and I arrived.' When Anton's frown deepened Maria assumed it was because he was trying to place her. 'She had red hair, was doing some laps. You probably didn't notice her, but she's actually been in the hotel since yesterday, posing as a jewellery designer from Sydney here in Melbourne to showcase her work…'

'She's a *detective*?' Anton's voice was a hoarse whisper as realisation hit. Closing his eyes for a second, he replayed the morning's events. With the benefit of hindsight, his mouth tightened in rage. 'You are telling me that that woman is in fact a police officer?'

'No, Mr Santini,' Kevin answered patiently. 'For the next couple of days, according to everyone she meets, Lydia is a jewellery designer visiting Melbourne and is here to target some new clients. However, given that the hotel is full, she's checking out this morning. The bellboy is bringing her luggage down as we speak.'

'I thought you said that she was staying with me?'

'She is.' Kevin nodded, enjoying seeing this supremely powerful man momentarily flailing as he explained the carefully laid plans. 'Initially she was going to hang around the hotel until lunchtime but, given that you've arrived early, we've had to move things forward. You're going to chat her up, and after a brief exchange you'll invite her to stay with you. From our homework, sir, I don't think any of your staff will be remotely surprised to find you with a young lady *in situ* by the time they get here. By all accounts you're a pretty fast operator.'

Anton pressed his lips together, fighting back a smart retort because, though it galled him to admit it, Detective Bates was speaking the truth—no one would turn a hair if they arrived to find a beautiful woman on his arms. After all, it had happened on numerous occasions before.

'Once you're alone, Lydia will give you more details and try and glean any information from you that might give us some insight as to who this person might be. She'll also brief you about how the next few days are to be handled. But that conversation can only take place in your hotel room, and even then only when Lydia is satisfied that the room is secure and that you're definitely alone. Whenever you are out of your room or there is another person present you are to act as if you're lovers…'

Kevin paused for a moment, giving Anton time to digest the instructions. He was slightly bewildered by the stunned expression on Santini's face—the fact that his life might be in danger hadn't initially evoked even a hint of reaction, but now, Kevin decided, clearly shock was setting in and the truth must be starting to hit him. The Detective's voice was a touch gentler as he continued. 'Now, to make your initial contact look accidental, we thought you could make your way over to the breakfast bar—'

'What do you mean—*initial contact*?' Anton sneered,

desperately trying to regain some semblance of control, forcing himself to drag his mind away from Lydia and back to the conversation. What on earth was he talking about? Did this buffoon not realise it had already been made? That the *initial contact* had been well and truly taken care of?

But just as he was about to correct him, he checked himself. Long ago Anton had learnt that any knowledge, however unimportant it might seem at the time, was a vital tool that could be used later. That to keep the upper hand one had to be constantly ahead of the game. So instead he changed tack.

The sneer still in place, he voiced a different question. 'Why on earth would I go over to the breakfast bar? I do not serve myself. Did you think of that when you were making your plans?'

He didn't get an answer. The room fell quiet as Kevin's mobile phone trilled. 'She's ready.' Kevin nodded, quickly ending the call and nodding to Maria. 'Okay, Mr Santini, there are two detectives coming up in the lift. Their names are Graham and John. Don't talk to them—just treat them as you would any strangers—they're going to take the lift down with you and watch until you're in the restaurant. Once you're there, Lydia will walk in. Perhaps you could—'

'I do not need to be told by *you* how to chat up a woman,' Anton sneered, appalled now by what had taken place this morning, and more than ready to face this undercover detective and give her a piece of his mind. 'Come.' He snapped his fingers impatiently. 'Let's get this over with. Let's make this *initial contact*!'

CHAPTER FOUR

ORDERING his breakfast Anton glanced around the room, bracing himself for her entrance. To anyone watching he would look supremely in control as he flicked open the paper and read through the business section, but inside he was seething.

She had *used* him, had been playing a mere game with him; she was the one who had been in control this morning, and it stung like hell to admit it. A bitter taste of his own medicine had been served, and it was almost choking him to swallow it down.

What the hell had he been thinking anyway? Anton demanded of himself—aside from the fact she was a detective, what the hell had he been doing, practically making love to a stranger in a pool with no thought to birth control, no thought to the consequences?

She could have been anyone!

Anton's jaw tightened.

She was a damned detective!

He looked up from his paper and his racing mind stilled as a pale woman walked into the restaurant. His anger momentarily faded as he watched her cross the room. Maybe the bright early-morning Australian sun that streamed through the windows had dipped behind a cloud for a moment, shadowing the bright skylights of the restaurant because all of a sudden the vast sun-drenched restaurant seemed to dim. Even the noise seemed to fade—the clatter of knives and forks against plates, the rustle of newspapers, the chatter of his fellow diners, all blurring in the distance as Lydia became the sole power source.

Lydia, filling each and every one of his senses, her presence so electric, so consuming, it was as if he could taste again the cool decadence of her kiss, inhale again the sweet pungent fragrance of her arousal. Her presence was so potent that as Lydia crossed the room it was as if everything bar her had been plunged into darkness, as if they had been catapulted back to the weightless intimacy of the pool. Anton felt hollowed out with lust as he watched the long, slender legs that had been wrapped around him just a short while ago cross the room. His body responded like some testosterone laden adolescent's, as he took in every last detail. The naked flesh that had seared his was encased now in sheer silk stockings; the feet that had been bare, the soles that had dusted his skin, were delicate in high strappy sandals; the feather-light toned body he had pressed his own against was draped in a burnt orange dress—a brave move, with her colouring, yet it clashed divinely. Exquisitely tailored, it skimmed the length of her torso, the superb, subtle cut of the fabric divinely accentuating the enticing swell of her breasts, and the jut of her nipples caused Anton's fists to clench as he quelled the tirade of desire that swept through him. The inappropriateness of his arousal was thankfully hidden under the table, but still he fought to douse it, willing himself to move, to reach for a drink, to do something to break the spell. But he simply couldn't drag his eyes away. The flame of hair cascading down her shoulders captivated him like a roaring fire—until sensibility took over.

This was the woman who had used him.

Even though her back was to Anton's table, Lydia could feel the searing heat of his eyes on her as he crossed the room. Horribly exposed, she felt like a helpless creature being quietly stalked, and though her senses screamed danger, although every fibre in her being warned her of his approach, because her colleagues were sitting at a table just a few feet away, because this was her job, somehow she feigned nonchalance.

Concentrating on keeping the tongs in her hand steady, she spooned strawberries onto her plate and carefully selected some canteloupe and Kiwi fruit. Her heart was in her mouth, every nerve was screaming, warning of his approach. Her fight or flight response kicked in, willing her to run, to flee this dangerous predator. But she stood her ground, her confidence inwardly wavering but determined to thwart the emotional attack Anton would surely deliver and deal with him professionally.

'We meet again.'

His voice was a low, silken drawl. The scent of him reached her even before his words did, making the hairs on her neck static in their response to him, yet she refused to turn, refused to jump, refused to let him glimpse how much he moved her. Instead she carefully piled two more strawberries onto her plate before finally offering her response.

'We do.'

'This is a pleasant surprise!' He was impossibly close now. She could feel the heat from his body, the suffocating, intoxicating power of his presence as he moved deeper into her personal space, and Lydia knew it had to be *now*—that if she were to have any chance of fulfilling her assignment, any hope of controlling any dangerous situation they might confront, then she had to assume control, had to wrestle her self-respect, her authority, back from this consuming man.

'Hardly a surprise.' A tiny nervous swallow went unnoticed with her back still towards him. She dragged in air, forced her face into a smile and, tossing her long red mane, she faced him. She registered with a surge of triumph the flicker of confusion in his eyes at her confident response and yet this newly found confidence almost instantly dissolved as the beauty she had witnessed earlier seemed multiplied now. His thick jet hair was still damp, and the heavy, opulent scent of his cologne filled her nostrils. The near naked body that she had been pressed against was dressed now, but even a sharp, exquisitely tailored charcoal-grey suit did nothing to detract from the body beneath. If anything his clothes accentuated his perfection—the heavy white cotton shirt a contrast against his olive skin, the luxurious gold tie expertly knotted around his neck the only splash of colour apart from his eyes—dark, liquid navy, a perfect deep blue. The colour was as dense as a bottle of ink—no silver flecks, no flashes of green, just a velvet blue that caressed her.

The sharp, sculptured planes of his bone structure, from the straight Roman nose to the almost Native

Indian slant of his cheekbones and the jaw that had bruised the tender flesh of her face, was smooth now, with just a smudgy shadow beneath the skin—a subtle, powerful hint of what lay beneath…the beauty of this man in the morning.

In a flash of self preservation Lydia flicked her eyes away, forced herself to look downwards. But there was no solace there from the brutal masculinity of him, and her eyes worked the length of his body, from the wide shoulders and broad chest to the flat, lean planes of his stomach, the long, muscular legs encased in superbly cut trousers. She was the predator now, flecks of gold sparkling in her amber eyes and her voice even when she spoke, the nerves that had threatened to drown her abating now as with relish she delivered a question. 'Did you enjoy your swim?'

For a beat he didn't answer. Two vertical lines formed between his eyes—her detached stance was clearly not what Anton Santini was used to. 'I did.' He gave a curt nod, his voice deep and confident. The telltale frown between his eyes was gone now, but Lydia knew she had confused him, knew he had been expecting a different reaction entirely. 'Aren't you supposed to throw a glass of water over me?'

A smile parted her lips a fraction, her eyebrows darting up at his questionable humour. If she'd had any more money in her purse she'd have cheerfully handed it all over to Karen. Whether or not the make-up had worked she still wasn't sure, but the confidence an impossibly expensive jar of make-up gave was proving invaluable—coupled with the assurance in her mind that her hastily formed plan would work.

'That was before...' Lydia said in a low voice, enjoying the confidence of her *alter ego,* enjoying playing the part of a beautiful spoilt woman used to dealing with rich men.

'Before what?'

'Before,' Lydia repeated, watching his harsh expression soften momentarily and feeling her own aloof façade recede a touch as the intimacies they had shared just a short while ago reared in their minds. 'We can't talk about it here.'

'Where can we talk about it?'

He was back in control now, taking the loaded plate from her with one hand and guiding her towards his table with the other. She was infinitely grateful that he'd taken the small breakfast plate. Even that tiny task would have been too much for her now. She could feel the heat from the palm of his hand in the small of her back as he led her across the room like a puppet on a string, dancing to his tune again. As he pulled back a chair for her, as a waiter appeared and spread a thick napkin across her lap, Lydia glanced across and saw Graham and John just a few feet away, seemingly engrossed in their newspapers. But she knew they were watching, knew that their eyes were on her and Anton and the seemingly initial contact they were making, and it gave her the impetus to centre, to focus on the task in hand instead of the man opposite...to face her burning shame with clear, unwavering eyes.

Nodding a vague thanks as the waiter filled up her coffee cup and melted into the background, Lydia waited till they were alone before answering his loaded question.

'Before the plans changed,' she responded. 'Before

I realised that you'd come on an earlier flight and contact had to be made sooner.'

'Contact!' His word cracked the air like a whip, but Lydia deliberately didn't flinch.

'Convincing contact,' she elaborated with a hint of wry smile. 'I was merely following procedure.'

'Procedure?' Jet eyebrows shot into his hairline, his accent thick, every word loaded with menace. 'Is making love to your subject part of your job? Is this what you expect me to believe? I was told you were a police officer, not some *prostituta*.'

As vile as his words were, Lydia swallowed them. His version was far safer than the truth. If Anton even glimpsed the effect he had on her then both their lives could be in danger.

Selecting the plumpest, ripest strawberry, Lydia drizzled a spoonful of sugar over it, watching as the white crystals dissolved, refusing to jump to his impatient command. Taking her time to ensure her answer to his accusation was the right one.

'I was following your procedure...' Gold eyes glittered as she confronted him. 'To make it look convincing I was following yours—see a girl and pick her up...' Lydia's voice had a taunting ring. 'I'm not the easy one here, Anton—it's you.'

'No.' Angrily, proudly, he shook his head. 'You try to tell me that it was a set-up? That you engineered what happened, because of some threat—'

'We'll talk about this later,' Lydia broke in. His anger, his impending indiscretion were so clearly visible that even Graham was folding his paper, glancing over with a questioning look as Lydia quickly brought the situation under control. 'I refuse to discuss it here, Anton.'

And something in her eyes halted him, told him that she was serious. His tirade, but not the question in his eyes, abated as a concierge appeared, wringing his hands in abject apology as he clearly recognised Lydia's breakfast companion.

'Miss Holmes, I have made a provisional booking for you in a nearby hotel. It's just a few streets away…'

'Why can't she stay here?' Anton's question was curt, authoritative, and had the poor concierge stammering as he tried to answer. 'Are you telling me there isn't a single vacant room in the place?'

'There is,' the concierge attempted. 'But only standard rooms are vacant. All of the luxury suites are booked, sir. I explained this personally to Miss Holmes when she checked in—I told her that the suite she is occupying now was only available for one night, and that after that it would have to be a standard room—which naturally isn't suitable for her needs.'

'Then find her a room that is!' Anton's voice had an ominous ring to it, and for a moment Lydia forgot that he was acting, her top teeth nervously chewing her bottom lip as he voiced his demands. He was clearly used to getting his own way, clearly expecting his demands to be met, and from the tension in the concierge's face, from the nod of his head, they were about to be. Lydia realised with a start that despite Anton's convincing protests, separate rooms were actually the *last* thing either of them wanted.

'I will see what I can arrange…' Nervously, he addressed Lydia. 'Miss Holmes, would you have any objection to staying in one of our mini-suites? They aren't as luxurious as the suite you are in now, but I could ask the staff to—'

'No,' Lydia broke in, and the concierge's hastily arranged solution thankfully disintegrated. Clearly Inspector Bates hadn't fully factored in Anton's enviable pull when he had dreamt up this particular scenario, and she swallowed her guilt as she fixed the concierge with her most withering superior stare. 'I'm not interested in being *downgraded!* Could you please arrange a car?'

Standing, she smoothed her dress, picked up her shoulder bag and started to walk towards the foyer, deliberately avoiding her colleagues' panicked looks, praying inside that Anton would take his cue and rescue the situation.

'Move Miss Holmes's belongings to my suite.' His deep, commanding voice stilled her, and, turning, she watched Anton stare unblinking at the concierge.

'To *your* suite, sir?' The concierge checked, his eyes swivelling from Anton to Lydia.

'That's what I said,' Anton responded.

'You want luggage in taxi?' The bellboy's Italian accent had none of the liquid notes of Anton's, and his attempt at English was crude as he loudly approached the table, causing a couple of diners to look up. Lydia bit down on her lip in mortification as the concierge corrected him.

'No, there's been a change of plan. Miss Holmes will be staying with us after all. Could you take her luggage to suite 311?' The concierge's behaviour was impeccable as he addressed the bellboy. Not by a flicker did he betray what he was surely thinking.

'Suite 311?' The dark features of the bellboy screwed into a frown. 'But that's Mr Santini's suite—'

'Take the bags now, please,' The concierge broke in, clearly irritated that the bellboy had voiced the obvious to anyone within earshot.

As realisation dawned on the junior staff member, the contempt in his black eyes was visible as his gaze met Lydia's. The background chatter on the nearby tables stilled for an impossibly long time as in one crushing moment she changed from executive to escort, and not even the latest make-up direct from New York could fade the blush that spread over her face, over her entire body. Even her hands seemed to burn as she clenched them by her sides and willed this uncomfortable moment to be over.

'Now, come here.'

The derisive tone to his voice as Anton addressed her was like a slap to her cheek. With a flick of his hand, he summoned her to his table, gestured for her to sit down, and even if it was part of the plan, even if he had done the right thing, even if it was her job, Lydia felt a sting of humiliation as she walked back towards him. A burning anger within her flamed at his arrogance, his presumption, and she fought the desire to turn tail and run, or to lift her hand and slap that mocking cheek as she witnessed the glint of triumph in his eyes at her apparent submission. She saw his lips twist into a cruel smile as she obeyed his command and sat down at his table and she was imbued with shame, acknowledging how it surely must appear to all who were watching.

'Take Miss Holmes's bags up to the Presidential Suite.' Anton's voice broke the heavy silence. He stared directly at Lydia as he spoke, and even though the flames of anger and shame licked the sides of her throat, still his voice caressed her, still he managed to fan her desire. Hollowed with unwelcome lust, her heart seemed to stop beating as Anton spoke on, caressing her with each dangerous word, terrifying her with each skilfully seductive syllable. 'She is to be my guest—my very special guest—and I expect her to be treated as such.'

CHAPTER FIVE

'Will that be everything, sir?'

Lydia paced uncomfortably as the last of her bags was deposited into the room by the bellboy. Clearly Anton had a lot of questions to ask, and after his arrogant performance Lydia certainly hadn't been in the mood for chit-chat over breakfast. The sooner Anton Santini heard the ground rules the happier she would be—and once the bellboy was gone, finally they would be alone.

'Not quite,' Anton clipped. 'Can you tell my team that I'm not to be disturbed? I'll meet them as arranged—I've booked one of the boardrooms for twelve.'

'I will make sure they are aware of your wishes.' The bellboy gave a small nod, but still didn't make a move to leave, staring instead at Lydia. Again she was uncomfortable under his scrutiny, embarrassed at what he perceived her to be. 'Would you like the butler to come and unpack for you?'

'I would like to be left alone. Put the "do not disturb" sign on the door on your way out,' Anton retorted briskly. Then, when still he didn't move, Anton pulled out his wallet, pressing a fold of notes into the younger man's hands, whistling an impatient, *'Grazie,'* through gritted teeth.

'Thank you,' the bellboy responded, and Lydia found herself frowning at his response, given that both men were clearly Italian. 'Enjoy your stay.'

Even though there were plenty of things she wanted to say to Anton, even though angry words bobbed on her tongue, as the door closed behind them Lydia still couldn't say what was on her mind. The room had been thoroughly checked only a couple of hours before, but it was up to her to ensure it was still safe. After locking the door and putting the chain on Lydia made idle small talk as she did just that.

'Gorgeous room,' she said, her voice casual. 'The bathroom's divine.' Her words were utterly at odds with her actions as she unzipped her shoulder bag and pulled out a handgun, placing it in the bedside drawer before carefully checking the suite, opening each and every door, looking under the bed, behind the mirrors and pictures, even in the lush arrangements of fresh flowers. Anton frowned, clearly bemused by her actions.

'Is all this really necessary?' When Lydia didn't deign to respond, instead carrying on with her careful check of the room, Anton's palpable impatience upped a notch. 'I asked you a question.'

'I think we need to set some ground rules,' Lydia responded crisply. 'Firstly—I'm here for your protection, Anton, and believe it or not I do happen to know what I'm doing. So please don't question my every move.'

'Suppose these people come into the room at three a.m.?' Anton retorted. 'I hate to tell you your job, but what good is a gun in a bedside drawer with its owner asleep?'

'None at all,' Lydia answered. 'I won't be sleeping, Anton. I'll rest during your meetings.'

'So at night you stay awake?'

'That's right,' Lydia said crisply.

'At night you watch me sleep?' The question was delivered in the same direct manner, his eyes still holding hers, and not by a flicker did he change his expression, but somehow Anton managed to shift the tempo, somehow he managed to reignite the crackling sexual tension, and Lydia moved quickly to douse it.

'I won't be watching you, Anton; I'll be watching the door.'

'It will be a long night for you.'

'I'm used to it,' Lydia said, attempting to be dismissive. 'I don't mind at all.'

'Why not? Do you get paid overtime?'

Her pay packet was none of his damn business. But it wasn't so much the question that infuriated her as the almost imperceptible implication, and the anger that had suffused her downstairs when he'd summoned her to his table emerged again.

'That's none of my business.' Anton answered his own question, then moved swiftly on. 'Secondly? I assume there's more?'

'You are not to leave this room without informing me—either I will accompany you downstairs—'

'Am I allowed to go to the bathroom by myself?'

Ignoring his facetious comment, Lydia attempted to continue with the brief, but Anton wasn't listening. He'd turned his back to her, pulling a small silver laptop out of his case in a clearly insolent gesture.

'I haven't finished yet,' Lydia said. But instead of

turning around to face her, infuriatingly, he opened up his computer and turned it on. 'I'm talking to you, Anton.'

'Then talk.' Anton shrugged, ignoring the warning note in her voice. 'I do not have to see you to listen.'

This only enraged her more, and gave her the final impetus to say what was on her mind. 'Finally, let's get one thing very clear—I know you don't want me here, Anton, and I know you think I'm clearly not up to the job, but don't you ever treat me the way you just did downstairs.'

'I assume we're talking about the restaurant rather than the pool?' Anton asked, pulling up files on his screen, long dark fingers stroking the keys, absolutely refusing to turn around. 'Because from memory you seemed to be enjoying yourself...'

'I'm talking about in the restaurant,' Lydia snapped. 'Insinuating that I'm some sort of escort, trying to embarrass me...'

Lydia wasn't sure what she had expected from Anton—contrition, perhaps, or an attempt at an apology—but the anger that had been simmering inside her exploded out of control as he threw his head back and had the audacity to laugh.

'It isn't funny.'

'I am told that I have to chat you up. I am told by your seniors that I am to arrange for you to stay in my room after only the briefest of meetings.' Finally he faced her, the computer forgotten as he stood up and turned around. 'Tell me, Lydia, how the hell were you supposed to come out of that encounter looking anything other than a cheap tart? Did you expect to come out of it looking like a rescued nun?'

'Of course not,' Lydia retorted but Anton hadn't finished and he walked two dangerous steps towards her. There were several metres still between them but even the slightest forward motion of this man had her mentally ducking for cover, had the vast Presidential Suite shrinking to a broom cupboard as he held her with his eyes.

'You say that people are watching.' His voice was coarse and direct. 'You say that that I have to act normally, that these people will know if I act in a different way.'

'Yes,' Lydia croaked, her mouth impossibly dry, her eyes wide as still he came closer. She tried to stall him with words, tried to put her point across while there was still space between them. 'And maybe you're used to women who—'

'Oh, I'm used to women,' Anton broke in, still a couple of feet away, but suffocatingly close now. 'I *know* women,' he breathed. 'I know all the games they play…' His voice trailed off, a muscle flickering in his cheek as he stared down at her. 'And believe me, Lydia, I have never once needed to pay for the pleasure of a woman's company—and anyone watching, anyone who knows about me, knows that to be true.'

'So what was that about downstairs?' Lydia pushed. 'Summoning me to your table, ordering me to sit. If I hadn't been on duty, Anton, I'd have walked—'

'You'd have sat,' Anton cut in. 'And that isn't a compliment.'

'I don't take it as one,' Lydia retorted. 'You're so damn sure of yourself,' she choked, appalled at his arrogance. 'You're so sure that with one crook of your finger you can have any woman you want—well, you're wrong. I'm here because of work, Anton, and believe me, I'm not enjoying myself.'

'You were a couple of hours ago,' Anton pointed out. 'Don't try and tell me otherwise.'

'You're a great kisser.' Somehow she kept her voice even, somehow she stayed calm. 'Maybe practice does make perfect after all—but it was strictly work for me.'

'Liar.' Anton smiled slowly, playing his trump card, recalling Inspector Bates's words and carefully watching her reaction as he relayed them. 'I spoke with your boss. I know that you weren't expecting me in the pool—the same way I wasn't expecting you, Lydia. This morning wasn't about work. It was about attraction.'

'No.' Slowly but surely she shook her head, red hair shimmering as the morning sun captured it. 'I thought you had been briefed, that you were fully aware I was a police officer. I was told that our initial meeting had to look authentic. I was just glad that as luck would have it Anton Santini didn't turn out to be five foot two with a beer belly. I guess even in the dirtiest of jobs there are flashes of silver.'

'So that kiss we shared…' He didn't look so assured now, his voice trailing off, those dark eyes for the first time confused.

'Was for the cameras.' Lydia finished for him. 'At least it was on my part. Though I have to admit—' she gave a small laugh '—it was extremely pleasurable.'

'We nearly made love,' Anton pointed out. 'We nearly—'

'No, Anton, we didn't.' Every word was a lie, every word a supreme effort, but a necessary one. She knew with certainty that she had to take the heat out of this encounter—had to somehow erase all that happened. And this was the only way she knew how. 'I pulled back—remember? I might have to crawl into your bed for the next couple of mornings to make things look convincing when the maid comes in. I might have to hold your hand as we walk down the hotel corridor, or even kiss you in front of a crowd, but don't for a minute think that it's about you and I. This is what I do for a living. I'm an undercover cop, and immersing myself in a role is something I'm used to. You were the one who kissed me, Anton,' Lydia reminded him. 'You were the one who swam over to a virtual stranger for no other reason than sexual attraction. I, on the other hand, was working.'

'Prostituting yourself!' Anton sneered.

'Trying to save your life,' Lydia countered. 'Though I have to admit sometimes I wonder why I bother.'

'I didn't ask for your help,' Anton pointed out. 'In fact, if it were up to me I would prefer to take my chances alone rather than have a—' He didn't say it, stopped himself before it continued, but the word was as audible as if he'd shouted it.

Lydia shook her head as yet again he questioned her competence and she finished the sentence for him.

'Than have a *mere* woman protect you?'

'I didn't say that,' Anton refuted. 'But if you insist on the truth then, yes—I admit that is how I feel.'

And Lydia could only grudgingly admire his honesty as he elaborated, because finally here was someone who actually voiced what half the station she worked at secretly thought. Here was someone who had the guts to speak his chauvinistic mind.

'I cannot possibly see how a woman half my weight,

who does not even reach my shoulders, has any hope of protecting me…' Anton's hands were gesturing wildly as he spoke, relegating her substantial height to that of a five-year-old. 'Maybe you are an expert at martial arts—who knows? But a black belt won't stop a bullet. This is not suitable women's work.'

Even making allowances for a rather poor translation, Anton's take on things was brutally obvious. His utter disregard, his sheer lack of respect for her had been made crystal clear.

'What *is* suitable women's work, Anton?' Lydia asked, her face chalk beneath her rouge, lips rigid with rage. 'Barefoot and pregnant in your kitchen?'

'You are being ridiculous,' Anton hissed.

'No more ridiculous than the assumptions you have just made about me—but at least my assumptions are based on fact. I've read up on you these past few days, Mr Santini.'

'What? You've flicked through a few glossy magazines to form an opinion?' Anton sneered. 'That would be about your level.'

'You arrogant bastard,' Lydia whispered. ' Maybe the only role you feel suitable for women is on our backs, with our legs wrapped around you, massaging your already over-inflated ego, but other people's lives may be at stake here—not just yours. There are innocent guests at this hotel, children staying here, and not for a second will I or my team allow their safety to be compromised. So you'd better start playing the game, Anton. For the next couple of days, like it or not, you're stuck with me—and whatever problem you have dealing with that fact, I suggest you bury it.'

Turning she headed for the bathroom, closing the door behind her and resting her shaking hands on the cool black marble, staring into the mirror at the made-up face she barely recognised, swallowing bile as she recalled the vile words that had hissed between them. Somehow they had managed to derogate the pure, naked beauty that had shrouded them this morning, had taken away the raw pleasure of that intimate moment until all that was left was a filthy smear of shame.

Flicking on the cold tap, Lydia ran her wrists under the water, willing herself calm, collecting her thoughts before heading back into the sumptuous room. She was expecting a second onslaught. Expecting Anton's fury to have been exacerbated by her absence and for the onslaught of questions to start again. But as she stepped into the lounge, her stilettos not making a sound on the thick woollen carpet, for a second Lydia felt as if she were intruding.

His back to her, Anton was gazing out of the massive windows, but there was a loneliness to him that hadn't been there before, a weariness she was sure she hadn't seen, and it unsettled her—a flash of fragility in this fiercely proud man, a tiny chink in his armour that she was sure he hadn't meant to reveal.

'Anton?' The brittle edge had gone from her voice, but she waited for his mask to slip back on, for his haughty indifference to emerge as she crossed the room, but still he stared out of the window, and his voice was low and soft when finally it came.

'I apologise.'

Not for a moment had she expected an apology. The best she had hoped for was a tense stand-off. But somehow Lydia knew his words were heartfelt, somehow she knew that a man like Anton wouldn't apologise unless he meant it.

'I go too far.'

'You do?' Lydia gave a tiny, tight smile, taken aback by the sudden change in him. 'I do too,' she admitted.

'This morning has been…' She watched as he struggled to find the appropriate words, his hands clenching in frustration, and Lydia said them for him.

'A shock?'

He gave a slow nod.

'More often than not these security alerts come to nothing,' Lydia explained, more gently now. 'Certain events trigger alarms and we have to explore every avenue. It doesn't necessarily mean that—'

'That isn't what is bothering me,' Anton said with a tiny flick of his head.

'Then what is?'

Slowly he turned, the pain in his eyes hitting her with such intensity she took a step backwards. But he recovered in an instant, his stance snapping back to normal, a brittle smile inching over his lips as he scathingly answered her question. The mask had slipped back on with practised ease, just as she had known it would.

'Anton—' Lydia's voice was wary '—do you have any idea who it is that might want to harm you?'

'No.'

'Do you have any enemies?' Lydia pushed, frowning when he shrugged dismissively.

'Too many to name—'

'Anton, if you have any idea who might be behind all this, then it's imperative that you tell me. If you think—'

'My thoughts are my own, Lydia,' Anton snapped. The mask was firmly back in place now—no glimpse of the pensive side to him she had just glimpsed. 'Not even *you* can access them. Now, if you can let your colleagues know, I'd like to head down to the boardroom and get on with my day.'

CHAPTER SIX

IT WAS a relief to leave him at his meeting—a relief to come back to the room, lock the door and finally let her own mask slip for a few hours. To undress and pull the curtains and slide into the massive bed that he would inhabit tonight, and force herself into a few hours of Anton-inspired restless sleep.

The vibration of the pager on her bedside table informed her that the meeting would soon be closing, told her to get dressed and make her way down to the bar. Eyeing her wardrobe, Lydia stared at her rather pale offerings. The faithful black dress that *always* fitted the bill seemed drab and lifeless now. Her wardrobe wasn't quite up to the sophisticated world Anton inhabited. She was unsure if she could get away with wearing the dress she had worn earlier—the one truly fabulous item in her wardrobe, which had been borrowed from her incredibly glamorous younger sister.

It would have to do.

Again!

Dressing quickly, and heading to the bathroom, Lydia rinsed her mouth and touched up her make-up and perfume. She carefully placed the gun in her specifically designed handbag—a holster was considered too much of a risk if it were seen—then took a moment to check her reflection in the vast full-length mirror. The controlled, elegant woman who stared back at her was the antithesis of how she was feeling—her emotions were as friable as an adolescent's—but her glittering eyes were the only indicator of the fizzing arousal he had so easily instigated.

Checking her bag was in position, feeling the heavy weight of the gun against her side, Lydia let her eyes linger on the massive opulent bed of the Presidential Suite. She tried not to picture his jet hair on the golden pillow... Tried not to visualise that haughty guarded face softened by sleep... Tried not to imagine herself lying beside him...tried and failed on all three counts.

As dangerous and unpredictable as the night might be, the real danger to her wasn't what lay ahead in the bar, or on the walk back to the suite. The real danger for Lydia would be right here in this room. She had to keep her guard up, had to remain eternally vigilant, had to watch out not just for his life, but for her heart.

There was no question of heading over to the bar and ordering her drink.

As Anton Santini's *special guest,* Lydia acted accordingly—taking a seat on one of the low, velvet lounges and barely looking up as an attentive waiter came and asked what she would like to drink.

'Strawberry daiquiri,' Lydia answered, glancing briefly over to the bar to ensure that Kevin had seen her arrival. It was important that no one suspected even for a second that she was carefully observing proceedings, and if she was being watched a glass of mineral water might raise suspicion. Kevin had been placed at the bar to work as a member of the staff. His seniority was needed to oversee things, and also to ensure that, as much as possible, all the undercover detectives' drinks remained alcohol-free.

As the VIPs started to drift in from their meeting, Lydia didn't even need to turn her head to know when Anton arrived. The noise of background chatter and laughter dropped a touch, conversation momentarily suspended as he entered. The staff snapped to attention and Lydia noted that even the most beautiful of women checked themselves. Their hands dashing to their faces, flicking their hair, pulling in already toned stomachs, tongues licking at beautifully rouged lips, eyes narrowing a touch as their gazes followed the focus of this beautiful man's attention. Because he filled the room as he stepped inside—brooding yet somehow charismatic, with an elusive quality that had everyone paying attention.

What Lydia had expected of Anton, she wasn't sure—perhaps for the same chauvinistic arrogance she had witnessed in the restaurant to emerge again, or a brief, distracted introduction to his colleagues and acquaintances. But his attention was solely on her, his eyes fixed on her and only her as he crossed the room, dismissing his entourage. Clearly whatever had needed to be said in the meeting had been dealt with, and Anton was now off duty.

And stunning, to boot!

As he crossed the room, his purposeful stride heading directly towards Lydia, his restless eyes focussed solely on her, it was all too easy for a tiny dangerous moment for Lydia to indulge herself, to pretend that this was her reality—that the elegant, intimate smile softening his mouth was truly for her.

'How was your meeting?' Lydia asked as he sat down beside her on the low couch. The forced closeness was more intoxicating than any liquor, his thigh pressing against hers, his voice low and deep. Because of the background noise, Lydia had to lean forward to catch it.

'That is not how you would greet me if you were my woman.' His warm hand slid behind the curtain of her hair, his fingers massaging the back of her neck. Tiny pulses of energy flicked through her body as his mouth moved towards hers. '*This* is how you would greet me.'

He tasted of danger.

His kiss was a dangerous, teasing elaboration of the fantasy she had just harboured. And, as sexist and chauvinistic as his words were, they caused a flutter of excitement in the pit of her stomach—to be *his* woman, to greet this divine man with the deepest of kisses, had Lydia literally trembling inside. His tongue slid around hers, and his utter lack of inhibition, the complete inappropriateness of his actions, caused a shrill of excitement in her groin.

'That's better!' Pulling back, he lifted the drink that had been placed before him, completely calm, seemingly unmoved.

Lydia's eyes darted to Maria's, and she tried vainly to ignore the shocked but gleeful expression on her colleague's face.

'Now, how about we head for the restaurant?'

'I'd rather eat in the room,' Lydia attempted, the detective in her anxious to get him away from the crowd and to the relative safety of his suite. But when Anton shook his head and headed for the restaurant Lydia had no choice but to follow, her lips tight as Kevin delivered an annoyed frown in their direction.

Naturally Anton made an entrance as he entered the restaurant, with every face turning to look at the dark, brooding gentleman as he was whisked away to a discreet corner table.

There was an uncomfortable moment as Lydia ignored the chair that was pulled out for her, choosing instead the one that was being held out for Anton—to enable her to face the room and watch out for any irregularities.

'Sorry, I forgot,' Anton said as she sat, and for a second she was privy to one of his most charming smiles. Not for the first time Lydia wondered how on earth she was going to get through this—because Anton wasn't the only one struggling to remember why she was here. His gaze was so captivating, his company so overwhelming, it took all her strength to remain focussed, to break away every now and then and work the room with her eyes instead of staring into his. Waiters were hovering, pouring water, spreading a huge napkin over Lydia's trembling knees as Anton dealt swiftly with the wine list.

'Red?'

'Just water, thank you.'

'Water?' Anton looked truly appalled, but Lydia was insistent, taking the massive menu and trying to quickly make her way through it—which, after such a thorough kissing, was a feat in itself. Somehow Lydia stumbled through it, choosing a simple risotto as Anton ordered a massive rare steak, making small talk as the waiters flurried around them, but once they were alone Lydia managed to say what was on her mind.

'Don't do that again, Anton. If I say we go to the room, then that's what we do.'

'You like your work?' Anton asked, completely ignoring her anger.

'I love jewellery,' Lydia responded tightly, her eyes working the room, but relaxing slightly when she saw John and Graham being guided to a nearby table.

'Have some wine,' Anton pushed. 'It's really very good.'

'I can't drink any alcohol,' Lydia answered, her eyes imploring him to understand. Anton just frowned back at her, but thankfully changed the subject.

'So, your boyfriend—what does he think of your job?'

Not so thankful perhaps!

Giving him a tight smile, Lydia reluctantly answered—realising they would arouse suspicion if they sat in silence, but not too sure how much of herself to reveal. 'My ex-boyfriend hated it.' Lydia gave a tight smile. 'Even though he was in the jewellery business too. I've had a bit more success than he has lately—I think he may have been jealous.'

'Or concerned?' Anton quipped, and Lydia gritted her teeth. 'I wouldn't like my woman in that kind of work.'

'Your woman?' Lydia gave a tight smile. 'Whatever you were trying to say, Anton, it didn't translate very well.'

'It translated perfectly,' Anton answered, not remotely fazed. 'It's not a very feminine job—though I have to say you look amazing tonight. That dress, however, is a touch familiar. Maybe tomorrow I take you shopping.'

If it had been a real date she'd have slapped his damned face. 'Maybe not!' Lydia snapped.

'You are...' He paused for a second as he chose his words. 'One of those feminist women, yes?'

Lydia's jaw dropped at his cheek. 'What I am and what I believe in has absolutely nothing to do with you—'

'But we are on a date!' Anton flashed a devilish grin. 'Surely we are supposed to be getting to know each other better, Lydia?'

He had a point—and, given that her colleagues were close, and that the background noise of the restaurant meant there was no chance of them being overheard, by the time their meals arrived Lydia had relented a touch, dropping her defensive guard a notch, but only so as to find out more about *him*.

'Do *you* enjoy your work?' Lydia asked, picking her way through her risotto, her usually healthy appetite the size of a sparrow's under Anton's scrutiny.

'Most of the time.' Anton nodded. 'It does not leave me much time for myself, though...' He frowned as Lydia raised a slightly questioning eyebrow. 'It doesn't!' he insisted.

'From what I've gleaned, you've found the time to maintain an incredibly active social life, Anton.'

'It really isn't as good as the magazines make out.' Not remotely embarrassed by her inference, Anton gave an easy shrug. 'A lot of those so-called relationships were nothing more than a few dinner dates.' Lydia's eyebrows were practically in her hairline and Anton managed a wry laugh. 'So I don't like to sleep alone. I wasn't aware it was a crime!'

'I never said it was,' Lydia replied, but despite the hair and make-up, despite the flickering candlelight and the presence of this stunning man, her mind was still alert. The detective in her was carefully placing the pieces in this difficult, complicated jigsaw, and, shooting him a direct question, she carefully watched his reaction. 'What happened twelve months ago, Anton?'

Watching his face still, Lydia knew her hunch had been right—knew that she'd hit a nerve.

'Nothing.' To most people it would have seemed his recovery was instantaneous, but Lydia noted that his eyes were no longer able to meet hers. His hand reached for his glass and he took a sip as, to Lydia's trained mind, he played for time. 'Why do you ask?'

'I'm just curious,' Lydia said casually, but her mind was anything but. 'It would seem your *social life* became rather more active around then…' Momentarily she took her eyes from him. After ensuring no waiter was hovering she pushed the conversation a touch further, sure that her vague hunch was right—sure that somehow she was on the right track. 'And so did those telephone calls.'

'The two are not related,' Anton said quickly—too quickly for Lydia's liking. His rapid response told Lydia it was something he'd already considered.

'How can you be so sure?' Lydia asked.

'I just am,' Anton retorted, abruptly ending the conversation, clearly irritated by her intrusion.

The slightly more amicable air they had created was

history now and they stumbled on in silence. Pretty soon dinner was clearly over. His steak barely touched, Anton dropped his knife and fork with a clatter, screwed up his napkin and tossed it onto the table.

'You walk me back now?' He gave a tight smile, and Lydia wasn't sure if it was an apology for his bad English, or the embarrassment of his date looking out for him.

'Do you want to go out in the gardens for coffee—or a brandy, perhaps?' Anton asked as they walked through the hotel foyer. And though it could have been mere politeness that had engineered the question, though she was in no doubt he offered the same to every woman after a meal—brandy and coffee in some delectable surrounds—Lydia had a feeling he was delaying things. She realised that maybe, just maybe, Anton was dreading heading upstairs as much as her—dreading the stuffy confines of his bedroom—even if it was in the Presidential Suite. A night in each other's company, a night denying the attraction that leapt between them, would be an almost impossible feat.

'No.' Lydia shook her head. The gardens were the last place she wanted to be with a potential hitman on the loose. 'I think we really ought head back.'

'And I think I could really use a brandy,' Anton said sharply, snapping his fingers at the young woman on the desk, who immediately made her way over, completely refusing to follow the rules that had been so carefully spelt out.

All Lydia knew was that if she didn't get control here and now then she might just as well walk away from the job—unless Anton accepted that for now she was the one in charge, then both their lives would be in danger.

'Darling—' Smiling sweetly, Lydia took his hand as he relayed his orders to the young woman, choking back a gurgle of laughter as Anton's words abruptly halted. 'I really am tired. Let's forget about the brandy and head for bed.'

It was a credit to his strength that he didn't make a sound, his expression almost bland as Lydia's hand coiled around his and, in a subtle but supremely painful manoeuvre she had learnt years ago—one that would have bought most people to their knees in a matter of seconds—pushed his thumb up firmly against his wrist. Briskly, she walked her reluctant partner towards the lifts. For all the world they looked like any other couple heading for bed. No one could have guessed the agony Anton was in as she marched him across the foyer.

'What the hell was that?' Anton glowered as the lift doors closed and Lydia's grip finally loosened. She held back a smile as he let out a long breath and mumbled a few choice words. She didn't need a translation to guess that he was cursing her in Italian as he bent over slightly and held his hand between his thighs. 'You just about broke my thumb back there.'

'And you just about broke our cover,' Lydia said sharply. 'When I say move, Anton, we move—got it?'

He didn't answer—didn't even let her go first when the lift door opened—just marched ahead of her.

'Manners.' Lydia grinned at his tense back.

'You want it both ways?' Anton barked, pulling out his swipe card to open the hotel room. 'Well, you choose, Lydia—if you want to act like a man in a bar then that is how I will treat you. Don't act all tough one minute and then demand I hold doors open for you or step aside.'

In angry silence they entered the suite, and Anton stood with his back to the wall, eyes narrowed. as again she checked and secured the room.

'Have you ordered Room Service for the morning?' It was Lydia who broke the silence with a brisk question which Anton clearly had no intention of answering. 'I need to know, Anton, because if there's going to be someone coming in with breakfast then I'm going to have to tidy away my stuff and unlock the door…' For a beat of a second she paused. 'It will have to look as if we're sleeping together—but don't worry, I'll be fully clothed!'

'I have coffee and papers delivered to the room at five-thirty,' came the surly response. 'I can cancel if you prefer.'

'No need,' Lydia breathed. 'Don't change your routine on my account.'

'Maybe I should ring down now for some ice packs and plaster of Paris. We could spend the night making a few limb splints for me, just in case I step out of line again!'

'You're being ridiculous, Anton,' Lydia retorted. 'I was doing my job.'

'I know…' A ghost of a smile twitched on his angry mouth. 'That really hurt, you know.'

'It's supposed to,' Lydia answered, but her own mouth was curving into a smile as her anger dimmed, a tiny giggle escaping as she replayed the scene in her mind. 'Are you okay?'

'I'll survive.' Anton shrugged. 'I'm not sure if it's my thumb or my ego that's bruised.'

'Probably both.' Lydia grinned. 'I'll go and make myself comfortable and hopefully I won't disturb you—just pretend I'm not here. Carry on as you would normally.'

'Suppose I want a shower?' His voice was almost defensive. 'Suppose I want to ring for ice cream and watch the late night movie...?'

'Then do it,' Lydia replied, rather more nonchalantly than she felt. 'Anton, I've slept all afternoon, I'm not even remotely tired, so if you want the lights blazing all night that's fine. If you want Room Service dropping by, go for it—just carry on as you usually would and just forget that I'm here.'

'Forget?' A tiny mocking laugh met Lydia's ears and she watched as he peeled off his jacket and sat on the massive bed, kicked off his shoes and then wrestled with his tie, loosening it enough to slip it over his head and toss it on to the floor—undoubtedly sure that someone would pick it up in the morning, that someone would untangle whatever mess he'd created.

The analogy was as welcome as the relief that flooded Lydia—he was her problem, but only for now.

This impossible, beautiful, incredibly spoilt man was only in her life for a very short while, and she mustn't forget that for a moment.

'Forget I'm here, Anton,' Lydia affirmed, and, dragging a chair to beside the bed and swivelling the night light behind it, grabbing the magazines that were thoughtfully arranged on the coffee table, she set up her small corner for the next few hours. 'Just carry on as normal—I'm here to protect you, that's all. You certainly don't have to entertain me.'

'Fine,' Anton clipped, peeling off several thousand dollars' worth of suit and dropping it to the floor.

Lydia forced herself to concentrate on her magazine—trying to read about creating the perfect eyebrow shape as Anton wandered around the room, pacing like a restless animal. He was dressed only in a pair of boxers and his white shirt now, and he had the attention span of a two-year-old—flicking on the television, lifting up the phone and then changing his mind and replacing the receiver, even rummaging through his toiletry bag and producing his razor.

'You don't mind?'

Glancing up, Lydia rolled her eyes as he held up the offending article. 'Be my guest.'

As he began shaving, Lydia stole a tiny glimpse—and immediately wished she hadn't. The white shirt had been replaced by a white T-shirt now, emphasising his broad chest. Dark, olive-skinned legs were accentuated by the navy silk boxers, and somehow Anton Santini made the simple act of shaving look impossibly sexy—dark hair flopping over his forehead, the skin around his eyes creasing in concentration, a very pink tongue poking out of his full, sensual mouth.

But even that wasn't enough to calm his restless mood. Drying his face on a fluffy white hand towel, he headed to the window and, pulling back the curtain, stared out at the night city skyline. He watched the moon drifting past the Rialto Towers, his fingers drumming on the window ledge, while Lydia sneaked a peek from behind the safety of her magazine, looking at his haughty profile, noting the tension in his shoulders, the grim set of his jaw. She decided to reiterate what she had said.

'I know it's uncomfortable for you having me here, but you really don't have to—'

'I'm not uncomfortable,' Anton broke in.

'You were pacing before,' Lydia pointed out. 'You haven't even lain down.'

'So?' He shrugged, still staring out of the window, his fingers still drumming their silent tune on the ledge, tension etched in his every feature. 'This is how I am.' He gave another tight shrug. 'I don't sleep much—is that a problem for you?'

'Of course not,' Lydia replied, returning her attention back to the magazine—but Anton prolonged the conversation.

'I want a coffee.'

'Sorry?' Lydia blinked at him—no wonder the guy had trouble sleeping!

'I want a cup of coffee.'

'You don't expect me to make it for you, do you?'

'Of course not,' Anton snapped, clearly irritated by her response. 'But if I ring Room Service, then you have to put the gun away, move your chair, make it look as if…'

'That's no problem at all,' Lydia said assuredly. 'Anton, you can ring Room Service every hour, on the hour, for all I care—believe me, moving a chair a few times doesn't faze me at all. In fact, compared to what I usually have to do—'

'I'll make it myself,' Anton interrupted, and Lydia returned to her magazine, assuming, as one would, that making a coffee was no big deal.

Unless it was Anton making coffee!

From the noise coming from the tiny kitchen area Lydia could have been forgiven for thinking he was attempting to whip up a five-course meal! Just how hard was it to flick a switch on a kettle and peel open a sachet of coffee?

'You pull the plunger out first, Anton!' Lydia

snapped, watching in disbelief as he went to pour the filter coffee straight in.

'What difference does it make?' Anton bristled.

'None.' Lydia shrugged. 'If you don't mind picking the grinds out of your teeth all night.'

She certainly hadn't wanted to interfere—if he was so mollycoddled he didn't even know how to make a pot of filter coffee it was certainly time he learnt—but his restlessness was irritating Lydia now. The sooner he had his blessed drink, the sooner he would get into bed, and the sooner Lydia would find out how to turn her pale eyebrows into something that would rival Audrey Hepburn's.

'I know what you're thinking.' Bringing over his pot of coffee and a cup, and placing them on the bedside table, Anton stretched out on the bed, propping himself up on one elbow. Even though Lydia wasn't looking at him, she could feel him staring at her. 'You're thinking that I don't even know how to make a cup of coffee.' There was a smile behind his heavily accented words, but Lydia refused to reciprocate, just stared at the blurring words before her and attempted a vague answer.

'I wasn't.' Lydia shrugged.

'Yes, you were.'

'Believe it or not, Anton—' still Lydia didn't look at him '—I wasn't thinking about you in the least. I was actually trying to read.'

'I thought you were supposed to be on guard.'

'I am.' Lydia whistled through her teeth, giving him a taste of his words from earlier. 'I can read and listen at the same time!'

'Well, just in case you *were* wondering,' Anton carried on, to his most unresponsive audience, 'I actually make a very *good* cup of coffee. But normally I make it on the stove…' The tiniest of smiles flickered on her lips and Anton picked up on it in a second. 'What is so funny?'

'I suppose you chop your own wood too?'

'Sorry?'

'To heat the stove?'

'You are being sarcastic, no?'

'Yes, I'm being sarcastic.' Giving in, Lydia put the magazine down and finally looked at him. 'It's nearly two a.m., Anton.'

'So?'

'You flew across the world last night—you were in the swimming pool at six.' At least he had the grace to blush, Lydia noted. 'And the maid's coming in at five-thirty. You really don't sleep much, do you?'

'Hardly at all.' Anton grimaced, taking a hefty belt of his treacle-coloured drink.

'Doesn't it bother you?' Lydia asked. 'I mean, I'd be a nervous wreck if I had to chair an important meeting tomorrow and had barely slept a wink.'

'I'm used to it,' Anton said, as he simultaneously stretched and yawned.

'Maybe if you cut down on the caffeine, it would help…' Lydia paused for a moment as his stretching movement offered her a rather delicious view of a very flat, very toned stomach.

'Maybe,' Anton said. 'But then again, an armed detective by my side and the knowledge that someone wants me dead isn't exactly conducive to a restful night.'

'Touché,' Lydia smiled.

'Actually…' He yawned again, his eyes squinting as

he attempted to focus on her, and Lydia realised just how tired he must be. Even if it had been in the utmost luxury, the man had crossed from the other side of the world less than twenty-four hours ago, had been briefed by detectives, then sat in a meeting for hours, and managed to make it to a restaurant for dinner when most people would have been asleep by now. Somehow he wore it well, but his voice was a touch slower now, his accent a shade heavier as he spoke. 'If I were at home now I would have been asleep hours ago. It's not you, or the guns or the threats that bother me—it's the hotel.'

'But it's gorgeous,' Lydia admonished. 'You're thinking about buying it!'

'No doubt I will.' Anton groaned. 'And I'll be the one to sign off on the glossy advertising that calls it a home from home for the busy executive. But how can it be home when that tiny little bottle of shampoo is always full…?'

Lydia found herself smiling at his sleepy logic.

'How can it be home when every time you walk in it's as if you have been erased—clothes hung up, the newspaper you were reading neatly folded… I'm tired of hotels.'

'I suppose after a while the novelty would wear off,' Lydia agreed, her fingers twirling her red curls, long legs stretched out. So relaxed was their conversation that she barely noticed when her robe fell open a touch. She was completely engrossed in this intriguing man.

'Can you answer me something honestly?' Anton asked, pulling back the duvet and slipping inside, his eyes almost closed now.

Lydia's guard dropped another couple of notches. Not against the danger outside—her senses were still on high alert for any intruder that might approach—but the man before her now didn't pose any danger. Jet lagged, exhausted, after an age of fighting, the only thing on Anton's weary mind was sleep.

'It depends what you want to know,' Lydia answered easily, but the smile on her lips faded, her throat constricting when he voiced his question, and her mind whirred for an appropriate response.

'When we kissed this morning, when you were in my arms, was it merely another day in the office for you?'

It was an age before she answered—weighing up her answer, truth versus a lie—but somehow with his eyes half closed, with that delicious, vicious mouth relaxed now, it was so much easier to be honest, so much easier to answer his question.

'No.' Her throat felt like sandpaper, her honesty startling her, but it was countered with relief at finally being able to admit the truth. 'It was *nothing* like a normal day in the office.'

'Good,' Anton answered softly, a small, lazy smile on his face, and Lydia wondered if he was recalling it now, was going to sleep with that scorching encounter on his mind.

'Can you answer me something, Anton?'

'Hmm?' He was almost asleep now.

'Was it just another day in the office for *you*?' She watched a lazy frown form about his closed eyes. 'I mean, I know you've had lots of...' Her voice trailed off. She didn't actually want to go there, Lydia realised. Didn't want to think about the women he treated so casually, didn't want to be associated with that formidable list of conquests. But Anton spoke anyway, his voice thick with sleep.

'I like company.' Anton yawned. 'And I hate sleeping alone, hate having time to think about...'

'About?' Lydia pushed, intrigued.

'It doesn't matter.' Anton shrugged.

'Have you ever been in love?' Lydia asked—and, yes, it was personal, but so was what they'd shared that morning. 'I mean, do any of those relationships mean anything to you?'

'One did.' His navy eyes snapped open and Lydia stared into them, her breath held in her throat as she awaited his response. She knew, just knew, that her gentle line of questioning combined with his sheer exhaustion was allowing him to open up—knew she was going to get the answer to the question she had versed a couple of hours before.

'Or I thought it did, I guess. Even I get things wrong sometimes. You should have been a psychologist, Lydia, not a detective—you were right downstairs: something did happen twelve months ago. But it has nothing to do with this, nothing to do with the phone calls I have been getting...'

'How can you be sure?'

'I just am.'

'Who was she?' Lydia asked, nervous of pushing too hard but needing to know more. And it wasn't all down to the fact she was a detective—she needed to hear for herself the name of the woman who had moved this man so. A rush of jealousy washed over her as she heard the pensive note to his voice.

'Her name was Cara...'

'Was?' Lydia whispered, picking up on the past tense, berating herself for her envious feelings as she registered his pain. 'Did she die?'

'No.' He gave a tiny shake of his head and Lydia assumed that was it, that the conversation was over and already he'd revealed more than he'd intended, but Anton hadn't finished yet. 'Sometimes, though, I wish that she had.'

It wasn't the viciousness of his words that shocked Lydia, but the certainty behind them.

And she'd have loved to hear more, willed him to go on—but, exhausted, he had fallen asleep mid-sentence. Those astute navy eyes had finally closed on a world that would have left any other mere mortal asleep hours ago.

Lydia tried so hard to focus on the snippets of information she had gleaned, tried so hard to concentrate on the job instead of the man, but over and over her gaze drifted to where he lay, watching that haughty, sculptured face, gentle now in sleep. And finally, when the moon had long since gone, when the deep silent hush before dawn hummed around the room, Lydia slipped out of her seat, ready to face the moment she had simultaneously been awaiting and dreading.

Moving the coffee table to its original place, she pushed the chair back against the wall, placed her gun carefully under the pillow and unlocked the door. Dressed in nothing more than shorts and a small crop top, she slipped in bed beside him, shivering on the cool cotton sheets and awaiting the maid's entry, bracing herself for intrusion, for danger…

CHAPTER SEVEN

IN SLEEP he reached out for her.

Heavy forearms dragged her rigid body to the soft warmth of his side of the bed. For a moment she fought it, but her shivering and exhausted body gave in. She relaxed a touch as his knees pressed into the back of hers, as she felt the dust of his thigh against her skin, the idle stroking of her ribs as he edged her closer, spooning his body into hers.

It could be any woman lying beside him, Lydia reminded herself, and his response would be the same—men like Anton weren't used to sleeping alone. Men like Anton were way too used to sharing their bed. His response to her was automatic.

A soft knocking on the door had Lydia's heart pounding in her chest. To an onlooker she would have looked asleep, but the tumble of hair over her face concealed eyes that were wide open, taking in every detail of the shadowy room. One hand was underneath the pillow, its fingers curled around the gun, and her body was locked in a fight or flight response as the door creaked open. Her ears were on alert, not for a moment fooled by the reassuring sounds of cups being arranged and drinks being poured. She made sure that she could only hear one set of footsteps—that no one else was taking this opportunity to plant themselves in the room.

Anton slept on, seemingly unaware of the danger. Downstairs there were armed police, and undercover detectives, ready to watch his every move, and even if a potential attacker was unaware of the fact, it was unlikely that they would choose a visible high-profile arena to attempt an attack. It was here, behind closed doors, where an attack was more likely—and Lydia was acutely aware of that fact, knowing that whenever a staff member entered the hazard was heightened.

Stirring slightly, as if awakening from a deep sleep, Lydia repositioned herself, her hand still on the gun. She watched as the maid first opened the curtains, then headed back to the table, arranging the morning's newspapers, moving the sugar bowl an inch or two before discreetly heading for the door.

'Your coffee's been poured, Mr Santini.'

Deep in sleep, unaware of the possible danger he had been in, Anton didn't even stir, and Lydia's attention remained solely focussed on the door until it closed behind the maid. Looking around the room, she ensured in her mind that everything was in order, that nothing was out of place. Only then did her hand move from the gun, only then did she finally relax.

'We're alive, then?'

Startled, Lydia turned her head to face him, auburn hair tumbling on the pillow, a frown marring her brow as Anton, wide awake, raised an eyebrow at her response.

'I thought you were asleep.'

'I thought that was the idea.' Anton shrugged. 'But

if I'm about to meet my maker, I'd at least like to be aware of the fact!'

Wriggling from his embrace, Lydia jumped free, busying herself by sugaring her coffee. She deliberately avoided looking at him as he jumped from the bed, yawning and stretching, and pulled on his bathers.

'What are you doing?' Lydia blinked.

'I'm going for my swim, as I always do.' Anton shrugged. 'I assume you'll be joining me?'

'You assume wrong!' Lydia answered, putting on her massive white robe and slippers, then carefully placing her gun in the pocket, her fingers coiling around the cool metal. 'This time I'll just be watching—supposedly in rapt admiration.'

'Supposedly?' Anton gave a knowing smile, and without a word headed out the door.

With some difficulty Lydia feigned nonchalance, relaxing on a lounger that faced the pool's entrance. But Anton was wrong for once—there was no time to admire his toned body as he dived into the pool and started his arduous swim. Well, maybe a second or two, but the pool and gym were far busier this morning and Lydia's attention was focussed instead on the hotel patrons. She carefully observed their movements, ensuring that no one was taking more than a vague interest in the man whose life she was guarding, and it was a relief to get Anton safely back to his room.

Whatever profit the hotel might make because Anton didn't like the intrusion of a butler they would lose in their water bill. The full half-hour he spent in the shower gave Lydia plenty of time to dress, hoping that the black pants and sheer top that she'd normally go out on the town in would suffice for breakfast with Anton.

God, he was taking for ever! She spent ages on her make-up—there was even enough time to plug in her ceramic hair straighteners and attempt to recreate the sleek, glossy look Karen had achieved so easily until finally he came out. The steam following him from the bathroom made him look like an angry genie emerging from a bottle, and the collar of his robe was turned upwards, as if he were about to step out into the snow. His eyes were two slits in his swarthy face as he took in her clothes.

'I'll take you shopping later.'

'How rude!' Without Karen's magic green powder Lydia blushed an unflattering shade of pink, utterly appalled at his rudeness. Because even if her top and trousers didn't suffice, how dared he say it? Anton didn't appear remotely bothered by her angry reaction, just gave an easy shrug and turned on his computer.

'What's rude?'

'Saying that my clothes are inadequate.'

'I didn't,' Anton replied easily, then ran a lazy eye over her as she stood there, simultaneously bristling and mortified. 'But now you come to mention it...' He gave another easy shrug before continuing, 'I always buy my girlfriends' clothes—and till now not one of them has complained. I thought women liked shopping. Anyway, you were the one who said I should carry on as normal—and *normally,* if my date only had four items in her wardrobe, I'd do something about it. Not that it often happens. I'll ask Angelina to ring a couple of boutiques, so they can close.'

'Close?' Lydia frowned. Somehow he'd boxed her into yet another corner. Somehow he'd left no room for manoeuvre. Anton Santini could be as rude as he damn well liked and it was her job to take it!

'I hate crowds when I shop.' Anton smiled. 'And, given the nature of your job, so should you! What time is it?' he added, clearly bored with the conversation.

'Six-thirty,' Lydia answered through pursed lips, though she wasn't entirely sure the question had been directed at her. She watched as Anton fiddled with his heavy-looking watch for a moment, before facing his computer.

'So it's mid-afternoon in New York and night-time in Italy?'

'I have no idea,' Lydia admitted. 'I assume you're not asking because you need to ring your mother and don't want to wake her?' She expected a smart retort, but instead she got a smile, and somehow it melted her—somehow she forgave him.

'Do you want to ring down for some fresh coffee?'

'Can we go back to bed for when the maid arrives?' Anton asked hopefully.

'No.' Lydia grinned as he turned back to the computer. He tapped out responses to seemingly hundreds of red-flagged e-mails, then delivered rapid messages into his Dictaphone—no doubt Angelina would have to decipher them later—before tapping into a calculator impossibly long numbers without even looking. She could only admire his staying power. On less than four hours' sleep, Anton had dealt with almost a day's work before he had eaten breakfast.

'Do you always get so many e-mails?'

'Always.' Anton rolled his eyes. 'I hate them—people expect an instant response.' He shook his head. 'I'm sounding sorry for myself.'

'No, you're not.' Lydia nodded knowingly. 'I know exactly what you mean. Take the telephone—I hate it.'

'You hate the phone?'

'Absolutely.' Lydia nodded. 'And I dread the day we all have video phones, when you can't pretend that your flat doesn't look like a bomb just hit it when someone rings you, or that they didn't just wake you, and have to peel off your face pack... It's just so invasive,' Lydia finished weakly, but Anton was smiling now, clicking off his inbox and swinging around on his chair to face her.

'What are you going to do with yourself today?'

'Sleep, hopefully,' Lydia offered. 'After breakfast I'll come back to the room and have a shower—assuming you haven't drained the entire hotel of hot water—and then I'll crawl into bed. When I wake up I'll get my hair and make-up done, so I can look suitably gorgeous to hang on your arm for the night—it's hell being rich.'

'Do you come down to breakfast with me?'

'I'm afraid so.' Lydia nodded.

'And if I need to leave the meeting? If there is an adjournment—?'

'I'll be told,' Lydia broke in, glad that he was finally taking her being here seriously. 'If there isn't time for me to come down and meet you in the bar, or if that would look too suspicious, then just come up to your room as you normally would. One of the detectives you first met will take the lift with you.'

'Your boyfriend?'

'My *ex*-boyfriend,' Lydia corrected, unplugging her

beloved ceramic hair straighteners and standing up. 'How did you guess?'

'Easy,' Anton answered. 'It's supposed to be me he's watching, but he cannot take his eyes off you. Take it from me—he doesn't want to be your ex!'

'Then he'd better get used to the fact that we live in the twenty-first century and realise that women are capable of holding down a demanding job,' Lydia snapped.

Anton deftly swooped. 'Another chauvinist?' He raised a knowing eyebrow, and, tongue firmly in cheek, he terminated the discussion. 'My God, Lydia, the world's full of them!'

As Lydia raced for a suitably crushing response, Anton swiftly changed the subject. 'Why don't you have your shower now, then you can just go straight to bed after breakfast? I'll let the desk know and they can service the room straight away. You must be tired.'

'I am,' Lydia admitted, the wind taken out of her sails, surprisingly touched by his thoughtfulness. 'But if I even so much as step into that bathroom my hair will frizz, and any attempt to look like your sophisticated lover will evaporate as quickly as my hair serum!' Her rapid English must have been too fast for him, because from the expression Anton gave her he clearly had no idea what she was talking about. 'I'll shower *after* breakfast.'

'As you wish.' Anton nodded and went to turn away but changed his mind, clearly something on his mind. 'Won't it look suspicious?'

'What?'

'You are supposedly in Melbourne to work. If you just come back to bed—'

'After your little display yesterday,' Lydia broke in, a tight smile on her lips, 'I'm sure the staff will all assume that I *have* been working—all night! They'll be *expecting* me to crawl into bed exhausted.'

'I really am sorry about that.'

'I know,' Lydia replied, though not particularly graciously.

'I was embarrassed,' Anton admitted. 'And I overreacted.'

'I know.' This time her response was kinder. Perhaps for the first time she was seeing things from his side—the humiliation he must have felt when he had found out their entire meeting had been engineered, that the woman he had practically made love to was in fact being paid to be with him. 'Let's just forget it, shall we?'

'I'm trying to.' Anton shrugged. 'I'll get dressed, then.'

'Fine.' Lydia nodded.

'Fine,' Anton agreed.

Not for the first time an appalling awkwardness descended, the Presidential Suite diminishing in size as Anton located his clothes and Lydia turned her back and feigned nonchalance. She picked up that blessed magazine and tried reading again how to shape her eyebrows as he pulled off his robe and began to dress. She tried not to imagine that gorgeous body stripped naked, had to actually concentrate on not turning her head for even a second, and wondered for the millionth time how she was going to get through this—how she could possibly keep her mind on the job when her body screamed out for Anton.

'Done.'

'Good,' Lydia responded, placing her gun in her

handbag before turning to face him, wondering how, dressed in yet another white shirt and dark suit, he could still make her catch her breath. 'Ready, then?'

'Not quite.'

No wonder he always smelt gorgeous, Lydia thought, as practically half a bottle of cologne was splashed on his cheeks.

'I'll always be able to find you.' Lydia smiled. 'If I lose you, I mean.'

'I do not know what you are talking about,' Anton replied, raking a comb through his damp hair, then filling his pockets with his swipe card and wallet. He picked up his laptop and placed it under his arm, and Lydia noted that he didn't even check his final appearance in the mirror—but then again there was no need to. He looked, as always, completely immaculate.

'There's no greater shame in my job than losing someone you're supposed to be watching—but all I'd have to do is follow your scent, or, at worst, wave that bottle under a sniffer dog's nose. Though it would probably render him unconscious.'

'Do you always talk so much in the morning?'

'Always.' Lydia grinned, stepping out of the suite and into the corridor, having to half run to keep up with his incredibly long stride.

But despite the casual chit-chat she felt incredibly shy when they were in the lift, nervous of being back on show with him, for the act to resume… Because it had been on hold, Lydia realised as the lift swooped down to the first floor. Yes, she'd been on duty, and yes, there had been a gun by her side and a two way radio, but for a while there it had been about them—about a man and a woman mutually attracted and getting to know each other a bit better.

'Anton—over here!' Angelina waved a heavily jewelled hand as they entered the restaurant, signalling them over to where she sat with a rather pained-looking Maria. 'Join us!'

'Oh, no,' Anton muttered out of the side of his mouth. 'That's all I need.'

'Looks like you're going to have to learn how to be sociable in the morning.' Lydia laughed as Anton managed a brief wave and smile and headed over to their table.

He did no such thing! In fact Maria and Lydia were completely forgotten as an impromptu breakfast meeting ensued, with Angelina and Anton commandeering most of the table, pulling out their laptops and mobile phones, talking loudly. Had she really been his girlfriend, Lydia would have walked off in a matter of minutes, but instead she took the opportunity for a quick catch up with her colleague.

'You have no idea what I'm going through,' Maria groaned.

'Nor you of what *I'm* going through.' Lydia sighed, but, catching Maria's expression she felt a smile break out on her tense mouth. 'What's wrong?'

'Nothing.' Maria shook her head. 'Anyway, we shouldn't be seen talking.'

'Ah, we can be seen talking now,' Lydia corrected. 'Angelina called Anton and I over—we certainly didn't engineer this meeting. We're just two women who've been introduced and are having a gossip—no one can hear what we're saying. So come on, Maria, tell me what the problem is.'

'It's nothing to do with...' Maria's voice trailed off. Words like 'the case' or 'bribes' were clearly out of bounds, even if it appeared that no one was listening, but Lydia got the unspoken message.

'Salacious gossip isn't my forte,' Lydia reminded her.

'I know.' Reaching over to the bread basket, Maria selected a croissant before finally talking, her voice so low Lydia had to strain to catch it. 'They should have made us *sisters*.'

'Sisters?' Lydia frowned. 'But you're way too young to be her sister. It would have looked...' Her voice trailed off as she remembered to keep the conversation vague.

'I'm not talking about being her sibling.' Maria shuddered. 'I mean...' As Maria broke open a croissant Lydia saw that her hands were shaking. Her jaw dropped a mile.

'She *fancies* you?'

'I think so.' Maria's face was scarlet, clearly in serious need of a green-based foundation and Lydia did the only thing she could—burst into a fit of giggles. Finally, Maria joined in.

'Something amusing?' Anton glowered across the table.

'Just chatting, honey,' Lydia said sweetly, blowing him a kiss and enjoying the flicker of annoyance that passed over his face before he turned back to his computer.

'There is a glimmer of hope.' Using her serviette to dab her face, Maria let her giggles fade and she sounded like any PA's assistant from the world over as she carried on talking. 'Apparently Anton raced through things yesterday. The hotel's figures tally with his external audit, so, with a bit of luck, they'll be finished by the day after tomorrow and then they can head back to Italy.'

It was as if a bucket of water had been thrown over Lydia. The laughter that had been so therapeutic faded in an instant, realisation shrinking her momentary good humour.

'The day after tomorrow?' Lydia checked.

'Hopefully,' Maria countered, spreading jam on her croissant, so relieved to have shared her predicament she didn't even notice Lydia's rigid expression. 'And then we can all go back to our lives.'

'I'm going to the meeting room.' Closing his computer, Anton stood up and made his way around the table.

'You should slow down a touch—at least enjoy your breakfast properly,' Angelina chided. 'You work far too hard.'

'I pay you to assist me,' Anton clipped. 'Not mother me.'

'Come, Maria, we have work to do,' Angelina said, not remotely fazed. Clearly she was used to being snapped at by Anton.

As he stood up Lydia held her breath, wondering what he was going to do this time—kiss her possessively on the mouth again, as he had last night, perhaps? Remind her to get a lot of sleep because she'd be needing a lot of energy? She was sure, given his previous exploits, that he'd do something, anything to embarrass her, but she shivered inside with excitement all the same.

She was way off with her predictions—he didn't even bother to say goodbye, just stalked out of the restaurant without a backward glance, followed by his entourage. And Lydia realised, as she sat there with cheeks flaming, stinging from his dismissal, with the heavy scent of him lingering long after he'd gone, that she'd rather have been humiliated than ignored.

Swiping her card to open the door to the Presidential Suite, Lydia understood a little more where Anton was coming from—every trace of him, of them, had been erased. The clothes that had littered the floor were all back in the closet, coffee cups and glasses had been washed and replaced, the rumpled bed was made and taut. All this Lydia took in as she carefully performed her routine check, noting that even the heady scent of Anton had been erased. Opening the heavy glass bottle of cologne, she inhaled his fragrance and shivered a touch at the images his scent conjured.

She didn't want to go back to her life.

Didn't want this fairytale to end before it had even begun.

And it had nothing to do with the clothes and the hair, nothing to do with luxurious surroundings or having eager staff at her beck and call.

It had everything to do with Anton.

The real Anton—not the brash, chauvinistic version she had encountered so many times, but the deep, sensitive, incredibly sensual man she had glimpsed.

Her exhausted, sleep-deprived brain waged a weak argument.

Anton hated her job as much as Graham did.

But Anton had the guts to admit it, Lydia countered; Anton didn't hide his sentiments in the way most men did.

He made her feel like a woman. Not the weak, pale

version Graham and the men before him wanted—a woman who needed protection, a woman who needed a strong partner—instead he made her more.

More.

Sitting on the edge of the bed, Lydia buried her tired face in her hands and tried to qualify what she was thinking. More feminine, more sexy, more vibrant. He made her feel more than she had ever felt in her life. In one day and a night it was as if her life had been transformed—as if he'd dipped her in some wonderful primer, bringing out the best, the shiniest, the most beautiful qualities she held, not attempting to hold her back or reel her in.

She was literally drooping with exhaustion now, ready for a quick warm shower and hoping that it wouldn't revive her. The last thing Lydia wanted was a second wind. Her few precious hours alone needed to be used wisely, and sleep was her top priority if she was going to stay alert over the next couple of days.

The bliss of hot water on her tired body was unrivalled. She washed away the conditioner, the hair serum, the subtle yet heavy make-up, stripping away the chic woman she was portraying. Her hand reached out for the shampoo bottle, a gurgle of laugher escaping when, as Anton had predicted, it was full!

She didn't even have the energy to dry her hair—just rubbed a towel over it and then listlessly brushed it and tied it back, grateful that Karen would sort out the inevitable tangle later. After pulling the curtains and slipping off her robe, Lydia peeled back the immaculately made bed, placed her gun under the pillow, and climbed inside.

* * *

God, she looked beautiful.

Walking quietly across the room, he took a moment or two to adjust his eyes to the darkened room, to adjust his psyche to the peaceful stillness after the noise and commotion downstairs, the high that charged him at work ebbing away as he stared down at Lydia.

Quite simply, she *was* beautiful.

More beautiful than he had ever seen her.

The make-up was gone, freckles he hadn't noticed before dusting over her perfect, slightly snubbed nose. Her hair till now had always been straight, either dragged by the pool's water, or sleek from a trip to the salon, but now it was pulled back in a ponytail, wispy burnt reds and oranges spilling from the tie and framing her delicate face. The colours even in the semi-darkness were like the night sky falling over his beloved home town.

He had seen her without make-up in the pool, but now, seeing her so relaxed, he realised just how tense she had been. It was like seeing her for the first time, so young, so vulnerable, and it stirred something far deeper than lust in him—something he was scared to interpret, something that made his heart almost still in his chest for a moment. He was scared—not for him, but for her—scared at the casual price she placed on her life, the job she did, the bastards she exposed herself to in the name of duty.

Someone was watching her.

That feeling that someone was in the room, that she was being watched, had Lydia struggling into consciousness, like a deep-sea diver being forced to rapidly ascend.

Disorientated, confused, still her mind worked on

autopilot. Resisting the urge to snap her eyes open, she pretended to stir, her hand reaching under the pillow. It took less than a second, but it felt like for ever.

'Why,' came an angry, familiar voice, 'are you lying here asleep without the door chain on?'

Her fingers relaxed around the gun, anger overtaking her as her brain finally made the connection with the voice.

'It's not a good idea to creep up on me like that, Anton,' she bristled. 'Especially when I'm sleeping with a gun under my pillow.'

'But I could have been anyone. It is not safe, you up here alone.'

'They're after you, not me,' Lydia pointed out. 'And the door has been left unlocked so that you can come directly in—if someone *were* following you, the very last place you'd want to find yourself is locked outside your suite, knocking on the door, waiting for me to wake up!'

'I don't think it is a good idea,' Anton insisted. 'You put yourself at too much risk.'

'That's not your concern,' Lydia answered, staring up at him from the bed as he towered over her.

'It shouldn't be,' Anton countered. She watched as his harsh expression softened, watched the bob of his Adam's apple as he swallowed, those knowing eyes almost confused as he stared down at her, his usually strong voice thick with emotion when he spoke on. 'But all of a sudden it is.'

The magnitude of his words should have came as little surprise—after all, she was feeling it too—but the fact that Anton Santini was standing over her, baring his soul, telling her he was scared for her, concerned for her, was almost too much to comprehend.

'I hated the restaurant this morning,' Anton said, his voice gruff. 'Up here it's just us, isn't it?' When she didn't respond he elaborated, each word revealing the depth of his feelings, each word telling Lydia that she hadn't been imaging things, that Anton Santini felt it too. 'But as soon as we step outside that door I'm reminded again that it's all just an act.'

'Anton...' she started, but her voice trailed off, the absolute impossibility of their situation starting to hit home. They lived on opposite sides of the globe, had careers that demanded all from them, were two separate people from two different worlds, and nothing could change those facts. 'In a few days you're going back to Italy...'

'We should be finished here the day after tomorrow.'

Even though Maria had unwittingly warned her, still the words fell like a guillotine—the death sentence to their fledgling relationship.

'I fly back to Italy in a couple of days' Anton affirmed. 'I have come now to get some files that I hadn't thought would be needed today because things have moved on far more quickly than any of us expected. All we have to do now is go through some more figures, a few more presentations, then it will be merely a case of signing on several hundred dotted lines. There is no reason to stay longer.' Anton stared down at her. 'I don't think your colleagues would be too thrilled if I told them I was staying on in Melbourne for an impromptu holiday! Why don't *you* do it, though?'

'Do what?'

'Come back with me?' Anton stared down at her. 'We could spend some time together—some *real* time together…'

'It's not that easy, Anton.' Lydia almost snapped the words out, terrified that if she didn't stay strong she might give in—might lose her head and take him up on his offer. 'I'm up for promotion. I can't just take a couple of weeks off when I feel like it.'

'If you have no holiday time left I can…' Seeing her face harden, he stopped talking, but he needn't have bothered. The offer, even if hadn't been voiced, was there.

'Pay for my time?' Angry eyes glittered as she spoke.

'You are twisting my words. I like you, Lydia, and I want to spend time with you. I was just trying to come up with some way to do that.'

'You don't know me, Anton,' Lydia pointed out. 'You see this groomed, elegant woman, who's at your beck and call—a woman who supposedly has nothing better to do than sit in her room and wait for your meetings to finish. That isn't the real me.'

'I'm aware of that. That is why I want to spend time with you, and get to know the real Lydia.'

'She's nothing like this!' The words were delivered with a defiance that startled even herself. 'The real Lydia wears jeans and sneakers. The real Lydia works twelve, sometimes twenty-four-hour shifts, and she certainly wouldn't take being spoken to the way you saw fit yesterday.'

'I'd already guessed that.' A tiny smile ghosted his lips as he gazed down at her. 'And, at the risk of enraging you further, you're not looking particularly groomed or elegant now!'

Bastard!

Too livid even to blush, Lydia spoke through pursed lips, challenging him with her eyes. 'Would I suffice, Anton?' she asked. 'If I couldn't be bothered with make-up or the hairdresser this afternoon? If I pulled on my inadequate black trousers and off-the-peg top to join you for dinner, would you still want me?'

Anton didn't answer, just ran an eye over her unmade-up face and messy hair, the expression on his face unreadable. 'Come with me, Lydia. Let's get to know each other better.'

'There's no point.' She almost shouted the words, angry at the impossibility of it all, angry at Anton, too, for pretending they might stand a chance when they both knew it would be over before it even started.

'You're quite sure of that?'

There was dignity in his question—no argument, no pleading his case, no fanciful lies to attempt to sway her, just a tiny chance for Lydia to retract.

She dragged her eyes from his, staring fixedly at the ceiling, terrified that if she looked at him she'd waver. 'I can't come.'

'Can't or won't?'

'Both.' Lydia held her breath, watching as Anton's eyes narrowed. 'I can't come because of my work and I won't because…' Her argument ended there, because quite simply there wasn't one.

'You want me as much as I want you.'

Anton spelled it out to her, delivering irrefutable facts, but in a stab at self-preservation somehow Lydia managed a denial, knowing that if she gave in now, if she followed him, yes, it would be wonderful, yes, it would be divine—but it could never, ever last. A man like Anton would eat her up and spit the pips out afterwards—she'd read his bio.

She knew the score.

'No, Anton.' Somehow she managed to look at him as she lied. 'For a while there I thought I did, but no.' She shook her head firmly. 'You're not what I want.'

She watched as he opened his mouth to object, but there had been a finality to her voice that must have reached him, because snapping his mouth closed he gave a curt nod of his head, and she knew as he turned to walk away that that was that.

Men like Anton weren't rejected twice in a row.

He'd offered her the trip of lifetime and she'd refused; now she had to live with the consequences.

'I'll be back in a couple of hours to take you shopping.' He stared long and hard at her. 'Maybe you should get your hair and make-up done in the meantime.'

CHAPTER EIGHT

'Blowdry and make up?' Karen beamed as Lydia walked into the salon and wearily she nodded, lying back on the familiar chair, waiting while Karen transformed her into a suitable escort for Anton. 'Are you doing anything nice this afternoon?'

'Shopping,' Lydia replied tightly, and then checked herself, forcing her frozen face into what she hoped was a bright smile. 'Anton's taking me shopping.'

'Lucky you!'

She tried hard to enjoy it—tried so hard to just accept this surreal moment, to push aside the logistical nightmare Anton had created with this brief expedition. Armed detectives walked discreetly behind them as they wandered down Chapel Street and into the trendiest, most exclusive boutique that was closed to everyone except her and Anton. But even with the doors safely bolted, with Lydia able to legitimately drop her detective mode for a short while, she found it impossible to relax.

Anton had said that he wanted to get to know her better, to see the real Lydia, and then promptly ordered her to get her hair done. And now, after selecting several dresses that he considered suitable, he had guided her to the changing area—a changing area like Lydia had never seen before. It was a huge room with floor-to-ceiling mirrors, and Anton was now sitting, long-limbed and relaxed, on a leather lounge, thumbing through glossy magazines as Lydia changed again and again for him in one of the cubicles, opening the doors every now and then, utterly humiliated, parading in front of him.

'I don't like it.' Defiantly she stared at him and lied through her teeth yet again. This dress was in fact one of the most gorgeous things she'd ever laid eyes on, but she certainly wasn't about to tell Anton that! 'Anyway, red clashes with my hair.'

'It isn't red, it's more burgundy—anyway, I like it,' Anton said, as if that should be reason enough for her to want it. 'Try the grey now.'

Since their confrontation in the hotel room his mood had been wretched. Clearly unused to rejection, Anton had taken it in bad part, and had returned at his most bloody and chauvinistic, flouting the rules she had carefully laid down, demanding that she hurry up if she wanted to escort him, then walking out of the hotel with little warning, forcing Graham and John out of their newspapers and out into the street. And now he was taking out his toxic mood on her—demanding that she fit his extortionate bill, choosing shoes, perfume, even underwear for her as if she were some sort of mannequin it was up to him to dress. He was letting her know in no uncertain terms that if she was going to escort him tonight then she'd damn well better look the part.

Pulling on a crushed velvet dress, Lydia wrestled with the zipper, scowling at her reflection—furious that yet again Anton had somehow managed to choose the perfect dress, wondering how he got it so right over and over.

'Where's the assistant?' Peering round the cubicle door, Lydia called to Anton. 'I want her to help me with my zip.'

'I told her that we wanted some privacy,' Anton said, levering himself out of the couch and boldly walking into the cubicle. 'I will help you.'

This was not the plan, Lydia thought frantically as his hand met her waist and he turned her around so that her back was to him, This was *so* not the plan!

'It's on the side,' Lydia hissed. 'It's a concealed zip...'

'Oh, yes.' But he didn't move, and neither did she.

Lydia eyed his reflection in the mirror, frozen still as his hand located the tiny zip she hadn't been able to manage. He should have pulled it up. Even as she stood staring Lydia knew that by now the dress should be done up. But instead his hand was parting the soft fabric, warm fingers stealing in, softly stroking the exposed flesh. The sensible thing would have been to stop him, to push his hand away, to tell him she could do it herself or call loudly for the assistant. But quite simply she didn't want to—didn't want the feather-light strokes on her stomach to abate.

The only sound of a zipper Lydia could hear was Anton's, coming down.

'Someone might come in...' she whispered, her voice a mere croak as his hand moved lower, but Anton shook his head.

'I told you—I asked for privacy.' And what Anton asked for he got, Lydia realised. It would be more than the assistant's job was worth to come in now.

'They'll surely know,' Lydia begged, though she ached for him to go on.

'So?'

So?

The word resonated in her mind. Her body was a squirming mass of desire at his touch. She felt empowered by the knowledge that this sensual, desirable man wanted her just as much as she wanted him, and even if it was just for now, even if they could never, ever make it, somehow she wanted this moment, wanted the bliss of him inside her, wanted to follow her instincts, to take this dangerous step and finish what they'd started in the pool.

It was the most reckless, decadent decision of her life, but for now, for Lydia, it wasn't just the right one, it was the only one she could make—to go with her instincts, to heed the call of her body, to sate the desire that had overwhelmed her since Anton had come into her life.

Maybe then she'd have clarity, Lydia begged of herself, as his fingers moved in ever decreasing circles. Maybe once the frenzy he so easily generated had abated she'd be able to see things more clearly. But for now all she was could see was Anton's navy eyes, holding hers in the mirror's reflection, and transfixed she stared back at him, stared back at the beautiful man who stood behind the beautiful woman he had created.

Thoughts of the assistant waiting for them in the store, of the detectives standing out in the street, instead of horrifying her, aroused her. She could feel his hand stealing down towards her knickers, watched as he pulled the velvet material of the dress upwards and slid her knickers down. She stared at her own image, watched as his fingers parted moist, delicate flesh, and all she could see was beauty, her fascinated eyes widening as he stroked her most intimate place, the pink of her labia. And the swell of her clitoris was a sweet contrast to the angry swell of his arousal, jutting against her.

'I thought you said you didn't want me…' His fingers slipped inside, and she was so welcomingly moist, the tiny gasps in her throat so needy, it was absolutely pointless to persist with the lie.

Almost a spectator, she watched in the mirror as his other hand pushed the spaghetti strap of the dress down, watched his lips kissing her pale shoulder so deeply that surely he must bruise her. He massaged her erect nipple as his fingers still worked on below, and Lydia felt herself tip into oblivion, felt her soft mound trembling in his hand, and knew she wouldn't last more than a second longer.

Neither would he, Lydia realised, and in one swift movement he turned her around, lifting her so she was slightly above him, his fingers bruising the peach of her buttocks, his mouth working the pale, tender skin of her shoulder.

She didn't have time to process the thought, didn't have time for anything as he nudged at her entrance. All Lydia knew was that she was coming, her whole body rigid as he plunged deep within her, spilling at her entrance as she dragged him in. She could see their entwined bodies in the mirror—pearly white thighs a contrast against his dark suit, her toes curling in her strappy sandals as they scratched the cubicle wall, his fingers parting her buttocks as he stabbed deeper within—and it was all she had imagined it would be and more, the most dizzy, exhilarating ride of her life.

When it was over, when she was coming back down to earth and he was lowering her to shaky ground, there was no awful thud of shame. Dragging her against his chest and pulling her in, tenderly he held her, wrapped his arms around her till she found her balance.

Maybe she should have felt used, should have burned with shame for what had just taken place. But even when he let her go his eyes were still holding her with a softness she'd never witnessed in Anton, and his mouth for once was tender as he smiled down at her.

'I'd better buy you that dress.'

'You'd better.'

It was the most heady feeling of her life, walking back into the hotel lobby with Anton, as the bellboy rushed to relieve them of their bags, her body tingling from their union, the whole world sharper, more colourful now.

'Anton!' Angelina pounced on them as they headed for the lift, followed by a long-suffering Maria. 'I need to talk to you. Some figures don't add up—nothing major, though. We can do it over coffee at the bar—it shouldn't take long.'

'Why don't you go on up?' Anton called over his shoulder, heading towards Angelina, then stilling as Lydia did the same—and they both knew why: for a tiny slice of time he had forgotten that she was on duty, truly forgotten that she was here to protect him.

'I'll stay, if you don't mind,' Lydia said, forcing a smile and following him through the foyer with Maria, wishing that it really could be so, and knowing that Anton was thinking exactly the same.

It didn't even take five minutes. In fact, by the time

the waiter had come over to take their order Anton had cast his astute eyes over the figures and nailed the problem. 'Cross-reference that figure, but I think you'll just find that someone missed a zero on the end. Not for me, thanks,' Anton added to the waiter, standing up. 'I'll see both you ladies tonight at the cocktail party.'

'Will it be very grand?' Lydia asked as they headed out of the lift and towards Anton's suite.

'Probably.' Anton shrugged, swiping his card and opening the door to let her in. 'Why don't you get your hair put up? I think it would suit you!'

But Lydia wasn't listening—instead her mind was on her job, her hand in her bag, wrapped firmly around her gun, hazel eyes checking out the suite as she entered, standing stock still, the hairs on the back of her neck standing on end as instinct told her something wasn't right.

As Anton went to breeze past her Lydia moved quickly, deliberately stepping in front of him, halting his progress, her slender frame shielding him.

'What the…?' Anton's voice trailed off as the bellboy came into view, stepping into the hallway, his black eyes meeting Lydia's.

'Would you like me to unpack?'

'Unpack?' Lydia frowned. Her breath was coming in short, rapid bursts but her voice was even.

'Your shopping bags,' the bellboy explained. 'I have placed them on the bed—'

'We'll be fine.' It was Anton talking now, taking over the conversation and side-stepping Lydia, walking past her, pressing a tip into the bellboy's hand. *'Grazie.'*

'Enjoy your evening,' the bellboy responded, nodding briefly before quietly exiting.

'What the hell was that all about?' Anton demanded once they were alone, but Lydia said nothing for a while, checking the room meticulously before finally sitting down on the bed surrounded by the pile of shopping bags they had acquired on their expedition.

'I knew someone was in the room,' Lydia answered, raking her hand through her hair. 'Anton, I don't like him…'

'He's the bellboy, for heaven's sake!' Anton flared. 'But that's not the point. Suppose he *had* been an attacker, suppose his intention *had* been to hurt me—what on earth were you doing stepping in front of me?'

'It's my job, Anton,' Lydia answered, but her response was vague, her mind still going over and over the brief encounter, instinct still telling her that something didn't fit, that something wasn't right.

'To take a bullet?' His hand gripped her arm, jerked her around to face him. 'And I'm not going to flatter myself that it has anything to do with feelings, anything to do with what just happened. You'd do it for anyone wouldn't you?'

Lydia didn't respond. She didn't have to—they both already knew the answer.

It was the longest night of her life. Dressed in the same strappy number he had taken her in, her hair skilfully put up by yet another hairdresser Anton had summoned to the room, Lydia felt her nerves jangling more loudly than Angelina's ostentatious earrings.

His simmering black mood was palpable—the incident with the bellboy had been a non-event, yet the result had been devastating. Anton had seen with his own eyes the lengths she was prepared to go to in the name of duty, and he had confirmed for Lydia what she had known already deep down—Anton would never accept her work. The tension in the suite had been unbearable. After escaping to the bathroom before coming down to the cocktail party she had checked her shoulder for the bruise his weighty kiss must surely have left and found nothing. But even if there were no visible signs of their lovemaking his mark on her was indelible. Her whole body felt deliciously bruised, Anton's touch still reverberating through every tender muscle. Eyeing her unfamiliar reflection carefully in the mirror, taking in the sleek hairdo, the heavily made-up eyes, the sophisticated, groomed woman who stared back, mocking over and over the trembling child inside, she had wrestled with the biggest decision of her life.

'I'm going downstairs now!'

He had summoned her with a sharp knock on the bathroom door, told her in no uncertain terms that if she intended to join him she'd damn well better come now.

And—because it was work—she'd complied.

Now, watching the room, Lydia sipped at yet another fake daiquiri as Anton held court—easily a head above the rest. And though he listened intently to the conversation in progress, occasionally smiled as the people around him loudly laughed, his aloofness, his air of superiority had never been more evident.

All Lydia knew was that she didn't want it to end—didn't want to go back to the world she had inhabited just a short while ago. And it had nothing to do with the jewels and the clothes. Nothing to do with the sumptuous surrounds and the lavish wealth that swathed her now. Instead it had everything to do with the man who had transformed her life the second he had stepped into it—the man who, quite simply, had taken her heart the second she had laid eyes on him.

'You're quiet,' Maria observed as they stood on the outskirts of the entourage. 'Not that I blame you—I'm just about dying with boredom. Even when they're not working, it's all they talk about. I don't know how Anton manages to retain all those figures. He's like a human calculator.'

She so ached to confide in her friend. Not to find an answer—Lydia knew there wasn't one—but for some moral support. But now was neither the time nor the place. 'How's your boss?' Lydia asked instead.

'Like my dog when it's on heat!' Maria's mouth twitched as she took a sip of her drink. 'I should be armed with a stick to keep her at bay. Not that I'm complaining. I'm having the best time really—I've booked myself in for a hot stone massage tomorrow, which sounds divine! And so is he…' Maria breathed as Anton looked over in their direction and started to make his way over.

'Maria,' he gave her a curt greeting before facing Lydia, 'I'd like to go back to the room.'

A bucket of champagne was cooling in a silver bucket, and as Lydia closed the door behind them Anton opened the bottle with ease.

'Lock the door,' Anton said, pouring two glasses and offering her one, frowning as Lydia shook her head.

'I'm not supposed to drink alcohol on duty.'

'You had three strawberry daiquiris downstairs,' Anton pointed out.

'Which were made by one of my colleagues.' Lydia gave a tight smile. 'They were non-alcoholic, to ensure that I'm able to keep my mind on the job.'

'You weren't exactly concentrating this afternoon…'

'The shop was secure…' Lydia swallowed hard. 'But you're right. That wasn't my finest career moment. But my work *is* important to me Anton…' She watched his face darken.

'It's too dangerous.'

'It's who I am.'

'No.' He shook his head firmly. 'I saw the *real* Lydia this afternoon.'

'No, Anton,' Lydia said softly. 'You've never met the real me.'

'Come here,' Anton said softly, and Lydia knew that it was now or never, knew that he was testing her. If she joined him in his bed then he'd expect her to join him in his life, and Lydia knew that she couldn't do it. A night in Anton's arms, being held by him as she slept, seemed far more intimate somehow than what they had already shared. It would make the inevitable loss that would follow greater somehow if she glimpsed his tender side.

'Come to bed, Lydia.' It was practically an order, and it took a supreme effort to defy him, to pull over the chair and resume her guard.

'You go to bed if you want, Anton. I'm working.'

CHAPTER NINE

'ANYTHING from Angelina?' Lydia asked as Maria closed her eyes and rested back on the wooden slats of the sauna wall. Both women were delighted to be able to drop their guards for a few minutes—the only reminder they were detectives were the pagers nestled in their bathrobes that would trill if they were needed.

'Nothing—she's safely tucked up in the salon, getting her beard waxed, with Graham beside her.' Maria let out a gurgle of laughter. 'He's having a facial and a manicure, can you believe? Strictly so that he can watch Angelina while we catch up, of course, but I think he's enjoying it just a bit too much—maybe *that's* why you really broke up.'

'You're obsessed!' Lydia laughed.

'No, I'm not.' Maria sighed. 'You're looking at the new laid-back me, courtesy of the hot stone massage—Lydia, you simply have to try it. They place these warm stones all over you and wrap you up in this little cocoon, and when you're cooked, when you think you could never be more relaxed in your life, they oil you and massage you with the stones—it's bliss—sheer bliss. I swear, nothing will ever faze me again—not even

Angelina and her none too subtle advances. I couldn't be more relaxed!'

'Any news on the background check for that bellboy?' Lydia asked.

'Nothing out of the ordinary.' Maria yawned. 'He's a backpacker who's worked for the hotel a couple of months. No criminal history…'

'Where's he from?'

'Florence,' Maria answered. 'Well, that's the last address they've got on him—and given Anton's from Sicily, and works mainly in Rome, there's nothing suspicious there. They're still running checks, but it doesn't look as if he's involved in this.' Maria gave a lazy shrug. 'I'd forget it if I were you, Lydia.'

'I don't like him,' Lydia insisted. 'Tell Kevin I want them to keep looking in to him.'

'No problem.' Maria nodded.

'Anton wants me to go back to Italy with him.'

Lydia blurted the words out, watching as Maria's eyes peeped open, a tiny frown puckering on her newly relaxed brow as she eyed her agitated colleague. 'He wants me to join him there for a holiday.'

'He wants *you* to join him!' Maria gaped.

'Is it really that unbelievable?' Lydia snapped.

'Of course it is.' Maria shook her head as if to clear it. 'Lydia, this is *Anton Santini* we're talking about. And you're telling me that he wants to whisk you away for a holiday! What on earth did you say?'

'No, of course.' Sitting forward on the bench, Lydia raked her hands through her rapidly frizzing hair. 'If I take a few weeks off to jet to the other side of the world I can practically kiss my promotion goodbye—my career, too, probably! I mean—' Lydia's hands flailed like windmills as Maria listened intently '—Graham was offering me marriage and I said no. Why on earth would I give everything up for a fling with Anton?'

'Why are you so sure it would be just a fling?' Maria asked.

'Because flings are what Anton does best—the man's a serial flinger!'

'Is there such a thing?' Maria grinned.

'I don't know,' Lydia admitted, reluctantly smiling back. 'But there should be—it should be listed in the dictionary and when women look the word up there should be the name *Anton Santini* written beside it!

'It could never work,' she added, even though Maria hadn't asked. 'I mean, just look at his reputation! And he's made it very clear he hates my work. He doesn't even know me—he *thinks* he knows me,' Lydia carried on, talking nineteen to the dozen as Maria sat patiently listening, 'but he doesn't. I'd be an idiot to go.'

'Then don't,' Maria said, closing her eyes and sinking back into relaxed oblivion. 'Just chalk it up as one of the nicest offers you've ever had! And be grateful that you didn't lose your head and do something daft like sleep with him.'

Lydia sat back on the bench beside Maria, closing her eyes and dragging in the hot air, her silence speaking volumes.

'Lydia!' It was Maria who was agitated now, the warm volcanic stones a distant memory, staring at her friend, aghast. 'Tell me you didn't sleep with him!'

'Well, we didn't exactly sleep...' Lydia grimaced.

'But you've only know him a couple of days,' Maria wailed.

'That's a bit much, coming from you,' Lydia retorted.

'We're not talking about me—heavens, Lydia, it took Graham *weeks*...'

'Months,' Lydia corrected.

'Months, then,' Maria choked. 'So what the hell happened with Anton? How on earth did he...?' Maria's voice trailed off as Lydia broke down, and at the sight of her friend's devastated face Maria wrapped an arm around her. 'This isn't love, is it?'

'I think it might be,' Lydia gulped. 'But, like I said, he doesn't even know me.'

'Then show him you,' Maria said firmly. 'Show him the amazing woman you are, Lydia.'

'You think I should go with him?'

'Hell, no.' Without hesitation Maria shook her head. 'You're Detective Lydia Holmes, and he'd damn well better get used to it.' A cheeky smile inched across Maria's pretty face. 'Give him a taste of the real you, Lydia. Don't compromise yourself, and don't play by his rules. You never have before, so why start now? I guarantee that even if he leaves he'll soon come back!'

'And if he doesn't?' Maria stared at her friend and she answered her own question. 'Then it wasn't meant to be.'

Finally she knew what to do.

Back in the Presidential Suite, like a child creeping into her mother's room, Lydia faced the mirror alone. Armed only with her rather paltry make-up bag, she slicked her lashes with mascara and rubbed some gloss on her full mouth. She tamed her wild curls with some mousse, and pulled her long red locks into some sort of acceptable shape. If Anton thought she was dressing down then he was wrong, she was actually dressing *up*.

Nerves truly hit her as her pager buzzed, alerting her that the meeting was nearing its end and to head downstairs in fifteen minutes.

It would have been so very much easier to pull on one of the dresses Anton had chosen for her, to dab her pulse-points with the expensive perfume he had bought and to strap on the perfect new shoes that lay nestled in tissue paper, courtesy of their shopping expedition, but it wasn't her.

Flicking through her wardrobe, Lydia bypassed the expensive designer gowns, settling instead on her own faithful black dress—the one staple in every woman's wardrobe. It was the same black dress she had worn for the police Christmas party, the same black dress that had seen her through plenty of first and last dates—the one dress she felt good in. Slipping it over her head, Lydia fiddled with the zip and then pulled on a pair of her own high strappy sandals. Rummaging in her handbag for her own scent, Lydia dabbed it on, her hands shaking so much she spilled most of it.

'Calm down, Lydia,' she scolded herself, placing her gun in her bag and heading for the door, stopping for just a moment to check her reflection.

And her nerves disappeared. A strange relief flooded her as she witnessed the familiar reflection, and even if she wasn't quite as elegant, quite as exquisitely packaged as she had been, somehow it felt right, it felt real, it felt honest.

Tonight she would face him as the woman she was.

Closing the door behind her, she headed for the lift, pushed the call button and stepped inside, shaking her curls, straightening her shoulders. She was on duty now, bracing herself for any eventuality, ready to face whatever tonight might bring.

Only it wasn't the thought of a security breach or the fact that her life could be in great danger that terrified her. It was the thought of Anton's reaction that caused her stomach to tighten, her throat to constrict as she stepped out of the lift and walked across the sumptuous foyer, heels clicking on the marble tiles…

Anton's reaction when he saw the real Lydia.

'Lydia!' Draped in some hideous multi coloured kaftan, Angelina summoned her over while simultaneously ramming tiny slivers of pâté-drenched toast into her mouth. 'You look fantastic—love the hair. Did you have a perm? What a brave move!'

'Thanks.' Lydia forced a smile, and then shook her head as Angelina thrust a glass of champagne at her.

'No, thanks, it gives me the most appalling headache.' Glancing over at the bar, she checked that Kevin had seen her arrival before summoning a waiter. 'I'd like a strawberry daiquiri please. Extra sweet,' Lydia added, then waved a finger in Kevin's direction. 'He knows how I like it.'

'Certainly.'

'Where's Anton?' Lydia asked Angelina, happy that her drink order had been taken care of.

'He's just signing some papers—he should be out soon,' Angelina said, summoning back the waiter Lydia had just spoken to and exchanging her empty champagne glass for a full one.

Lydia was grateful for the momentary reprieve and turned with a beaming smile to Maria, kissing her on the cheek.

'You look fabulous!' Maria said.

'Really?'

'Really.' Maria grinned. 'You'll knock his hundred-dollar socks off!'

'We've done well.' Angelina was back, draining her glass in one gulp. 'The deal is finalised, so tonight we can party before we head for home.'

'Or maybe we can get some sleep!'

His dry, deeply accented voice practically sent her already shot nerves into orbit. Her spine tensed as she felt the heat of his hand on the small of her back, radiating warmth through her dress, and, turning her cheek, she closed her eyes for a second, relishing the dizzy brush of his lips against her cheek as he joined the gathering.

'You look stunning.' His low tones were for her ears only, and, carrying on the intimate mood, she turned to face him. 'Stunning,' he said again, his eyes dragging over her face as if slowly taking in each freckle, lingering on her full lips, the riot of curls that framed her face. 'Your hair's amazing—did someone new do it?'

'Yes.' Her eyes glittered back at him, taking in every flicker of his reaction as she delivered her words. 'Me.'

It was only the two of them. Angelina's loud voice faded, the crowd, the waiters seemingly melted away, leaving just the two of them facing each other. 'I did my own hair and make-up—this is me you're seeing, Anton.'

'Hello, you.'

Two little words, husked from his lips. His mouth had barely moved as he spoke, but one hand reached up to her hair, catching a heavy ringlet and coiling it around his finger in a curiously possessive gesture. His eyes ravished her, caressing each feature, taking in the almond-shaped eyes, the delicate snub of her nose, as if truly seeing her for the first time.

'Will *you* join me for dinner?' He offered his arm, clearly certain she would accept, a quizzical smile on his lips as she slowly shook her head.

'No, Anton, will *you* join *me*?'

'Where?'

And she'd have loved to take him by the hand, to lead him away from the grandeur of the hotel and out into the hustle and bustle of Melbourne's streets, to show him her favourite restaurant and later, to wander hand in hand along the river—would have loved, even more, to take him to her home.

To invite him in for coffee, so to speak.

But this was the strangest of first dates, and protocol didn't allow such luxuries.

A wry smile twisted her lips at the incongruity of her thoughts—they were, after all, in practically the most luxurious hotel in Melbourne, with a legion of staff to attend to their every whim, their every need, but right now true luxury would be her own little flat and Anton. There would be no one watching, no guidelines to follow, no conversations to steer. Just the sheer, decadent luxury of being truly together.

But instead she invited him to the one other place they could be themselves—the one place they could really let down their guard and talk without fear of being overheard.

'I've ordered food to be delivered to the room.' Her voice was so low he had to lean forward to hear her, his cheek dusting hers as she leant in and spoke. 'I thought perhaps we could talk…' She gave a tiny nervous swallow, trying to summon up the courage to lay down some guidelines. 'Talk,' she said again. 'Get to know each other a bit more. If you still want to, I mean.'

'There's nothing I want more,' Anton said solemnly, but his mouth twitched in a small private smile. 'Well, one thing, perhaps. But there are things we need to take care of first, yes?'

'Yes.' Lydia nodded, sharing his smile with one of her own, but blushing as she did so.

'I'll go and say my farewells, and then…' His eyes held hers. 'Then we will spend some time together, Lydia.'

'Is everything okay?' Maria cornered her as Anton made their excuses, spoke to his colleagues and bade them farewell for the night.

'Everything's fine. Anton wants to have dinner upstairs in his room,' Lydia said as lightly as she could. 'And I have to admit I'd be a lot happier away from the crowd.' Even though no one appeared to be listening, still Lydia chose her words carefully. But Maria got the thinly disguised message, delivering a tiny encouraging wink in her friend's direction.

'I just hope to God Angelina doesn't get ideas and suggest an early night herself. Frankly, I'd rather take my chances down here!'

'I don't think you need to worry.' Lydia smiled, watching as Angelina monopolised another drinks waiter. 'A couple more champagnes and she'll be out like a light!'

CHAPTER TEN

'HAVE YOU changed your mind about coming to Italy with me?' Anton asked when finally Lydia had checked the room and placed her gun on the bedside locker, when finally they were truly alone.

'No.' She faced him, revealing a little more of herself that perhaps he didn't know. 'I don't change my mind very often, Anton.'

'Neither do I.'

And it could have been checkmate—two proud, stubborn people unwilling to make the first move—but for now Lydia wasn't thinking about tomorrow. Instead she was thinking about the here and now, revelling in what they had, determined to enjoy the moment.

'What's this?' Frowning, he watched as Lydia lifted the heavy silver lids on the table, revealing two white boxes and a brown paper bag already shiny from its greasy contents. 'Noodles?'

'Not just any noodles,' Lydia corrected. 'The best noodles in Melbourne—when I'm on night shift I always grab a box, and generally there's enough left over for breakfast in the morning. I had them delivered, then asked the chef to heat them up—I don't think he was very impressed.'

'And these?' Anton peered into the brown paper bag.

'Spring rolls.'

'Not like any I've ever seen.'

'Try one,' Lydia said, sitting down at the table and smothering a smile at the role reversal. Anton was staring at the cheap wooden chopsticks, clearly used to working cutlery from the outside in. 'They pull apart.'

'So they do.' Anton grinned, and with enviable ease worked his way through the noodles. It was the most wonderful meal of her life—the food divine, the conversation easy. They were getting to know each other a little better, laughing at each other's jokes, finding out what made the other tick.

'The chef would have a coronary if he could hear me—but that was an amazing meal.'

'I told you so.' Lydia smiled, but it was short lived. The light-hearted conversation that had filled the room was fading as the seriousness of their situation hit home.

'So you're not coming?'

'No.' Lydia shook her head.

'Then how…?' Anton started.

'I don't know.'

Crossing the room, he took her in his arms, held her so fiercely, so closely, that for that moment the problems they faced barely mattered. All she could feel was him, and it felt so right it hurt. The cradle his solid arms provided comforted her, his masculinity enhanced her femininity. His arms swathed her, holding her so close, their roles easily reversed—Anton the protector, Anton trying to tell her that it would all be all right, that somehow they could make it work.

'Would it make things easier if I gave some sort of commitment…?' His English was faltering but his intention was clear, and Lydia pulled back from his embrace.

'A diamond isn't going to solve this, Anton,' Lydia said. 'It isn't that easy. But let's not think about it now…' Leaving the warmth of his arms, she headed for the door and double checked it.

'What are you doing?'

'Making sure it's secure.' There was a tiny tremble in her voice, her simple answer loaded with complicated meaning as she moved a chair and wedged it firmly in front of it. 'So I don't have to watch it.'

'The maid comes in at—'

'I already cancelled,' Lydia said, because he made her feel bold, made assertion possible, because finally she had found in a man what she needed. A man so comfortable in his own skin, so confident in his own abilities, his own sexuality, that he wasn't threatened by hers. She turned and faced him. The doubts, the questions in her mind were still there, but despite the internal wrestling, despite playing over and over the worst case scenarios of losing him in her mind, one constant remained—she wanted this night with him.

'Come here,' Anton said softly, using the same two words that had enraged her just a few days ago. But he was summoning her to his bed now, not his table, and his voice was so thick with lust, his eyes so loaded with desire, there was no question of feeling humiliated. Actually, Lydia realised, there were no questions at all in her mind—just want and need, propelling her those last few steps to his bed.

Her nerves caught up with her just a touch as he pulled back the bedlinen and, taking her trembling hand, guided her towards him. He held her close for a moment, the gesture somehow reassuring, stroking her long slender neck, the nub of his index finger exploring the pulsing hollows of her throat, then working down, slowly down, tracing the rigid prominence of her clavicle as his mouth finally found hers.

He undressed her slowly, savouring every slip of the fabric with his tongue, and with every kiss, every tender word he made her feel beautiful, feminine *and* beautiful—which sometimes was the hardest thing in the world with a job like Lydia's. No matter how fit, how assertive, or how much she craved the adrenaline and the danger of her work, sometimes all she wanted was to feel like a woman. And Anton achieved that just by looking at her.

There was no haste in his movements, no hurried gestures, so blatant, so potent was the chemistry between them. Long, deep kisses that made everything okay, made everything suddenly all right, giving her the impetus to undress him, her trembling fingers working the buttons of his shirt, Anton helping her, until for the first time they faced each other naked.

Quite simply he was more beautiful than even her mind had allowed, and the giant step to his bed was easy now, desire guiding her as he laid her down beside him. His fingers caressed the pale flesh of her breast and she could feel it swell in his hand, warm to his divine touch, to his finger slowly, slowly stroking her nipple, drawing it out to its needy length as still he kissed her. All Lydia could do was shiver at his skilful touch—submit to the pleasure he so easily generated. His touch was electric on her cool skin as he connected again the unbreakable circuit he instigated with one flick of his hand. And though her exposed body craved his touch he made her wait, taking a long, decadent moment to admire her naked beauty, slowly taking in every intimate feature, from the riot of titian locks on the pillow down to the golden curls that covered her womanhood.

She should have felt horribly exposed, should have felt embarrassed, but instead under his adoring gaze she felt beautiful. Her eyes closed in unbridled pleasure as his lips lowered to her chest, tracing with his tongue where his fingers had been. His hand was still moving, but to a far more intimate place, sliding into her needy warmth. Tiny gasps escaped from her throat as his fingers moved slow and rhythmic on her hidden jewel. His tongue was hot and teasing on her swollen breasts, his legs scratched as he parted her taut thighs with his own, cupping her buttocks in his hands, and his heated length plunged into her, filling her exquisitely.

Long, deliberate strokes consumed her, his body gliding against hers, tension meeting tension, no give, no time to relent. They were utterly absorbed, taking their time this time, revelling in the feel of each other's bodies, locked in delicious union, moving to a beat of their own, to the grind of his hips against hers. She could feel her legs shaking, her neck arching backwards, a flush of heat spreading along her spine, and she gave in then—gave in because she had no choice. Her whole body trembled as he came deep within her, as he called out her name, and her own contractions pulled him in deeper, dragging each precious drop from him until there was no more to take and he had nothing left to give.

Spent, exhausted, but still deep inside her, Anton rolled them onto their sides, his eyes never leaving hers, not even attempting words as their flushed bodies came down to earth together, knowing, just knowing, the pleasure had been entirely mutual.

'I'd better get up,' Lydia whispered, but Anton wouldn't hear of it.

'The door's locked and the chair's against it. No one can get in without us hearing.'

No one could, Lydia realised, relaxing in his arms, allowing herself to enjoy the remains of what might well be their last night together. And if their lovemaking had been divine, then falling asleep in his arms, being held by him, was a feeling that was unsurpassed.

'Anton?' Lifting her head, blinking at the harsh morning sun, Lydia heard his low grumble, felt his arm try to pull her in closer as she tried to pull away. But she wriggled free, smiling as he struggled to wake up. His body slowly stretched beside her, though his muscular legs wrapped her tighter, and she revelled in the warm, intimate cocoon of their entwined bodies, gazing down unashamedly as his navy eyes attempted to open—a sharp contrast to the sudden awakening of yesterday. 'Your plane's in a couple of hours—we ought to think about getting up.'

'It's ages yet.' Anton yawned.

'No,' Lydia corrected. 'It's almost ten.'

'No—' Anton started, but after he'd squinted at his

watch the evidence was irrefutable. 'I never oversleep,' Anton said in disbelief.

'You do now,' Lydia whispered, not even resisting as his arm wrapped around her again, jumping as the cool metal of his watch met the warm skin on her back.

'Come here.'

As he drew her back into his embrace Lydia relented for a moment, truly meaning to get up in just a couple more minutes. Her cheek was now back where it had been so comfortable, on the firm cushion of his chest, and, indulging her senses, she let him hold her. The slow, rhythmic thud of his heartbeat in her ear hastened a touch as one lazy finger circled the silk of jet hair that whirlpooled around one dark mahogany nipple, as the pad of her finger kneaded the small area of flesh. She felt it stiffen beneath her touch as the divine scent of him filled her nostrils; the last husky note of his cologne had disappeared, leaving in its place a headier, tangier, more sensual scent—the lusty fragrance of shared intimacy, *their* shared intimacy.

Schedules didn't matter any more, and her last sense was indulged as she moved her mouth a few delectable inches, her hair draping his chest, hungry lips dusting his chest, her tongue searching for the hard pad of flesh her fingers had created, lips tasting his delicate flesh.

A low, throaty moan escaped him as her lips worked their magic. She was bold now, empowered by the desire she had instigated, and her thigh moved seductively against his. The scratching warmth of his leg was against hers, deepening her arousal, and, gently straddling his body, she felt his morning glory swelling against the soft warm flesh of her inner thigh. She lowered herself a fraction to accommodate it.

Amber eyes on navy, she slid down that delicious length. And eyes closed in mutual bliss as the sweet warmth of her vice-like grip filled them—how easy it was to be herself with him inside her, to move her body against his, to *know,* just know that their pleasure was mutual.

Their lovemaking was slower now, they were taking their time because they'd only just been there, and there was no rush as she climbed that decadent hill. His fingers pressed into the flesh of her buttocks, his cool tongue exploring her, tasting her sweet flesh, biting on her fruit as she moved above him, gliding over his silken body—coveting him even while possessing him. It would have been so easy to lose herself to the moment, so easy for Lydia to let Anton take her ever higher, but the sound of her pager vibrating on the bedside table broke the moment.

Lydia grimaced at the intrusion and Anton tried vainly to ignore it.

'I have to get it.'

'You don't,' Anton grumbled, but the moment was gone.

Lydia moved across the bed and, locating the offending article, punched numbers into her phone, rolling her eyes as Anton did the same.

'John and Graham are on their way up.' Lydia's voice was flat as she pulled on her track pants and struggled with the clasp on her bra. 'You'd better get dressed.'

'So had you,' Anton whispered, taking over the bra, deft fingers finding the tiny metal clasp. He planted a kiss on her shoulder as Lydia leant forward to retrieve her T-shirt and asked, for what Lydia knew was the final time, 'Will you come?'

Picking up her T-shirt, Lydia pulled the cotton over her head, welcoming the fact that as she asked the most difficult question of her life her face was covered.

'Will you stay?'

The lift must have just been serviced, because it seemed a matter of seconds before someone knocked at the door. Peeping through the spyhole, Lydia could feel the time that had been theirs escaping like air from a leaking balloon.

'Get rid of him,' Anton said. 'And then we'll talk.'

As Anton headed for the bathroom Lydia let in her dark-suited colleagues, listening intently as they brought her up to date.

'Where is he?' Graham asked, his eyes working the room, taking in the rumpled bed, and Lydia spoke quickly to distract him.

'He's in the shower.' She feigned a shrug.

'Well, his flight leaves in just over an hour. He'd better step on it.'

'I'm not his keeper,' Lydia pointed out. 'He doesn't seem in any hurry to catch the plane.'

'Well, he needs to be,' John Miller said sharply. 'At midday his protection ends, so the sooner we get him to the airport and on his plane the better!'

'What's going on?'

Her throat thickening, Lydia watched as Anton emerged from the bathroom, rubbing his hair with a massive white towel, feigning surprise at the intrusion.

'Problem?'

Voicing the question, even dressed in a bathrobe, he was still the one in control.

'On the contrary, sir.' Graham cleared his throat.

'Things have gone extremely well: the conference has passed without event and we've got a car waiting to take you to the airport.'

'Sorry?' Anton frowned, but Lydia knew that despite his slightly confused expression he had understood every word. 'I wasn't aware that I *had* to check out—in fact, given that I practically own this hotel, I would have thought I would be most welcome to stay on here for a few days and actually *see* a bit of the place.'

'It's not that straightforward...' Graham attempted, but John Miller stepped in, his tone slightly more authoritative than Graham's.

'The security threat would seem to have passed—your stay has gone off without a hitch—'

'Maybe there *was* no security threat.' Anton glowered.

'Maybe there wasn't,' John admitted—but, refusing to be intimidated, he soon rallied. 'Or maybe someone got wind of the massive security operation that was underway and thought twice. But until you're out of the country we can't completely relax—'

'So it would be easier for you if I leave?' Anton interrupted, cutting straight to the point in his brutal, direct way.

'Yes,' John admitted, without apology. 'It *would* be easier for us if you leave. We've arranged a car to take you to the airport now, sir. We'll provide security for you till you're safely on the plane.'

Still rubbing his hair on a towel, Anton didn't seem in any hurry to go anywhere, and he certainly didn't look like someone who was about to pack his bags on command. But John Miller stood firm.

'We'll meet you downstairs in fifteen minutes; the bellboy is on his way up now to collect your things, so I suggest you get packing.'

'You were saying?' There was a wry smile on Anton's face once they were left alone. 'I don't think I have much choice other than to leave, Lydia.'

'I know.'

Sitting down on the rumpled bed, raking a hand through her hair, Lydia let out a long breath, watching as Anton peeled open a massive leather suitcase and started throwing things inside. Divine, superbly ironed shirts were given the same treatment as socks, tossed into the suitcase with no thought for the journey. No doubt he would be happy to let someone else unpack for him when he arrived in Rome. She watched with mounting despair as he walked around the room, erasing every trace of himself—tightening the stopper on his cologne and throwing it into a toiletry bag, gathering cufflinks and comb and putting them in his case. His progress was interrupted by a knock on the door, and Lydia moved to the bed, her hand edging under the pillow to feel for her gun as Anton peered through the peephole.

'It is the bellboy,' Anton informed her, and waited for Lydia to give the nod before he opened the door.

'I'm not quite ready,' Anton informed him. 'You'll have to come back—I'll ring down when I'm ready for you.'

'I can pack for you, sir.' Lydia could hear the conversation taking place, could feel the whole world pushing her to make a decision. These last, vital minutes alone with Anton were slipping away. 'I was told there's a car waiting for you and to bring your belongings straight down.'

'Fine,' Anton snapped, clearly not remotely impressed with Detective Miller's haste to get him to the airport. 'My suits need to be packed—there is a holder…'

'I'll find it, sir.'

'And my shaving stuff,' Anton added, and as the bellboy set to work he crossed the room back to Lydia and resumed the conversation. 'Talk to me Lydia,' he insisted. 'Tell me what you are thinking?'

But it wasn't that easy. Unlike Anton, who was so used to endless staff attending to his needs that he could probably carry on making love while a maid opened the curtains, Lydia felt incredibly uncomfortable revealing her feelings with anyone else present. She was acutely aware of the bellboy's presence, and despite Kevin's assurances she was still wary of him. She watched his every move as he zipped up the suit holder and gave a helpless shake of her head, her eyes gesturing the reason she couldn't talk now.

'Could you get my shaving stuff?' Anton asked, pressing some money into the young man's hand. 'And maybe take your time?'

'Of course, sir.'

Alone again, she faced him.

'I'm being silly,' Lydia whispered. 'I just thought if we could have a couple of days here—if I could show you where I live, the things that are important to me—maybe then…' She couldn't elaborate, couldn't paint a picture of the future without knowing if Anton wanted it as much as her.

'We can do all that, Lydia,' Anton said softly and hope flared in her eyes. 'But when the time is right…'

His voice trailed off and Lydia stiffened, her eyes narrowing as the bellboy came out of the *en suite* bathroom.

'You could always stay on here for a couple of days.'

The bellboy's voice, intruding on this most personal conversation, had Lydia's hand tightening like a reflex action around the gun under the pillow. Anton swung around, clearly appalled at the intrusion. But even as her hand gripped the cool metal of her weapon Lydia knew she couldn't use it.

The bellboy's semi-automatic pistol was already pushing into the back of Anton's neck, and, no matter how rapid her response, she knew that the bellboy's would be quicker—and probably fatal.

'In fact, why don't you ring down and tell your assistant you've decided to spend the next few days in bed with your *prostituta*?'

For the first time he addressed Lydia, shouting his orders as he kept the gun trained on Anton. 'You. Over there. Sit over there.'

He waved his free hand towards the window and in that split second Lydia knew she had to comply—knew that for now she had to obey, do exactly what he said. Only when the situation was calmer could she begin to control it—from the mad look in the bellboy's eyes, Lydia knew he wouldn't have any hesitation in using the gun, and probably not just on Anton. Her hand loosened its grip on her own gun beneath the pillow, taking some small comfort as she crossed the room that he didn't check the bed, didn't remove the weapon.

'Strap her hands behind her back.' Thrusting a roll of tape at Anton, he gave more orders.

'Do it, Anton.' Lydia said firmly, determined to keep

things calm, and something in her voice must have reached him.

Anton reluctantly took the tape and bound her wrists, his hands supremely gentle, his fingers giving her just one tiny reassuring squeeze before their captor became impatient.

'Now you ring your assistant,' the bellboy spat, his Italian accent pronounced, sweat pouring down his face as he jabbed Anton with the gun, towards the telephone. 'And tell them you're staying on with your slut.'

'What the hell do you want?' Anton snarled, refusing to pick up the phone, seemingly oblivious to the appalling danger of the situation, refusing to do anything until he got an answer. 'Who *are* you?'

'Don't you even recognise your own family?'

'Family?' Anton gave a superior derisive scoff. *'You?'*

Lydia watched the nervous tic in the young man's left eye, could see the anger and hatred twisting his features. She wanted so badly to warn Anton not to inflame him, not to fuel this crazed man's anger, but even a single word from her lips could prove dangerous, could cause enough panic in their captor for him to pull the trigger. So instead she bit her lip, held in the words she wanted to say. Instead she mentally willed Anton not to antagonise him.

But clearly Anton's mind wasn't feeling particularly receptive. His mouth curled in a superior sneer as he eyed his captor with loathing. 'You're no Santini.'

'My nephew Dario is, though.'

Up to that point Lydia hadn't really been scared. Her actions were being fuelled by pure adrenaline, her professional mind too busy working overtime, assessing the situation, to really process fear, But watching the colour drain out of Anton's face as the bellboy responded to his taunt terrified her. Seeing the strong, immovable man literally pale before her, seeing the flash of panic in Anton's navy eyes, Lydia caught the first whiff of her own terror. And as their captor introduced himself further she realised that the threat to Anton had nothing to do with politics or even money, but was in fact born from the most dangerous vendetta of all—pure, unadulterated hatred.

'I'm Rico,' the bellboy sneered. 'I'm your son's uncle.'

CHAPTER ELEVEN

'THEY'RE NOT going to believe me if I suddenly say that I'm staying on.' All the certainty had gone from Anton's voice. His eyes swung to Lydia's and she saw his jaw tighten as he looked at her, saw the apology in his eyes as he held her gaze, and she knew that he felt responsible, knew at that moment that Anton was terrified—not for him, but for her. 'If I ring down and suddenly say that I'm staying in Melbourne for a few days, then they're going to know that something's up.'

'Then you'd better make them believe you,' Rico snarled.

'There's a car waiting...' Anton attempted to argue, and Lydia knew she had to step in, knew she had to calm things down—and quickly.

'Tell them you've changed your mind.' Running a dry tongue over her lips, Lydia spoke to Anton, relieved to see that Rico was nodding as she urged Anton to follow his orders. 'Make it sound convincing—if they argue, tell them it's none of their damn business. That's what you'd usually do.'

She watched as his reluctant hand moved for the phone, and knew that somehow she had to get a message out. Anton's arrogance might cause some annoyance, but it wouldn't come as any surprise, wouldn't necessarily ring alarm bells. Somehow she had to let her colleagues know that they were in desperate trouble up here. Taking a deep breath, she weighed up the risk of inflaming Rico further against the horror of being left here alone and no one even knowing.

'And tell them that we want some drinks sent up.'

'No one comes up!' Rico screamed, furious at her suggestion, but Lydia held her ground, carried on talking over his hysterical ranting.

'It will sound more convincing. Tell them you want drinks sent up but that we're not to be disturbed—that's what you usually do. Anton, you have to make them believe us. Tell them I want a strawberry daiquiri just as you would normally.'

'She's right.' Rico was nodding frantically again, saying the words over and over. 'She's right…' Waiting for Anton to pick up the phone, he gave his orders. 'Tell them to send the car away and that you're staying on. Tell them to bring up drinks, but to leave them outside. You're not to be disturbed. And you are to put the phone on speaker so I can hear the conversation.' His voice was growing louder with each and every word. 'So that I know you are not playing games! Talk to them like they're dirt, the way you always do!' Following Anton's gaze, clearly sensing his weakness, Rico crossed the room and held the gun to Lydia's head. 'Do as I say or she gets it.'

Lydia could feel her heart thumping in her chest as Anton's snobby, derisive voiced reeled off his orders—his words so coolly delivered there was no way the receptionist could possibly envisage the sheer terror on the other end of the line, no way she could even begin to fathom just how vital each word was. Lydia winced as Rico pressed the gun harder into her temple and the voice of the receptionist filled the room.

'How much longer will you be staying, Mr Santini?' The receptionist's purring voice filled the room.

'A day—maybe two,' Anton answered. 'I do not need the car—tell Mr Miller that I am grateful for his offer, but I will not be needing the car to take me to the airport. I will make my own arrangements.'

'Certainly.'

'And send up some drinks; just leave them outside— two coffees…' Lydia felt her throat tighten at his unwitting error, but thankfully Anton retrieved it easily. 'Actually, make that one coffee and one strawberry daiquiri—and make sure it is made properly, not like that poor effort last night.'

'I'll have those brought up directly.'

'And I am not to be disturbed. Is that clear?'

Whatever her answer was, they didn't get to hear it. Rico crossed the room and slammed his hand down on the phone, terminating the call. He nudged Anton nonetoo gently across the room and instructed him to sit.

'Hands behind your back,' he ordered.

'I might need to get the door,' Anton attempted, but Rico was having none of it.

Holding the gun with one hand, he bound Anton's wrists together with the tape, only putting the gun down when his wrists were secured and then carefully checking his handiwork. He reinforced the tape to ensure that Anton couldn't free himself, and in an appalling act of defiance slammed his fist into Anton's face.

Lydia stifled a scream, watching as Anton took the blow as if he somehow deserved it, not a sound escaping from his lips. Her eyes widened in sickening horror as she saw the jagged welt Rico's ring had left on his cheek, watched as blood poured down his face and onto his white bathrobe, and she winced as Rico's rough hands taped her ankles to the chair, and then repeated the humiliating act on Anton.

'What do you want, Rico?' Anton asked, spitting out the blood that had spilled into his mouth.

But Rico was clearly tired of talking—clearly didn't feel he needed to explain anything. He just headed across the room and sat on the bed, his gun pointing at both of them, and even if she couldn't see it Lydia could feel the hatred blazing in Rico's eyes.

The wait for their drinks to arrive was endless and the silence deafening as Rico's eyes bored into them. A thousand questions raced through Lydia's mind—questions she needed answers to. Who was Rico? Was he really related to Anton? And, most importantly of all, why did he hate him so much?

'You'll be okay.' Anton's voice was a low, gentle whisper.

'Shut up, Santini,' Rico called, but Anton wasn't to be deterred.

'It's me he wants, not you.'

Why? She didn't say it, but her eyes begged the question. She dragged them away, focussed instead on his shoulder, hoping that Anton would take the hint and not answer just yet—they needed Rico to calm down, for his agitation to abate a touch before they spoke further.

A soft knocking on the door had them all jumping. Rico shot out of his seat and stood over them as Lydia's eyes darted to Anton's. She almost wept with relief when Maria's voice filtered into the room.

'Your drinks are outside, Mr Santini.'

'Thank you!' Rico hissed in Anton's ear. 'Say thank you.'

'Thank you,' Anton called.

'Do you need anything else, sir?'

'Nothing,' Rico breathed, pushing the gun into Lydia's face until Anton repeated the word.

'Nothing.'

A tense silence followed. Rico stood rigid over them, ears on alert until finally the sound of the lift pinging told him that the 'maid' had gone. For the first time since he'd produced the gun Rico relaxed. He flicked on the television, pulled open the bar fridge and lined up the contents. He was ramming chips into his mouth, pouring spirits down his throat. Lydia prayed that he would continue, infinitely grateful that they were in the most luxurious suite in the hotel and that Anton's bar fridge wasn't the usual mini-version, but held full bottles of liquor that would hopefully anaesthetise him.

Seconds ticked away like minutes.

Minutes ticked away like hours.

As the sound of a children's cartoon filled the room and Rico laughed loudly, clearly engrossed, finally Lydia voiced her question. 'Why?'

'He's sick,' Anton said quietly. 'I've never met him before, Lydia. I just know of him.'

'Why does he hate you?' Lydia said quietly. 'If he's never even met you?'

'I know his sister.'

He didn't need to elaborate. One look at his stricken face and Lydia guessed the truth: the one woman who'd touched him, the one woman who'd got close to him, seemed to be wedged between them now, inextricably linked to this appalling nightmare.

'Cara?' Her voice was hoarse as she whispered the word, and she closed her eyes for a second when he nodded. 'And who's Dario?'

And she watched—watched as his eyes darted, watched as he paused for just a second too long before answering. And she knew, because it was her job to know, that even if Anton wasn't lying, he wasn't telling her the entire truth.

'Dario is Cara's son.'

So many questions she hadn't even voiced were answered then—such as why Rico had always spoken in English: no doubt he hadn't wanted Anton to recognise his local dialect, hadn't wanted to give Anton even a hint as to who he was.

There was plenty of time to think—to go over Rico's abhorrence of her in the restaurant, his reluctance to deliver her bags, his disinclination to leave the room that first morning. The hunch she had tried so hard to rationalise, to explain to her colleagues, was easy to explain now, with the benefit of hindsight.

Helpless, in abject misery, she watched the man who sat before her—the man who hour upon hour took without complaint Rico's demented beatings. She watched that beautiful face darken with bruises, his astute eyes become so swollen they were practically closed, trying to work out how to get them out of there safely, trying to keep her emotions in check as that dignified head tried to stay up, as somehow, despite the appalling situation, despite the appalling evidence to the contrary, each time Rico finished his vile tirades, Anton would mouth to her that he was okay; as still he tried to comfort her.

With supreme effort she pushed her personal feelings aside, forced her exhausted mind to focus, to concentrate solely on ending this nightmare, on saving the life of the man she had been entrusted to protect.

The ringing of the telephone was intrusive, and when Rico ordered Anton to answer he pulled it over to where they sat and pressed the receiver to Anton's ear. Lydia felt her heart hammering in her chest, anticipating Rico's vile reaction when he realised that the police knew of their plight.

'They want to speak to you.'

'Me?' Rico ripped the phone from Anton and his demented rage returned. He cursed into the receiver, slamming it down, and then headed for the bed. He rocked against the bedhead, the black of the gunmetal facing his nemesis, and for the first time Lydia heard him speak in Italian. But the beauty of the language was entirely lost as Rico spat out his churning, hate-fuelled words.

'Dicono che vogliano parlare, vogliano negoziare!'

And even if Lydia's Italian only ran to naming pastas she picked up on what Rico was saying—knew what her colleagues would have said to him.

'Talk to them,' Lydia implored. 'They can help you.'

'How they know?' Rico demanded of her.

'They just do, Rico,' Lydia said calmly. 'And now

you have to deal with that fact. So talk to them—tell them what it is you want.'

'There is nothing to talk about,' Rico spat. 'Because there is nothing to negotiate.'

On and on the phone rang, till even Lydia wished it would it stop. Wished that the people outside would just go away, would let her sleep, would let her close her eyes on this nightmare for even a moment.

Darkness filled the room, but Lydia knew it would end soon. Knew because her eyes were fixed on the massive floor-to-ceiling windows, her head lolling from side to side in exhaustion, her body jolting each time she succumbed. Her eyes tracked the moon on its inevitable path through the interminable night, watching as it somehow found the only cloud in the night sky and momentarily dipped behind it. That same moon had guided her thoughts last night, the same moon that would rise again tomorrow—and all Lydia knew was that she wanted to be there to see it, wanted to live her life.

'I need to go to the bathroom.' Her strangled plea dragged Rico out of his fitful slumber.

'Then go,' Rico taunted. 'Go where you sit!'

'Please,' Lydia begged. 'I have to go to the bathroom.'

'Just go here,' Anton said softly, his lips swollen, his eyes two slits in his ravaged face. 'Don't be embarrassed. There is nothing you can do.'

'Please,' Lydia begged again, noting with quiet relief that if Anton believed her, then surely Rico would too. 'I have to go to the bathroom, Rico. Please let me. It's my time, you can't just leave me sitting here…'

From her training she knew that if one thing could

make Rico weaken it was her femininity—knew that a man like Rico wouldn't be able to deal with it.

'Periodi mestruali,' Anton snapped as Rico's eye tic resumed. 'Let her go to the bathroom, for God's sake.'

Offering a silent prayer of gratitude, Lydia stared at Anton as Rico untaped her arms, barely registering the pain as the tape tore at her flesh, just pleading with her eyes as Rico moved to her legs. Lydia mouthed one single word—*Wait.*

Finally in the bathroom, Lydia knew she had seconds, maybe a minute to work. Eyeing the contents of the bathroom, the tools she could work with, she turned on the taps as she sat on the loo, mindful of the semi-open door, knowing that Rico was timing her.

Picking up Anton's razor, she set to work, shaving her wrists, disposing of the tiny invisible hairs, barely wincing as the blade nicked into her dry flesh, and as she flushed the loo she grabbed at one of the tiny bottles Anton so despised, squeezing a slug of hair conditioner onto her wrist and massaging it in.

'Out!' Rico shouted, bursting through the door, impatience etched in every feature. He dragged her back to the hateful chair by her hair, rough hands forcing her to sit before layering the tape around her wrists. He paused when the phone rang and, Lydia noted with relief, forgot to tie her ankles.

'Why don't you answer it?' Lydia suggested. 'Surely it can't hurt just to hear what they have to say?'

'I don't care what they say!' Rico shouted.

'If you really don't care,' Anton said coolly, his voice a thinly veiled taunt, 'then you'll answer it.'

And finally, just when Lydia was sure he wouldn't,

Rico gave in, knocking the receiver out of its cradle and putting the phone onto speaker.

'Rico!' John Miller's voice boomed over the speakerphone, imploring Rico to calm down, to listen to reason. 'We understand you're upset…'

Lydia tuned out, concentrating instead on her wrists. The hair conditioner she had applied, the smooth skin she had created, was allowing her a fraction of room to move, and hands were working as Rico swore at the telephone and knocked it back on the hook.

'Rico.' Anton's voice was amazingly calm. 'Why don't you let Lydia go and then we can talk?'

'Pay me off?'

'If that is what you want,' Anton offered.

'You really think money will fix everything,' Rico sneered. 'That fat bank account of yours will save your soul. Well, not this time, Anton.' He slammed the gun into his cheek and Lydia choked back a scream, watching as the harsh metal tore through Anton's flesh, heard again the sickening sound of metal on bone.

'What do you want from me?' Anton breathed.

'To see you suffer,' Rico answered coolly. 'No more, no less.'

'Then let Lydia go.' Somehow his voice was calm, somehow he managed to deliver the words as if it were almost a natural assumption that she should be freed. Lydia's eyes darted to Rico, fear gripping her as she awaited his response—not at the fact she might be held, more at the prospect of being freed, of leaving Anton with this crazed captor. It was a torture she couldn't fathom.

'She stays.' Rico's response was unequivocal, but Anton demanded an explanation.

'What possible good could it do?' Anton demanded, and even though his face was as white as marble, with blood streaming down his cheeks, his hands were bound and the collar of his robe was saturated with blood, there was a tortured dignity about him. His presence was still commanding, his voice firm, controlled as he reasoned with the impossible. 'You say you want to see me suffer—no more, no less. So what benefit can there be in making her stay? The police will treat you more favourably if you release her, and it is me you want after all. So let Lydia go…'

'You're not listening to me.' Rico's voice verged on hysteria. Anger and hatred blazed in his eyes as he snarled at Anton, who somehow didn't flinch. 'I said I wanted to see you suffer.'

'I heard you.' Anton's was the voice of reason but it only served to incense Rico further.

'I don't think you understand,' Rico screamed.

'I'm trying to.'

Lydia watched as Anton's eyes struggled to focus. He was squinting, fighting the pain, the nausea, the sheer exhaustion. He ran a dry, pale tongue over even dryer lips, beads of sweat forming on his brow. Not just the collar but the entire top of his robe was drenched now with his own blood, and her fear multiplied. She knew that she had to do something, that it wasn't a single bullet that would kill them both, but the slow torture of death from a thousand cuts: the pain, the injuries, the torture Rico had inflicted over the last day and night were culminating now, slowly squeezing the life force out of them.

'You have to stop the bleeding.' Lydia spoke to Rico,

trying to keep the fear from her voice, to somehow restore a strange normality. 'You need to apply pressure to his cheek, Rico—wrap something around it—he's losing too much blood.'

'Shut up.' A stinging slap blistered her cheek, but Lydia was too numb to register the pain. 'You don't know what it is to suffer, Anton Santini, so now I will tell you. Suffering is watching someone you love, watching someone you care about, robbed of their dignity, crying in pain night after night, watching Cara—'

'Speak to me in Italian.' Anton's voice cut in and sent a shiver down Lydia's spine.

'Why?' Rico's voice was a mocking taunt. 'Are you scared that she will think less of you if she knows the truth about you?'

'We will discuss this in Italian.' Anton's voice was still loud, but she heard him waver. Her terror intensified as the situation escalated, as she sensed Anton's tension—as, for the first time since the ordeal began, she saw true naked terror in his eyes. 'We discuss this in Italian because Lydia has nothing to do with this!' Anton shouted.

'Oh, but she does,' Rico said softly. 'You care about her—more than you care about yourself, more than you ever cared about my sister. And as I explained before, I want to see you suffer.'

The gun that had been pointed at her for so many hours now was out of sight, but she could feel the cool metal against her chest. The feel of the solid object pressing into her flesh didn't compare to the vile touch of Rico, the savage drag of his fingers along her cheek, the rubbing of the nub of his finger against the bitten flesh of her bottom lip.

'She is very beautiful.'

'Don't touch her,' Anton breathed, but his words fell on deaf ears.

Rico's crazed eyes bored into her as he addressed Anton. 'Tell her!' he shouted. 'Tell her how you made love to my sister—tell her how you promised you would be there for her, that you would marry her. Tell her how you cried tears of joy when your baby was born, when you held your son in your arms for the first time…'

'Rico, we can talk about this. I can explain…'

'Then do,' Rico spat. '*Explain* how when your son was sick, lying near death's door, you walked away. You told Cara that you weren't ready for fatherhood, paid my sister off with a cheque. Explain that if you can!'

And it wasn't the gun or Rico that scared her now, but Anton's response. Her eyes dragged across the room as she willed him to refute the accusations, begged him with her eyes to tell her that it wasn't true, that the man she had started to love could never leave a woman so cruelly, could never walk away from his own flesh and blood.

'I can't,' was Anton's paltry response.

'I hate you, Santini,' came Rico's menacing whisper. 'I've been tracking you since the day you left, watching your every move and waiting for this moment.'

'Why here?' Anton stared back at him. 'Why now?'

'You've caused my sister enough shame, so I'm taking care of it well away from her. You won't bring any more shame to our village, because *I'm* the one dealing with things now.'

'You're sick.' Somehow Anton held it together, somehow he kept his voice even. 'Rico, you're not well—you need help. This isn't the way to deal with things.'

'Oh, but it is. I hate you, Santini—hate the way you treat women, the way you treated my sister, the way you walked out on your own flesh and blood. I've hated you for so long now, and today I'm going to show you how much—'

'You'll never get away with it,' Anton broke in. 'The place is swarming with police.'

'Ah, but I'm sick.' Rico's smile was pure malice. 'You said so yourself. Which means none of this is my fault. How can I be responsible when I don't know what I'm doing?'

'Let Lydia go.' Anton's voice was crystal-clear. 'You're wrong about one thing, Rico. I don't give a damn about her. She's not my girlfriend—she's a police officer…'

'Liar!'

'Look under the pillow,' Anton roared. 'That's her gun you'll see. She means nothing to me, she's just someone paid to watch me. You can believe what you want, Rico, it doesn't make a scrap of difference to me—I'm dead anyway. But think about it. Think about facing a jury with a police officer's blood on your hands. I don't give a damn about her.' Anton said it again, conviction lacing each and every word.

'The same way you didn't give a damn about my sister?' Rico asked.

'The same way.' Anton met his captor's eyes.

'Rico!'

The booming voice through a megaphone outside in the hallway only exacerbated the tension. The voice that filled the room was way louder, way more invasive than the speaker phone had been, and the gun waved manically in Rico's hand as his fragile mind was toyed with.

Lydia knew that he couldn't go on much longer, that

in a short time things were going to come to a head. Furiously she worked to free her wrists, oblivious of the raw bruised skin. She rubbed them together, feeling the tiniest give in the tape, and concentrated on keeping her face expressionless as her hands worked on behind her back.

'We have someone on the telephone who wants to speak with you. If you don't pick up I'm going to play her voice over the loudspeaker.'

Rico just shouted, screaming into the stale air, every word, every action more crazed, more terrifying, more unpredictable than they had ever been.

'Rico…' The tearful rasps that filled the air stilled him, and a soft woman's voice crackled into the room, desperately urging Rico in Italian to pick up the phone, to talk to her, to end this madness. Every word inflamed Rico further. He was pacing the room now, shouting at people who weren't even there, and Lydia wished it would all just stop, wished that everyone would just go away and let her deal with it. And it wasn't Rico's response that worried her, but Anton's. She watched as the strong mask finally slipped, as thick tears coursed down his cheeks. They told Lydia without question that the woman talking was Cara.

Finally Rico kicked the phone across the room, then crouched to pick it up, and for a tiny hope-fuelled second Lydia envisaged it being over—surely Cara would sort things out? But Anton's words tore that last vestige of hope from her, and she watched in stunned silence as he addressed Rico.

'Don't pick it up, Rico. Talk to me, not her.'

'Anton?' Utterly bemused, Lydia questioned him. 'Rico surely needs to speak with his sister—'

'Shut up,' Anton's snarl was as loaded and as angry as Rico's had been, but it hurt twice as much. Lydia recoiled on her seat as if she'd been slapped, totally confused, and every last avenue seemed closed to her as Anton's verbal assault continued. 'This has nothing to do with you.'

'Yeah, shut up.' Rico sneered. 'I need to think.'

'She doesn't know *how* to stay quiet.' Anton's voice was a jeer. 'Nagging all the time, telling me what I'm supposed to be doing.'

The delirium, the paranoia that was clouding her mind, lifted a touch as she realised that Anton was somehow still in control, that Anton was trying to save her, trying to get her out before Rico finally succumbed to the mounting pressure. To free her before the appalling bloody climax that would surely ensue when Rico spoke with Cara. But Lydia didn't want her freedom—not at that price. Her job was to protect Anton, not to leave him at the mercy of this madman. Whatever game Anton was playing, it was surely the wrong one. Cara was their only hope, Lydia reasoned. The only person who could talk Rico down. This dangerous game Anton was playing would see them all killed.

'Deal with me, Rico,' Anton pushed. 'Don't listen to Cara. Don't let her talk you out of what you want to do. Deal with me, man to man.'

'Speak to Cara, Rico,' Lydia begged, shooting a furious authoritative look at Anton as she worked on to free her bound wrists. 'Don't listen to Anton. He left your sister. Why would you listen to a man who walked out on his own child?' The truth was too hard to contemplate, the words she was saying just too horrible to comprehend, but she said them anyway, knowing deep down that this was their last chance. 'Listen to what Cara has to say.'

She saw Rico waver, and though she despised him a flash of sympathy flared in her as she witnessed his pain, saw the blind confusion in his eyes, smelt the stench of his fear. And, as finally her hands slipped from the tape, Lydia knew that this was her only chance—that if she didn't do something now they were all going to die.

Lunging across the room she tackled Rico, felt the wedge of flesh against her as she wrestled him to the floor. She felt a searing pain as her head hit the floor, but it barely registered. All she could feel was the tension in Rico's hands as she fought for control. All she could hear was the release of gunshots as they whistled across the room. And then the shrill of a scream—her own scream—filled her ears as she heard, sensed, Anton thudding to the floor.

There was nothing she could do, not a single blessed thing she could do, other than go on holding Rico's wrists high above his head, refusing to let go. She didn't release her grip even as the door slammed open, even as her colleagues swarmed the room and finally secured the scene. She held onto his wrists even as Kevin held her shoulders and told her it was all over, that she was going to be okay, only letting go when everything started to blur, the shouting voices around her started to muffle.

Unconsciousness. A welcome reprieve from the pain.

CHAPTER TWELVE

'YOU'RE OKAY.' Graham's face stared down at her, familiar but strange, and Lydia struggled to place him, trying and failing to work out where in her life he belonged.

'Was I shot?'

'No.' Graham shook his head. 'You lost consciousness for a while—you had a nasty bang on your head and the doctor said that you are concussed—but you definitely weren't shot.'

'Anton?' Her voice trembled around the word. She was terrified of the answer but needed to know all the same, panic rippling through her as she again recalled the sound of the gun going off, the relentless sound of bullets in a confined space, and then worse, far worse, the thud of Anton falling behind her, the silence that had followed.

'He's fine—or at least he will be soon. They're just stitching him up, and he's getting some IV fluids…'

'He was shot!'

'He wasn't shot.' Graham sounded irritated. 'The bullet barely nicked his arm.'

'He's right.' That thick, unmistakable accent filled the room, and even in vivid green hospital-issue pyjamas he still cut a dash—even with a broken nose and a massive row of sutures in his cheek he was quite simply beautiful.

'What happened to Rico?' Lydia's voice wavered and she struggled to check it. She knew that Graham would be thinking she had gone soft, but she didn't care. Rico was sick and needed help—and, Lydia recalled sadly, the hatred that fuelled him, even if it had been appallingly displayed, wasn't entirely without reason.

'Locked up. Which is way less than he deserves. We knew you were in trouble even before you called down— some information came in that he had a psychiatric history, was actually from the same village as Santini—and we were just ringing up to warn you, calling in for back-up, when your call came through.' Graham's mouth twisted with suppressed rage. 'If it was up to me, they'd—'

'He's sick, Graham,' Lydia broke in.

'Don't ask me to waste any sympathy on him,' Graham retorted, gripping her hand, his fingers squeezing her bruised flesh. 'I thought I'd lost you for a moment there, Lydia.'

Wriggling her hand away, she stared up at him. 'You lost me ages ago, Graham.'

'Lydia…' Graham shook his head. 'You're exhausted. You've been to hell and back. In a couple of days—'

'I'll feel exactly the same,' Lydia interrupted.

And it was the easiest thing in the world to tell Graham to leave—easy because Lydia knew that she didn't love him. But as he quietly left she knew that now came the difficult part: saying goodbye to someone she would love for ever.

Impossibly shy, she gazed up at Anton, taking in the row of black sutures along his cheek, the swollen and bloodied lips and the purple bruises surrounding his near closed eyes.

'Green doesn't suit you.'

'Believe me, I don't intend to stay in them for long.' His voice grew more serious. 'You were asking about Rico?'

'I know I shouldn't care.' Lydia closed her eyes, picturing his tortured face. 'But he's sick.'

'He's very sick,' Anton agreed. 'Apparently he bought a round the world ticket and he has been watching my itinerary, getting work in each hotel I was due to visit for a couple of months before I arrived.'

'He was in Spain?' Lydia frowned.

'And New York.' Anton nodded. 'And to my shame I didn't recognise him. He was just another bellboy. Apparently he was determined to deal with me away from our village. '

And she wanted to ask why, but she simply didn't have the strength to face the answer.

'I've been on the phone to his psychiatrist in Florence…'

'Florence?'

'He moved there a while ago.' He didn't elaborate further. 'I've also arranged a good solicitor for him. Rico will get the help he needs soon.' Anton was silent for a moment and Lydia ached for him to go on, to refute Rico's awful accusations, to tell her it had been his crazed mind talking. 'Angelina's just been in. She sends you her love. She's booking my flight…'

'But you've just been shot! Surely you shouldn't even be *thinking* about flying?'

'I wasn't shot.' Anton played down his wound the same way Graham had. 'It just scratched the surface.'

Sitting down on the bed, he took her hand, stroking the pale, translucent flesh for a moment before bringing it up to his lips. Tears filled his eyes as he kissed her slender fingers. 'I didn't even feel the bullet. It threw me back off my chair, apparently, but I'd lost a lot of blood and passed out. Somehow I heard you scream, and I thought you were dead.'

'I thought *you* were!' Lydia admitted through chattering teeth. 'But we're both okay.'

'No, Lydia, we're not.' Dark eyes held hers, and Lydia knew that he wasn't talking about the nightmare they'd just been through but the one that was about to follow. Anton's voice was thick with regret. 'I'm flying to Rome tonight.'

'Tonight? But you're not well enough…' And even though that wasn't the reason he shouldn't go it was the only one she could voice right now. Her emotions were too raw for exposure.

'I'll be fine,' Anton said assuredly. 'I'll be in first class, sleeping all the way. I have to go now—there are things I need to do, things I need to sort out. I have a lot of unfinished business to deal with.'

Defeated, she sank back on the pillow, too tired, too exhausted to truly comprehend the magnitude of her loss—too damn weary to ask the thousand questions that she should be asking, just knowing it was over.

'We'd never have worked out,' Anton said, a regretful smile on his lips as he gazed down at her.

The fingers on his good hand traced her bruised, swollen cheek and she'd have loved to push him away, to tell him that he was right, that no man who called the child he'd walked out on 'unfinished business' could ever earn a place by her side, but she didn't have the strength to move. She just stared back at him, tears pooling in her amber eyes as he touched her for the last time.

'I guess you're going to have to just keep on looking, Lydia.'

'Looking?' Lydia sniffed.

'For that man who can somehow accept what you do for a living. Especially after...' His lids closed for a second, and he was visibly moved as he recalled the private hell they had shared. 'I just don't think I'd be able to deal with it,' he reiterated.

Brushing his hand from her cheek, Lydia turned her head away. 'Well, you don't have to deal with it, Anton, because I'm not your problem. Would you please just go?'

CHAPTER THIRTEEN

'READY for briefing?'

Maria popped her head around the washroom door as Lydia rinsed her face.

'Sure. I'll be there in a moment.'

As the door closed Lydia splashed her face again with cold water and then, taking a deep breath, headed to the briefing room.

'One for the ladies!' Kevin called as Lydia slipped into the room, taking a seat beside Maria. 'We've got a new pimp strutting his stuff and causing grief amongst the regulars. We're going to put an officer in undercover—deep undercover.'

'How deep?' Graham asked as the inevitable cheers and jeers filled the room.

'Enough, guys.' Kevin's voice was serious. 'This could get nasty—you don't need me to tell you about the recent shootings. Naturally we'll have men in place, do everything we can to ensure protection...'

'I'll do it.' Maria's hand shot up and her chocolate-brown eyes darted around the room. She was clearly expecting Lydia to have beaten her to it. 'I'll do it,' she said again, frowning at Lydia's lack of response.

Somehow Lydia muddled through the rest of the briefing. Somehow she asked intelligent questions, jotted down relevant notes, even laughed along with some of the lewder jokes, but even as the group were dismissed, even as they all headed outside, Lydia knew she was going to be called back.

'Is everything all right, Lydia?'

'Everything's fine, Kevin,' Lydia responded, grateful that he was using first names, grateful that he had taken the lead and made it clear that this conversation was off the record. 'I know you were expecting me to put my hand up back there, and I know that normally—'

'You were held hostage, Lydia,' Kevin said gently. 'There are bound to be repercussions.'

'Six weeks on?' Anguished eyes met her senior's. 'It's been six weeks, and still I keep playing it over and over in my mind.'

'You'll still be doing the same in six years' time,' Kevin said, squeezing her arm in support. 'Not as much, perhaps, but it's never going to leave you.'

That was what terrified her the most. She was waiting for the day, waiting for the moment when she didn't wake up thinking about it—waiting for the day when it would all be behind her. And as much as Kevin might think he understood—he didn't. As she had with her counsellor, Lydia was keeping her pain private.

'Lydia, we all laugh in here—we all make out we're tough. But at the end of the day you were the one bound up, you were the one held against your will with a gun to your head. Don't feel bad because you can't just shrug it off. Have you been keeping up with seeing your counsellor?'

'Sort of.' Tears sparkled in Lydia's eyes but she blinked them back. 'She's very good. It's just...'

'She doesn't really get it?' Kevin offered and Lydia nodded, words failing her as she struggled to hold back tears. 'Go home,' he said firmly. 'Take the rest of the day—the rest of the week off. Take as long as you need.'

'I've already had some time off,' Lydia pointed out. 'I thought if I came back to work things would be better.'

'Are they?'

'They were for a while.' Lydia gulped. 'It's just...' She shook her head, not able to go there.

'Go home,' Kevin said firmly and Lydia knew he was telling her—not suggesting.

'And then what?'

'That's up to you,' Kevin said more softly. 'Just take your time, Lydia.'

When she stepped off the tram, even the length of her street looked liked a marathon. Dragging her feet along the warm pavers, Lydia screwed her eyes against the hot afternoon sun, too listless to cross to the other side of the road to the shady retreat of the gum trees.

She understood now.

Understood Anton's refusal to accept her career.

Understood the fear that gripped him, because now she felt it too.

But the decision that was forming in her mind, the thought of stepping down from her position, had nothing to do with him and everything to do with her.

Anton was gone...

...and good riddance.

Straightening her shoulders, Lydia picked up her feet

and walked more purposefully now. How could she ever respect a man who would walk out on his own child? She'd had a lucky escape!

Dodging the sprinklers, Lydia rummaged in her bag for her keys, trying to recall some poem she had learnt years ago in school. Unable to remember the beginning, she recalled the end, a smile forming on her lips as she replayed it in her mind…

> *To love you was pleasant enough,*
> *But, oh, it's delicious to hate you!*

And it was. So much more delicious to hate than to grieve, so much easier to hang the blame for their demise on him rather than her.

'Lydia.'

So sure was Lydia that she was imagining it, she didn't even turn around—just pushed her key into her lock and turned it, willing the images that haunted her to just go away, to leave her alone so she could get on with her life.

'Lydia.'

And she knew she wasn't imagining things then. Knew because in her dreams he always wore a suit—every image she had of him was immaculate—and yet here he stood, dishevelled and unshaven, dressed in jeans and a T-shirt, that immaculate dark hair practically unruly now, dark curls flopping over his forehead.

And never had he looked more beautiful.

'I thought you were in Italy.' Amazingly her voice was even—amazing because her heartbeat was well into triple figures. Her lethargy dissipated as she pushed open the door and led him inside, through her tiny hallway and into her lounge room. She watched as tired, bloodshot eyes took in the scruffy couch she'd been meaning to replace, the mountain of cushions to freshen it up until she could afford to do so, the endless photos that lined every available space, and the complete and utter lack of the recent presence of a vacuum cleaner.

'I've been home.' When Lydia didn't respond, just moved a pile of magazines so that he could sit, Anton elaborated, 'I went to see my family.'

'And Cara?'

'And Cara,' Anton agreed, sitting down in the space she had cleared. 'What have you been doing since—'

'Working,' Lydia broke in. 'It's busy, as always—I had a few days off after…' Neither could bring themselves to say it, the pain of their ordeal still too raw to fully reveal. 'It didn't help. I was just sitting around feeling sorry for myself, going over and over all that had happened.'

'And all that could have happened?' Anton asked perceptively, and Lydia knew he wasn't talking about them, but about the terror of the aftermath—the horrible tricks one's mind played as it replayed a hundred and one scenarios. Even if it hurt to see him, would be agony to say goodbye all over again, for now at least she was glad that he was here—glad for five minutes in the same room with the only person on God's earth who truly knew what she'd been through.

What *they'd* been through.

'I knew that I had to go back to work. Had to get back on the horse, so to speak.'

'On the horse?'

And somehow, in the most horrible of conversations, they managed a small laugh.

'It's a saying, Anton—the sooner you get back on a horse after a fall…'

'Thank God.' Anton grinned. 'For a minute there I thought you might be in the mounted police. Actually, come to think of it, you'd look good on horseback…' The joking ended then, with a tiny shake of his head to let her know he couldn't make light of it, and his voice was heavier now. 'It's your job.' Anton shrugged, and she was grateful that he didn't pretend to understand, didn't offer her false sympathy.

'It is.'

There was a horrible pause, each waiting for the other to speak. She wished he'd just get it over with—tell her what he'd come for and leave, give her the bad news so she could begin to pick up the pieces and sort out whatever was left of her life.

'You have a nice home.'

God, she hated this stilted, forced attempt at conversation. She almost wished he hadn't come if this was what they were reduced to.

'How's Dario?' She watched as he paled, watched as guilt caught up with him, pathetically grateful that she still had the upper hand.

'Beautiful.' His jaw quilted with emotion. 'Cara showed me some pictures. I have set up a college fund for him…'

'Great!' Lydia didn't even attempt to disguise the bitterness in her voice. 'Just wave your chequebook, Anton, and it will all be fine.'

'Lydia—'

Even the sound of him saying her own name irritated

her now. Furious, she faced him. 'Don't try and justify it to me, Anton. Don't you dare try and justify to me how you could walk out on your own son!'

She'd never expected to reduce him to this—had never thought that she, Lydia, could make this beautiful, vital man literally crumble before her. But that proud, dignified face slipped and the delicious navy eyes filled with tears as he said words that she'd never, even in her most far-fetched of scenarios, contemplated.

Oh, and she *had* contemplated. Tried to fathom reasons, excuses to justify a man walking away from his son—yet however hard she'd tried, still she hadn't quite been able to manage it.

But now, as Anton spoke, he threw every excuse, every reason she'd concocted in his favour on those long, lonely nights into a heap as he admitted his agony.

'He isn't my son.'

And such was the pain behind the simple sentence that in that instant she believed him—knew from the abject agony on his face that this wasn't a lie. She had interviewed too many witnesses, seen too much raw emotion in her time. And if it had taught her one thing, it was to recognise the truth when it finally came.

Lies were complicated, sinister. They slipped off a guilty tongue in defiance and were delivered with tears that beggared belief. But the truth, when it really hurt, was always so much harder to reveal.

'That's why I didn't want Rico to pick up the telephone—why I told him to listen to me instead of you. I knew if Cara revealed the truth to him he'd really go crazy, that it would be the end for us both.'

She sank to her knees and held his hands as he told

her the appalling tale, and knew way beyond the reasonable doubt she normally lived by that these raw, anguished words came right from his soul.

'I thought Dario was my son. I thought he was mine...' Navy eyes met hers. 'She let me love him as if he were my own—and I did love him, Lydia. I loved him more than I thought it possible to love another...' His face twisted in pain, balled fists ramming into his temples as he revisited his private agony.

She didn't know what to say. Truly didn't know what paltry words she could offer in the face of such painful truth.

'Nearly two years ago I found myself with four weeks off work.' Anton's voice was distant, almost void of emotion now, but his body was rigid beneath her touch. 'I never get four weeks off—*never*,' he added, just to make sure Lydia understood the rarity of it. 'But a trip to the States was suddenly cancelled, and a hotel I had been considering buying was sold from under my nose, and suddenly I had four weeks rubbed out of my diary. So I decided to go home. Even though I live in Italy, I rarely get back to my village—something I always feel guilty about—so I decided to take the time and use it wisely, to catch up on my family.'

She felt his shoulders relax a touch, saw his face soften as for a second he was back there, back at the beginning of the dream before it had turned into a nightmare.

'My mother is brilliant at two things: cooking and talking—and believe me, Lydia, that is not a sexist comment. She is amazing at both! It took about a week of solid eating and talking just to bring me fully up to date on our family, and gradually things moved on to friends. She told me about a family in the village. The elder brother was in hospital with mental health problems. They needed money for his treatment, but the family were too embarrassed to ask for help.'

'Rico?'

Anton nodded. 'There was a clinic in Florence that the doctors thought might be able to help him, but the family didn't have any health insurance, and the cost of relocating him there would have been too much for them. I went round to see what I could do. They were family friends of my mother, and she told me how good they had been to her during difficult times...' His voice faded to a whisper. 'That is when I met Cara—she was Rico's younger sister, and I guess we...'

'Fell in love?' Lydia finished for him, hating the jealousy those words flared within her. But as Anton shook his head she felt as if a knife was being pulled from her side.

'That happened two years later,' Anton said softly. 'Love came to me when you did.'

It was the most beautiful thing anyone had said to her, but there was no time to dwell on it. It didn't answer the questions that buzzed in her brain.

'It was nice. For three weeks we were together, but it was never going to go anywhere. Cara never wanted to leave, and in truth I didn't want to stay, but for a short time it was special.'

'She got pregnant?'

Anton nodded. 'I didn't know. We didn't keep in touch or anything. But months later she called me, said that she'd been working up the courage to tell me. She'd concealed the pregnancy but now it was out in the open and her family was furious—mine too. I flew home straight away. I told her I would stand by her, that we would be married before the baby was born…'

'You married her?'

'No.' Anton shook his head. 'The baby came prematurely, a few days later, before we'd had time to arrange things.'

'But you would have married her.' Lydia frowned. 'Even though you didn't love her?'

'I cared for her, and believed she was carrying my child.' Anton made it sound that simple—and maybe it was. 'People have married for less. But it never got to that.' She could feel the tension in his body, looked down at his clenched fists as he relived his tale. 'Cara was rushed into Theatre. The baby was tiny, so tiny, and yet my lawyer was telling me he was big—too big to be my baby. He told me to ask for a DNA test.'

'Did you take one?'

Anton shook his head. 'I thought there was no need. I knew he was mine. I trusted Cara. I believed every word she was telling me.'

'She was lying,' Lydia said, and it wasn't a question, just a sad, sad statement. And as Anton gave a slow, leaden nod, in that moment all Lydia could feel was hatred. Hatred for a woman she had never met, for the agony her deceit had caused.

'Dario got sicker. He had been in Intensive Care since he was born, and when he was four weeks old he needed an urgent transfusion in the middle of the night. He has a rare blood group, and because Cara's type was different the pathologist told me that mine would be suitable. He took my blood and said that he would rush through all the tests, that the blood would be ready soon—that it was quicker this way than waiting for it to be flown in. We waited for that blood for hours.' Anton's face was pale beneath his suntan, and there were black rings around his eyes as he forced himself to go on. 'I didn't match. I can still remember the pathologist sitting with me, telling me that there was no way I could help Dario because he wasn't my son.'

A hundred emotions, words, tumbled in her mind as she tried to imagine his horror, his devastation, tried to comprehend what he had been through.

'I confronted Cara and it all came out. Apparently she'd had a brief fling before we met, with a married man in the village; she knew there was a chance the baby was his, but it was easier to say the baby was mine.'

'Easier for who?' Lydia flared, but when Anton just shook his head she knew she didn't really understand.

'For everyone. If the truth had come out she would have broken up a respectable family, her own family's name would have been shamed…'

'So she shamed you instead?'

'I offered because I could take it.' Anton swallowed hard, all the lies, however well meant at the time, finally catching up with him. 'I told Cara she could say I had said I wasn't ready for fatherhood, that I didn't want to be tied down, but that I'd given her money to support Dario.'

'Why?' Lydia begged. 'Why would you say such a thing after all she'd done to you? After all the lies?'

'Because even if I was able to walk away from Cara, I couldn't bring myself to just walk away from Dario. I had to be sure he was going to be okay. That is why I gave her money—so she could provide for him.'

'He's not your responsibility,' Lydia argued, but even as she said them she knew the futility of her words—knew that when a man like Anton loved, he loved for ever.

'I held him, Lydia. I cut his cord when he was born. Even if he is not mine he will always matter to me.'

'And Cara?' God, it hurt to ask—hurt almost more than she could bear. But Lydia needed answers.

'We have made our peace,' Anton said softly. 'The anger is gone now. She was scared; she didn't know what else to do…'

'So she tried to con you!' Lydia retorted. 'I'm sorry.' Pulling her hands away, she stood up. 'It's not for me to judge, and I'm glad you've made up…' She forced a smile. 'I hope you'll both be happy.'

'Both?' Anton frowned.

'All three of you, then,' Lydia snapped, wishing he would just leave, wishing this torturous agony would soon end so that she could give in to the tears that were appallingly close.

'Why would I want to be with Cara?' He sounded genuinely bemused. 'Why do you think—?'

'You said you'd made your peace.'

'It doesn't mean I slept with her.' He was back in control now, his flip response more the Anton of old. 'Lydia, why do you think I am here?'

'I don't know.' Her hands flailed in the air. 'To "make your peace" with me, perhaps? Well, save your breath, Anton. I'm doing fine.'

'Are you?' Gripping her wrists, he stared down at her, taking in a face that was way too pale, way too thin, watching those once confident eyes darting nervously, appalled at the fragility beneath his fingers. 'Lydia, why do you think I left?'

Hadn't he humiliated her enough? Tears filled her eyes and she gave an ungracious sniff as she struggled to hold them back, refusing to cry in front of him—there would be plenty of time for that later.

When she didn't answer, when the words strangled in her throat, Anton spoke for her. 'I left for you, Lydia.' He watched a tiny frown pucker her taut face. 'I left because that day I felt real fear and I truly thought that I couldn't do it—thought that I couldn't be the man you wanted me to be. And I knew if I stayed a moment longer I would try to dissuade you, would beg you to give up your work, and I also needed to talk to my mother about Cara, to explain things face to face…'

'That was the unfinished business?' Wide-eyed, she stared back at him. 'I thought you meant you were going to see Cara.'

'I had to deal with that too. But it is really finished now. Things are better now they are out in the open,' Anton explained. 'Rico is having the treatment he needs, and our families finally know the truth—or most of it.'

'Most of it?'

'I didn't slip in the bit about emigrating, and taking over our Australian franchise. My mother's heart isn't quite what it used to be.'

'Emigrating?' The frown on her face deepened as she whispered the word back to him.

Anton continued—because Lydia couldn't. 'And I admit I omitted to tell her that my future wife is an inspector in the police…' Registering her confusion, he ignored the issues he'd raised and focussed on the one that really mattered. Cupping her fragile face in his hands, all joking and flip comments over now, he bared his very soul. 'I thought I couldn't do it, Lydia. Couldn't imagine, after all we'd gone through, ever being able to wave you to off to work, ever allowing you…' His translation skills stalled and she watched as his mind raced to find the right words. He settled for, '…to be you,' and it worked beautifully. Tears spilled from her eyes unchecked now as Anton Santini opened the door to his heart and invited her to step inside.

'These past weeks I have worked on myself—does that make sense?'

It made perfect sense. Because she'd worked on herself too. Had spent sleepless nights facing the bigger issues, had grown up more in these past six weeks than she had in her entire life.

'At first I thought it was pride—what sort of man would I be, allowing my wife to do such work?—and maybe that was a factor. But not now.'

His hands still cradled her face, the nub of his thumb hushing her as she opened her lips to speak, to reassure him that finally she understood, that she knew exactly how he was feeling. But it wasn't that that silenced her. Instead it was respect and need—respect for his heartfelt words that deserved an audience, and a need to know how he really felt.

'I couldn't bear the thought of losing you, Lydia. I couldn't bear the thought of some bastard doing to you what Rico did—and maybe far, far worse. I almost managed to convince myself that it would be easier to walk away, to let you live the life you want and I would live mine. It took me six damned weeks to realise why it hurt so much. Six long weeks to work out why I was still in so much pain—because in walking away I'd made my own worst fear come true. Either way, I had losed you.'

'Lost me,' Lydia corrected, but, seeing the pain flicker on his face, she begged an explanation. 'Either way you had *lost* me.' A gurgle of laughter spilled from her lips, in contrast to the tears streaming down her face. 'I was correcting your English, Anton, not telling you it's over. You could never lose me—never in a million years. Because as long as I'm breathing I'm going to love you.'

'You mean it?'

Hope flared in his eyes and his mouth searched for hers, but Lydia pulled away. They had their whole life ahead of them. Kissing, loving, sharing could all come later. Some things needed to be said, and it was Anton's turn to listen.

'You don't have to tell your mum about me being an inspector—'

'I want to be honest now,' Anton broke in.

'So do I.' Lydia nodded, but changed midway, shaking her head against the hands that still held her face. 'I can't do it any more, Anton. I've lost my nerve.'

'You'll get it back,' he said assuredly. 'It will just take time. In a few weeks you'll be back to normal, kicking arse…'

Lydia could scarcely believe what she was hearing—here was the man who hated her job more than anyone encouraging her, almost pleading with her to go back.

'I understand.' Lydia silenced him with two tender words. 'I understand how you feel because I feel it too.

I understand that when you love someone, when you care about someone more than you care about yourself, all you want to do is protect them.' Trembling hands met his, guiding them from her face to her stomach, and she watched in silence as the news filtered through.

'A baby?' His voice was incredulous as the warmth of his hands seeped through her flimsy top, radiating love to the tiny life within.

'Our baby,' she affirmed. 'I didn't take the promotion, Anton. I couldn't. When there was only me to worry about I could take the risks, but not now. I understand how you feel...' Lydia whispered, closing her eyes as his lips met hers, closing the door on the horrors that were behind them, glimpsing a beautiful future ahead.

With Anton protecting them both.

EPILOGUE

'Lydia!' Anton's urgent voice had her running. Taking the steps of their smart Melbourne home two at a time, she raced into the living room, preparing herself for any appalling eventuality, skidding to a halt as a smiling face greeted hers.

'I think Alexandra has a tooth.'

'It's milk,' Lydia said in a matter-of-fact voice, peering into her eight-week-old daughter's gummy mouth.

'It's a tooth,' Anton insisted.

'It's *regurgitated* milk,' Lydia said, wiping away the offending dot to confirm her point, smiling as she did so. The innocent, never-ending smiles from her tiny daughter never ceased to move her.

Or Anton.

He was as proud of Alexandra as he was dedicated to her—bathing her, singing tunelessly to her, changing the most vile of diapers with barely a word of protest. The only concession to his abhorrent wealth was a night-time nanny.

From seven through to seven it was just about them.

Apart from many final kisses goodnight.

Apart from the night feeds.

Apart from the times Anton nudged her in the ribs when Alex's piercing screams filtered through to their bedroom around three a.m.

Over and over he loved them—loved the two redheaded women in his life; again and again he surprised her.

She'd handed him an envelope ten days after their daughter's birth, because given what he'd been through he deserved it. She'd handed him the irrefutable proof that confirmed that Alexandra was 99.99 per cent his, and he'd handed it back unopened.

No proof of identity needed when none was required.

Trust was easy to achieve with love on their side.

'We're lucky.'

'Very,' Lydia agreed, snuggling into the sofa beside him, watching as he fed a greedy Alex the last remains of her bottle.

'Some children aren't.' Anton gave a rather too dramatic sigh—the sort of sigh that had Lydia frowning; the sort of sigh that had her senses on high alert. 'Don't you wish you could help them?'

'Who?'

'I don't know.' Anton shrugged, way too nonchalantly. 'Kids that maybe have been abused, babies that have no voice…'

Which wasn't exactly idle conversation—wasn't the type of thing Anton usually said at all. In an instant Lydia had worked him out—Anton hadn't developed a social conscience all of a sudden, he'd been snooping where he shouldn't.

'You've been reading my e-mails!' Appalled, she confronted him. 'Don't try and lie to me, Anton—you've been reading my mail.'

'I read one e-mail,' Anton retorted. 'By complete accident.'

'Please!' Lydia snorted, two spots of colour flaming on her cheeks. Because even though she was in the right, even though she had every right to privacy, for some reason she felt as if she'd just been caught with her hand in the cookie jar, felt horribly guilty for not telling Anton what had been going on in her head for the last two days.

'Is there anything you want to tell me?'

'I've been offered a job. Well, I've been invited to apply for a job.' Lydia gulped, staring at her divine daughter and wondering how she could even contemplate leaving her, wondering how she could bear to think about going back to work so soon. 'Kevin phoned me a couple of days ago to see if I was interested, then e-mailed me the job description. It's only part-time.' Lydia breathed through it, bracing herself for his reaction. 'I wouldn't be starting for a couple of months yet. It's as an inspector on the Child Protection Unit.'

'You need to work, don't you?' Anton smiled, and for the thousandth time she was taken aback by his insight.

'I do,' Lydia admitted. 'I guess I must need a bit of guilt back in my life…' Seeing Anton's frown, she elaborated. 'It's no fun buying shoes when you don't need to hide the receipt.'

'Why would you want to hide the receipt?' Anton asked, clearly bemused.

'It's a girl thing,' Lydia said airily. 'We like to feel as if we're doing something we shouldn't.' But her voice changed as she answered seriously the issues going back to work raised. 'I feel awful even thinking about leaving Alex. But, Anton, it's a great job—and it's a lot safer than what I was doing before.'

'No guns?' Anton checked, and Lydia nodded. Then she gave a tiny, hesitant wince.

'Not like before, Anton. But there probably will be a few situations where guns will be present—you've seen the news, you know what goes on. But I'm not going to be armed.'

'It could still be dangerous.'

'Of course it could,' Lydia agreed. 'But it's probably one of the safer jobs that still manages to interest me, and at the end of the day…'

'Don't tell me again how you could get run over by a bus.' Anton gave a tight smile, but his mind was clearly elsewhere. He stared at his gorgeous daughter for an age, before turning to her mother. 'And you need it?' Anton asked. 'You need to work?'

'I do,' Lydia admitted. And it didn't feel wrong saying it but it didn't feel right either. It just…

…was.

'But I can't do it without you fully behind me, Anton. You have to know that there will be sacrifices, that even though the job's part-time I might be late home sometimes. I might have to stay—'

'I do work too,' Anton broke in, and Lydia braced herself, sure that he was about to point out how important his work was, how much more he earned, how he wanted his wife home for dinner. But, as always, Anton surprised her. His next comment told her that he genuinely seemed to understand the problems she might face. 'I do know that it's not always easy to just get away. You don't have to justify that to me.'

'I *know* we don't need the money, and I *know* that there will be days I hate my job more than anything in the world. But that won't mean I want you telling me to leave it, that we don't really need me to be there…' Her voice faded and she stared at his strong, handsome face, listening to the contented sounds from a dozing Alex and wondering for the millionth time how she'd ever got so lucky.

'Go for it, then.' Anton smiled, snapping her out of her trance and back to beautiful reality.

'You're sure?'

'I'm sure.' Anton nodded, but a tiny frown puckered his brow, his face clouding over as he conjured up one horrible prospect. 'On one condition.'

'What?' Lydia was frowning now too.

'No night duty.'

'No night duty!' Lydia cried, rolling her eyes at the appalling concession he was forcing her to make, trying not to over-act too much, but hard pushed to keep the smile off her face. 'Well…' she gave a dramatic sigh '…I suppose if that's what it takes to go back to work…'

'That's what it takes,' Anton insisted, pretending not to notice as Lydia shared a conspiratorial smile with her gorgeous daughter.

'Then I guess that's how it will have to be.'

'Nights,' Anton said, putting Alex in her crib and joining Lydia on the sofa, pulling her close and taking her in his arms, 'are for you and I.'

UNDERCOVER CONNECTION

HEATHER GRAHAM

For Lorna Broussard – with love and thanks for all the help and support for…well, many years!

Chapter One

The woman on the runway was truly one of the most stunning creatures Jacob Wolff had ever seen. Her skin was pure bronze, as sleek and as dazzling as the deepest sun ray.

When she turned, he could see—even from his distance at the club's bar—that her eyes were light. Green, he thought, and a sharp contrast to her skin. She had amazing hair, long and so shimmering that it was as close to pure black as it was possible to be; so dark it almost had a gleam of violet. She was long-legged, lean and yet exquisitely shaped as she moved in the creation she modeled—a mix of pastel colors that was perfectly enhanced by her skin—the dress was bare at the shoulder and throat with a plunging neckline, and back, and then swept to the floor.

She moved like a woman accustomed to such a haughty strut: proud, confident, arrogant and perhaps even amused by the awe of the onlookers.

"That one—she will rule the place one day."

Jacob turned.

Ivan Petrov leaned on one elbow across the bar

from Jacob. Ivan bartended and—so Jacob believed thus far—ran all things that had to do with the on-the-ground-management of the Gold Sun Club. The burning-hot new establishment was having its grand opening tonight.

"I'd imagine," Jacob said. He leaned closer over the bar and smiled. "And I imagine that she might perhaps be…available?"

Ivan smiled, clearly glad that Jacob had asked him; Ivan was a proud man, appreciative that Jacob had noted his position of power within the club.

"Not…immediately," Ivan said. "She is fairly new. But all things come in good time, my friend, eh? Now you," he said, pouring a shot of vodka for Jacob, "you are fairly new, too. New to Miami Beach—new to our ways. We have our…social…rules, you know."

Jacob knew all too well.

And he knew what happened to those who didn't follow the rules—or who dared to make their own. He'd been south of I-75 that morning, off part of the highway still known as Alligator Alley, and for good reason. He'd been deep in the Everglades where a Seminole ranger had recently discovered a bizarre cache of oil drums, inside of which had been several bodies in various stages of decomposition.

"I have my reputation," Jacob said softly.

Ivan caught Jacob's meaning. Yes, Jacob would follow the rules. But he was his own man—very much a *made* man from the underbelly of New York City. Now, he'd bought a gallery on South Beach; but he'd been doing his other business for years.

At least, that was the information that had been fed to what had become known as the Deco Gang—so called because of the beautifully preserved architecture on South Beach.

Jacob was for all intents and purposes a new major player in the area. And it was important, of course, that he appear to be a team player—but a very powerful team player who respected another man's turf while also keeping a strict hold on his own.

"A man's reputation must be upheld," Ivan said, nodding approvingly.

"While, of course, he gives heed to all that belongs to another man, as well," Jacob assured him.

A loud clash of drums drew Jacob's attention for a moment. The Dissidents were playing that night; they were supposedly one of the hottest up-and-coming bands, not just in the state, but worldwide.

The grand opening to the Gold Sun Club had been invitation only; tomorrow night, others would flow in, awed by the publicity generated by this celebrity-studded evening. The rich and the beautiful—and the not-so-rich but very beautiful—were all on the ground floor, listening to the popular new band and watching the fashion show.

Jacob took in the place as a whole, noting a balcony level that ran the perimeter, with a bar above the stage. But that night all the guests were downstairs, and Ivan Petrov was manning the main bar himself.

The elegant model on the runway swirled with perfect timing, walking toward the crowd again, pausing to seductively steal a delicious-looking apple from the hands of a pretty boy—a young male model, dressed as Adonis—standing like a statue at the bottom of the steps to the runway.

"I believe," Jacob told Ivan, turning to look at him gravely again, "that my business will be an asset to your business, and that we will work in perfect harmony together."

"Yes," Ivan said. "Mr. Smirnoff invited you, right?"

Jacob nodded. "Josef brought me in."

Ivan said, "He is an important man."

"Yes, I know," Jacob assured him.

If Ivan only knew how.

JASMINE ADAIR—JASMINE ALAMEIN, as far as this group was concerned—was glad that she had managed to learn the art of walking a runway, without tripping, and observing at the same time. It wasn't as if she'd had training or gone to cotillion classes—did they still have cotillion classes?—but she'd been graced with the most wonderful parents in the world.

Her mother had been with the Peace Corps—maybe a natural course for her, having somewhat global roots. Her mom's parents had come from Jordan and Kenya, met and married in Morocco and moved to the United States. Jasmine's mom, Liliana, had been born and grown up in Miami, but had traveled the world to help people before she'd finally settled down. Liliana had been a great mom, always all about kindness to others and passionate that everyone must be careful with others. She had believed that words could make or break a person's day, and truly *seeing* people was one of the most important talents anyone could have in life.

Declan Adair, Jasmine's dad, was mostly Irish-American. He'd been a cop and had taught Jasmine what that meant to him—serving his community.

They had both taught her about absolute equality for every color, race, creed, sex and sexual orientation, and they had both taught her that good people were good people and, all in all, most of the people in the world were good, longing for the same things, especially in America—life, liberty and the pursuit of happiness.

They sounded like a sweet pair of hippies; they had been anything but. Her father had also taught her that those who appeared to be the nicest people in the world often were not—and that lip service didn't mean a hell of a lot and could hide an ocean of lies and misdeeds.

"Judging people—hardest call you'll ever make," he'd told her once. "Especially when you have to do so quickly."

He'd shaken his head in disgust over the result of a trial often enough, and her mother had always reminded him, "There are things that just aren't allowed before a jury, Declan. Things that the jury just doesn't see and doesn't know."

"Not to worry—we'll get them next time," he would assure her.

Jasmine scanned the crowd. Members of this group, the so-called Deco Gang, hadn't been gotten yet. And they needed to be—no one really knew the full extent of their crimes because they were good. Damned good at knowing how to game the justice system.

Fanatics came in all kinds—and fanatics were dangerous. Just as criminals came in all kinds, and they ruined the lives of those who wanted to live in peace, raising their children, working…enjoying their liberty and pursuing their happiness.

That's why cops were so important—something she had learned when sometimes her dad, the detective, hadn't made it to a birthday party.

Because of him, she'd always wanted to be a cop. And she was a damned good one, if she did say so herself.

At the moment, it was her mother's training that was paying off. As a child, Jasmine had accompanied her mom to all kinds of fund-raisers—and once she was a teenager, she'd started modeling at fashion shows in order to attract large donations for her mom's various charities. She had worked with a few top designers who were equally passionate about feeding children or raising awareness when natural disasters devastated various regions in the States and around the world.

So as Jasmine strutted and played it up for the audience, she also watched.

The event had attracted the who's who of the city. She could see two television stars who were acting in current hit series. Alphonse Mangiulli—renowned Italian artist—was there, along with Cam Li, the Chinese businessman who had just built two of the largest hotels in the world, one in Dubai and one on Miami Beach. Mathilda Glen—old, old Miami society and money—had made it, along with the famed English film director, Eric Summer.

And amid this gathering of the rich and famous was also a meeting of the loosely organized group of South Beach criminals that the Miami-Dade police called the Deco Gang.

They had come together under the control of a Russian-born kingpin, Josef Smirnoff, and they were an equal-opportunity group of very dangerous criminals. They weren't connected to the Italian Mafia or Cosa Nostra, and they weren't the Asian mob or a cartel from any South American or island country. And they were hard to pin down, using legitimate business for money laundering and for their forays into drug smuggling and dealing and prostitution.

Crimes had been committed; the bodies of victims had been found, but for the most part, those who got in the way of the gang were eliminated. Because of their connections with one another, alibis were abundant, evidence disappeared, and pinning anything on any one individual had been an elusive goal for the police.

Jasmine had used every favor she had saved up to get assigned to this case. It helped that her looks gave her a good cover for infiltration.

Her captain—Mac Lorenzo—probably suspected that she had her own motives. But he didn't ask, and she didn't tell. She hadn't let Lorenzo know that her personal determination to bring down the Deco Gang had begun when Mary Ahearn had disappeared. Her old friend had vanished without a trace after working with a nightclub that was most probably a front for a very high-scale prostitution ring.

She could see Josef Smirnoff in the front of the

crowd; he was smiling and looking right at her. He seemed to like what he saw. Good. He was the man in charge, and she needed access to him. She needed to be able to count his bodyguards and his henchmen and get close to him.

She wasn't working alone; Jasmine was blessed with an incredible partner, Jorge Fuentes.

Along with being a dedicated cop, Jorge was also extremely good-looking, and thanks to that, he'd been given leeway when he'd shown up at the Gold Sun Club, supposedly looking for work. Jasmine had told Natasha Volkov—manager of the models who worked these events or sat about various places looking pretty—that she'd worked with Jorge before and that he was wonderfully easygoing. Turned out the show was short a man; Jorge had been hired on for the day easily. They'd cast him as Adonis and given him a very small costume to wear.

Jorge had been trying to get a moment alone with her as preparations for the fashion show had gone on. Jasmine had been undercover for several weeks prior to the club's opening night, and briefings had been few and far between. The opportunity hadn't arisen as yet, but they'd be able to connect—as soon as the runway show part of the party was over. She was curious what updates Jorge had, but they were both savvy enough to bide their time. Neither of them dared to blow their covers with this group—such a mistake could result in instant death, with neither of them even aware or able to help the other in any way.

Her cover story was complete. She had a rented room

on Miami Beach, which she took for a week before answering the ad for models. She'd been given an effective fake résumé—one that showed she'd worked but never been on the top. And might well be hungry to get there.

After a lightning-quick change of clothes backstage, she made another sweep down the runway. She noted the celebrities in attendance. South Beach clubs were like rolls of toilet paper—people used them up and discarded them without a thought. What was popular today might be deserted within a month.

But she didn't think that this enterprise would care—the showy opening was just another front for the illegal activities that kept them going.

She noted the men and women surrounding Josef Smirnoff. He was about six feet tall, big and solidly muscled. His head was immaculately bald, which made his sharp jaw even more prominent and his dark eyes stand out.

On his arm was an up-and-coming young starlet. She was in from California, a lovely blue-eyed blonde, clearly hoping that Smirnoff's connections here would allow her to rub elbows with the right people.

Jasmine hoped that worked out for her—and that she didn't become involved with the wrong people.

Natasha was with him, as well. She had modeled in her own youth, in Europe. About five-eleven and in her midfifties, Natasha had come up through the ranks. One of the girls had whispered to Jasmine that Natasha had always been smart—she had managed to sleep her way up with the right people. She was an attractive woman, keeping her shoulder-length hair a silvery-white color that enhanced her slim features. She kept tight control of the fashion show and other events, and sharp eyes on everyone and everything.

Rumor had it she was sleeping with Josef. It wasn't something she proclaimed or denied. But there were signs. Jasmine wondered if she cared for Josef—or if it was a power play.

Jasmine had to wonder how Natasha felt about the beautiful women who were always around. But she understood, for Natasha, life hadn't been easy. Power probably overrode emotion.

The men by Smirnoff were his immediate bodyguards. Jasmine thought of them as Curly, Moe and Larry. In truth, they were Alejandro Suarez, Antonio Garibaldi and Sasha Antonovich. All three were big men, broad-shouldered and spent their off-hours in the gym. One of the three was always with Smirnoff. On a day like today, they were all close to him.

Victor Kozak was there, as well. Victor was apparently the rising heir to receive control of the action. He was taller and slimmer than Josef, and he had bright blue eyes and perfectly clipped, salt-and-pepper facial hair. He was extremely pleasant to Jasmine—so pleasant that it made her feel uneasy.

She knew about them all somewhat because she had talked to Mary about what she was doing. She had warned Mary that there was suspicion about the group on South Beach that ran so many of the events that called for runway models or beautiful people just to be in a crowd. Beautiful people who, it was rumored, you could engage to spend time with privately. Mary had described many of these players before Jasmine had met them.

Before Mary had disappeared.

The club manager was behind the bar; he didn't often work that kind of labor himself. He usually oversaw what was going on there. He was like the bodyguards—solid, watching, earning his way up the ranks.

Still watching, Jasmine made another of her teasing plays with Jorge—pointing out the next model who was coming down the runway. Kari Anderson was walking along in a black caftan that accented the fairness of her skin and the platinum shimmer of her hair. Jorge stood perfectly still; only his eyes moved, drawing laughter from the crowd.

As Jasmine did her turn around, she noted a man at the bar. She did not know him, or anything about him. He was a newcomer, Kari had told her. A big man in New York City. He was taller and leaner than any of the other men, and yet Jasmine had the feeling that he was steel-muscled beneath the designer suit he was wearing. He hadn't close-cropped his hair either; it was long, shaggy around his ears, a soft brown.

He was definitely the best looking of the bunch. His face was crafted with sharp clean contours, high defined cheekbones, a nicely squared chin and wide-set, light eyes. He could have been up on the runway, playing "pretty boy" with Jorge.

But of course, newcomer though he might be, he'd be one of "them." He'd recently come to South Beach, pretending to be some kind of an artist and owning and operating a gallery.

The hair. Maybe he believed that would disguise him as an artist—rather than a murdering criminal.

When she had made another turn, after pausing to do a synchronized turn with Kari, she saw that the new guy had left the bar area, along with the bartender. They were near Josef Smirnoff now.

Allowed into the inner circle.

Just as she noticed them, a loud crack rang out. The sound was almost masked by the music.

People didn't react.

Instinct and experience told Jasmine that it was indeed a gunshot. She instantly grabbed hold of Kari and dragged her down to the platform, all but lying over her. Another shot sounded; a light exploded in a hail of sparks. Then the rat-tat-tat of bullets exploded throughout the room.

The crowd began to scream and move.

There was nothing orderly about what happened—people panicked. It was hard not to blame them. It was a fearsome world they lived in.

"Stay down!" Jasmine told Kari, rising carefully.

Jorge was already on the floor, trying to help up a woman who had fallen, in danger of being trampled.

Bodyguards and police hired for the night were trying to bring order. Jasmine jumped into the crowd, trying to fathom where the shots had been fired. It was a light at the end of the runway that had exploded; where the other shot had come from was hard to discern.

The band had panicked, as well. A guitar crashed down on the floor.

Josef Smirnoff was on the ground, too. His bodyguards were near, trying to hold off the people who were set to run over him.

It was an absolute melee.

Jasmine helped up a young man, a white-faced rising star in a new television series. He tried to thank her.

"Get out, go—walk quickly," she said.

There were no more shots. But would they begin again?

She made her way to Smirnoff, ducking beneath the distracted bodyguards. She knelt by him as people raced around her.

"Josef?" she said, reaching for his shoulder, turning him over.

Blood covered his chest. There was no hope for the man; he was already dead, his eyes open in shock. There was blood on her now, blood on the designer gown she'd been wearing, everywhere.

She looked up; Jorge had to be somewhere nearby. Instead she saw a man coming after her, reaching for her as if to attack.

She rolled quickly, avoiding him once. But as she prepared to fight back, she felt as if she had been taken down by a linebacker. She stared up into the eyes of the long-haired newcomer; bright blue eyes, startling against his face and dark hair. She felt his hands on her, felt the strength in his hold.

No. She was going to take him down.

She jackknifed her body, letting him use his own weight against himself, causing him to crash into the floor.

He was obviously surprised. It took him a second—

but only a second—to spin himself. He was back on his feet in a hunched position, ready to spring at her.

Where the hell is Jorge?

She feinted as if she would dive down to the left and dived to the right instead. She caught the man with a hard chop to the abdomen that should have stolen his breath.

He didn't give. She was suddenly tackled again, down on the ground, feeling the full power of the man's strength atop her. She stared up into his blue eyes, glistening like ice at the moment.

She realized the crowd was gone; she could hear the bustle at the doorway, hear the police as they poured in at the entrance.

But right there, at that moment, Josef Smirnoff lay dead in an ungodly pool of blood—blood she wore—just feet away.

And there was this man.

And herself.

"Hey!" Thank God, Jorge had found her. He dived down beside them, as if joining the fight. But he didn't help Jasmine; he made no move against the man. He lay next to her, as if he'd just also been taken down himself.

"Stop! FBI, meet MDPD. Jasmine, he's undercover. Jacob… Jasmine is a cop. My partner," Jorge whispered urgently.

The man couldn't have looked more surprised. Then, he made a play of socking Jorge, and Jorge lay still. The man stood and dragged Jasmine to her feet. For a long moment he looked into her eyes, and then he wrenched her elbow behind her back.

"Play it out," he said, "nothing else to do."
"Sure," Jasmine told him.
And as he led her out—toward Victor Kozak, who now stood in the front, ready to take charge, Jasmine managed to twist and deliver a hard right to his jaw.

He stared at her, rubbing his jaw with his free hand.

"Play it out," she said softly.

The Feds always thought they knew more than the locals, whether they were team people or not. He'd probably be furious. He'd want to call the shots.

But at least his presence meant that the Feds had been aware of this place. They had listened to the police, and they had sent someone in. It was probably what Jorge had been trying to tell her.

Jacob was still staring at her. Well, she did have a damned good right hook.

To her surprise, he almost seemed to smile. "Play it out," he said. And to her continued surprise, he added, "You are one hell of a player!"

Chapter Two

"Someone knew," Jorge said. "Someone knew that Smirnoff came in—that he was selling them all out."

"Maybe," Jacob Wolff said. He was sitting on the sofa in Jasmine's South Beach apartment.

She didn't know why, but it bothered her that he was there. So comfortable. So thoughtful. But it hadn't been until now, with him in her apartment, that she really understood what was going on.

Two weeks ago, Josef Smirnoff had made contact with Dean Jenkins, a special agent assigned to the Miami office. Jenkins had gone to his superiors, and from there, Jacob Wolff had been called in. Among his other talents, he was a linguist, speaking Russian, Ukrainian, Spanish, Portuguese and French, including Cajun and Haitian Creole. He also knew a smattering of Czech and Polish. And German, enough to get by.

Maybe that's why she was resenting him. No one should be that accomplished.

No, it was simply because he had taken her by surprise.

"Maybe someone knew," Wolff said. He added, "And maybe not."

"If not, why—?" Jorge asked.

Wolff leaned forward. "Because," he said softly, "I believe that Kozak set up that hit. Not because he knew about anything that Smirnoff had done, but because he's been planning on taking over. Perhaps for some time.

"Smirnoff came in to us because he was afraid—he'd been the boss forever, but he knew how that could end if a power play went down. He was afraid. He wanted out. Kozak was the one who wanted Smirnoff out. And he figured out how to do it—and make it look as if he was as pure as the driven snow in the whole thing himself. He was visible to dozens of people when Smirnoff was killed. He played his cards right. There were plenty of cops there today, in uniform. What better time to plan an execution, when he wouldn't look the least guilty? In *this* crime ring, he was definitely the next man up— vice president, if you will."

"The thing is, if Kozak figures out something is up, we're all in grave danger," Jorge pointed out. "Undercover may not work."

"Jorge, undercover work is the only thing that might bring them down," Jasmine protested.

She was leaning against the archway between the living-dining area of the apartment and the kitchen. It was late; she was tired. But it had been the first chance for the three of them to talk.

After the chaos, everyone had been interviewed by the police. Stars—the glittering rich and famous and especially the almost-famous—had done endless interviews with the press, as well. Thankfully, there had been plenty of celebrities to garner attention. Jasmine,

Jorge and Jacob Wolff had all managed to avoid being seen on television, but still, maintaining their cover had meant they were there for hours.

She'd been desperate to shower, and her blood-soaked gown had gone to the evidence locker.

In the end, they'd been seen leaving together, but that had been all right. Everyone knew that Jorge was Jasmine's friend—she'd brought him into the show, after all.

And as for Jacob Wolff...

"You shouldn't have made that show of going off with us in front of Victor Kozak," she said, glaring at Wolff. She realized her tone was harsh. Too harsh. But this was her apartment—or, at least, her cover persona's apartment—and she felt like a cat on a hot tin roof while he relaxed comfortably on her rented couch.

She needed to take a deep breath; start over with the agent.

He didn't look her way, just shrugged. "I told Ivan, the bartender, I wanted to get to know you. They believe I'm an important player out of New York. Right now, they're observing me. And they believe if they respect me, I'll respect them, play by their rules. I'm supposed to be a money launderer—I'm not into many of their criminal activities, including prostitution or any form of modern slavery. My cover is that of an art dealer with dozens of foreign ties.

"Before all this went down tonight, I was trying to befriend Ivan, who apparently manages the girls. I'm trying to figure out how the women are entangled in their web. Apparently, they move slowly. Most probably, with drugs. Before all this went down tonight, I'd asked about you, Jasmine, as if taking advantage of the 'friendship' they'll offer me. He said you weren't available yet, but that all good things come in time, or something to that effect. He'll think I took advantage of the situation instead—and that I'm offering you all the comfort a man in my position can offer."

"Really?" Jasmine asked. "But I was with Jorge."

Wolff finally looked at her, waving a hand in the air. "Yes, and they all know you two are friends, and that it's normal you would have left with Jorge. But Jorge is gay."

"That's what you told them?" Jasmine asked.

"I am gay," Jorge said, shrugging.

Jasmine turned to him. "You are? You never told me."

"You never asked. Hey, we're great partners. I never asked who you were dating. Oh, wait, you never do seem to date."

Jasmine could have kicked him. "Hey!" she protested. Great. She felt like an idiot. She and Jorge were close, but…it was true. They'd been working together for a while, they were friends. Just friends. And because of that, she hadn't thought to ask—

It didn't matter. They'd both tacitly known from the beginning as partners they'd never date each other, and neither had ever thought to ask the other about their love life.

She had to draw some dignity out of this situation.

"At least we did the expected," she said. "I guarantee we were watched. Oh, and by the way, Ivan Petrov controls the venue. But Natasha really runs the models. She gives the assignments, and she's the one who hands out the paychecks."

Wolff looked at her. "You're going to have to be very careful. From all that I've been told, she's been with this enterprise from the beginning. She may be almost as powerful as Kozak himself. When Natasha got into it, she wasn't manipulated into sex work. She used sex as an investment. She came into it as a model, slept with whomever they wanted—and worked her way up to Kozak."

"I am careful," Jasmine told him. "I'm a good cop—determined, but not suicidal."

"I'm glad to hear it. So, this is all as good as it can be," Wolff said, shaking his head. "What matters most here tonight is that we've lost Smirnoff, our informant. And we've still got to somehow get into this and take them all down. We have to take Kozak down, with all the budding lieutenants, too. My position with this group is pretty solid—the Bureau does an amazing job when it comes to inventing a history. But the fashion show is over. The opening is over. The club will be closed down for a few days."

"I'll have an in, don't worry. The last words from Natasha this evening had to do with us all reporting in tomorrow—for one, to return the clothing. For another, to find out where we go from here." Jasmine hesitated.

"They haven't asked you to entertain anyone yet?" Wolff asked.

"New girls get a chance to believe they're just models. After that, they're asked to escort at certain times, and, of course, from there..."

"We'll have this wrapped up before then," Jorge assured her.

"And if not, you'll just get the hell out of it," Wolff said.

"You don't have to be protective. I've been with the Special Investigations Division for three years now, and I've dealt with some pretty heinous people," Jasmine told him.

"I've dealt with them, too," Wolff said quietly. "And I spent this afternoon up in the Everglades, a plot of godforsaken swamp with a bunch of oil drums filled with bodies. And I've been FBI for almost a decade. That didn't make today any better."

"I'm not saying anything makes it better. I'm just saying I can take care of myself," Jasmine said.

She really hadn't meant to be argumentative. But she did know what she was doing, and throughout her career, she'd learned it was usually the people who felt the need to emphasize their competency who were the ones who weren't so sure of their competency after all. She was confident in her abilities—or, at least she had thought she was.

With this Fed, she was becoming defensive. She hated the feeling.

"Guys, guys! Time-out," Jorge said.

Wolff stood, apparently all but dismissing her. "I'm heading back to my place. Most days, I'll be hanging around a real art shop that's supposedly mine. Dolphin Galleries."

He handed Jorge a card, then turned to look at Jasmine. "Feel free to watch out for me. In my mind, no one cop can beat everything out there. We all need people watching our backs. I'm more than happy to know I have MDPD in deep with me."

His words didn't help in the least; Jasmine still felt like a chastised toddler. What made it worse was the fact he was right. They did need to look out for one another.

She wanted to apologize. They had met awkwardly. She wasn't brash, she wasn't an idiot—she was a team player. But despite his words, she had the sense that he was already doubting her.

"I'll be hanging as close as I can," he said. "The woman managing the shop, Katrina Partridge, is with us. If you need me and I'm not there, just ask her. I trust her with my life."

He didn't look back. If he had done so, Jasmine was certain, it would have been to look at Jorge with pity for having been paired with her.

When Jacob was gone, she strode to the door and slid the bolts. She had three.

"Jerk!" she said. She turned back into the room and flounced down on the sofa.

"Not really. Just bad circumstances," Jorge said, taking a seat beside her. "I, uh, actually like the guy."

She looked at him. "I don't dislike him. I don't really know him."

"Could have fooled me."

She ignored that. "Jorge, how did it happen? We were all there. The place was spilling over with cops.

And someone shot and killed Smirnoff—with all of us there—and we don't know who or how."

"They were counting on the place being filled with cops, Jasmine. Detectives will be on the case and our crime scene techs will find a trajectory for the bullet that killed him. We do our part, they do theirs. Thing is, whoever killed him, they were just the working part of the bigger machine. We have to get to the major players—Kozak, whoever else. Not that the man or woman who was pulling the trigger shouldn't serve life, but… it won't matter."

"No, it won't matter," she agreed. What they needed to do was find Mary. She nodded.

He took her hand and squeezed it. "You're just thrown. We weren't expecting to take them all down tonight."

"We weren't expecting Smirnoff to get killed tonight. I—I didn't even know he'd gone to the FBI!"

"I knew but couldn't tell you. And I didn't know that Smirnoff would be killed before I had a chance to loop you in. I'm sorry—I put you and Wolff both in a bad position. At least you didn't shoot each other. You know you're resenting him because he had you down."

"He did not have me down."

"Almost had you down."

"I almost had him down."

"Ouch. Take a breath," Jorge warned.

She did, and she shook her head. "I worked with a Fed once."

"And he was okay, right? Come on, we're all going in the same direction."

"He was great. Old dude—kept telling me he had a granddaughter my age. Made me feel like I should have been in bed by ten," Jasmine said and smiled.

Jorge arched his brow at her.

"Okay, okay," she said. "I resent the fact he almost had me down. But really, I almost had him, too." She squeezed his hand in return. "How come we never have discussed our love lives and this stranger knew more about you than I did?"

"'Cause neither of us cares what our preferences are, and we work well together—and we enjoy what we're doing. And Wolff for sure had all of us checked out before agreeing to work with us. He'd need to know our backgrounds and that we're clean cops. Also, you're a workaholic and even when we're grabbing quick food or popping into a bookstore, we're still working."

"Not really," she told him. "Honestly, not until this operation."

He nodded. "Mary," he said softly.

"Jorge, I'm so afraid she's dead." She paused. "Even more now. Do you have any details about the oil drums they found today? All I've seen is what has been on the news. Captain Lorenzo was even with the cops doing the interviews at the show, but I didn't get to ask him anything. Obviously, I did my best to be a near hysterical model."

"You were terrific."

She laughed. "So were you." Jasmine tried to smile, but she was searching out his eyes.

"Mary wasn't in one of the oil drums," he said.

"You're sure?"

"Positive. The bodies discovered were all men."

"Oh, thank God. I mean… I'm not glad that anyone was dead, but—"

"It's all right," Jorge assured her. "I understand. So, tomorrow will be tense. I'm going to get out of here. Let you get some sleep." He started to rise, and then he didn't. "Never mind."

"Never mind?"

"I'm going to stay here."

"I don't need to be protected," she said. "Bolts on the door, gun next to the bed."

"You don't need to be protected?" Jorge said. "I do! Safety in numbers. Bolt the door and let's get some sleep."

She rose. "Okay, I lied, and you're right—anyone can be taken by surprise. And I have been a jerk and I don't know why."

"I do," Jorge said softly. "You really shouldn't be working this case. You have a personal involvement. And in a way, so do I. I've met Mary."

Jasmine nodded. "I don't feel that I'm really up to speed yet, despite what we learned from Wolff. I'll get you some pillows and bedding," she told him.

"What time are we supposed to be where?" he asked her as she laid out sheets on the sofa.

"Ten o'clock, back at the club."

"I'm willing to bet half of it will still be shut down."

"We won't be going to the floor. We'll be picking up our pay in the offices, using the VIP entrance on the side to the green room and staging areas."

"You know that we can get in?"

She nodded. "I wound up with Natasha and the other girls in a little group when the police were herding people for interviews. Natasha asked the lead detective—Detective Greenberg is in charge for the City of Miami Beach—and he told her that they'd cordon off the club area until they finished with the investigation. Owners and operators were free to use the building where the police weren't investigating."

"Then go to bed. We'll begin again in the morning."

Jorge was clearly thinking something but not saying it.

"What?" she pressed.

"I didn't know until today that the FBI was in on this case—the briefing was why I arrived late. MDPD found the group operating the Gold Sun Club to be shady, as did the cops with the City of Miami Beach. But there's been no hard evidence against them and nothing that anyone could do. I know you've been talking to Captain Lorenzo about them for a while, but…we just found out today that Smirnoff was about to give evidence against the whole shebang. I'm just—"

"Just what?"

He grimaced. "I like the Feds. They have more resources than we do. They have more reach across state lines. Across international lines. And I don't know how long I'll get to be one of the models—if the big show ended in disaster, I could be out fast. And then I won't be around to help you."

"I'm willing to bet the Deco Gang will keep planning. Kozak will say that all the people who had been hired for jobs at the club will still need work. He'll go forward in Smirnoff's name—Smirnoff would not want to have been frightened off Miami Beach. We'll be in."

"You will be. I may not. So, I'm just glad that… well, that there's another law enforcement agent undercover on this case. Speaking of undercover…" Jorge grabbed his blanket and turned around, smiling as he feigned sleep.

Jasmine opened her mouth to speak. She shook her head and went to the bedroom. Ready for bed and curled up, she admitted to herself that she just might be glad for Jacob Wolff's involvement, too.

She had assumed the group was trading in prostitution, turning models into drug addicts and then trafficking them.

She hadn't known about the bodies in the barrels. And she hadn't suspected that Smirnoff was going to die.

So she was glad she would have backup if she had to continue getting close to these dangerous players. Otherwise she probably should back right out of the case.

Except she just couldn't. They had Mary. They had her somewhere.

And Jasmine had to pray her friend was still alive.

Chapter Three

Jacob could remember coming to South Beach with his parents as a child. Back then, the gentrification of the area was already underway.

His mom liked to tell him about the way it had been when she had been young, when the world had yet to realize the beauty and architectural value of the art deco hotels—and when the young and beautiful had headed north on South Beach to the fabulous Fontainebleau and other such hotels where the likes of Sinatra and others had performed. In her day, there had been tons of bagel shops, and high school kids had all come to hang out by the water with their surfboards—despite a lack of anything that resembled real surf.

It was where his parents had met. His father had once told him, not without some humor, that he'd fallen in love over a twenty-five-cent bagel.

The beach was beautiful. Jacob had opted for a little boutique hotel right on the water. Fisher House had been built in the early 1920s when a great deal around it had been nothing but scrub, brush and palms. It had been completely renovated and revamped about a decade ago and was charming, intimate and historic, filled with framed pictures of long ago. The back door opened to a vast porch—half filled with dining tables—and then a tiled path led to the pool and beyond down to the ocean.

Jacob started the morning early, out on the sand, watching the sun come up, feeling the ocean breeze and listening to the seagulls cry. The rising sun was shining down on the water, creating a sparkling scene with diamond-like bits of brilliance all around him.

It was a piece of heaven. Sand between his toes, and then a quick dip in the water—cool and yet temperate in the early-morning hour. He loved it. Home for him in the last few years had been Washington, D.C., or New York City. There were beaches to be found, yes, but nothing like this. So, for the first hour of the day, he let himself just love the feel of salt air around him, hear the lulling rush of waves and look out over the endless water.

There was nothing like seeing it like a native. By 9:00 a.m., he was heading along Ocean Drive. The city was coming alive by then; roller skaters whizzed by him and traffic was heavy. Art galleries and shops were beginning to open, and tourists were flocking out in all manner of beach apparel, some wearing scanty clothing and some not. While most American men were fond of surf shorts for dipping in the water, Europeans tended to Speedos and as little on their bodies as possible. It was a generalization; he didn't like generalizations, but in this case, he was pretty sure he was right.

A fellow with a belly that surely hid his toes from his own sight—and his Speedo—walked on by and greeted

Jacob with a cheerful "good morning" that was spoken with a heavy foreign accent.

Jacob smiled. The man was happy with himself and within the legal bounds of propriety for this section of the beach. And that was what mattered.

He stopped into the News Café. It was a great place to see...and be seen. Before he'd been murdered, the famous designer Gianni Versace had lived in one of South Beach's grand old mansions. He had also dined many a morning at the News Café. Tourists flocked there. So did locals.

Jacob picked up a newspaper, ordered an egg dish and sat back and watched—and listened.

The conversation was all about the shooting of Josef Smirnoff at what should have been one of the brightest moments in the pseudo-plastic environment of the beach.

"You can bring in all the stars you want—but with *those* people—"

"I heard it was a mob hit!"

"Did you know that earlier, like in the morning, three bodies were found in oil drums out in the Everglades?"

"Yeah. I don't think anyone had even reported them missing. No ID's as of yet, but hey...like we don't have enough problems down here."

People were talking. Naturally.

"Told you we shouldn't have come to Miami."

"Hey, mobsters kill mobsters. No one else was injured. Bunch of shots, from what I read, but only the mobster was killed."

Someone who was apparently a local spoke up.

"Actually, honestly, we're not that bad a city. I mean, my dad says that most of our bad crimes are committed by out-of-towners and not our population."

Bad crimes... Sure, like most people in the world, locals here wanted to fall in love, buy houses, raise children and seek the best lives possible.

But it was true, too, that South Florida was one massive melting pot—perhaps like New York City in the last decade. People came from all the Caribbean islands, Central and South America, the countries that had once comprised the Soviet Union, and from all over the world.

Most came in pursuit of a new life and freedom. Some came because a melting pot was simply a good place for criminal activity.

While he people-watched, Jacob replayed everything he had seen the day before in his mind. He remembered what he had heard.

Witnesses hadn't been lying or overly rattled when they had reported that it seemed the shots had come from all over. From the bar, he'd had a good place to observe the whole room. And then, as Ivan had muttered that they could go closer and see, they had done so.

The shooter hadn't been close to Josef Smirnoff—Jacob had been near him and if someone had shot him from up close, he'd have known.

He was pretty sure that the shooters had been stationed in the alcoves on the balcony that surrounded the ground floor, just outside the offices and private rooms on the second floor. The space allowed for customers to enjoy a band from upstairs, without being in the crowd below.

When he'd looked up at the balconies earlier, he hadn't seen anyone on them. The stairs might have been blocked.

Would Jasmine have known that detail? Or would they have shared that information with a new girl?

Jasmine had, beyond a doubt, drawn attention last night. She had been captivatingly beautiful, and she had played the runway perfectly, austere and yet with a sense of fun. She was perfect for the role she was playing.

The band, the models, the excitement... It had all been perfect for the setup. It was really a miracle that no one else had been hit.

He had thought that Jasmine was going after Josef Smirnoff when he had seen her lunge at him—getting close to see that the deed was done, that he was finished off if the bullets hadn't done their work. He'd never forget her surprise when he had tackled her...

Nor his own shock when she had thrown him off.

He was surprised to find himself smiling—he wasn't often taken unaware. Then again, while he'd known that MDPD had police officers working undercover, he hadn't been informed that one of them was working the runway.

A dangerous place.

But she worked it well. She had an in he could never have.

He pictured it all in his mind again. There had been multiple shooters but only one target—Josef Smirnoff.

Create panic, and it might well have appeared that Smirnoff had been killed in a rain of bullets that could have been meant for anyone.

Jacob paid his bill and headed out, walking toward Dolphin Galleries. He felt the burner phone in his left pocket vibrate and he quickly pulled it out. Dean Jenkins, his Miami office counterpart, was calling.

"You alone?"

The street was busy, but as Jacob walked, he was well aware that by "alone," Dean was asking if he was far from those involved with the Deco Gang.

"I am," he said.

"They're doing the autopsy now. Someone apparently had a bead on the bastard's heart. It's amazing that no one else was hurt. Oh, beyond cuts and bruises, I mean. People trampled people. But the bullets that didn't hit Smirnoff hit the walls."

"They only wanted Smirnoff dead. Kill a mobster, and the police might not look so hard. Kill a pretty ingenue, a pop star or a music icon, and the heat never ends."

"Yep. I wanted to let you know that I'm on the ground with the detective from the City of Miami Beach and another guy from Miami-Dade PD. Figured if I was around asking questions I'd be in close contact, and you could act annoyed and harassed."

"Good."

"You met the undercover Miami-Dade cops, right?" Dean asked.

"I did. We've talked."

"Good. The powers that be are stressing communication. They don't want any of you ending up in the swamp."

"Good to hear. I don't think I'd fit into an oil drum. Don't worry, we've got each other's backs."

"Have you been asked to move any money for the organization yet?"

"On my way in to the gallery now," Jacob said. "I expect I'll see someone soon enough."

"It may take some time, with that murder at the club last night, you know."

"A murder that I think they planned. I'd bet they'll contact me today."

"You're on. Keep up with MDPD, all right? Word from the top. Both the cops and our agency are accustomed to undercover operations, but this one is more than dicey."

"At least I get to bathe for this one," Jacob told him.

"There's a bright spot to everything, huh?"

"You bet."

He ended the call, slid the phone back in his pocket and headed toward the gallery.

The sun was shining overhead. People were out on the beach, playing, soaking up the heat. The shadow of last night's murder couldn't ruin a vacation for the visitors who had planned for an entire year.

Besides, it was a shady rich man, a mobster, who had been killed.

He who lives by the sword...

Jacob turned the corner. Ivan Petrov was standing in front of the gallery, studying a piece of modern art.

Moe, Curly and Larry—or, rather Alejandro Suarez, Antonio Garibaldi and Sasha Antonovich—were upstairs when Jasmine arrived with Jorge at precisely 10:00 a.m. the next day.

Alejandro was at the top of the stairs. Sasha was at the door to what had once been Josef Smirnoff's office and was now the throne room for Victor Kozak.

Jasmine had made a point of greeting both Alejandro and Sasha. She presumed that Antonio was in the room with Victor, which he was. She saw him when the door to that inner sanctum opened and Natasha Volkov walked out.

The door immediately shut behind her, but not before Jasmine could see that Victor Kozak was seated at what had been Josef Smirnoff's desk.

The king is dead; long live the king, she thought.

This had shades of all kinds of Shakespearean tragedy on it. Apparently, Josef Smirnoff had known that someone had been planning to kill him—he just hadn't known who. Maybe he had suspected Kozak but not known. And he probably hadn't imagined that he'd be gunned down at the celebrity opening for the club.

She knew that Smirnoff hadn't exactly been a good man. She had heard, though, that he wasn't on the truly evil side of bad. He'd preferred strong-arm tactics to murder. He'd rather have his debts paid, and how did a dead man pay a debt?

Jasmine couldn't defend Smirnoff. However, she believed that Kozak was purely evil. It made her skin crawl to be near him. She had a feeling he'd kill his own mother if he saw it as a good career move.

"Ah, you are here! Such a good girl," Natasha said, slipping an arm around Jasmine's shoulder and moving her down the hallway. She turned back to Jorge. "You come, too, pretty boy. You are a good boy, too."

Jorge smiled.

Natasha opened the door into a giant closet–dressing room combo. There were racks of clothing and rows of tables with mirrors surrounded by bright lights for the girls to use. Before the show the day before, the room had been filled with dressers, stylists and makeup artists.

"So sad. Poor Josef," Natasha said, admitting them through the door and then closing it. She made a display of bringing her fingers to her eyes, as if she'd been crying. Her face was not, however, tearstained.

"We are all in shock, in mourning today," Natasha added. "So, let me pay you for last night and we will talk for a minute, yes? Maybe you can help."

"Definitely," Jasmine said. "Talking would be good. Mr. Smirnoff was so kind to all of us. It's so horrible what happened."

"Terrible," Jorge agreed.

"So." Natasha grabbed a large manila envelope off one of the dressers and took out a sizable wad of cash. She counted off the amount for each of their fees. When Natasha casually handed it over, Jasmine saw it was all in large bills. It seemed like a lot of cash to have lying around.

Natasha indicated a grouping of leather love seats

and chairs where models and performers waited once their makeup was complete.

Jorge and Jasmine took chairs.

"You—you were very brave," she said, looking at Jasmine. "I was behind the curtain, but I saw the way you protected Kari and tried to help poor Josef."

"Oh, no, not so brave," Jasmine said. "When I was a child... I was with my parents in the Middle East, and my father taught me to get down, and get everyone around me down, anytime I heard gunshots. It was just instinct."

"I tried to get to Jasmine," Jorge said, "because she's my friend."

"Of course, of course," Natasha said. "But you two and Kari were the ones who were out on the runway when it all happened. What did you see? Of course, I know that the police talked to everyone last night, but... we're so upset about Josef! Perhaps you've remembered something...something that you might have seen?"

Jasmine shook her head. "Oh, Natasha. This is terrible, but I was only thinking about saving myself at first. I didn't see anything at all." Jasmine wished that she wasn't lying. She could easily be passionate because her words were true. She wished to hell that she had seen something—anything.

She had just heard the bullets flying. And seen Josef Smirnoff go down.

"I'm so, so sorry," she said. "Of course, I suppose this means that... Well, if you need anything from me in the future, I'd be so happy to work with you again."

Natasha smiled. "Jasmine, you must not worry. We

will always have a need for you. We are a loyal family here! And, Jorge, of course, you, too."

"Thank you," Jorge said earnestly.

"But nothing—nothing at all?" Natasha persisted. "Tell me about your night, from the time you stepped out on the runway."

"It was so wonderful!" Jasmine said. "At first, I could hear the crowd. We were having a great time on the runway, and I heard people laughing and having fun... and then, that sound! I didn't realize at first that I was hearing bullets. And then...then it was as if I knew instantly. My past, maybe," she whispered. "And I went for Kari, and when I saw Josef down on the floor, I wanted to help... He'd been good to me, you know? Then that man—a friend of Josef's, I think—thought that I was trying to hurt Josef, and he...he tackled me."

"And you were angry, of course," Natasha murmured.

"Well, at first, of course, but it was okay after. He apologized to me. He told me he thought that I wanted to hurt Josef. He was very sincere. So apologetic."

"He saw to it that we got back to Jasmine's place safely. I liked him," Jorge said.

"And you, Jasmine? Did you like him?" Natasha asked.

"After we talked, of course. He was very apologetic. He told me that he's new to Miami Beach—new to Miami. He was working up north, but he got tired of snow and ice and had some connections to help him start up in business down here, and so...he was sad that his first time really heading to a fine event ended so tragically."

"So. He made moves on you," Natasha said softly. She wasn't pleased, and Jasmine recognized why.

Jasmine was now a commodity—one controlled by Natasha—even if she wasn't supposed to really understand that yet. This newcomer needed to go through Natasha—her and Victor Kozak now—if he wanted to have Jasmine as his own special escort.

"Oh, no, he didn't make moves," Jasmine said.

"He was a gentleman. Almost as if he was one of your security people. He just saw that we got home safely," Jorge said. He looked at Jasmine. "I thought maybe he liked me better."

"Oh?" Natasha said. "Interesting."

"No, no, Jorge—he didn't like you better!" Jasmine said. She knew that Jorge was smirking inwardly, and yet he was playing it well. They were both saying the right things in order to be able to stay close with Jacob as they ventured further into the world of Deco Gang.

They needed everyone in on this—Federal and local. Jorge had been right.

"You found him to be a nice man?" Natasha asked.

"Very," Jorge said before Jasmine could answer.

"Jorge, I am sorry, I don't think that he's interested in you," Natasha said. "He did express interest in Jasmine. But we shall see. Be nice to him, if he should see you or try to contact you. But if he does so, you must let me know right away."

"Of course," Jasmine said, eyes wide. "I know that you'll watch out for me."

"Yes, of course. We will watch out for you," Natasha said. She smiled. "We are family here. So, now, come with me. There will be another event soon enough. We will mourn Josef, of course. But so many are dependent on us for a living, we cannot stop. We will have a memorial or something this weekend on the beach. You will be part of it. We are family, yes? We don't let our people...down. For now, you will give Victor Kozak your...condolences."

Give him their condolences. If this had been happening just years earlier, they might well have been expected to kneel and kiss Kozak's ring.

She and Jorge both smiled naively. "Definitely," Jasmine said.

They rose; Jasmine led them down the hall.

Antonio and Alejandro were by the door to the office. Jasmine knew that Sasha Antonovich had to still be guarding the door.

Natasha tapped on the door to the office. Kozak called out, "Come in," and they entered.

He was alone, poring over papers that lay on the table before him.

"We're so sorry for your loss," Jasmine ventured timidly when Kozak didn't look up.

"The police are still in the club downstairs," he said, shaking his head. "They want to know about the balconies. I want to help them. I want to find the person who did this to our beloved Josef. But the balconies were closed off. Just with velvet cords, of course, but... Ah, Jasmine! We were all so enchanted with your performance," he said, looking up. "And you, too, of course. You were the perfect foil for the girls," he told Jorge.

"Thank you," Jorge murmured.

"I don't know who was on the balcony," Victor went on. "We'd said there would be no one on the balcony."

"Maybe the police have ways to find out," Jorge suggested in a hopeful voice.

Victor Kozak waved a hand in the air. "Maybe, maybe not. We'll keep up our own line of questioning. Anyway…"

He seemed to stop in midthought and gave his attention to them. "Please, I know that you were hired by Josef, but…it is my sincere hope that you will remain with us. We pay our regular models a retainer, which you will receive while we wait for this…for this painful situation to be behind us. That is, if you still wish to be with us."

"For sure!" Jasmine said.

"Retainer? Me, too?" Jorge asked hopefully.

Kozak glanced over at Natasha. She must have given him her approval with the slightest nod.

"Yes, you were quite the centerpiece for our lovely young girls. We have a reputation for always having beautiful people in our clubs. All you need to do is be around, available to us, and maybe meet some people we'd like to introduce you to. Please, we will be in touch. You may come in tomorrow for your paychecks."

They both thanked him profusely. Natasha led them down to the street.

As they were going out, Kari Anderson was just arriving. She threw her arms around Jasmine, shaking.

"I don't think I had a chance to thank you. You saved my life!" Kari told her.

"Kari, I just made you get down," Jasmine said, flushing and very aware that both Natasha and Sasha were watching the exchange. "Instinct!" she added quickly. "And we're all just so lucky...except for poor Josef."

"I know, it's so terrible," said the young blonde, her empathy real. Jasmine liked Kari. She was an honest kind person who seemed oblivious to her natural beauty. "Josef was always nice. It's so sad. Terrible that people do these things today! Terrible that poor Josef was caught in it all."

Naive—just like Mary, Jasmine thought. Not lacking confidence but unaware of just how much they had to offer.

"Come on up. We will straighten all out with you, Kari," Natasha said. "We will be all right. Victor will see to it," she added. "Now, you two run along and try to enjoy some downtime. Kari, come with me. We will have work for all of you—you needn't stress."

"See you, Kari," Jorge said, waving.

He and Jasmine started down the street while Natasha led Kari past Sasha and up the stairs.

"I worry about her," Jasmine said.

"I worry about all of us," Jorge said. "I was worried about the two of us unarmed during the show. We were taking a major chance."

"We knew there would be cops all over."

"Right. And Josef Smirnoff is dead and bullets were flying everywhere."

She couldn't argue that.

"So, tomorrow, we go back for our checks. Our retainer checks," she murmured.

"And you know we're going to be asked to do something for those checks."

"At least I don't think they're remotely suspicious of us," Jasmine told him.

"Not yet. We're still new."

"Kari came in just ahead of me," Jasmine said. "She…she was a replacement for Mary, I think."

"Here's the thing—what do we do when they want something from us that we don't want to do?" Jorge asked. "We haven't gotten anyone to admit to any criminal activity. If they ask you to be an escort, that's actually legal. So, you go off with someone they set you up with—and that guy wants sex. What do you do? Arrest the guy? That won't get us anywhere. And you sure as hell aren't going to compromise yourself."

"You may be asked first."

"I'm pretty—but not as pretty as you are."

Jasmine laughed. "Beauty is in the eye of the beholder, you know."

"Trust me on this. You'll be first. They'll tread a little more lightly with me."

Jasmine shook her head. "We have to get in more tightly, hear things and find something on them. You're right. They'll deny they have anything to do with illegally selling sex—I'm sure they've got that all worked out." She sighed. "I guess that our FBI connection will do a better job—he'll find out what they're doing with the money."

"How do we prove murder?" Jorge asked softly.

Jasmine lowered her head.

Jorge took her shoulders and spun her around to look at him. "We don't know that Mary is dead."

"I know," she whispered.

She was startled when her phone started to ring; it was a pay-as-you-go phone, one purchased in her cover name, Jasmine Alamein.

She looked at Jorge. "It's Natasha."

"Answer it!"

"Ah, Jasmine, my darling," Natasha said. "I'm so glad to reach you so quickly."

"Yeah, no problem," Jasmine said.

"We have a favor to ask of you. It includes a bonus, naturally."

"What is it?" Jasmine asked. Jorge was staring at her, wary.

"That friend of Josef's—Mr. Marensky. He is new in town. He has asked if you would be so good as to show him around. We'd be happy if you could do so— he came to us, instead of trying to twist our arm for a phone number. You will take him around town, yes? I said that wrong. He wishes to take you to dinner and perhaps you could show him some of the beach. And report to me, of course."

"Yes, for sure. Where do you want me to be when?" Jasmine asked.

"He will call for you at your apartment. Please, make sure your friend is not there when he arrives."

"What time?"

"Eight o'clock tonight."

"Thank you, Natasha. I will be ready."

"Wear something very pretty." Natasha didn't mean pretty. She meant *sexy*.

"I will. Thank you. Thank you!"

"My pleasure. Tomorrow morning you will come back in here."

"Yes, Natasha." Jasmine hung up. Jorge was staring at her. "My first date."

"I was afraid of this."

"She doesn't want you hanging around when my date comes for me."

"Like hell!"

"It's Jacob—*Marensky*."

"Oh." Jorge breathed a sigh of relief.

"I'm just a little worried," Jasmine said.

"About Jacob?"

Jasmine laughed. "Not on that account—I'm not sure he's particularly fond of me."

"You were acting badly."

"I was not—"

"You were."

"Never mind. I'm just wondering what good it's going to do if we just wind up watching one another."

"Trust me. That man has a plan in mind."

"I hope you're right. I'm so worried."

"Jasmine, we just went undercover. You know as well as I do that often cops and agents have to lead a double life for months to get what they're after. Years."

"This can't take that long," she said softly. She didn't add the rest of what she was thinking.

If it did…they might well end up dead themselves.

Chapter Four

Jacob arrived at Jasmine's apartment at precisely 8:00 p.m. She was ready, dressed in a halter dress and wickedly high heels. The assessment he gave her was coolly objective. And his words were even more so.

"You know how to play the part."

"Hey, I'm just a naive young model willing to let a rich guy take me out for an expensive dinner," she told him.

"Jorge?"

"They told me not to have him here."

"What is he doing tonight?"

"Catching up on his favorite cable show," Jasmine said. "Playing it all low."

"At his studio?"

Jasmine nodded and turned away.

Her captain had gone along with this at her say-so. But the FBI seemed to know way more than the police. She was certain that Jacob Wolff knew all about her fake dossier and Jorge's fake dossier, and she felt woefully late to the party.

"Hey." To her surprise, he caught her by the shoulders and spun her around. "This isn't a jurisdictional pissing match, you know. The FBI started planning the minute we heard from Smirnoff. You didn't know because we didn't inform the cops until it was absolutely necessary they knew we were in town. We had no idea you were in the middle of an undercover operation—we've had an eye on these guys for a while. Smirnoff coming in was the opening we needed."

He was right; they'd both had separate operations going on. And she'd wanted this case. She'd talked her captain into it being important. The bodies in the oil drums had proved she was right. Provided they could link them back to the Deco Gang.

"I'm sorry," she murmured.

"I worked something like this in New York not that long ago," he told her. "The Bureau crew I wound up working with hadn't known about me. It's always like that. A need-to-know basis. Fewer people to say things that might get you killed."

"Yes, but now—"

"Now, we're in it together. And now we need to head out. Where would you like to have dinner?"

"Wherever."

He grinned. "I'm supposed to be a very rich guy, you know. Oh, and with the power to push ahead at any given restaurant."

"How rude!"

"Yes, absolutely. But we're playing parts. And we need to play those parts well."

"How have your people gotten to so many restaurants?" Jasmine asked.

"They haven't," he said. "No one will say it, but everyone is afraid of the Deco Gang."

"Ah," Jasmine said. "Well, then, we're in the middle of stone crab season. I say we go for the most popular."

"Sure."

As they left her apartment, he slipped his arm through hers. Jasmine stiffened.

"Play along," he murmured.

"You think they're watching?"

"I think they could be at any given time."

She didn't argue that.

"I didn't bring a car. Taxi or an Uber?" he asked.

"I'm fine walking."

"In those shoes?"

She shrugged. "Not my favorite, but we're going about seven blocks. Over a mile in these? I'd say taxi or Uber!"

They walked past T-shirt shops and other restaurants with tables that spilled out on the sidewalk. It was a beautiful night. Balmy. It had to be in the midseventies. Jasmine could smell the salt on the air, and, over the music that escaped from many an establishment, she could hear the water—or at least she could imagine she heard the waves crashing softly up on the shore. Here where they walked, the sand and water were across busy Collins Avenue; the traffic was almost always bumper-to-bumper. She knew young people often came just to cruise the streets, showing off their souped-up cars.

She didn't get it; never had cared for fancy cars.

People in all styles of dress thronged the sidewalks. Some were decked out to the hilt, planning to visit one of the clubs or see a show. Others were casual, out just to shop or dine in a more casual fashion. While the South Beach neighborhood of Miami Beach was trendy and filled with great deco places, boutiques and more, heading farther north, one crossed Lincoln Road, a pedestrian mall and beyond that, a lot of the more staid grande dame hotels from the heyday era when Al Capone and his mobsters had ruled, and later the fabled Rat Pack had entertained, along with other greats.

The beach was like a chameleon, ready to change for every new decade.

At an old and ever-popular restaurant, known for its stone crabs while in season, they did find they were welcomed by a hostess and discreetly—but far too quickly—shown to a table. Jacob had managed, even with the lines outside wrapping around the building, to get them a private table in a little alcove.

Jacob made a pretense of studying the wine menu. He had known, she was certain, exactly what he wanted from the beginning. He wound up ordering champagne—and club soda, as well. She knew as the evening progressed, the champagne would disappear into leftover club soda.

The waitress was gone—they had both ordered the stone crab claws—and he leaned toward her, taking her hand from across the table, rubbing his thumb lightly over her flesh.

"You talked to your people?" he asked softly.

She nodded. "This afternoon. The three men in the oil drums...one has been there, they estimate, about three years. One several months…and one maybe two weeks or so."

Jacob smiled lightly, his expression expertly at odds with their conversation. "Do you know who they might be? They'll be testing, checking dental records. But so far, they don't match anyone reported missing down here." He hesitated. "We're a land of promise, but… people take advantage of that. I recently worked a case in New York… Here's the thing, and the cause of half the world's problems. When you have nothing at all, you have nothing to lose. People from war-torn countries might be desperate and can be drawn in and then forced to do just about anything." He was quiet for a minute. "Some wind up in oil drums."

"And some," she said, "just want more and more—like Victor Kozak."

"So it appears."

"What do you mean, so it appears?"

"Kozak became kingpin. But when Josef Smirnoff came in to the Bureau, he didn't know who intended to kill him. He just…he was afraid. He ruled so much, controlled so much, and yet must have felt like an ancient king. Someone wanted his throne."

"Just like an ancient king—who could plan to overthrow him unless they had a right to follow in his line?"

"That's true. But… I can't get over how lovely you look in that dress," he said suddenly.

She saw that the waiter had arrived, bearing a large silver champagne bucket filled with ice and a bottle.

"You clean up all right yourself," she said softly. And he did. He was wearing a casual soft taupe jacket over a tailored white shirt. He was a handsome man, she thought—with a bit of the look of a Renaissance poet, except she was certain that while his appearance was that of a tall lean man, he was composed of wire-tight muscle beneath.

The waiter smiled and poured their drinks, and they acted like a couple happily out on a date.

Jacob leaned closer to her again, smiling as he lifted his glass to her. "Josef Smirnoff admitted to dealing drugs, arms dealing, prostitution and money laundering. He swore up and down that he didn't order murder."

Jasmine lifted her glass with a dazzling smile, as well. "And yet, one of those bodies discovered had been there a very long time."

"So, someone might have been getting rid of people without Josef Smirnoff knowing."

"And how could that happen?"

"I don't know. We weren't able to get to Smirnoff for more conversation before he was killed. This had all just sprung into being, you know. It's been a complicated case for us. Smirnoff managed to get hold of an agent in the Miami office, but they didn't have anyone down here that they were certain couldn't be compromised—wouldn't be known by anyone. They appealed to the head offices in Virginia. From there, they called on me. I spent a week immersed in everything related to the Deco Gang, and we were lucky that we could arrange paperwork so it appears that I—as Jacob Marensky—own the Dolphin Galleries."

"So, you didn't know Josef Smirnoff?"

"I can't say that I knew him. But I know what he

told people. And he was set up with the US Marshals' office—he would have disappeared into witness protection as soon as we had finished our investigation."

Their dinner was arriving.

"Do you really like stone crabs?" she asked him, hoping that her smile was flirtatious. "They're more of a local delicacy. And here's the thing—the crab lives! They take the claw and toss the crab back in. The claw regrows. That's why they're seasonal."

He lowered his head. His smile was legitimate. "Yes, I've had them, and I actually like them very much."

"Can I get you anything else?" their waiter asked. They had their crackers, mustard sauces and drawn butter.

"I think we're just fine," Jacob said.

"Lovely," Jasmine agreed.

The waiter left them.

"So, you think someone other than Victor Kozak arranged the murder? You know that the press—and half the people in the country—think he was caught in another act of random violence."

He nodded. "And we have nothing to say."

Jasmine cracked a claw. A piece of shell went flying across the table, hitting Jacob on the left cheek.

"Oh! Sorry!" she said, somewhat mortified.

He laughed. "Not a problem."

"These really aren't date food," Jasmine said. "But then again, we aren't really on a date." She frowned, then made a show of dabbing at his face and laughing. "So, if not Victor Kozak, who would have the power to pull off such a thing as the murder of Josef Smirnoff?"

"It might have been Kozak. If not, there's Ivan Petrov, bartender and manager."

"You think he's high enough on the food chain?"

"Depends on who is in on the coup."

"The only people as close to management as Ivan are the bodyguards—I like to think of them as the Three Stooges."

"On steroids," Jacob said.

"Yes, deadly Stooges," she agreed.

"So, Victor Kozak, Ivan Petrov, Natasha Volkov—and the Stooges," he said.

"I just wonder about the bodyguards. The others are all Russian or Ukrainian, but Alejandro is Colombian, and Antonio is Italian."

"Half Italian," Jacob told her. "His mother is English."

"You do know more than I do."

"They are equal-opportunity crooks," Jacob said drily. "Any group down here can find power elsewhere—even elsewhere around the country."

"Their bookkeeper is from Atlanta," Jasmine murmured.

"Good old Southern boy."

"Girl."

"Pardon?"

"Good old Southern girl," Jasmine said. "And yet…"

"Yet?"

"I don't think she really knows about the criminal enterprises. She gets money after it's been laundered. As far as paperwork goes, they're enterprising citizens, paying their taxes."

"Well, Ivan is deep into it all," Jacob told her. "He was waiting at the gallery when I went in this morning. We made arrangements for the sale of one of the paintings in the gallery."

"As a way to move money?"

"Yeah. He paid way more than the painting is worth. The funds will go into an offshore account. It's all setup."

"So they believe in you?"

"For now…"

He had been studiously cracking a shell. This time, his piece of shell flew across the table—catching Jasmine right in the cleavage.

"Sorry!"

She caught the shell quickly before he could. But the gentleman in him came through; he started to move but stopped. The two of them laughed together. Honest laughter, and it was nice.

"Not really date food," he said. "Unless I were more accomplished at this, of course."

"I don't think you could be much more accomplished," she muttered, afraid that a bit of envy and maybe even bitterness might have made it through in her voice. She caught his curious look. "You speak half a dozen languages," she explained.

He shrugged. "I was just lucky. My family—much like yours—is a mini United Nations. Everyone from everywhere. And I love language. It gets easier to pick up another, if you know the Romance languages, the Latin base always helps for reading, even if it takes a bit. But all languages have rules—well, except for English! It's the hardest. Luckily, it was my first."

"Still...it's impressive."

"You speak Spanish."

"Picked up from growing up in South Florida. Half of my friends are Cuban, Colombian or from somewhere in the islands or South America."

"Or Brazil."

"I do also know a bit of Portuguese," she agreed.

They both smiled again. "So...we're equal-opportunity law enforcement, dealing with equal-opportunity criminals," Jasmine mused.

"So we are," he said. "Let's wander on down Washington Street. We'll stop and have dessert and coffee somewhere else."

"You think we're being followed?"

"I think we're definitely being watched in one way or another."

He paid the check and they left.

"You're from here, right?" he asked her.

"You know all about me, right?" she returned, looking at him.

"Well, I do now. I swear, when I tackled you... I didn't."

"You knew there were cops on the scene."

"They didn't tell me that one of the cops was a woman—modeling as if she were accustomed to the runway. But then you are, correct?"

"You received a full dossier on me after the fact?" Jasmine asked. "I wish that the powers that be might have returned the favor."

"I'm an open book," he told her.

"I'll bet."

"I knew from the time I was a kid I wanted to be in the FBI," Jacob told her. "I had a great uncle who was gunned down—for having the same name as a criminal. He was killed by mistake. Anyway, I got into a military academy, served time in the army and immediately joined the FBI. I've done a lot of undercover work. I seem to blend in well with an accepted and ambiguous foreign criminal look."

"Or latent hippie," she told him.

He grinned.

"If you want to see some of South Florida, I can show you around," she told him.

He smiled, lowering his head. "Great. I grew up here. But you know South Florida better than I do."

She grinned. "I was born here."

"Oh?"

"We traveled a lot—but always lived here. Well, not *here*, but in Miami, in Coconut Grove."

"There are so many areas… An amazing city, really. I think, just four decades or so ago, the population of the area was about three hundred thousand. Now, we're looking at millions." He cast a grimace her way. "Populations always lead to crime," he added.

He could be incredibly mercurial. He slipped an arm around her shoulder and pointed to a café before them. "They're known for their crème brûlée. Shall we?"

"Crème brûlée," she agreed, frowning slightly.

He lowered his head close to hers. "We are being followed," he said, pretending to nuzzle her forehead.

"Ten o'clock, just down the street. Our dear friend Alejandro Suarez."

She was careful not to look right away, but let out a tone of delighted laughter and planted a kiss on his cheek.

"Let's have dessert," she said louder.

He took her arm and led her into the café.

"Well," she said as they sat close together. "I'm not sure if we've gotten anywhere, but the stone crab claws were delicious, and this is wonderful crème brûlée."

"Definitely better than some of the undercover work I've done before," he told her. He made a face. "Homeless detail. Sleeping in boxes—and for dinner, French fries out of the garbage."

"Yuck."

"You do what's called for."

"I would have…for this," she murmured.

"So, tell me about Mary. Tell me why you're on this case."

She stared up at him, startled. Somehow, he seemed to know everything. She hesitated and then shrugged.

"Our watchdog has stayed outside," he said softly.

She nodded. He was good at observation; she trusted him.

"Mary," she began. "The Deco Gang has been on our radar for a long time—they've operated out of restaurants, bars and even dry cleaners, moving on all the time. My usual cases keep me on the mainland. MDPD comes in on cases in many of the cities—Miami-Dade County is made up of thirty-four cities now, with more incorporating all the time. Not all the smaller cities have their own major crime divisions, and so we handle a great deal of it. South Beach does have a major crime unit, but the powers that be approved of us taking over this case. Miami Beach cops had a greater risk of being recognized, even undercover. It's not that they tried to hand off work—it was just a better plan. And honestly, until the bodies were found... I might have been the detective taking it the most seriously. Jurisdiction on this is complicated. The oil drums you saw were discovered up in Broward County, by a Seminole law enforcement official."

"There's the Florida Department of Law Enforcement. They could have taken over."

"And those guys are great. But going in on this, it fell to something Miami-Dade would do. We were investigating a disappearance. We were suspicious of the Deco Gang. And when it came to finding a way to slip in and be close enough, the models the clubs use all the time seemed a good cover. I approached my captain about it."

"You were in."

She shrugged. "In all honesty, I was afraid if I mentioned that a friend of mine had been working with the gang's models and then disappeared, it would be a strike against me in terms of being able to take the case. But it actually worked in my favor—I really knew her, I could talk about her and maybe get some information from the other young women working with them. And Mary, well, she's one of the nicest people you'd ever hope to meet. She looks for the good in everyone. Since I'm a cop, she thinks I'm jaded—though I actually think I'm pretty nice, too. Cops don't have to be asses."

"No, they don't," Jacob agreed, clearly somewhat amused.

"But Mary's problem is that she does look for the good. She has to be slapped in the face by bad to see that it exists."

"She probably is a very good person."

"Kari Anderson—the girl on the runway with me when Josef was shot—reminds me of Mary. They're both natural blondes with huge blue eyes and a trusting manner to go with them. Mary was working dinner theater, but not making much money. She saw the ad for models. She did a few shows with the group—Smirnoff's group is behind a number of entertainment offerings. They've been doing legitimate business, too. They own a bunch of other nightclubs. Anyway, Mary got swept up with Natasha and Josef and what she was doing...and saw no evil in it. And she was excited to get paid so well. Florida is a right-to-work state, so dinner theater may be a group requiring Actors' Equity, but then again, it may not be. She was thrilled. She paid her rent two months ahead with her paycheck from one show. And then there was the regular retainer just for being at the clubs, filling them with beautiful young people... It was easy money at first."

"Did she say anything to you about being nervous?"

Jasmine shook her head. "Never." She hesitated. "The last time I talked to Mary, she was excited. She was going to be a star attraction, working their next show. Which was the opening of the club the other night."

"The one you starred in instead."

"Yes. Look, Mary never said anything to me. She wasn't nervous, as far as I know. She just disappeared. A few weeks ago, she was supposed to meet me for lunch. She didn't show up. Mary's parents passed away when she was eighteen. She's on her own, an only child. She and I have been friends forever—we went all the way through grade school and high school together. We have other friends, but no one else has any other information about her. I don't even know how long she's actually been missing. After she missed our date, I called and called. We had an officer from Missing Persons go in to talk to Josef and Natasha, and they both appeared mystified—according to the officer."

"Have you gotten anything?"

"Not yet. The girls are still getting to know me. No one expected what happened to Josef. But apparently, we're all on retainer. Including Jorge."

"Retainer," Jacob murmured.

"I'm not sure what's next. Jorge and I can go in for checks tomorrow."

"Good. I'll stop by at some point." Jacob leaned back. "Well, I believe I'm supposed to walk you back now."

She nodded, oddly sorry that the evening was ending. It was work. Dangerous work.

Work to find Mary.

"You think we're still being watched?" she asked.

"I do."

He paid, stood and drew out her chair. He very politely took her arm and opened the door for her as they exited the café. He slipped an arm around her shoulders.

"Alejandro still around?" Jasmine asked.

"I think he was sitting at one of the outside tables... that's the back of his head behind us. Nope, he's rising now. I'd say he's going to make sure that I take you home and then leave—not overstepping my bounds."

They walked at a lazy pace, his arm around her but with all propriety.

"Interesting," she murmured.

"What's that?"

"How I'm going to discover that they keep control. I mean, as far as they know, I'm just a girl trying to get ahead in modeling. What if I just liked you and wanted to be with you?"

"I don't know. But if I went outside the rules..."

"I'm wondering if we'd both wind up in oil drums. I can see how they'd blame you. You're officially on the inside. But—"

"You're just an innocent. Well, in their eyes."

They'd reached her apartment. She was in a charming place, ground floor, almost in front of the pool. He walked her to the door and then paused. She wound up with her back against the wall by her door. He had a hand on the wall and was leaning against her.

He lowered his face toward hers and gave her a slow careful kiss. She allowed a hand to fall on his chest, and she wished that she didn't feel that there was absolutely nothing wrong with him. His scent was clean and masculine, mixed with the salty cool ocean air. His chest was vital and alive and yet like a rock. His lips were...

He drew away from her.

"I think that was just right. You might want to smile and laugh and then go in."

"Alejandro is watching?"

"He's right out on the street."

"Lovely, what a lovely night," she said, letting her voice carry.

"I'm sure we'll see each other again," Jacob said. "If you're willing..."

"I just have to check my work schedule."

"Of course." He stepped back, and she turned and let herself into her apartment.

She swung the door shut and slid the locks. And then, she stood there for a long, long time. She brought her fingers to her lips. They felt as if they were on fire.

Chapter Five

"You will pay Mr. Chavez twenty-five thousand for the painting," Victor Kozak told Jacob.

They were seated in the office at the rear of the gallery Jacob was pretending to own. Jacob nodded sagely to Kozak. They had already been through the niceties. They both sat with little demitasse cups of espresso. Kozak had admired the shop. Jacob had expressed his appreciation for Kozak's patronage.

"I don't know this artist," Jacob said.

"Trust me. He is excellent."

"And my commission?"

"Fifteen percent."

Jacob let that sit. He smiled at Kozak. "No disrespect. Twenty percent." He was pretty sure that in all such haggling—legal and illegal—Kozak had a higher limit than the figure he'd started with.

"Eighteen," Kozak said.

"I'm looking forward to working with you. Seeing that wonderful art arrives in our country. But if we're to go forward in the future, I believe we need a set rate now. I will be an excellent gallery to procure all the right artists—but I need to survive. The overhead here is quite high," Jacob told him.

Kozak was thoughtful. "All right, then. Twenty percent."

He rose; their dealings were complete. Jacob stood as well and the two men shook hands.

"Have the police come up with anything as yet regarding the shooter? Or shooters?" Jacob asked.

"No, nothing they have shared. You said *shooters*. You think that more than one man was involved?"

"We both know guns," Jacob told Kozak. "Yes, the shots were coming from at least two angles, maybe three."

"Accomplices," Kozak said, shaking his head. "So much violence in this world." He sighed as he lowered his head in sorrow. "Josef was a good man." He shrugged, a half smile on his face. "A good man—for all that we are. He was simply a businessman, and he had integrity in what he did."

Drugs and prostitution, if not murder. But sometimes, even criminals had their ethics.

"All the security," Jacob said, "and still—"

"Don't worry. What the police don't discover, we will," Kozak assured him.

"Naturally," Jacob said.

"I'm so sorry that this happened. Josef…was your friend?"

"We had a few business deals years ago. Art, you know, is always in the eye of the beholder. He'd commissioned a few pieces through me in my galleries before. When I wanted to come south—no more chipping ice off windows, you know—I looked down here and saw that Josef was opening a club. It's always prudent to establish relationships before opening a business anywhere," Jacob said.

"Josef told me about you." Kozak smiled. "And we do nothing without checking out references. I know that Josef trusted you. But now…his body will be released on Friday, they tell me."

"And there will be a funeral?"

"Yes, it will be at a little Russian Orthodox church in the city, not on the beach. A private affair. But you will be invited."

"I appreciate the honor and privilege of saying goodbye to an old friend," Jacob told him. "And with your permission, I will be by this afternoon with a small token for our new friendship."

"That will be fine. The club will reopen Friday night, but invitation only. A very small group to begin. We must show the world that we're now a safe place to be."

"This violence… It can happen anywhere. Lightning doesn't usually strike the same place twice. I believe the club will be fine."

Kozak gave him a rueful grin. "Sometimes, such events make a place a curiosity. Think back to the '80s. Paul Castellano and Thomas Bilotti were gunned down in a hit ordered by Gotti in front of Sparks Steak House in New York. The restaurant is still going strong. Down here, Al Capone was often in a suite at the Biltmore Hotel in Coral Gables. The suite is very expensive, and people still love to take it—even though Thomas 'Fatty' Walsh was gunned down at the hotel, supposedly over a gambling dispute." His smile deepened. "The hotel did go down after hurricanes and the Depression. It became a veteran's hospital. It was empty—and very haunted—but it's back to being very chic today."

"Let's hope we don't all have to go down first."

"Not to worry about us. Josef created a strong group of business associates. We will be fine." With that, Kozak took his leave.

Jacob walked him to the door. They both smiled at Jacob's "assistant," who was busy behind the old art nouveau desk that served as their register and counter. Katrina smiled back and waved.

She was a perfect choice for this role. Katrina Partridge had been with the Bureau for nearly twenty years. She was in her midforties, attractive and able to carry off both charm and a completely businesslike demeanor. She also knew the art world backward and forward.

When Jacob was gone, she shook her head, indicating they shouldn't talk in the gallery. She pointed to his office, and he followed her there.

"He was walking around a long time. I think he touched a few of the frames, and… I could be wrong. But he could have planted some kind of a bug."

"Good observation, thank you. So, we're being given our first commission," he told her.

"But that's not enough," Katrina said.

"We could bring him down," Jacob told her. "But there will be a work of art, and who is to say what a work of art is worth?"

"Someone who knows art," she said drily.

"But art is subjective."

"So true. Yes, you're right."

"We're after killers," he said softly. "That's what we want to nail them on."

"I know," Katrina said. "And hey, what's not to like about this assignment? I don't have much going on yet—I'm enjoying my downtime. Sand, beach, lovely weather…"

"Still, be careful, Katrina. We can never know when something may slip. They gunned down a man in a room full of cops and security."

"I'm always careful," she said. She smiled, indicating her back.

She was dressed in a fashionable skirt and blouse ensemble with a handsome tailored jacket. Despite the tailoring, he could see—when she indicated her back—that she was not without her Glock.

He smiled his acknowledgment but found himself worrying about Jasmine Adair.

Modeling. There was no hiding a weapon when dressers were around, making sure that a gown was being worn properly. And she was into it on a personal level—something that was dangerous from the get-go.

He had no right to interfere; her operation had begun before his and they were now required to work together. He had no problem working with police.

It was just that he was attracted to her. He didn't think it possible not to be. She was unique; elegant and a bit reserved, and yet when she smiled, when she laughed, she was warm, vibrant and sensual.

He turned his mind from thoughts of her.

"I'll bring the caviar over in about an hour," he told Katrina.

"All ready, in the container in back. I've dressed it up beautifully, if I do say so myself."

"I'm sure you did," he told her.

They moved back into the gallery. Jacob made a point of informing her that they were commissioning a piece, one that had a buyer already, who was in love with the artist's work.

She made mention of a local up-and-coming artist the buyer might like, as well.

A real customer sauntered into the room. Jacob returned to his office but found himself sitting and doing nothing but thinking.

He had to find a way in that was tighter; he had to be close to Jasmine.

He was still wary, of course. She hadn't turned him into a fool.

Maybe she had. Jacob hadn't felt such an instant attraction…almost a longing…in years.

Not since Sabrina.

"Ah, you are so beautiful, even in mourning," Natasha told Jasmine, admiring the way the draped black dress fell in sweeps to the floor. "Remember, at this, you will be quiet. You will help our guests with their drinks and food but keep a distance. Victor has ordered that this be a solemn occasion. You understand?"

"Yes, Natasha," Jasmine assured her.

Natasha looked over at Jorge, handsome in a conservative black suit. "You two will do well, I believe."

She called to the little seamstress who hurried over. "I don't think that the hem needs to come up, but at the waist…a half an inch?"

"Yes, ma'am, of course," the seamstress said. She poked and prodded at Jasmine for a minute, pinning the waist and then nodding.

Jasmine thanked her. The tiny woman helped her slip out of the dress, and carried it away.

As Jasmine reached for her jeans and T-shirt, she was aware that Natasha was assessing her again—as she might assess meat in a market.

"So, last night, you were charming?"

"Yes, he took me for a nice dinner, and I told him about the beach."

"Very good. He likes you."

"I believe so."

Natasha turned away. "You could be asked to do much worse," she said, almost to herself, rather than to Jasmine. "So, now…jeans and a T-shirt. You must dress more…ah, how do I say this? Much prettier, to come in here."

"Business clothes."

"No, the halter dress you wore last night. Very pretty. And heels. No sneakers."

"Definitely, whatever you say."

"Victor would like to see you. I wish there was more time…time for you to go home. Ah, what am I thinking? I still have clothing from the show!" Natasha beamed, and caught Jasmine's hand. "No, no. Don't put your jeans back on."

"Oh…okay."

Natasha left her standing on the little podium where dresses were fitted and headed back to the racks of clothing that remained hanging in the massive closet space. She searched through the racks until she evidently found something that pleased her.

When she returned, she had hangers that bore a sleeveless silk blouse and a red skirt. "These will do," she said.

The skirt was short. Very short.

Jasmine donned the clothing. She smiled, hoping to show that she was feeling friendly with Natasha. "I don't think that the sneakers go with this so well."

"Ah, but of course not! You're an eight and a half, American size, in shoes?"

"Nine," Jasmine told her.

A very large shoe size, apparently, in Natasha's opinion. "Ah, well, you are tall."

She was five-ten. Natasha would be appalled by Jasmine's mom—just five-eight and she wore an eleven.

Natasha brought shoes—four-inch stilettos. "These will be beautiful," she said.

Jasmine slipped on the shoes. She was well over six-feet, now.

"So, come. Victor is happy with you." She turned to Jorge. "You—you will come on Friday evening. The service is at two. Josef will be interred after, and then we will be arriving here."

"Yes, ma'am," Jorge said.

Natasha studied him for a minute and then smiled. "We may have more work for you soon. Showing people Miami Beach—and all its pleasures."

Jasmine knew Jorge well. He didn't miss a beat. "Thank you," he said.

"And, now, you..." Natasha took Jasmine's hand. "Come and see Victor."

"For sure, a pleasure," Jasmine said.

"I'll wait here," Jorge said cheerfully.

"No, Jorge, you are done for today. Antonio will see you out."

Antonio was standing at the door to the large dressing room.

"Call you later!" Jasmine told him cheerfully.

She wasn't feeling so cheerful; she was caught here with nothing, no backup—and she was off to see Victor. She wasn't worried for her life. If she was going to be taken out, they'd have gone after Jorge, too.

Had she done too well with Jacob "Marensky"? Was she now going to be asked to entertain another of their associates?

There was really no choice but to play it out. She had to wonder if this was where Mary had stood—right before she had disappeared.

With a smile, Jasmine watched Jorge go—and she accompanied Natasha to Victor Kozak's office.

Victor Kozak was not alone.

There was a man in his office. A tall man, he wore a designer suit in charcoal gray. He was perhaps in his midfifties, with iron-gray hair and mustache and watery blue eyes.

They'd both been sitting; Victor behind the desk, the new man in one of the upholstered chairs set before it. They stood politely.

"Ah, Jasmine. I'd like you to meet Mr. Connor," Victor said. "He's visiting from England and knows nothing about Miami Beach. He's hoping you will show him the beach, and to the finest hotel."

Jacob was already on his way to the club when his phone rang. He glanced at the number; he hadn't saved any in his contacts, but rather memorized the last four digits of those he needed to know.

Jorge Fuentes was calling.

"Where are you?" Jorge asked.

"Heading to the club. Why?"

"Head faster. I think they've taken Jasmine in to entertain a client. I mean, she can handle herself, but this is happening way too fast."

"Picking up the pace," Jacob moved forward quickly. "I'll be back in touch as soon as possible."

He didn't run; he might have been observed. But he could walk fast as hell and he did so. He came to the corner of Washington Street and rounded it, heading to the employee side entrance to the club.

This time, Antonio was leaning against the wall by the door, smoking a cigarette, watching the day.

"Those things will kill you," Jacob said.

"Mr. Marensky. I don't believe we were expecting you."

"I have something for Mr. Kozak. He was just in the shop, you know. I need to get right up there."

Jacob didn't wait for Antonio to respond but hurried past him in a way that meant the goon's only action could be to physically accost him, and the man would still be trying to figure out if Jacob was important enough or not to get through.

Suarez was in the hall.

Jacob made a point of striding past him with a huge grin on his face. "Present for Victor!" he declared, lifting the ice chest filled with caviar that Katrina had so beautifully decorated with multicolored ribbons.

He burst into the office before he could be stopped.

Kozak immediately stood, reaching toward his jacket—and the weapon he surely carried there, Jacob thought. But he didn't draw the weapon.

Good. Jacob was trusted.

Jasmine was there, outfitted like the very expensive and exclusive call girl she was apparently expected to be.

A man had just been leaning over her—either inspecting her or seeking a better look at her cleavage. He was tall and solid, though his face was lined—perhaps from years of worriedly looking over his shoulder. His eyes were a strange, cool blue. Like ice.

"Victor! A present. Forgive me for interrupting. My source delivered this just this morning, and after we spoke—" He paused. "Excuse me, sir. No disrespect intended. I was in a rush— Jasmine!" he said, breaking up his own run of words. "Hello, and thank you again for last evening. You were a wonderful tour guide."

"I was conducting business with Mr. Connor—" Kozak began.

Jacob brought a frown to his face, and then allowed himself to appear deeply disturbed. "No, sir," he said, addressing Connor.

Connor straightened and stared at Kozak. "Kozak, I want—"

"I'm afraid I already have an interest," Jacob said softly.

"She's just a woman," Kozak muttered beneath his breath.

Jacob was glad that Jasmine appeared not to have heard the words. "Forgive me, but, Mr. Kozak, you're a very busy man. This arrangement was made. Yesterday. And at the show, before he was killed, I received promises from Josef Smirnoff."

"Smirnoff is dead," Connor said.

"But not forgotten," Jacob said.

Kozak was, of course, in a tight position. If he hadn't murdered Josef Smirnoff and was taking over as a natural progression, he had to respect promises made by his predecessor.

"Not forgotten, no. And honored," Kozak murmured. Jacob had given him an out—and he was glad to see that the man wanted his "business" and was willing to take the out.

Jacob turned to Connor.

"I'm new, but... I understand this. Miss Alamein and I had dinner last night and arranged for a sightseeing tour this evening. I had forgotten to tell Mr. Kozak about my tickets, but I'm afraid that I did specify this... young woman."

"I can make even better arrangements for you, Mr. Connor," Kozak said. "You must understand, we are in mourning right now. And in honor of Josef, I must follow through on all his promises."

"Fine. Call me when you have found a suitable companion," Connor told Kozak. He was looking at Jacob. Sizing him up. Apparently, he determined that the companionship of a certain woman was not worth a battle. He turned and left without another word.

"So, before you came to me... Josef had promised you this woman," Kozak said.

Jacob didn't look at Jasmine. Knowing her as he was coming to know her, he was amazed that she was managing to just sit still.

"When I saw her on the runway," he said, his voice husky, "I knew I wanted her at that moment. I believe she might have been his last promise."

"Then I will make no other arrangements. But you must remember, Miss Alamein is in my employ. And she will appear when she is needed."

"That is understood."

Kozak walked over to Jasmine. "You will honor this arrangement?" he asked her.

Jasmine stood. In the heels she was wearing, she was eye level with Kozak. She smiled sweetly. "As you wish, Mr. Kozak."

"Fine," Kozak said. "Just remember, you work for me," he added softly.

"Always," she told him earnestly. Jasmine's smile deepened. "And thank you, sir. Thank you. Mr. Marensky and I were able to have the most delicious dinner last night. Far more easily than I might have ever imagined!"

Even Kozak seemed caught by her charm. "My pleasure. So, I believe that Natasha wanted to talk with you one more time. And…" he gave his attention back to Jacob "…Miss Alamein will be ready for you tonight, for these tickets you have."

"I'll wait and escort her home now," Jacob said. "Sir, if you have a minute, the present I brought… I believe you will enjoy it immensely. It is Almas, from the beluga sturgeon—supposed to be some of the finest caviar. I must admit, I am not an expert, but I have been assured by those who are that this is delicious."

"Then you must sit and enjoy it with me," Kozak said. He waved a hand at Jasmine. "See Natasha, see what she needs from you."

Jasmine was dismissed. She left the room.

Jacob looked at Kozak. "I thank you for respecting me—and Josef's memory," he said. "And I would like to do more."

"Oh?"

"I am not without certain skills. I would like your permission to look into Josef's death myself."

Breathing was difficult.

Jasmine's heart was pounding. She'd been so sure of herself, even in Kozak's office with the very strange *Mr.* Connor all but pawing her, that she'd been figuring out ways to handle the situation herself. Alone with the man, she'd have figured out something…

And blown her cover. And all hope of finding out what had happened to Mary.

She hurried down the hall—smiling at Sasha, on duty there now—to the dressing room. Natasha was at one of the tables, studying her face in the mirror.

She looked at Jasmine, and as she did so, Jasmine had to wonder if the woman's eyes could stretch out of her head, or if she had ears that could extend down a hallway.

Natasha already knew what had happened.

"It's not good," she said. "It's not good at all. One man should not become so possessive."

Jasmine shrugged. "Does it matter?" she asked. "Does it matter if the money is the same?"

"Ah, child, you're new to this," Natasha said.

"Yes, I am. And I am ignorant but willing to learn."

Natasha seemed pleased with her reply. "He will start to think that he owns you and that he would be better off just spiriting you away somewhere. You must be careful and declare your loyalty to us at all times, do you understand?"

"Yes, Natasha. And I am loyal, I promise you."

"And," Natasha added, "you like this Jacob Marensky?"

"He's clean and he smells good. And he is younger."

Natasha waved a hand in the air. "Yes, he is clean and young and smells good. And young can be good. Old men, with their hopes and their prayers and their pills… They have no idea how often those they think they control sit there and do nothing but laugh at their faulty efforts." She shook her head; Jasmine had the feeling she had experienced the worst and earned her way out of it.

"So then, you may have your jeans and your T-shirt. Apparently, Mr. Marensky is a more casual man and you are going on a sightseeing tour." She shuddered as if a sightseeing tour might be akin to torture.

"Thank you," Jasmine said. "I must admit, the shoes…the heels are a lot."

"They make you very tall. Then again, Mr. Marensky is very tall." She waved a hand in the air. "Josef admired the man. Victor believes that he is an admirable man as well, who understands our business but demands that we respect his. You will, of course, report to me."

"Yes, I will."

Jasmine heard voices. A few of the other girls had arrived.

Kari Anderson came into the room, carrying a bundle of clothes. Behind her were Jen Talbot, Renee Dumas and Helen Lee. They were like a palette of beauty—Kari so pale, Jen olive-skinned, Renee almost ebony and Helen extraordinary with her mix of Eurasian features and lustrous long black hair. They were beautiful on a runway.

They had also been hired to please all tastes.

Thus far, though, she hadn't seen any of the women forced into anything. Just pretty girls with an understanding that they could be paid well for their company. She had sat silently herself as Victor had introduced her to Mr. Connor and informed her that he needed a guide and an escort for the evening. What if she had protested?

Had Mary protested?

"I'll just grab my things and change and get out of here," Jasmine said. "And hang these up."

She fled over to the hangers, finding that her clothing had not been hung—just folded as if with distaste and left on the shelving above the racks. She eased out of the shoes and slid out of the skirt.

Kari walked in. "I'm going to need that skirt, I hear," she said.

"Oh?" Jasmine handed her the skirt on its hanger and shimmied the blouse over her head.

"I'm going to go see Mr. Connor," Kari said. She sounded slightly nervous.

"Are you afraid of him?" Jasmine asked in a whisper. "If so—"

"No, no. He's supposed to be very nice."

"I thought he was new."

"No. Mary went out with him. Just dinner. She said he was very nice. Oh, sorry, you didn't know Mary. She was great, but... I guess this wasn't for her. Me, I want the runway. And if it means dating a few losers..." Her voice trailed. "Dating," she repeated drily. "Okay, having sex with a few repulsive specimens... Well, I managed to choose a lot of losers on my own! Might as well have it be worth something in the end, I guess."

"Kari?" Natasha called.

"Excuse me," Kari said to Jasmine. "I have to run!"

Jasmine caught her hand. "Kari—please. Will you call me tomorrow and let me know that you're all right?"

Kari seemed surprised. "Of course, I'll be all right. But thank you. And I will call you—we can maybe have lunch or something?"

"I'd love to have lunch," Jasmine assured her. She hesitated. "It's allowed?"

"Oh, yes. They like us to be friends. Sometimes..."

"Sometimes?"

"Kari!" Natasha called again.

"Later!" Kari told her, and with a swirl of blond hair, she was gone.

Kozak had opened a bottle of his special "very Russian" vodka to go with the caviar. Jacob was careful to pretend to sip as much as the crime tsar but imbibe as little as possible.

His time with the man was proving to be very interesting.

Kozak talked about growing up in Russia—about the KGB coming for his father in the middle of the night.

"That must have been very hard on a child," Jacob said.

Kozak shrugged. "My father, he was a killer. When it all broke apart, though…everyone was running. The kind of crime was brutal, from all manner of directions. My mother, bless her, got us out. I never understood. Business is business, but…"

He paused and looked hard at Jacob, very sober despite the vodka he had all but inhaled. "You think you can find Josef's killer?"

Jacob weighed his words carefully. "There have been certain…events in my past that required me to take a closer look at them. I have a talent for uncovering things." He paused. "You really have no idea who killed him?"

Kozak frowned.

"No disrespect," Jacob said quickly. "I liked Josef. We did very good business together. But perhaps, something was going on with the group that was dangerous to all."

"You're talking about the bodies discovered in the Everglades," Kozak said. "There is talk of little but that and the shooting on the news these days. We have even ceased to care about politics, eh? When people are scared…"

He paused and shrugged again. "We had nothing to do with those bodies. Not Josef, not me. And I do not know who killed him. Me, I have kept my boys close—Sasha, Antonio and Alejandro. I have played the game, I have become the king. But you are a newcomer. Down here, that is. Josef trusted you. You know how to stand your ground. You tell me—who killed Josef?"

"I don't know, but as I said, with your permission, I will find out."

"You have my permission—and my blessing. What else do you need?"

"Permission to speak with your boys. And Ivan and Natasha. Whether wittingly or not, Victor, one of them helped the killers."

There was a tap at the door.

"It's me, Mr. Kozak," Jasmine said in a small voice.

"I will see her home," Jacob said, rising and heading to the door. "And I will begin tomorrow. I will find the killer, I promise you."

"Then most definitely, the woman is yours—along with my gratitude," Kozak told him.

Jacob nodded and opened the door. And capturing Jasmine's hand, he hurried down the stairs, Jasmine in his wake.

Chapter Six

"I should have gone with him," Jasmine murmured.

The look Jacob gave her could have turned her to stone. She supposed, in his mind, he had managed not only to save her from a fate worse than death—or actual death, for that matter—but to keep up their undercover guises, as well.

"No, no," she amended quickly. "You were wonderful, magnificent. I mean, you pulled that off, and normal circumstances—"

"Just wait. Wait until we reach your apartment," he said. "At this point, I'm pretty sure it's okay if I come in."

"Are we being followed?"

"Maybe. You never know."

She was surprised when he pulled out his phone. He had such a grip on her with his left hand that she could hear the voice of the man he was calling from his phone in his right hand.

"You got her out?" the voice asked.

Jorge.

"Yes." Jacob glanced her way. "I need tickets, fast. Some kind of sightseeing trip. First available."

"Call you right back."

"Tickets?" Jasmine murmured.

"Tickets."

They were almost to her apartment when the phone rang again. This time, Jorge was speaking more softly.

"Lincoln Road Mall," Jacob relayed.

"We can walk it," Jasmine suggested.

"Then keep walking."

He was angry; she hadn't had a chance to explain yet what she'd meant about wishing she'd gone with Mr. Connor. And on the street the way they were, unaware of how things might go, despite the stand Jacob had just made, he clearly didn't want her talking.

His pace was urgent; she had long legs, and she could trek it, but he was moving fast. They were some distance from the club on Washington Street when he finally seemed to slow—perhaps having burned off some of his energy.

She managed to retrieve her hand from his hold and slide an arm through his, drawing herself close and speaking softly, as if she whispered a lover's words.

"I may have found out how Mary disappeared—and with whom," she told him.

He turned and frowned at her.

"I finally got a second with Kari. She's probably going to wind up going off with this man, Connor. Jacob, Mary met with Connor. She met him—and then she disappeared."

"And you were willing to take that kind of a chance?"

Jasmine swallowed, leaning on his shoulder. "That's what I'm here for. But I didn't find out until after you came and got me out of the room. I saw Kari when I went back to get my own clothing. That's when she told me...and they're going to send her in to be his escort. Jacob, we have to find a way to follow that man. Maybe Jorge—"

"No, Jorge still has an in. And they'd wonder what he was doing. Let me call my office. They'll get someone on it."

He pulled out his phone again. They'd reached Lincoln Road Mall—a pedestrian walkway that offered dozens of shops and restaurants, fun places to dine and enjoy a coffee, a drink, entertainment or an evening.

"It's a private tour company," Jacob said, pointing to a spot by the theaters on Alton Road. "They'll pick us up there."

He veered in that direction, speaking quickly to someone on the phone and giving them the information they had on Connor. Jacob described him to a T. But Jasmine knew he had little else to go on.

She heard rapid questions in return, and then assurances.

"I believe that's ours," Jacob said, pointing to a limo with a sunroof.

The vehicle made a U-turn and pulled to the corner. The driver, a young man in a suit, hopped out and offered them a broad professional smile. "Marensky?" he asked.

"Yes, thank you, Jasmine and Jacob," Jacob said, sliding his phone back into his pocket.

"I'm David Hernandez, your guide for the day!" he said cheerfully. "I'm at your disposal. Now, I understand you're new to the beach, so I'll give you a few suggestions. My first pick is the Ancient Spanish Monastery, but that's north on the beach, so…"

"That's fine," Jacob said quickly. "Is that okay, honey?" he asked Jasmine, and then he told their guide, "Jasmine knows the place. Me, I'm new."

"I love the Spanish Monastery!" she said. "But I'm not sure I'd be the best guide."

David looked at his watch. "Well, if we move, you can have a couple of hours there. Your assistant ordered a driver and guide until midnight, so—"

"We'll start with the Spanish Monastery," Jacob said.

They slid into the car. With the beach traffic, it was going to take them a few minutes to reach what Jasmine considered to be one of their most intriguing destinations.

"I grew up here, but not on the beach," Jasmine told David.

"Cool. I grew up in the city, by the old Flagler Dog Track—Magic City Casino now," David told them. "People say Miami is young, no history. But we've got tons of it. I could go on forever. But—"

"Please, do, go on forever," Jacob said.

He leaned back in the plush seat of the limo, closing his eyes for a minute. It was the only indication Jasmine had seen that his world could cause him pressure.

He had come in, guns blazing, for her.

She leaned back, as well. She really needed to talk

to Captain Lorenzo and give her report. Lorenzo could get cops out after Kari and Connor.

"Of course, South Beach itself is a tourist attraction," David said. "Did you know that it was the original area that was populated? Believe it or not, the beach started out as farmland. The City of Miami itself incorporated on July 28, 1896. Julia Tuttle, our founding mom, had sent an orange blossom to Henry Flagler, convincing him to bring his railroad down—we were almost always frost free!

"The City of Miami Beach was incorporated on March 26, 1915. Now, Miami Beach is comprised of natural and man-made barrier islands. In 1870, Henry and Charles Lum—father and son, by the way, bought a lot of the bracken, sandy, nothing land that's worth billions today. There was a station to help shipwreck victims up north of where you're staying, closer to where we'll be today. They started off with a coconut plantation, but that didn't go so well. Enter some rich Yankees, and the beach started developing.

"Collins Avenue is so named because of an entrepreneur called Collins. He mixed up the crops and got things going. Then with Miami up and running, the railroad coming down and Government Cut created, people were on their way to thinking it would make a great resort area. Enter the Lummus family, who were bankers, and Carl C. Fisher from Indianapolis, who worked with the Collins and Pancoast group, and by the beginning of the twentieth century, Miami Beach was on its way."

David had a great voice—informative, interesting

and soothing. Jasmine hadn't realized she had closed her eyes, too—until she opened them and discovered Jacob was looking at her.

"We're on it," he said softly. "The Miami office will speak to your captain and see that the police are aware of this new player."

"I just..." Jasmine paused, looking to the front.

David was going on, talking about the development of the area for tourists. The entrepreneurs had started off developing their crops—avocado, for one—and taking tourists on day trips from the City of Miami. Then came food stands and finally, the Browns Hotel, which was still standing.

"What if this man, Connor, is...a killer?" Jasmine asked quietly. "One of those men who can only get off if he strangles or stabs a woman. What if...?"

"He'll be followed and watched, Jasmine. And, they'll do the same with him as they did with me—just a date, first. Just a date. We'll find out about him, and Kari will be all right."

Kari would be all right. And that meant so much. But what about Mary? She'd been gone nearly a month now.

Jacob started fumbling in his pocket. She realized his phone was buzzing. He answered it in a quiet voice.

David kept speaking. "Collins needed money. He got it from the Lummus guys. He started construction of a wooden bridge. The beach areas went through a number of different names, but you can still find those founding fathers in street names here—and of course, we have Fisher Island, a haven for the very rich. If you really want to find a lot of these founders, we can do that another day.

"You should see the old Miami City Cemetery across on the mainland. It was north of the city limits in 1887 when it was founded. Julia Tuttle is buried there, and oh! If you like Civil War history, we've got some Confederates buried just feet from some Union guys—friends by then, I would think, since they died long after the war. Friends in death, if nothing else."

Jasmine looked at Jacob. He smiled tightly at her. "We have two guys on it. They're trying to dig up something on Connor, but we don't even have a first name for the man."

"He's English. He definitely had an accent."

"I told them that. Jasmine, they're watching Kari. She's at her apartment right now."

"She's an innocent... She's a Mary. She isn't worried about...about anything he might ask her to do. She said she's been with dozens of losers and might as well improve her career chances by going with men chosen for her by Kozak or Natasha. I'll never forgive myself if she gets hurt. I could have gone with Connor."

"She's going to be all right."

Jasmine nodded, taking a deep breath.

David talked on, telling them that when the South Beach area had fallen into a slump, Jackie Gleason had helped to change things doing his famous show from the beach, along with more entrepreneurs who saw the fabulous artistic value of the art deco hotels and buildings.

They were finally nearing their destination.

"The Ancient Spanish Monastery, known officially

as the Monastery of St. Bernard de Clairvaux, is really—well, ancient. Construction began in northern Spain in 1133, in a little place near Segovia called Sacramenia. It housed monks for somewhere around seven hundred years, and then there was a revolution and it was sold and became a granary and storage and...not a monastery.

"It came to be here because, in 1925, it was purchased by an American—you guessed it—entrepreneur, Mr. William Randolph Hearst. For a long time, it was known as the world's biggest jigsaw puzzle, because it was shipped to the US as thousands upon thousands of stones.

"Well, then Hearst had some financial problems. He'd wanted to rebuild it at San Simeon, but some of what he'd purchased of the monastery was sold off. The crates—about eleven thousand of them—were in storage in New York. Not to mention there had been an outbreak of hoof-and-mouth disease in Segovia, which meant the packing hay had to be burned and the crates had to be quarantined.

"And then poor Hearst died! More entrepreneurs invested, and all the crates were taken out of storage. Took about a year and a half, they say, to put all the pieces back together. Two businessmen bought them, had them put together and then couldn't afford the fact that the monastery didn't make it right away as a tourist attraction. Financial difficulties again.

"In 1964, it was purchased by Bishop Henry Louttit, who gave it to the diocese of South Florida, which split into three groups. Then it was owned by a very rich and good man, a billionaire and a philanthropist, Colonel Robert Pentland, Jr. He went on that year to give the cloisters to the Bishop of Florida, and voilà! Finally, a church and a tourist attraction. And now, while the monastery is still a great tourist attraction, it's still also an active church. I love going there. It's like stepping back in time."

They arrived. David quickly arranged for their tickets, and Jasmine and Jacob were in, admiring the old stone cloisters and hearing about the historic instruments that were often used in services, seeing some of the artifacts that had come with the monastery—and the carved coats of arms and other relics that had come from other monasteries and venues around Spain.

Then they were out in the gardens, arm in arm, and Jacob was back on the phone again.

"I did get the autopsy information on Smirnoff from my Miami counterpart," Jacob told her as they strolled.

"I realize autopsies are important, but I'm pretty sure I know how Josef Smirnoff died—bullets," Jasmine said.

Jacob nodded. "Yes. But I guess he didn't know he had cancer—colon cancer. According to the ME, Smirnoff must have had it for some time without knowing. He wasn't looking at a long life, even if he'd gone for treatment."

"So, someone murdered him for nothing," Jasmine said. "Kozak was next in line anyway."

Jacob was quiet.

"You don't think it was Kozak?"

"He would just be so obvious. And he denied having anything to do with the bodies in the oil drums."

"Have they finished those autopsies?" Jasmine asked.

Jacob nodded. "They are still waiting on testing. They've gotten fingerprints on the most recent body, but the two other corpses were too decomposed. They think one of the bodies has been there several years."

"I'm assuming they're also trying to trace the oil drums and whatever remnants of clothing they can find?"

Jacob nodded. "They don't have much hope on the oil drums. They were apparently dumped by a major oil company years ago. They were headed to the closest landfill, I imagine. Nice, huh? Anyone could have picked them up."

"But you said they got fingerprints off the most recent corpse?"

He smiled. "As soon as I know, you'll know. Easy now that I've staked my claim on you."

"It does make communication between us a lot easier," Jasmine murmured.

"And hopefully keeps the wolves from baying at your door—and forcing you to show your hand." He grinned at her. "I can appear to be extremely possessive."

She was afraid that her smile was a little fluttery. Because something inside her had fluttered, as well.

His phone rang. He answered and listened intently. "Okay," he said, hanging up. He looked at Jasmine. "Apparently, Mr. Connor doesn't believe in being fashionably late Miami Beach–style. He's at Kari's apartment now."

"So, they're heading to dinner now. We should get back down there—"

"Jasmine, agents are on it."

"I know, but—"

Her phone rang then. She glanced at the number; it was the number that Captain Mac Lorenzo was using for the operation.

"Checking in—and watching out for a valuable asset," he told her.

"I'm fine," Jasmine assured him. "I'm touring the Ancient Spanish Monastery."

"I've spoken with Jorge. We're not pulling either of you out yet. But I also have strict instructions from way high above not to endanger an FBI operation."

"We're not endangering it."

"And you're not to endanger yourself," he reminded her.

"Never, sir," she told him.

"Just make sure you remember the FBI has taken the lead on this, and they're calling the shots."

"I understand." She was careful to keep any remnant of emotion from her voice.

"You're doing all right with interagency communication?"

Jasmine glanced at Jacob. "We're doing just fine, sir."

Jacob must have heard. He arched his brows in a question and reached for the phone.

"Captain Lorenzo, how do you do? Jacob Wolff. We're working on this together well. I don't think we could have planned this out any better."

Jasmine didn't hear what Captain Lorenzo said after

that. Jacob handed the phone back to Jasmine and she quickly hung up.

"Thank you for that," she told Jacob.

He shrugged. "I think we are working well together."

"Yes, I guess we are."

"Hey, I'm pretty sure I would have liked you one way or the other. And I do admire your swing. That was a hell of a punch you gave me the other day."

"I didn't know—"

"Maybe that was better. That's the thing with undercover, really. Check in only when you need to or when you need help. Work everything on a need-to-know basis."

He was right, and she knew it. And she could have said she liked him, too. But suddenly, doing so seemed to be a very dangerous part of the operation.

She liked him too much.

Liked the deep set of his eyes, the tone of his voice... the way he touched her. She'd liked the feel of his lips on hers far too much... That brief touch was still a memory that lingered and haunted.

"I still think we should head back," she said.

He looked around. "It's beautiful here. Not just the monastery, I mean South Florida."

"Yeah. But how often do you get down here?"

"I go where they send me," he told her.

She nodded and turned away. Even with the undercover operation underway, they were ships passing at sea. It was disturbing that she was coming to care about him, and almost humiliating the way that she felt...

With him, she would have gladly taken a feigned relationship anywhere.

It was one thing to discover she found him attractive. More, even. Compelling, sensual…a man with the kind of masculinity that moved beyond sense and logic and simply reached into the very core of her being.

It just didn't work to be craving his touch while on the job.

"Well, we've checked in, Jorge knows I'm all right," she said, "and Connor will have Kari on the beach somewhere soon. I'd like to get back to South Beach."

"We can do that," he said.

He took her arm and they headed back. David Hernandez was waiting for them by the limo. Jacob told David he was great, and they would use him in the future, but for the moment, they'd decided just to head back to the hotel. They were going to wander the sand by night.

Hernandez thought that was fine, and he was grateful they'd call on him again. Of course, the man would be pleased. He had the night off now with full pay.

Jasmine and Jacob were both quiet during the drive back. When they reached the cute little boutique hotel where Jacob was staying, Jasmine admired the old lobby.

"You've never been in here before?" he asked her.

She grinned. "When I was in high school, we used to come out here and prowl a few of the clubs and maybe have soda or coffee at a few of the hotels. But I think I've only stayed out here a few times. I'm a native, but that doesn't mean I know every hotel."

"It's nice. Not a chain. And the owners seem to love the deco spirit of the place. I can have coffee on the balcony every morning if I want. I can hear the sound of the surf and watch the palm trees sway—before the rest of the world wakes up and the beach becomes crowded with bodies."

She smiled. "You will see some of the most beautiful bodies in the world out here, you know."

He was quiet for a minute.

"You disagree?"

He smiled awkwardly and shrugged, and then looked at her at last. His light blue eyes seemed to caress the length of her.

Her heart, her soul, her *longing* seemed to jump to her throat.

But he quickly changed moods. "Then again, it's not just perfect bodies. You know that, of course."

"You mean old and wrinkly? We'll all be there someday. I hope when I'm older and drooping everywhere, I still love the beach."

He laughed. "I'm with you on that. I hope when I'm creased and drooping everywhere I can still sit on the sand and watch the sway of the palms and not worry that someone is judging me. I believe everyone has to do what is comfortable for them—and that's part of what I love.

"Yes, there's beauty. Yes, there's the ridiculous. And there are quiet times, when the sun is rising, when you can look out and feel you're in a private paradise. And then you turn around and the neon of the hotels and the rush of the world comes on in. This place is ever changing, plastic in so many ways and yet real when it comes to the feel of the salt air and those moments when you're in the water, and it's just you and the waves and the sea and the sky."

"Yes," she said softly.

"So, let's take a walk," he said.

They headed out to the beach. Jasmine doffed her sneakers and Jacob rid himself of his shoes and socks, too. They left them by a palm.

Jacob's phone rang.

He listened, and then he told Jasmine, "Connor has Kari out to dinner. He took her to Joe's Stone Crab. They're fine."

"I'm afraid for when they leave. What do we do now?"

"Wait," he said.

"So hard!"

He laughed. "I've been undercover for months at a time. Watching, waiting. And for this case, well, the watching and waiting is a hell of a lot better than usual." He was quiet for a minute. "I recently worked a case where immigrants were brought in and used horribly. It was long on my part, but when it broke, we moved quickly. This may be the same. Thing is, right now, we could get them, or Ivan at least, on money. Then again, they can employ the best legal team known to man. So, we have to take them down big-time—with evidence that prosecutors can take to court."

Jasmine muttered, "So…we wait."

"And play the part," he agreed.

Nightfall was coming in earnest. The sky was fighting darkness and the sun was shooting out rays that seemed to be pure gold and magenta.

Jasmine wasn't sure what got into her. She suddenly broke away from him and ran down the beach, turned and kicked up a spray of the waves that had been washing over their feet.

She caught him with a full body splash, and he yelped and laughed with surprise. Then he came after her.

She squealed and turned to run, but he tackled her and bore her down to the soft damp sand. He leaned over her, looked down into her eyes and then murmured, "Good move. I just saw Sasha up on the boardwalk. We are being watched."

He eased closer. "Can I kiss you?"

Role-playing...

She tangled her fingers into the richness of his hair, pulling him in, and he kissed her.

And then he broke away, laughing, and pulled her to her feet. "I think we gave Sasha a good show, eh?" he asked softly.

"Oh, yeah," she whispered. Once again, her lips were burning.

As they retrieved their shoes and decided on a restaurant for dinner, she couldn't help but wish that the FBI had sent down a much less attractive agent.

Chapter Seven

"His full name is Donald McPherson Connor," Jacob told Jasmine. "He's living at that grand old place down from the club just off of Washington Street—a quiet and dark intersection. The whole sixth floor is his apartment."

They were at her place. He'd done a thorough search for bugs and hadn't found any, and with the way this gang seemed to work, he was pretty sure he wouldn't find anything. In Kozak's words, Jasmine was "just a woman."

Jacob had a feeling that Kozak might be pretty surprised.

Just a woman. In any kind of a fair fight, Jasmine would take Kozak.

But for them, at this moment, it bode well that Kozak and the members of his gang still seemed to live in an archaic world of chauvinism.

"And what else?" Jasmine asked.

"Born in Yorkshire, and he has dual citizenship."

"How does he make his money?"

"He inherited a nice sum and knows how to invest in the stock market."

"So, an older Englishman-turned-American, rich, with nothing to do. Wife? Kids?"

Jasmine had changed from her salt-spray-and-sand-covered clothing to a dark silky maxi dress. She'd come to perch on the sofa by him, hugging her knees to her chest as she looked at him.

"Wife died about ten years ago. They had a daughter but I can't find much on her."

"Criminal past?"

"Nope."

"Any hint of anyone disappearing when he's around?"

"He's been living in Savannah. He's just been down here about two months. They're still looking into him."

"And the agent saw him take Kari back to her apartment and then leave?"

"Yes," Jacob said.

He didn't have to read from his phone; one of his assets was his memory. He could retain what was told to him, which was probably why languages came to him easily. Then again, he loved languages, and all the little rules and differences and nuances within them.

He wished at that moment, though, that he was reading. Because he was left to meet her eyes.

He'd been right that first day, when he'd seen her from afar. Her eyes were green. A brilliant beautiful green, like twin emeralds in a sea of gold. Her face was so perfectly molded he was tempted to reach out and touch it, as he might be tempted to reach out and touch a classic sculpture. Her hair was free, freshly washed and tumbling around her shoulders, still damp. And in the maxi dress, she seemed exceptionally alluring—though he was sure she had donned the article of clothing because it covered her entire body. It felt like a reaction to the skimpy outfit she'd been forced to put on for the "date" with Connor.

"But according to Kari, Mary did escort him," Jasmine pointed out, "and then she disappeared."

"You're going to need to get closer to Kari."

"Well, we're both supposed to report to Natasha tomorrow—Kari and I."

"And I have an excuse to go in. I've gotten Kozak's permission to investigate Smirnoff's murder."

"Have the cops gotten anything? I guess not. I'm pretty sure that, even though the FBI has lead, I'd know about it if anyone had been apprehended for the murder."

"From what I've heard, they're still pretty much in the dark," Jacob said. "Trajectory shows the bullets were fired from the balcony. But everyone working there swears the balconies were closed off. Someone is lying, of course. But no one knows who."

"No guns were found, no casings...no nothing?"

"Nope. And the gunmen—two to three of them, best estimate—entirely disappeared."

Jasmine leaned her chin thoughtfully on her knees. "We could see all the major players when it happened. You were out there with Kozak, Ivan Petrov and the goons, Sasha, Antonio and Alejandro. And Natasha was backstage."

"The killers were hired, obviously. And they were guaranteed a clean getaway. We dusted for prints on the rails and so forth, but there are hundreds of prints. Workmen were there, of course, before the grand opening. Anyone who so much as delivered pizza might have left a print. Smirnoff, from what I understand, loved showing off the place and brought everyone out to those balconies to let them see how they looked down at the floor and the main stage."

She shook her head. "So, we're nowhere."

"No. We're moving forward. You're just impatient."

"I guess so. I mean, I have worked undercover before. But often just for a day or so, getting into the right place, talking to the right people. I admit—it was never anything like this."

"We just keep moving forward."

She nodded. "I guess… I guess I need some sleep."

"Go on."

"You're staying here?"

"I believe I'm entitled now—and I don't want to disappoint anyone by not taking my full measure."

"Ah." She stood, almost leaping away from him. "Pillow and blankets. If I'd known I was having nightly guests, I would have asked for a two-bedroom." She smiled awkwardly and hurried into her bedroom. A moment later, she was back. She plopped down two pillows, sheets and a blanket. "Not sure if you need the blanket, I don't air-condition the place too much. But… Anyway, all right. I'll see you in the morning. Start coffee if you're up first!"

She spoke quickly, almost nervously. It wasn't like her.

"Good night," he said softly.

She left him, and he wished he wasn't playing a role. More than that, he wished he wasn't working. She'd closed the door between them, but he could still see her in his mind's eye.

See her laughter as she kicked up the salt spray.

Feel her beneath him when he tackled her in the sand.

He could see the emerald of her eyes as she'd looked at him before she pulled him in for that blistering kiss.

And he couldn't help but wonder, in his misery, if she just might…just might…be wishing a little bit herself that they had met under different circumstances.

He spent the next hour reminding himself he was a special agent, he loved his job and he had made a difference… They were professional. They played their parts. They brought down the bad guys.

He thought he'd never sleep. He wondered why the hell he had stayed. She could take care of herself. She was trained.

But despite the logic, despite what he knew, he was afraid for her.

He could have returned to his apartment. He knew being here had nothing to do with being professional. If it came to it, he'd give anything to save her life if it was threatened in any way.

Why? He'd worked cases with so many beautiful women and never done more than acknowledge that fact.

Jasmine was different. She had touched something else in him. Something that was more than attraction, even desire.

She was...everything. Everything in a way he hadn't known in over a decade. Not since his wife had died.

Jacob was up when Jasmine emerged in the morning.

She'd spent the night...waiting. She'd thought the door to her bedroom might open at any time. She couldn't decide if she wanted it to or not.

But it did not, and when she finally rose, she found him already awake. He'd brewed coffee and was sipping a cup, leaning thoughtfully against the refrigerator.

He looked at her as she emerged, his eyes fathomless.

"Three more bodies last night," he said softly.

"What? Where?" she asked. Three bodies. Was one Mary?

He must have seen the fear on her face. "Three men again," he said quickly. "And they weren't found in oil drums. This time, they were found south of the Tamiami Trail. Miami-Dade County, on Miccosukee tribal land."

"Three. Maybe the hired gunmen? If they weren't in oil drums, if they're new... It's possible it isn't related. Will we get identities soon?" Jasmine said.

He hesitated. "No. The bodies are missing heads and hands."

"Oh."

"Cause of death?"

"Unknown, at this point. In my mind, logic suggests they were shot in the head."

"Logic?"

"Execution-style—then the heads were removed. Dumped them in the Everglades." He hesitated. "From what I've been told, they were well ravaged by the animal life. Among other creatures, the vultures had a feast."

"There are few better places to dispose of a body than the Everglades," Jasmine agreed. "But they were definitely...male bodies?"

"Yes, definitely male bodies."

She wandered to the coffeepot and poured herself a cup. She was shaken, but she didn't want to be. She was a detective in a major crime division. But this was personal.

Maybe she shouldn't have been working this investigation. But there had truly been no one better suited to the task of getting in with the Deco Gang.

Jacob came up behind her and placed a hand on her shoulders. "Jasmine, I believe the men found might well have been the shooters. If whoever planned this wanted to make sure no one talked, they had to get rid of the people who actually carried out the deed."

"Yes, that's my gut feeling on it, too," she said. Her hands were still trembling slightly as she held her coffee cup. And she was ridiculously aware of him, right there behind her, the heat of his body, the scent of him.

She had to spin around, composed and determined. "So, today, you start questioning everyone?"

"Today I start questioning everyone."

He had barely spoken when there was a knock on the door.

"Excuse me," she murmured.

As she headed to the door, she was aware Jacob had already showered and dressed completely for the day. He had his hand behind his back, ready to draw his weapon if the guest at the door intended to offer any danger.

No danger was forthcoming; she looked through the peephole. It was Jorge.

She let him in quickly. "Hey."

Jorge glanced at Jacob. He seemed to accept the man's presence as normal.

"I was bringing you the latest news. Captain said he didn't think you should be calling in, even on the burners. Too easy for one of them to catch the phone and check out numbers and get suspicious when nothing on you had an easily trackable number. But I imagine you've gotten the latest?"

"The bodies in the Glades?" she asked.

He nodded and looked at Jacob. "Who do you think did it? Is it Kozak? Natasha? Ivan?"

"I don't know. But I intend to find out." Jacob smiled. "Breakfast first. Somewhere obvious. Somewhere anyone who wishes can see the three of us—me and my escort, provided for me with their blessing, and you, my new love's best friend. Plenty of places in the area. Let's go for a walk and find good food."

"Okay," Jorge said slowly, frowning.

"Then Jasmine needs to check in with Natasha and assure her of my happiness and her own satisfaction with the arrangement—and I get to question the goons."

"And..." Jorge pressed. "Me?"

"I think it's fine if you come in today, just a cheerful dude happy to be with a friend."

"It's a plan," Jorge said.

It wasn't difficult for Jacob to pretend to be out with friends. He liked Jorge very much and thought he was probably a damned good cop. He knew how to fit in to what he was doing, and he didn't need to take the lead. He'd set up the tour for them yesterday in minutes flat and had managed to introduce him and Jasmine on the floor opening night at the club—at the end of a spray of bullets—without giving things away. Jacob also just liked the man.

And as for Jasmine...

He had to be careful.

When they were seated, Jasmine and Jorge were talking about Miami, and Jasmine was telling Jorge about their tour guide.

"He was a great guy—a super guide, knew his stuff," Jasmine said. "Friendly and informative without being annoying."

"Hard to imagine this place as a coconut plantation," Jacob said.

"Hard to imagine the whole south of the state as a 'river of grass,'" Jasmine said.

Jacob noted that there was a man seated at a far back table, eating and reading a newspaper. Watching them.

Jacob picked up his coffee cup and said softly, "Antonio Garibaldi is at the back of the restaurant."

"We were followed here," Jorge said casually.

"And here's the thing," Jasmine said, running her fingers up Jacob's arm and smiling sensually, "we don't even know who else might be in the employ of the new boss, be he Kozak or even someone else."

Jacob leaned closer to her. "We need to find out who

is calling the shots." He planted a quick kiss on her lips and looked at her lingeringly. Then he stood. "Think I'll visit the restroom."

He headed to the back of the restaurant and the restrooms. But he made a pretense of stopping, as if surprised and pleased to see Garibaldi.

"Hey! I guess I did choose a good place, if you're here," he said. He pulled out the chair on the other side of the table and sat.

"Yeah, they do a great breakfast," Garibaldi said. He was a big man with dark hair and a solid physique, built as a good bouncer should be. His eyes were quick and dark. His smile was pained.

"I'm really loving South Florida," Jacob told him. "And getting to work with Kozak. Of course, I'm as sympathetic as anyone over Smirnoff. He was a good man. What the hell do you think happened? I mean, forgive me, I know you guys are good at your jobs. But how the hell did shooters get up on the balconies?"

Garibaldi looked uncomfortable—he was on the spot. Then he leaned forward. "Hell if I know. Seriously. From the beginning, it was planned that the balconies be roped off. Crowd control. And that day... Smirnoff was giving us our orders. I was watching the front, Suarez had the stage and Antonovich was moving through the crowd. There were cops all over, hired for the occasion. I'll be damned if I can figure it out, and I've tried. Thing is, I was given my orders. The other guys were given their orders. We never saw anyone get up there."

"There has to be an entrance from the offices," Jacob said.

"Sure. There's a door across from Smirnoff's office. That way, when he chose to, he could be in his office, and when he wanted to be part of the crowd, he could come out on the balcony. The cops were all over it. But here's the thing. The door is kept locked. There's a key. And when the cops were all over the place right after the shooting, the door was still locked. Smirnoff kept the key."

"Duplicate keys can be made. I'm sure the cops checked on that," Jacob said.

Garibaldi shrugged. "Whoever may have had a duplicate key, I don't know."

"It was obviously well planned."

Garibaldi appeared to be honestly confused. "You know, sure, it could have been planned. But it seemed like one of those bad things, you know. Some disturbed person just out to hurt anyone—and getting Smirnoff."

"You don't believe that, do you?" Jacob asked.

Garibaldi's voice was soft and low. "I want to believe it," he said.

"But you don't."

"Kozak told us last night that he'd given you permission to question us, see if you couldn't figure something out. I'd like to help you. What do I know? I was in my position. And the shooting started. I was—well, hell. Hate to admit this. I was scared. I think I managed to get people out, get them down. But I got the hell out as fast as I could myself."

"You were armed?"

"I was. But the best gun in the world doesn't do you a bit of good if you don't know what you're supposed to be shooting at."

He seemed to be telling the truth. Jacob never took anyone at face value, but he also noted the man's expressions and body language. He'd have bet that he was being honest.

Garibaldi looked at him and seemed to judge him, as well. "I'm not in this for violence," he said softly. "The money is good..." He shrugged. "I mind my own business and don't care where it comes from. Drugs... People are going to buy them somewhere. The girls... They do what they choose. Natasha talked to Jasmine, and you all had an agreement. Cool. She seems to really like you. So, is that a crime? As for me, I do what I'm told and I keep my nose clean and stay out. I'm just security."

"So you're just supposed to report on us today?" Jacob asked him.

"Yeah. And it's cool. It's obvious you two have more than a business relationship going. That's the way Josef Smirnoff always rolled. Kozak said that it will be business as usual. Of course, he's scared now. Whoever killed Smirnoff could be gunning for him. That's probably why he said you could talk to people. Though, I already told the cops what I told you. The truth."

"Sure. Hey, next time you're watching us, just join us." Jacob shrugged. "She's a cool girl and I like Jorge, too."

"That wouldn't be the way the game is played," Garibaldi said.

"No, I guess not." Jacob stood. "You're a good-looking man with the right stuff. There are tons of other places on the beach that need bouncers, security. If this whole scene is too much for you."

Garibaldi shrugged. "I screwed up once. Didn't check an ID the way I should have. The girl's parents caused a stink. Josef gave me a job. Said I didn't need to ID anyone." He laughed suddenly. "Garibaldi. Nice Italian name. I was born here, my parents were born here and my grandfather came over from Naples to run a tailor shop. No mob ties whatsoever. He was in Worcester, Massachusetts. And didn't even have to pay anyone for a safe working environment.

"Alejandro Suarez, his family came over in the late 1880s. They were cigar makers up in Ybor City, Tampa area. And even Antonovich, he's a third-generation American. We're not…we're not mob. We're not mob-related. I'm here because I have a job. And I do it. Long hours, maybe, but so far, I haven't been asked to do anything other than protect people, watch people and break up fights."

"And what if you had to do something that was illegal?"

"It would depend on what that thing was." Garibaldi hesitated a minute. Then he said quietly, "Hey, man, you're buying art—that you haven't even seen. And we all know about your past."

Jacob nodded. "Yeah. But I play it the way Smirnoff played it. I don't go in for murder. Gets messy—and gets the cops on you."

"Yeah," Garibaldi agreed.

"Sounds like you're a good man. One I'd like to have on my side," Jacob said.

"Thanks," Garibaldi told him.

Jacob left him and returned to his own table. Jasmine and Jorge were having a conversation about the best spas in the area. When he sat down, Jasmine played it perfectly, stroking his arm.

He wished her touch didn't seem to awaken every ounce of longing in his body.

NATASHA WAS WITH Kozak when they arrived.

Jacob was allowed admittance to Kozak's office. Jasmine and Jorge were directed to the dressing room, where they were alone.

Jorge found a stereo system and turned on music. Phil Collins, "In the Air Tonight." Fitting. Shades of the old *Miami Vice* that had really put the area—and many myths about it—on the map.

"Natasha is sleeping with Kozak," Jorge said softly. "She might have been sleeping with Josef Smirnoff, too. At any rate, she was with him for years and years. Trusted. She could have gotten the key and had a copy made."

Natasha came sweeping into the room. She saw Jorge and frowned slightly, then shrugged. "I suppose you say anything in front of Jorge," she said. "Oh, by the way, Jorge, a man has been courting our business, one who may need some entertainment."

"Ready when you are," Jorge said.

"Now, Jasmine, about Mr. Marensky…"

Jasmine smiled and then decided to go another step. She walked over and hugged Natasha.

The woman was not used to hugs. She didn't push Jasmine away, but she didn't hug her back. She awkwardly patted her shoulders. "So, all went well," Natasha said.

"He's lovely," Jasmine said. "Best way to make some money I've ever known!"

"Yes, I believe you. You're very lucky such a man is so captivated by you. It's not always the case, but for you… Yes, I am glad that such a striking man—one whom Josef approved and Victor seems to admire, especially—has taken such a shine to you. But you must realize, my dear, he may tire of you. And move on."

"I know that," Jasmine said. "But for now…he's fun. He wishes to please me."

"And he is far from repulsive in bed, I imagine," Natasha said.

Jasmine didn't let her smile slip. "Oh, so, so, far from repulsive."

"Ah, she's a lucky one," Jorge said.

"Then you will continue as you have been doing. Don't forget… Friday night. Friday is the funeral. And at the funeral, you will be a hostess here, and you mustn't cling to Mr. Marensky at the gathering after the ceremony. After tomorrow night, the club may reopen. The workers will have cleaned up. No bullet holes will show in the walls by the ceremony. Now, you do understand about Marensky, Jasmine? First, we need you to be working. Second, it's important he remembers that he is graced with your company through us."

"Definitely," Jasmine said. "Understood."

"Then you are free for today. You may go. You, too, Jorge." She handed them each an envelope. Their paychecks. They had no choice but to thank her and leave.

As they walked, they noted they were being followed. It was Alejandro Suarez on their tail this time.

"So, straight to my place, I guess," Jasmine murmured.

"I don't think they're following me."

"What about phones?"

"I have a new one."

"I need to know about Connor. About Connor…and Kari."

Jorge sighed. "Jasmine, we have to trust our fellows. They saw last night that Connor left Kari at her apartment. No sex, nothing. She was fine."

Aware of their follower, Jasmine laughed as if Jorge had said something great and grabbed his arm in fun—as a friend might do. In contrast to her actions, her whisper was intense. "But what are they doing about him?"

"Watching. And waiting," Jorge said. "Jasmine, you knew this wasn't going to be an instant fix, that we'd be out of the loop much of the time. And—"

They had only come a half a block from the club when Jasmine saw Kari headed their way. She released Jorge's arm and cried out with delight, running to see the other girl.

"Kari!" She hugged her. She pulled away and asked softly, "All is well?"

"Fine, it's lovely. Mr. Connor is an absolute gentleman. I'll be seeing him tonight." Kari grinned and said, "Oh, he isn't young and hot like Marensky. But he's fine, very nice. Polite and courteous in a way I haven't seen in years. Happy to have some arm candy while he's out on the town, you know?"

"Good. Well, I guess you knew that, from what Mary said."

"I miss Mary. She was the sweetest!"

"Did she ever say anything to you," Jasmine asked, "anything about going away or even…even about being afraid?"

"No. She was just with us, and then one day she didn't show and didn't come back. Natasha was very upset. She was very fond of Mary, too. Speaking of Natasha, I've got to get in. She wants to see me." But suddenly, Kari gripped Jasmine's hands. "I'm telling you, Mr. Connor is so kind and caring, wanting to know my every wish."

Jasmine realized then that it was the man's very kindness that actually frightened Kari.

Someone so nice. What happened when he wasn't? What might he really want?

Further determined, Jasmine smiled. "Great, Kari," she said loudly. "I guess Jorge and I are going to go home and binge on repeats of *Desperate Housewives*."

"Have fun!"

"You're welcome to join us!"

Kari waved and headed off.

Jasmine headed back and grabbed Jorge's arm. "Something has to be done," she said firmly. "Before tonight!"

Chapter Eight

"I have had that door rekeyed," Kozak told Jacob. "The police asked about it, but it was locked. There was no sign that anyone had forced it. But...how? How did someone get through the balcony without being seen? There were dressers here, makeup artists... But when the show began, everyone was downstairs. Natasha was with the girls backstage. The band members were all downstairs. I didn't have the key! No one had the key—except for Josef Smirnoff."

"Someone obviously copied it," Jacob said flatly.

Kozak shook his head. "I have the only key now. No one knows where I keep it. And I don't intend to tell anyone. Including you. No offense or disrespect intended."

"None taken," Jacob said.

"You are free to look around, but I have to go. Josef's body is at the funeral home. I will make sure he is given the send-off such a man deserves."

"Where will the funeral be?"

"A small Russian Orthodox church, up the way on the beach. And then we will come here." Kozak hesitated. "Will you make the arrangements for it with me today?"

"I thought that I should stay here. We want to know what happened to Josef," Jacob reminded him.

"We do." Kozak sighed deeply. "Yes, you must speak with Antonio, Alejandro and Sasha. The thing is…"

"What is it?"

"They have their place. We work carefully. Of course, they are aware… But we never give them facts. They know people, they know who is important, but we have never given them much on the clients."

"They might have seen something," Jacob said. "Something they don't even know they saw. I've spoken with Antonio. You didn't tell me about the door and the key."

"I didn't. I had to make sure. Josef brought you in, and he assured me you were solid, that you were a powerful man with a long history. I had to come to know you myself." Kozak shrugged. "The police checked the door. They remain with nothing."

"But you know someone within your own ranks had to be involved."

Kozak looked unhappy. "Yes. But whoever did this, they were clever. They hired out. A man doesn't guard what he doesn't see to be in danger."

"No," Jacob agreed, trying to read Kozak.

"You must do what you will. I have hidden nothing on Josef's murder from the police. I will not hide it from you. But I must prepare to bury an old and dear friend."

It was evident that Kozak wanted company while he

made arrangements at the funeral home. Perhaps it was even important to go with him.

"I will go with you," Jacob agreed.

As it turned out, Kozak didn't want a driver with them. He had a big black Cadillac sedan, and he asked Jacob if he would do the driving.

"You don't want one of the guys to come along?"

"A bodyguard?" Kozak asked. "I think you will do."

They took Collins Avenue north and reached the funeral home. They were greeted by a solemn man in a suit, Mr. Derby, the current owner of Sacred Night Final Rest Parlor.

Derby expressed his condolences, offered them water or coffee and then tactfully suggested they needed to choose a coffin. The coffins ranged from a few thousand dollars to just about enough to buy a house—at the least, a nice automobile.

Jacob was surprised to see tears in Victor Kozak's eyes. He had either really cared for his friend, or he was able to pull off a feat many a Hollywood actor could not.

Then again, business was business. He could have loved the man—and still arranged for his death.

"What do you think, my friend?" Kozak asked Jacob.

"Personally?" Jacob asked. "I believe in a greater power, but I don't believe the body is anything but a shell. It makes no difference if a man is laid to rest in the finest mahogany or the cheapest pine, or if he's cremated and his ashes thrown to the wind. But if you're worried about the funeral, about our show of respect… then I'd say this."

Mr. Derby, the funeral director, was eyeing Jacob

with anything but kindness. Still, he seemed to perk up when Jacob pointed out a fairly expensive coffin, one that was both handsome, staid and possessed just the right amount of ornamentation.

"Perfect," Kozak said quietly. "This one is it, sir."

"All right, nice choice," Mr. Derby said. "Now, as to the wake—"

"No wake," Kozak said. "You will bring the body to the church. Closed coffin."

"Sir, my people have done an extraordinary job. You may have a wake. Mr. Smirnoff's face was not impacted, and his suit will cover—"

"No wake. No open coffin," Kozak said. "Josef will be honored and buried."

"As you wish, sir. As you wish. This is a painful time for you as a friend. I do suggest that you consider a viewing, for other friends—"

"No," Kozak said. "Our business is quite complete. We have our own cars for the services. You will bring Josef as arranged to the church. And arrange for the transport from there to the cemetery."

"Yes, Mr. Kozak. Arrangements have been made. He will be brought from the church to the cemetery. Now, the cemetery is over in Miami. You will need police officers for the journey as friends follow for the last services, something which, of course, we take care of for you."

Kozak waved a hand in the air. "Do what is needed."

He was anxious to leave; Jacob held back and assured Derby, "Someone will be by with the final check."

He then followed Victor Kozak back out to the car.

The man waited by the passenger's side as Jacob clicked the door open.

Kozak was trembling when he sat. Jacob hurried around to the driver's seat. He didn't have to push; Kozak appeared ready to speak.

"It's not real—I was there. I was there for a hail of bullets. I watched my friend fall, I saw the blood. And yet, it's not real. Not until you see he is laid into the ground. Yes, it is indeed a hard time. You know this. You have laid a wife to rest."

Jacob was still a moment.

A deceased wife was in his fake dossier. It was always best, when creating such a lie, to incorporate many details of life that were real. That helped an agent live the lie that was being created.

"It was a long time ago, right?" Victor Kozak asked.

Yes, a lifetime ago. He'd fallen in love with Sabrina Marshall the minute he had seen her. It had been tenth grade. They'd quickly become an item; he, a high school jock, Sabrina the smart one. They'd married and gone off to college together, and even after graduation when they'd planned their perfect life, talked about starting a family...

The cancer had found her. It had cared nothing about youthful dreams.

"It was a long time ago, yes," Jacob said softly.

A long, long time ago. Many women in between; savvy, bright women, some in business, some in politics, but none in law enforcement.

None like Jasmine, someone he had seen from afar

who had nevertheless seemed to enter into his soul. He barely knew her. Maybe, though, he knew her enough.

Maybe, when this was over... When this was all over, Jasmine would no longer be playing a role. She would go back to her passion, being cop in a major crime unit. And he would go where the Bureau sent him, because he was good at what he did, and he did believe, no matter what unbelievable things were going on in the world, that what he did was right. One good man, or maybe many good men, could make the world a better place.

Sabrina had believed that, too.

"I'm sorry," Kozak said.

"So am I," Jacob said softly. "So am I."

"But now, this woman, this Jasmine—she means something to you?"

"Yes," Jacob said simply.

"When Natasha brought her in, I knew, too, there was something about her. Women...most often, they are just part of business, and that's how it must be. So few have that inner fire. But, now and then...one enchants the mind, eh?"

"Yes," Jacob agreed. "This one in particular...there is something that appeals to me on many levels."

"She's all yours," Kozak said.

Jacob lowered his head. He was pretty sure he knew how Jasmine would feel about being granted to a man as payment for his friendship.

Heading back to Washington Street, Jacob cut down Meridian Avenue. As they neared the Holocaust Memorial of the Greater Miami Jewish Federation, Kozak made a little sound.

The memorial was a heart-wrenching, well-conceived artwork, created by survivors, respected and honored by a community. Statues and plaques told a story that tore at the human soul.

Jacob had been there several times through the years. His own past was a checkered piece of all manner of peoples, from the free world and from areas of great subjugation; his Russian mother had a background that included royalty, his Israeli father had parents who had barely made it out of Germany. Jacob was eternally grateful they had chosen the United States as a place to raise their own family—he knew he'd had a relatively easy and privileged start to life.

He was surprised when Kozak asked him to stop.

"You want to get out and walk around?" Jacob asked.

Kozak shook his head. "I just want to look."

Jacob sat next to him in silence.

"World War II. A brutal business. Hitler wanting to exterminate a race of people. Stalin…twenty million Russians were also killed, you know, between the enemy and Stalin."

"Yes, I am aware."

"Young people these days…they don't always know."

"Education is everything," Jacob murmured.

One of the sculptures at the outdoor memorial was especially poignant. It depicted a body, as many bodies had been found. Prisoners had not just gone to the death camps to be gassed and cremated; they'd gone to be a work force, and they'd been all but starved as they worked.

The body was skeletal and depicted in bronze. They

were a distance from the sculpture and couldn't see it completely. But Jacob had seen it before. And he knew that Kozak had, too.

Kozak turned to Jacob. "My grandmother survived by hiding in plain sight in Berlin. My grandfather was a Russian soldier, hiding the fact that he was also Jewish. When the Soviet Army closed in on Berlin, my grandfather found my grandmother, who was terrified. She had been in living with a Christian German couple who were appalled by the death and terror around them. She'd been told, however, there was less torture if you quickly admitted what you were. When he found her, she said, *'Juden.'* But you see, my grandfather said, *'Juden*, yes, I am *Juden*, too.' They were married, and they stayed married for the next forty years. They died in the same year. I believe he died of a broken heart when he lost her, because she passed away first."

"They had years together. It is still a beautiful story," Jacob said.

Kozak turned to him. "I have told you this story because maybe it will help you believe me. I don't kill people. I don't torture, and I don't kill."

Jacob couldn't help himself. Looking at Kozak, he said, "I beg to differ—slightly. Drugs kill."

Kozak waved a hand in the air. "Drugs kill, but people have a choice. But we do nothing where others have not made a choice. The addict must choose life. The drugs exist with or without my participation. We may as well get rich. Am I a good man? No. Am I a cold-blooded killer? No. Take what you will from that. But I did not kill my friend Josef."

Jacob nodded slowly.

Neither spoke for a moment.

He put the car back into gear and drove back south, to Washington Street and the club. They hadn't been away long.

"So, now," Kozak said, "you will find out what happened to Josef, yes?"

"I will do my damnedest," Jacob said.

JORGE REALLY DID put on a Netflix marathon of *Desperate Housewives*.

Jasmine nervously paced the room. "We should be doing something," she said.

"Jasmine, here's the thing. We are doing something," Jorge told her. "Okay, so, you're not a fan. What should we watch?"

"I can't. I can't sit still."

"You stink at this."

"Sorry!"

"All right," Jorge said. "I'll check in with Captain Lorenzo. Will that help?"

"Maybe."

He took out his phone and called. Jasmine watched him as he spoke, assuring Lorenzo they were both fine and they were proceeding with the work and their relationship with the FBI was moving along smoothly. Then he asked if anything else had been discovered, listened a while and then thanked Lorenzo and promised he'd be the one in touch.

"Well?" Jasmine demanded, burning with impatience.

"There's a Miccosukee village where they sell hand-made clothing, arts and crafts—and have alligator shows," he said.

"I know. It's out on Tamiami Trail, just west of Shark Valley."

"There's a fellow who lives not far from the village. He raises alligators, sells them to various venues for alligator wrestling. Handles them from the time they hatch." Jorge stopped speaking.

"And?"

"One of his young alligators died, and he didn't know why, so there was a necropsy done on the gator."

"And?"

"They found a hand. He reported it. And it's been brought in to the medical examiner, and they believe it belonged to one of the dead men found out there. They're hoping to get an ID. I don't know a lot about alligator stomach acids, but…well, they're still hoping to get something."

"I know what they're going to find," Jasmine said. "There won't be a match. I'm willing to bet that whoever is doing this is clever enough to have hired undocumented newcomers to do the deed."

"Maybe. Someone desperate and grateful for any work that doesn't go on the books."

Jasmine nodded. "Jorge, what do you think of Natasha?"

"She's all business."

"Yes. And she was in charge of the models. Of the show. And we all suspect she is sleeping with Victor Kozak, but—"

"Maybe she slept with Josef, too. And maybe she

was sleeping with Victor because Josef tired of her, and maybe—"

"Maybe!" Jasmine said. "If only we had a definite."

She started to pace again, thinking, trying to remember every move Natasha had made on the day of the show.

Jorge groaned and turned back to *Desperate Housewives*.

"Hey," Jacob said to Alejandro Suarez. He was on guard downstairs, at the door to the club offices and staging area.

"Hey," Suarez said. He studied Jacob. He was puffing on a cigarette, leaned against the wall. He grinned suddenly. "Are you some new kind of enforcer?"

"I'm just an art dealer."

Suarez studied him. "Sure. But hey, I just work here. Kozak said you were going to talk to us."

"Do you remember anyone—anyone you didn't know—at the grand opening?"

Suarez laughed. "Anyone I didn't know? What? Do I look like I rub elbows with the rich and famous regularly?" There must have been something ominous in Jacob's look, because he quickly sobered up.

"Did you see anyone upstairs?" Jacob clarified. "We know that the killers were on the balcony."

"Yeah, that's what the cops said." Suarez sighed, reaching in his jacket pocket for another cigarette. He lit it with his current smoke. The man was a few years younger than Garibaldi and maybe a few inches taller in height. "I came in through the upstairs. We all reported to Josef, who said the balcony would be closed off. That would leave all of us down on the floor with the hired cops—you don't do anything that big without hiring cops."

"Right."

"When I checked in, the girls were all getting dressed. The band members were in the green room, making cracks about the girls. I guess they planned on having them in to party later. That idea went all to hell, huh?"

"You saw the band, Josef Smirnoff, Natasha and the girls. Anyone else?"

"Ivan was already down at the bar. The caterers were never allowed upstairs. Oh, Victor Kozak was downstairs already when I came in, seeing to a last-minute check on the place. When I joined him, he pointed out that the balcony stairways—there's one set near the entrance on both sides—were roped off with velvet cords. They didn't want people up on the balcony. There's only one door up on the second floor, but it almost leads right into the office, and they didn't want anyone going up because of the office. And he didn't want anybody trying to grab selfies with the girls or the band or anything. If anyone headed toward the stairs, we were to politely stop them. And if they tried again, we were to politely escort them out."

"But no one tried to get up the stairs?"

"There were big signs attached to the velvet cords that said No Admittance. I think most people honor signs like that. Hey, it wasn't supposed to be... It was supposed to be a cool grand opening. No one expected any violence. If anything, we'd have had to throw out a drunk."

"But you saw no one. Nothing?"

Suarez shook his head. "No! I mean, I could have told you before the cops did their investigating that the shooters had to have been on the balcony. But there was a stampede. You know that. I admit, I froze for a second. Then I went to work getting people out."

"Was anyone on the back door—where we are now?"

"I'm assuming it was locked up tight. We were all on the main floor. But…"

"But?"

"I don't know what weapons were used. I was thinking that whoever was up there… Well, if they pocketed their weapons, in all the confusion, they might have come down the stairs and run out with everyone else. Or…" Suarez paused, shaking his head.

"What?"

"They could have come out the back, out of this door. But you see, I don't understand how that would be possible. Cops were already in here. They were crawling all over the area within minutes. I can't believe they wouldn't have seen three men with guns run out this door." Suarez seemed as mystified as Garibaldi had been.

Two down; one to go.

They were great liars—or they had planned their stories well.

Jacob thanked him, then turned and hurried back up the stairs. He found Sasha Antonovich outside the door to Kozak's office. Like Alejandro Suarez, he seemed at ease—bored, probably—as he stood by the door.

"My turn, eh?" Antonovich asked him. He shrugged. "We just look stupid. Kozak said you were going to try to do what the police seem be failing at. So. What can I tell you?"

"What *can* you tell me?"

Antonovich was older than both Suarez and Garibaldi. Remembering all the info he had been given, Jacob knew Antonovich had been with Josef Smirnoff the longest—well over a decade. His hair was beginning to gray, just at the temples. Fine lines were appearing around his light brown eyes, and he wore a weary look.

The man shook his head, his expression grim. "What do I know? That it wasn't just a random shooting? That someone was after Josef? I'm sure you believe that, too. How the hell did they get in? They had to have been on a guest list. I don't know who they were, what they looked like... There were hundreds of people here. They could have been with the caterers, they could have gotten in with the off-duty cops. The cops came from all over the city. Some of them, the Miami Beach guys, were naturally on duty, but in here... Josef wanted lots of security, so we hired people from all over the city. I've been thinking about it, too."

"A dirty cop? Is that what you're thinking?"

"Maybe. Or just someone dressed up like a cop. The other guys might not have known—they came from precincts all over the city. I keep thinking, though, that the guys investigating the shooting had to have thought of all this."

"I imagine they have. I would think they're working all angles."

"Three bodies found down off the Tamiami Trail—no hands, no heads. Sure as hell sounds like a hit to me."

"I agree. I'll bet just about all of law enforcement would."

"Definitely not just a domestic disturbance," Antonovich said, not amused at his own attempt at humor. "The door up here… I was the first one to check it, along with one of Miami Beach's finest. It was locked. If they came through that way, they had a key."

"It's been rekeyed."

"Yeah."

"Well, thanks," Jacob said. He started to walk away.

Antonovich called him back. "Hey," he said softly. "You get that son of a bitch. You get whoever killed Josef. He was all right. Yes, he sold drugs, he sold arms, he sold…women. But he was an okay guy, you know?"

"Sure," Jacob said quietly. He didn't agree that Smirnoff was "an okay guy," but he did believe that a murderer should be brought to justice. Antonovich seemed passionate about catching Smirnoff's killer.

"You're going to the funeral?" Antonovich asked.

"Yes, of course."

"I want to go over to the cemetery. It's old—and pretty big. Angels and archangels…and small mausoleums and large mausoleums."

"Places for a shooter to hide?" Jacob asked.

Antonovich nodded grimly. "I'll be checking it out," he said.

"Good. And good to know."

Jacob turned away. He knew the cemetery, on Eighth Street, or Calle Ocho, in the city. It was a beautiful cemetery. Gothic archways, handsome landscaping... and dozens of places for a shooter to hide—if Kozak was next in line, and there was still someone making a power play.

Antonovich appeared to be bitter about Smirnoff's death, as eager as any to pinpoint a killer. But Jacob just couldn't be sure what he felt he'd learned.

Either the goons were just hired muscle...or they had put together a trio of stone-cold killers, just waiting for the right moment to sweep in.

Which would mean that Victor Kozak was scheduled to die, as well.

Chapter Nine

Jorge left Jasmine's apartment at about 4:00 p.m. "I don't think I'm supposed to be hanging around here forever," he told her. "Despite the amount of fun and entertainment you're providing me, I've just got to go."

"What are you going to do?" Jasmine asked.

He smiled. "Hole up in my room with computer files. I'd rather hang around the beach. Check out the scene, hear what I can hear. But I guess that will be nothing. Rats. Guess I'll be hanging out with my computer."

"You don't think that's dangerous?"

"No, Bernie in tech helped me out. I hit a key, and only a genius could find my erased history or files or anything. I'll be okay. You'll be with a hot guy—I won't." He grinned at her.

She didn't grin back.

He walked over to her and hugged her. "Partner, I can feel it. Mary is going to be okay. And you're going to be okay, and I'm going to be okay. Okay? Oh, and pretty man is going to be okay, too."

That one, at last, made her grin. "I'm sure. Fine, go work. And I'll—"

"Keep pacing."

"Yep, I'll keep pacing."

Jorge was gone; she was alone.

She found herself pondering Jacob Wolff. He seemed to know everything about her. Of course, he was with the federal government. She was MDPD—not any lesser, but still, a total difference in privileges and responsibilities. She was, however, sure that if the operation had been planned differently, she'd know much more about him. She didn't even know anything about the fake man, much less the real Jacob Wolff. She was probably lucky she knew his real name.

He probably even knew that her parents were working with a charity rebuilding houses down in Haiti.

She was working up a fair amount of aggravation by the time Jacob Wolff arrived at her apartment; she didn't notice at first that he seemed worn and weary when he walked in.

"Anything? Do you have anything at all?" she asked. "I believe that Connor will be with Kari again tonight—and I'm very afraid for what will happen to her after that."

"We've got field agents watching Connor. They can find nothing to suggest that he's a murderer."

"Oh, really? So, in your usual line of work, people advertise the fact that they're murderers?"

The way he looked at her, she wished she could swallow the words back.

"I don't know anything yet. I have a firm belief that the men just found in the Glades were the killers. I believe they worked for someone who copied the key to the balcony, and they didn't bother to escape that way—they just blended with a panicked crowd that was trampling one another. I actually don't believe Kozak called the shots, but I can't be sure. What have you got?"

"Why do you believe Kozak is innocent—of murder, that is?"

Jacob was looking straight ahead, at the television. "I think he would do a great deal to make money, but I think he's seen enough of death."

"What makes you believe that?"

He turned to look at her. "He has a past very much like my own. My father was born in Israel to parents who barely escaped the Nazis. My maternal grandfather made it out of one of Stalin's purges. I was lucky. I was born here. Almost right here—Mount Sanai. But my parents had to work hard. We were always just scraping by. We were here several years, and then in New York. I went to high school in Manhattan, and on to Columbia University with tuition assistance through the military—and then after my service, the FBI. I've been under the direction of great men with the Bureau for years, always FBI, but recently, FBI in conjunction with Homeland Security—and I've seen what's really, really ugly. So, I allow myself to be wrong. But I talk to people. I try to hear what's beneath what they say. I'm not perfect. I have been fooled now and then, but not often."

"So, you're the only one with a tough past, huh?"

He didn't reply. He looked away. "We'll need a place to go to dinner. We're definitely being watched, and while I'm not worried about our three stooges—who aren't all that stupid, I don't think—we're being watched by someone else, as well. I'm itching to get to the cemetery, but I know I have to trust others. I've called ahead. Miami field agents will be in the cemetery, in the mausoleums, around every angel high enough to cover a man. So, for us, for now…"

She sat next to him. He looked over at her.

She hesitated and then said, "I'm sorry. My past was a piece of cake. My parents are as sweet and kind as a pair of over overgrown lovebirds. I wanted to be a cop because my dad was a cop, and he was influential in catching a serial rapist at work on Eighth Street near Westchester. He somehow managed to teach us about the evils of the world and see the beauty in it, as well. He never whined about me becoming a cop because I was a woman, and neither did my mother. I never wanted for anything. I was helped through college. I… I'm sorry."

He reached across the sofa and took her hand. And they weren't playacting for anyone, because no one was in the room.

"I know," he told her. He grinned. "I've seen your file."

"And I haven't seen yours. I don't even know… Are you married?"

"I was."

"Divorced?"

"No."

"Oh. I'm…sorry."

"It's been a long time," he said.

"Still."

He shrugged and smiled. "You would have liked her."

"I'm sure I would have," she said softly.

He was studying her, to a point where she flushed. "What?"

"I'm a classic case—that's what an analyst would say, I'm pretty sure. Married young, the sweet love of youth, lost that love, plowed into work, kind of a loner. Way too much time undercover for serious relationships..."

She was definitely blushing by then.

"So I've read your file, but there's nothing in there that explains the you that Jorge knows—and told me all about."

"I'm going to kill him."

"Don't. He's your partner. And he loves you."

"Okay, so I don't have a haunted history. And I didn't lose anyone. I mean, I didn't lose a husband or a lover. I just..."

"Well, if you don't go out, you don't meet anyone."

"Seriously, I'm going to kill Jorge."

He grinned. "I really like Jorge. So?"

"Okay, I don't often work undercover. But I do work major crimes. And even though you have shifts with other officers and you work with other agencies, there are times you have to be dedicated to the case instead of getting to know the people you're working with. When you're the one a loved one of a victim is depending on, or you're the one who's gained the trust of a young witness, or..."

Her voice trailed. His elbow was angled on the couch and he was smiling as he watched her.

"Many men find female police detectives to be intimidating," she went on. "And many of those who don't are a little scary themselves. It's not that I don't go out, or I don't believe in going out—"

"Just haven't found the right guy?"

She shrugged, rising nervously. She hadn't expected the evening to turn into a tell-all, especially when she sure as hell couldn't tell the truth about her feelings regarding him.

She walked over to the door. "I guess we'd better go to dinner. Let's see…where haven't we been?"

He stood and met her at the entry. "I don't know. Where do you suggest?" They were facing each other, ridiculously close.

And then, they both heard a shuffling sound, just outside.

"Someone following you?" she mouthed to Jacob.

He carefully looked out. "Maybe," he mouthed back. He drew his gun. He checked the door, and she saw that he had double-bolted it.

To her surprise, he threw the door open.

Night was falling. But the way the apartment building had been laid out, the pool and patio area faced the west, and while the night encroached, the lowering sun created a sky of bold beauty. Soon, the radiant colors would be gone, and it would be the darkness that reigned.

"Ah, what a lovely night. Maybe later…" Jacob said, his voice carrying. And then, still speaking with a full rich voice, he turned to her. "On second thought, why don't we order in tonight?" he asked.

Was there someone out there? A figure, to the side in the shadows, hunkered down in a lawn chair?

The door was fully open. They were on display, and he was looking down at her with his brilliant blue eyes, so handsome and so startling against his dark hair and bronzed face.

Jacob pulled her into his arms and kissed her. And this time, he pulled her close. His mouth came down on hers while his arms encompassed her, his hands sliding down low against her back, drawing her ever closer, his tongue parting her lips and slipping deep within her mouth.

The door slowly closed behind them while they backed inside the apartment, locked in the passionate embrace.

He was still kissing her as he eased one hand away, once again double-bolting the lock. She heard the sound as the bolts slid into place. And only then did his hold ease, his lips part from hers.

They were still so close. He looked down at her, and she could still feel the dampness of her lips, burning as they seemed to do when he touched her.

"I think…" she murmured, and he leaned closer, as if to hear her. His lips were almost upon hers again, his body was all but touching hers. To her amazement, she almost smiled, and she said softly, "Oh, screw this!"

She moved back into his arms. She was tall, but she moved up on tiptoe, the length of her body against his. She moved her mouth that one inch closer, found his lips and kissed him, parting his mouth, delving deep within it with her tongue, initiating all. She was stunned by her own movements, but more so by the depth of the longing and desire that was sweeping through her.

The kiss deepened and deepened. She pressed closer to him, flush against him, and felt his hands travel down the length of her body. The kiss broke, and he eased back slightly.

She felt she was panting like an idiot, and he had moved away. A flush of heat broke over her, and her limbs began to tremble. She had to force herself to bring her eyes to his, but when she did, she saw he was still watching her, intensely alert. He smiled slightly and said, "Ummmm." He was still holding her, and then he arched a brow and whispered, "Oh, screw this."

He swept her up, higher, into his arms. His mouth found hers again, but he moved as he kissed her, across the floor, toward the apartment bedroom. In seconds, they were lying down together on the bed. He braced himself over her, and said softly, "Only if it's what you really want."

She smiled. His pausing to question her, to be very sure, added to her sense of attraction and desperation.

She reached out, drawing his face down to hers again. She replied with her hands on his face, caressing his face as she drew him to her. "Yes. So much." They kissed again...just kissed, and then he straddled above her, doffing his jacket. The Glock he carried was evident then, and he reached back for the gun and holster, leaning over to set them on the dresser.

He looked down at her a moment.

"Mine's inside the bedside drawer, to the left," she

told him. Now they both knew where to reach if they were threatened in any way at any time.

That solved, he struggled from his shirt; she rose up to help him. He was still in trousers, socks and shoes. He halfway rolled from her, divesting his clothing, and she slipped out of the cool knit dress she'd been wearing, as well as her bra and panties.

To her surprise, he suddenly made an urgent sound, almost like a growl, rising to meet her again.

Naked flesh against naked flesh, he whispered, "So wrong of me. I knew the moment I saw you on the runway that you were extraordinary, you were grace and laughter and beauty, and I wanted you, but I didn't know what it would mean when I knew you…"

When his mouth found hers again, she felt the burn that had teased her lips become something of a raging wildfire that snaked down the length of her body. She allowed herself to roam free with her hands, loving the curve of his shoulders, the clench of muscle in his shoulders and down his back. She felt his body harden against her own, and she couldn't wrap herself tightly enough to him, to be both almost in his skin and touch him just the same.

They fell back on the bed together and she lay on top of him, landing kisses on his neck and his shoulders, the hard planes of his stomach, and moving lower against his body.

His hands grabbed her back, and they flipped in the bed. His mouth fell upon her throat and her breasts and lingered and teased and caressed. Those kisses continued downward, and she arched and writhed against him, finding his flesh and returning each touch of passion and hunger and longing.

She thought she would burn to a cinder, she was so alive, burning with a need unlike anything she'd ever known, wanting the play to go on forever, yet desperate that something be touched, that he be within her, as well.

And then he was, and they were moving, and moving, and moving...

They rolled, their lips melded together again and the rock of his hips was incredible. The sense of him within her was almost more than she could bear, the absolute sweetness, the rise of that fire, that longing to be ever more a part of him. Rising...and bursting out upon her like a flow of liquid gold.

The night seemed to sweep in all around her for long moments as she felt little bits of ecstasy shoot through her, ebbing bit by incredible bit, until she felt the damp sheen of their flesh, still so taut together, the rise and fall of her breath, the rock-hard pounding of her heart. And him, still holding her, still clinging in the darkness to the awesome beauty of what had been. So real, flesh and blood and pulse and their gasps for air...

They didn't speak at first; they just breathed.

And then he whispered softly, "I don't think I'll be putting that in the report."

She smiled and turned to him. "I understand you're often by the book. Forgive me."

"Forgive you?" He straddled her again, catching her hands and leaning low, his eyes alight with humor and tenderness. "Ah, my dear Detective Adair. It is I who must ask forgiveness. On second thought, no. Can't ask forgiveness. This was—"

"Incredible," she whispered.

"More than incredible. I don't know the words... Maybe there are none."

She pulled him back to her, and the kiss they shared was sweet and tender, and still, she knew, could arouse again at any second.

He pulled away and got out of bed suddenly. Light from the living room swept into the bedroom and she could see the full leanly muscled perfection of his tightly honed body in the doorway. He wasn't self-conscious as he padded out to the living room. Curious, she rose up on an arm.

Then he was back, every movement sleek and fluid, and he fell down beside her again. "Checking the door," he murmured.

"There's still someone out there?" she asked.

"Sitting by the pool. We'll order in," he told her.

He moved toward her and she jumped back suddenly, stricken. She'd been so enraptured with the man she'd been lucky enough to come to know that she had all but forgotten this wasn't an ordinary job.

She was looking for Mary. And even though Mary still seemed beyond her reach...

"Kari!" she exclaimed. "I'm worried, Jacob. What about Kari—and Mr. Connor?"

"I'll call in," he assured her. He found his jacket where he'd flung it earlier and dug his phone out of the pocket. After a minute, he had the info.

"Kari is back at her apartment."

"She's all right? And they're back inside?"

"Just Kari is back at her place. Connor took her out for a steak dinner and then a moonlit stroll on the beach. Then he brought her home. He left shortly, a smile on his face."

"Oh," Jasmine said. "Jacob, you don't think she'll be in any trouble with the gang for…for not sleeping with him?"

"No, I don't think she'll be in trouble."

Jasmine was still unsure. "He's being watched, Jasmine. Kari will be okay. Someone will get to Connor soon enough."

"Kari was worried though. I think she felt something was off. And I can't forget about Mary…"

"We'll find Mary. I swear it," he told her.

She believed him. And miraculously, she could move forward with her own night, grateful that the young blonde woman was all right. For now.

And there was nothing they could do. Not for the night.

She moved forward, catching his face, looking up into the dazzling blue of his eyes. "Thank you."

He kissed her again, that tender kiss… But the kiss deepened, and then it began to travel, and he was kissing her breasts again, affording each the most tender caresses, and her belly and thighs, bringing that erotic fire with every touch.

She let the night seize her again, and she returned his caresses, unable to stop seeking more and more of him, know the taste of his skin, the taste of him.

They embraced tightly, and he was within her, and

they rolled, and she was atop him, and this time they laughed and teased and whispered.

And then they lay together again, just breathing, still afrire, savoring the beauty of the darkness of the night, the coolness of the sheets beneath their bodies.

She was the one to sit up and straddle him this time.

He smiled, catching her hands with his. "Leave it to a cop to always want to be on top." He rolled her over, covering her with his body.

"And leave it to a Fed to think he must be in control."

"This Fed," he said softly, "is just happy to be with you."

She smiled back at him, wishing that the night would never end; that this was all they needed in reality and that the world would go away.

It could not.

He rolled from her, standing. "Food—we need to order food."

"I am hungry," she agreed.

She leaped out of bed, reaching to the foot of it for the caftan robe she kept there. He found his boxers but bothered with nothing else. He was already out in the living room, his phone drawn from his pocket. He looked at her. "I have a delivery service so, Chinese, Indian, Italian... Steaks? Seafood? What's your pleasure?"

You are my pleasure! she thought.

She managed not to say it out loud. "I'm easy. Food-wise," she added quickly. "Anything."

"Wow. I found one with pizza and champagne. Now there's an interesting combo. But I don't think that champagne... Not tonight."

"Not tonight," she agreed.

It was one thing to be drunk on desire when you were supposed to be drunk on desire. But quite another to have anything that might alter the mind with a goon outside on the porch.

"I don't believe we're in any danger, but I've seen things change quickly," he told her. "Ah, Thai food!"

"Perfect."

She stood near him and looked over his shoulder as he went through the offerings. They decided on one noodle dish and one rice dish.

Jasmine suddenly felt extremely awkward.

"Coffee!" she said. "I should make some coffee."

She started to walk into the kitchen. He caught her arm and pulled her back to him, holding her there, looking into her eyes. "Please, don't go away from me," he said softly.

She knew he didn't mean she shouldn't go into the kitchen and make coffee.

"I...it sounds like a line," she told him, "but I've never...in my life...just done this so quickly... I guess I don't know how to act."

"And I hope you believe me. I've always drawn a line. Until tonight."

She stood on her toes and kissed his lips lightly. "I won't go away," she promised.

She made coffee; Thai food arrived. Jacob made a point of answering the door still clad just in his boxers. He was careful to double-bolt the door again, and then to bring his Glock back out to sit on the table while they ate.

"You know, I'm a damned good markswoman," she told him.

He smiled at her. "I'd expect no less." He picked at a strand of the noodles. "Oh, by the way, Kozak gave you to me today." His smiled deepened as he saw her stiffen. "Sorry. All in a role."

She hesitated. "But in truth, I give myself where I choose."

"And so do I," he told her.

She laughed softly. Much of the Thai food went uneaten; they wound up laughing over a noodle they had both chosen.

And then they wound up in one another's arms again.

THERE WAS A knock on the door.

Jacob rolled out of bed, instantly awake. He grabbed his trousers and then his gun. Jasmine followed him out of bed in a flash, slipping on a robe, going for her own weapon.

He took a quick glance at the clock on the nightstand: 9:00 a.m. He headed out of the bedroom quickly, with Jasmine on his heels.

But one look out the peephole had Jacob unlocking the door. "It's all right. A friend," he told her.

Jorge stepped in, looked at both of them and then smiled.

"Method acting!" he said. "I like it. Just wondering what the hell took you two so long."

Chapter Ten

The funeral service was long. Speaking in Russian, the priest delivered the service with all respect and care—while the man might have known about Smirnoff and his deeds, he didn't judge when it came time for a man to meet his Maker. It was actually beautiful, though Jacob was sure many in the congregation had no idea what was being said.

Victor Kozak gave an emotional speech about his friend, and he did so in English for the benefit of the mourners who had gathered.

Many had come out to pay their respects—not so many would be invited to the celebration of life that would come later, at the club. Equally, not so many would travel with the funeral train that would follow the hearse to the cemetery.

Jacob had spoken with his Miami counterpart, Dean Jenkins. He knew agents were already waiting at the cemetery.

It would be a fine day for an attempt on Victor Kozak's life.

Jenkins also filled him in on what was happening

with events at the morgue, and with the local crime scene technicians.

"They identified one of the dead men, from the hand they got out of the alligator's gullet. Ain't technology great? Although, to be honest, it wasn't fingerprints or anything like that. One of my guys working in Little Havana recognized the ring.

"The victim was Leonardo Gonzalez—an undocumented Venezuelan immigrant. He and a few of his fellows had traveled through Mexico and, according to our agent, onto a cruise ship and into Miami. He'd been a contract killer at home and was looking for work in Little Havana. He was happy to work for anyone but was looking for connections in the Little Havana area because he didn't speak any English.

"Anyway...according to our sources, he was the kind of really bad guy taking serious advantage of the criminal activity going on down there right now, but he might have crossed another crime lord, meaning it was time for him to get out. But he had his own little gang. I'm working under the assumption our other two headless bodies are associates of his."

"Thanks— Anything new on Donald McPherson Connor?"

"We followed him. He was a perfect gentleman with the young lady. And he left her at her door. An agent is still outside. He could have followed Connor, or he could have kept his eye on her. He chose to protect the one we know to be an innocent. Anyway, we have a new crew out on the streets today. Oh, they're checking in at your art gallery, too, making sure that Special Agent Partridge is doing okay."

"Thanks. Hey, should I be getting a new phone?"

"Not to worry, I'm listed as a local artist. You any closer?" Jenkins asked him.

"I don't know. I'm going to see what happens at the funeral."

They ended their call, and Jacob joined the mourners, making himself one with Ivan Petrov and the three goons.

Jasmine was not invited to this part of the day; she would be at the club, preparing to work with the food and drinks that would be served. He tried not to worry. He knew she was an accomplished policewoman, and he believed she was an excellent markswoman. She was also vulnerable, though he had warned her that she should be wary at all times—and armed if any way possible.

She knew that, of course.

Kozak hadn't asked Jacob to drive to the cemetery; he wanted him next to him in his car, behind the driver, who would be Antonovich.

Jacob couldn't help but wonder if Kozak was afraid that Antonovich could shoot them both if Jacob was driving—he'd be easy prey for a man sitting behind him.

They arrived safely at the cemetery. It was just west of the downtown area known as Calle Ocho. The cemetery had recently joined with two different companies that had been offering funeral arrangements and grave sites since the 1850s back in Cuba. It was at the edge of a neighborhood close to downtown known as Little Havana.

But like most of Miami, anyone and everyone might be here.

They entered through Gothic arches. The grounds were sweeping, well tended and beautiful. Trees cast shady spots everywhere, and the park stretched for long blocks. They drove around a winding trail until they reached the canopy that stood over the area where the body of Josef Smirnoff would be laid to rest.

The cars parked; Jacob got out and waited for Kozak to emerge from the car, as well. He looked around. A lovely marble angel stood guard over a nearby family lot; a small family mausoleum stood about fifty yards away. Another, about a hundred yards farther out.

They were under a gracious old oak, near to a grouping of military headstones. Down a bit farther was a large concrete memorial to a man who had been a Mason and with the Mahi Shrine. His memorial gave witness to the fact that he had spent forty years as a Shriner, dedicating his time to raising funds for the children's hospital.

Probably a great guy. Right now, Jacob had to be certain that his memorial wasn't hiding a sniper.

He continued his scan of the area. The large mausoleum with its beautiful stained-glass windows, known to house many, many bodies, was perhaps a hundred yards behind them. A great place for a sniper to hide.

He reminded himself that the Miami agents knew this cemetery, where to be and where to watch.

And still he was on high alert.

"There, Mr. Kozak," Antonovich said, coming around to Kozak's side. "The chairs in front, sir. Those are for you and those who were close to Josef."

Sticking to Kozak's side like a piece of lint, Jacob led the man to the chairs.

Josef Smirnoff might not have been a cold-blooded killer, but he sure as hell had been a criminal. Victor Kozak had taken over from him, and while he might not be a cold-blooded killer either, he was also a major criminal.

But the showing of respectable people at the cemetery was large enough; the local news media brought trucks to the winding road that led through the very large cemetery—another place for a shooter to hide. Politicians and other respectable citizens arrived to say goodbye to Smirnoff.

Jacob sat back as the priest gave the graveside prayers. He had to have faith in his fellow agents. But just as he had settled—still alert and ready—a latecomer arrived at the grave site.

It was the man who so disturbed Jasmine.

Donald McPherson Connor.

The club was a bustle of activity when Jasmine arrived, even though it was early. The catering company personnel included two chefs, two wine stewards and six members of a cleanup crew.

Jasmine and Jorge reported right away to the dressing room. The servers were suited out appropriately— men in tuxes, women in similar versions with short skirts instead of pants—and shown the various food stations and the additional bars.

"Remember, today, you serve quickly, politely and quietly. We honor Josef," Natasha instructed. "You all understand? Behavior is beyond circumspect."

Stopping by one of the makeup tables where Jasmine had just harnessed her own hair in a braid at the back of her neck, Jorge told her, "Five City of Miami Beach cops, all aware to watch for trouble—hired on by Kozak." He lowered his head to her, pretending to smooth back a piece of her hair. "The chef at the first table is a plant—FBI. We have representation from MDPD as well—Detective Birch. You've worked with her. She'll be on the arm of one of our young politicians."

"Sounds good," Jasmine murmured. "Then again, how many cops were prowling the show when Josef was killed?"

"There's a cop at the balcony door. If anyone is going to start shooting, it won't be from the balcony." He leaned closer still, pretending to flick a piece of nonexistent lint from her brow. "FBI is crawling over the cemetery, too. Thing is, the killer must know. Unless he—or she—is really an egotistical bastard, nothing will happen today."

Nothing would happen. This would go on...

Jorge grinned suddenly. "You look different."

"I don't dress this way often."

"No, it's the way your eyes are shining."

"Jorge."

"It's nice to see you happy."

She looked at him and then lowered her head, ruefully smiling. "I'd like to see you happy."

"Hey, you may. I'm not watched, not the way you are," he told her. "I had some dinner out last night. Sat on the beach."

"Jorge, you have to be—"

"I was careful. Trust me."

He grinned, and she knew it was the truth.

"Jorge, I need you!" Natasha called. "Now, you will take the large silver tray—you have nice long arms. Move through the crowd but offer up the food. Do not interfere with people who are talking. You let them stop. Think of yourselves as courteous machines."

Jorge moved on. Jasmine saw Kari at the next dressing table and she stood, heading over to her.

"Need help with anything?" she asked.

"Nope," Kari said, looking up. "I never can do false eyelashes right, but Natasha says we shouldn't wear them today."

"They're miserable things anyway."

"I agree."

"So, how are you?" Jasmine asked her softly.

"Good. Great, really."

"Great?" Jasmine asked.

Kari smiled. "I know that he's old, but honestly, if I were, say, forty-five instead of twenty-two, well... He has such a great accent. He talked to me about books and plays and he told me so much history about this place that I didn't know... He's kind, Jasmine. So very kind."

"Great to hear. I thought he made you a bit nervous. Are you okay with him now? When do you see him again?"

"Tonight. Later, of course. I told him—and I'm sure Natasha told him—that the club models were working the funeral, and we wouldn't be available until the entire celebration of life came to an end. He told me that, no matter what the hour, he'd like to see me." Kari hesitated a moment and then whispered, "I don't know why I was worried. Jasmine, we had the best dinner. Such a lovely night. He's truly so well educated. And then I thought he would want more. I thought he would want me to sleep with him. Oh! And he talked about Mary. He said she was such a lovely person—he was sure she went on to resume her education. They had talked about school and always having a backup to modeling or acting. He believes she might have headed out to California."

California? Or the pit of an alligator's stomach, somewhere out in the Everglades.

"I guess he's worked with or been a client of these people for a while," Jasmine said.

"Not so long. He told me that the group here—well, Josef Smirnoff first, and now Victor Kozak—knew how to find the most cultured women. He likes to go to the theater and the opera and art shows, and…he needs the right escorts."

"How nice."

"He loves music and musicals, voices!"

The opera…or screams as a woman died beneath a knife?

"Jasmine, he's really such a gentleman. I thought he

might be the type to immediately demand that we sleep together, that…"

"What?"

"That he might want me to do weird things." Her voice dropped to a whisper. "You know, weird sexual things. Scary things." She swallowed. "You know…autoerotic asphyxiation, or maybe not even scary things, just disgusting things. But he didn't even press sleeping with me." She paused, seeming a little uncomfortable, then went on quietly. "We're not specifically *ordered* to sleep with the clients, but there's an understanding that they get what they want if they're paying the price. And that trickles down to us in money and…in prestige on the runway. It's no secret that Natasha's highest earners get the best gigs. But…this guy, no pressure. I'm babbling. I guess I am still maybe a little nervous."

"Kari, you have my number, right? If not, I'll make sure that you do now."

Kari pulled out her phone and Jasmine quickly gave her the number to her burner phone.

"We're having lunch, right?" Kari asked.

"Lunch, yes, but keep your phone near. If you're afraid at any point, you call me immediately!"

Kari frowned, but then smiled. "You can call me, too, you know, except that… Well! You seem just fine, and I imagine…" She broke off and laughed suddenly, leaning forward. "I might have been willing to pay some big bucks myself for that blue-eyed wonder who chose you."

Jasmine smiled weakly.

"You're okay, right?" Kari asked. "I mean, with him."

"Yes, I'm just fine," Jasmine managed.

"What is he like, that Jacob? Those eyes of his... If he ever looked at me the way he looks at you, wow. I'd be putty."

"Putty," Jasmine repeated. "That's me."

"Girls!" Natasha called. "Time to take your stations. Sasha has called—the services at the grave site are ending. We will be ready, the most gracious of hosts and hostesses."

And so, they were on. They all trailed out of the dressing room.

Natasha was by the balcony door; it was open for them to head down the stairs.

Jasmine smiled as she passed Natasha. Only Kozak was supposed to have a key. But Victor wasn't here. And Ivan was downstairs, setting up the main bar, giving orders to the catering company.

Jasmine hurried downstairs along with the others. She knew that somehow, she would get that information to Jacob.

Lightning didn't strike twice...

Unless sometimes, it did.

NO BULLETS RANG out at the cemetery.

The priest, resplendent in his robes, carried through the service. Women had been given roses; they walked past the coffin to drop them down upon it.

"I need a moment," Kozak told his companions.

He was at the coffin alone, except for the four cemetery workers who waited discreetly to see that the coffin was lowered six feet under. The hearse was preparing to leave. Antonovich, Suarez and Garibaldi waited while other mourners filed out to their cars.

Donald McPherson Connor was starting to walk away.

Jacob was a distance from Victor Kozak as it was; he wouldn't be any farther from the man if he walked toward Connor. He excused himself to the trio of bodyguards.

"Mr. Connor!" Jacob called out.

The man stopped walking and looked back at him, eyeing him distastefully. Jacob noticed that he was lean but fit.

Probably plenty strong. Certainly strong enough against a slim blonde girl.

Connor was evidently irritated at having been stopped—by Jacob, at any rate. "Yes, Mr. Marensky, what is it?"

"Well, I just wish to apologize, and I hope that we don't keep bad blood between us. I was, in fact, hoping that you found Miss Anderson to be up to your expectations."

"Miss Anderson is a truly lovely woman. I am enjoying her company."

Jacob forced a smile. "Excellent. She is quite beautiful."

"Not as intriguing as Miss Alamein though," Connor said. He was an oddly dignified man—soft-spoken. "So, Mr. Marenksy, what exactly do you do in relation to the Gold Sun Club?"

Then again, Jacob had seen some of the most innocent and soft-spoken men and women possible turn out to be vicious and as cold as ice.

"We have shared business interests. I run an art gallery," Jacob said.

"So I hear," Connor said, his British accent a little clipped.

"I'd welcome you for a visit. See if there's anything that catches your eye. Just what is your enterprise, sir?"

The man's smile tightened. "No enterprise—other than the stock market. Now there, sir, is bloody criminal action from the get-go, and yet quite legal."

"Ah, I believed that you had worked with Josef—and now Victor."

"I simply require a certain kind of companion."

"I see," Jacob said, still smiling. Just what was it that he required? "Well, sir, I shall see you at the club. I just wished to clear the air between us. Please understand, my arrangements had been made first."

"Oh, yes, I understand perfectly, Mr. Marensky." Connor was still looking at him with watery blue hatred.

"Jacob?" Kozak was calling to him.

"Excuse me," Jacob said, spinning around to return to Victor Kozak's side.

"We must be leaving now," Kozak said.

"Yes, of course."

"You and Connor are good then?" Kozak asked him softly.

"Oh, as good as we can be, Victor. As good as we can be."

"Please, then…" Kozak indicated the road through

the cemetery; theirs was the only car that remained. "Sasha, you will drive."

"Yes, sir," Antonovich said, sliding into the driver's seat.

Garibaldi took the front seat by him. Kozak slid into the back, between Suarez and Jacob. The car rolled out of the cemetery, onto Southwest Eighth Street and then headed for I-95 and the extension out to South Beach.

The funeral itself had gone off without a hitch. Now, all they had to do was make it through the reception—the celebration of life where the mourners would come together and Smirnoff would receive his last honors.

Smirnoff, Kozak and their peers really were criminals. Jacob had seen one too many a decent person cajoled into and then hooked on drugs. And abusing the trust of hopeful girls was reprehensible. But Jacob wanted Kozak prosecuted and locked away—not on a slab with a bullet in his head.

As the car rolled up to Kozak's special parking place at the back of the property, Jacob felt Kozak's hand wind into a vice on his arm.

The man looked at him, and there was fear in his eyes, quickly masked as Garibaldi came around and opened the door.

Jacob got out.

"My friend, I know you will change things!" Kozak said. He caught Jacob's arm again, turning to show him where they were. "Cops—down there, at the end of the block. That guy with the long hair and the beggar's cup at this end? A cop." He pulled Jacob along to show him the men to whom he was referring.

And then he whispered to Jacob, "Here. This is where they will try to kill me. Somewhere here, at the club."

Chapter Eleven

It always amazed Jasmine to see the people who came out for such an event—the last rites for a man they had to have known conducted criminal activities. She was also certain many people on the guest list had not sat through the long religious ceremony at the church, nor attended the final graveside services.

The club was busy within minutes of the door opening.

Ivan stood at the main doors dressed in his best designer suit. Natasha was at his side tonight, ready to greet everyone as they came in; she had finished her busywork, prepared her various crews and was ready to be the grand hostess.

Jasmine had been given a tray of canapés to carry around, and she did so smoothly and easily. Though maintaining her demeanor as a courteous robot was not as easy as it might have been—Kozak and the goons and Jacob had yet to come into the club.

When they finally did, she breathed an inward sigh of relief.

She tried to maneuver herself around to Jacob's position casually, making it part of her regular sweep of the room. When she made it to an area near the street entrance, he was still standing with Kozak and the bodyguards.

"Gentlemen," she said quietly, offering up her tray.

The bodyguards quickly reached for the little quiches. Jacob inclined his head slightly and took a canapé, as well.

Kozak turned to her. "What I need is a drink, Jasmine. Will you get me a vodka? I'm sure that Natasha has seen to it that our hired bartender knows what is my special reserve."

"Yes, of course," Jasmine said.

But Natasha swept by at that moment, giving her a serious frown. "Jasmine, you are to move among our guests."

"Yes, Natasha," she said.

"Natasha," Kozak said softly. "We have many people working the floor. I would like Jasmine to go and get me my drink."

"Victor, I can do that for you," Natasha said.

"You are the hostess. Let Jasmine go," Kozak said. "It's time that I...that I welcome our guests and give my little speech here, eh? But one vodka first!"

Jasmine headed off to the bar. The man there gave her an appreciative look and she smiled in return. "I need a drink for Mr. Kozak—his special reserve. He believes you'll know what it is."

"Yep," the bartender said. "I've been given the bottle and serious instructions. It's a unique vintage from Russia, not sold in the United States." He grinned at her, reaching beneath the bar for the bottle. He got a glass and said, "Just two ice cubes. Rich men and their drinks."

"Thanks," she told him.

"I live to serve. Come see me again!"

She nodded and started to hurry away but turned back. "Did you meet with Mr. Kozak before this event? Did he give you the bottle?" she asked.

He shook his head. "I met with the praying mantis. Oh, sorry—the entire catering company met with Natasha. She gave us strict instructions."

"And the bottle of vodka?"

"No, it was here where she said it would be when I came in. Hey, sorry, I hope she's not a friend of yours—I'm an actor and this catering company keeps me in cash while I'm pounding the pavement. I'm sorry. Please, I didn't mean to be offensive."

"You need to be a lot more careful."

"Please, don't get me fired."

"I won't, but... Never mind. Thank you."

Once again, she turned away, but then something about the situation seemed disturbing. "Would you mind? Give me four more drinks, just like this one but with regular vodka. Something good, just not Kozak's special reserve."

"Anything for you."

She smiled. And prayed that she and Jacob had come to know one another in their undercover roles as well as they had come to know one another personally.

Kozak and Jacob, with Garibaldi, Suarez, and Antonovich behind them, were heading toward the stage.

Jasmine took a step back, her heart pounding, wondering if she was wrong and if she might just cause the entire operation to implode—and put them all, including the guests, in serious danger.

But her hunch was strong. She had seen Natasha with the key.

Natasha was definitely sleeping with Kozak—but had she been sleeping with Josef Smirnoff before? Was she part of what came with taking over the business because she wouldn't be ousted herself?

Jasmine walked toward the men.

"Special for Mr. Kozak, and gentlemen, I believe it was a long day for you, as well. I hope I have not displeased you, Mr. Kozak."

She looked at Jacob, just lowering her eyes at the glass he was to take, and gave the barest shake of her head. He shouldn't drink it. He would know—surely, he would know!

Jacob's striking blue eyes fell on hers. Before Kozak could answer, he said, "That was very thoughtful of you."

"Nice, sweet, as always," Antonovich said happily, and he looked at Kozak.

"Definitely. One vodka, boss, eh?" Suarez asked.

"One vodka," Kozak agreed.

Jasmine dared look around as the men took their drinks. An up-and-coming beach politician was entering with a lovely young news reporter on his arm. Natasha was doing her duty and greeting them.

"I must get to the stage," Kozak said.

"I'll get you there swiftly," Jacob assured him.

Jasmine flashed a smile to all of them. "I'd best get to my canapés," she said. She started to walk away.

"A second?" Jacob asked, looking at Kozak for permission, as well.

"Yes, then you will walk with me, stand by me, at my back," Kozak said.

Jacob smiled and stepped away with Jasmine. She had her chance. "Natasha had the key tonight," she said. "Might be important. Kozak wasn't here. I don't think they plan a shooting."

"Poison in the vodka?"

"I could be wrong."

"Thanks. You gave it to me."

"You knew!"

"I knew," he assured her, and then he squeezed her hand and stepped back.

"To the stage," Kozak said. He seemed very nervous.

As he should be! Jasmine thought.

As he walked away, Kozak took a sip of his vodka. He frowned instantly. The man did know the taste of his special reserve.

And that wasn't his special reserve.

But Jacob guided him toward the stage. Jasmine saw Jacob casually and discreetly set his own glass down on a waiter's tray.

The waiter was Jorge. He looked across the room at her and nodded.

JACOB STOOD JUST behind Victor Kozak as the man took the microphone, thanking everyone for coming, and for honoring Josef Smirnoff. He told a few tales about his friend and talked about the way Smirnoff had loved Miami Beach and how the club had been a dream for him.

"Sparkling like the Miami sun!" Victor said. "He was my business partner. He was my friend. In his honor, we will rename the club—it will be *Josef's* when it opens to the public tomorrow night. While we faced senseless violence and his death here, we are a powerful people. We are South Floridians, whether we were born here or we were lucky enough to enter this country and find this paradise as our home. We are strong. And, in his name, we will prevail!"

As Kozak spoke, Jacob kept his eyes on the room. He also mused that Kozak didn't think that peddling escorts or drug dealing were really bad things to do. Illegal, but not bad.

He saw the police—in uniform, and undercover—and the agents in the room. And he knew each of them was watching for the first sign, so much as a hint, of the barrel of a gun or someone reaching into a pocket.

But he was pretty sure Jasmine was right; guns would not be blazing. A killer must right now be waiting for whatever poison might have been in the special reserve to work.

"Make it quick," Jacob managed to whisper.

Kozak took heed. He quickly asked the crowd to honor Smirnoff's memory and enjoy his dream. Then Jacob took his arm and led him from the stage.

"Tell your men you feel sick," he said. "That I'm going to get you upstairs."

Kozak heeded him once again. "I am unwell! Sasha,

you will watch the east stairs. Antonio, you will watch the west. Alejandro, you will take between them. I am… I must sit down. Alone. The day… It has been too long. Mr. Marensky will see me upstairs to my office. Tell Ivan and Natasha they must remain the finest hosts."

"Yes, sir," Garibaldi said quickly.

"Hurry, and stumble as we walk up," Jacob said quietly to Kozak.

Antonovich nodded to the policeman at the base of the stairs; the man noticed Kozak, nodded in return and unlatched the velvet barrier. Jacob set his arm on Kozak's back and they headed up the stairs. Halfway up, Kozak pretended to stumble.

"Good, good, we keep going," Jacob murmured.

They passed the expected security. They made it to the door, and Jacob passed through it quickly. A cop met them in the hall.

"Getting Mr. Kozak to his office," Jacob told him.

The cop nodded.

They opened the door to the office—despite the massive security, Jacob entered first.

The office was empty. He had expected it would be. The killer would be waiting for Kozak to fall downstairs.

And everyone would think the day had been just too difficult for Victor Kozak. The man drank, he liked his cigars, and maybe he liked some of his smuggled product, too. His heart could just give out, after a day like today.

And the poison wouldn't be found during an autopsy,

since such substances would not fall into the realm of regular tests.

Kozak sat behind his desk and sighed deeply. "I really could use a drink!"

"I'm sure you keep something in here. Then again, I'm sure there are others who know you keep something in here," Jacob warned him.

"So. I will not drink. What do I do?" Kozak asked.

"We wait here. We see if someone comes. Maybe we call an ambulance. We let the crowd know you're in the emergency room, barely hanging on."

Kozak drummed his fingers on his desk, smiling. He stared at Jacob.

"You are not an art dealer, are you, Mr. Marensky? As a matter of fact, your name isn't even Marensky, is it?"

THE NIGHT SEEMED VERY, very long.

Jasmine moved about the floor as she had been directed, watching the stairs now and then. She saw Jorge with one of the catering crew, an FBI plant, and knew the vodka was probably already on its way to be tested.

But the bartender, she was sure, had just been hired on for the night.

She saw the other girls milling about the room, doing exactly what they had been told to do. They were pretty and silent and moving like robots. She watched the stairs. And to her relief, people began to leave.

While the club had been open and music—soft, somber music, much of it Russian—had played through the night, there was no dancing. After the speech, after the food and free-flowing alcohol, there was little else to do.

People murmured about coming when the club was up and running again. Big names in music had been booked before Smirnoff's death—they were probably still on the agenda.

She was doing her last round with coffees and coffee liqueurs when she saw the man, Donald McPherson Connor, stop Kari Anderson and talk to her. Then he slipped out the door.

A moment later, Kari followed.

Jasmine walked back to the bar quickly, ready to dispose of her tray and head out.

But there was a man at the bar. A little man with big glasses, a nerdy smile and wild bushy hair. "Don't," he said softly, then called to the bartender. "Another, my friend!"

"Pardon?" Jasmine asked, setting her tray down. She didn't care what he was saying; Jacob had Kozak upstairs. Things were coming to a head. And Kari was leaving with a man who just might be a very sick murderer.

"No, we're on it," the little man said. He spoke more loudly. "I mean, man, you're not just a beauty, lady, you are really cool looking. Those eyes of yours—emeralds!" He lowered his voice while pretending to study her eyes. "Special Agent Dean Jenkins, working in association with Wolff. We have a man following Connor and Miss Anderson. Keep your cover."

"That's very nice of you, sir," she said. "I work for the club. We don't date customers."

Garibaldi came up behind her. "Is there a problem?" he asked, glaring at the man who had just identified himself to her as FBI.

Dean Jenkins lifted his hands. "No, sir. No problem. I'm totally a hands-off guy, just complimenting beauty."

"He was very sweet. No problem at all," Jasmine said quickly.

To her relief, Garibaldi ambled away.

Jasmine turned with her tray of coffee cups and coffee drinks.

Natasha was standing there. "All is well?"

"Yes, of course."

"Have you seen Mr. Marensky?" Natasha asked her.

"I believe he went up with Mr. Kozak. He wasn't feeling well."

"They are upstairs? Still?"

Jasmine didn't have to answer. She heard the sound of an ambulance screaming through the night. People began to chatter nervously.

"Oh, my God! Victor!" Natasha cried. She turned and raced for the stairs. She was stopped by Garibaldi, with whom she argued. But this time, Garibaldi had apparently been given strict instructions by Kozak himself.

The wailing sirens stopped.

Natasha kept arguing with Garibaldi. Ivan was coming to join her, a strange look on his face. Was he frowning…or was that a look of satisfaction?

No one was near Jasmine at that moment. She heard a soft whisper at her ear.

Dean Jenkins was standing just behind her. "Jacob

is with Kozak. They're heading to the hospital. Word will be out that he collapsed and that they're afraid of a heart attack."

Jasmine let him know she had heard him, nodding slightly, watching along with the others. She moved away from him. As she did so, she felt her phone vibrate in her pocket. She quickly made her way close to the bar, behind a structural beam, and answered it, halfway expecting Jacob.

But it wasn't Jacob.

"Jasmine!"

It was Kari Anderson.

"Jasmine, I need to tell you—"

"Kari, what? Kari?"

Jasmine looked at her phone; the call had ended. The line was dead.

"So, I will die. Or I will go to prison for the rest of my life," Kozak said, sighing softly. He shrugged. He was lying in the back of an ambulance. Comfortable.

It was a real ambulance. But they weren't real paramedics manning the vehicle, though they would really take Kozak to the hospital, where he would really be admitted.

Jacob had feared that Natasha or Ivan might have made their way upstairs before he'd managed to get Kozak out, but the ambulance had arrived just in time—and Kozak had been shoved right in and the vehicle had taken off into the night. Within moments of closing the ambulance doors, Jacob had revealed to him that he was FBI.

"Victor, the whole operation has to go down," Jacob told him. "I'm sure if you give the district attorney any help you can, he'll make the best arrangements possible."

"I can give you cartels. Names of the men who come and go with drugs and drug money."

"I'm not the DA," Jacob said.

"And I discovered that I do want to live, however long that may be," Kozak told him. He sighed. "My friend, will you do one thing for me?"

"This will be out of my hands now, Victor."

But Victor smiled. "This is a small thing. Before I am locked away, will you see to it that I get just one more…"

"One more what?"

"Shot of my good vodka!"

"I will do my best, Victor. I'm sure you have an attorney, and… I don't know. But for now, your best service is to give us the men who did put those bodies in the oil drums and who left the headless men in the Everglades."

"They want me dead."

"All the more reason we need anything you have to find out just who is calling the shots."

Jacob felt his phone vibrating in his pocket.

Jasmine? She had saved the night, somehow suspecting there might be poison in the vodka. But her cover might be jeopardized…

He answered the phone quickly.

It was Dean Jenkins. "She's gone after Connor, Jacob. Your detective associate."

"What? How? When?"

"The commotion started with the siren. She disappeared. And she saw Kari take off after Connor. We have a man on him, of course, and I'm on my way out, but—"

Jacob leaped up and hurried to the front of the ambulance. "Stop, let me out—quickly!" he said.

"Yes, sir. But—"

"Proceed, get him to a room, guards all around," Jacob said.

"Will do," the driver promised.

The ambulance jerked to a halt. Jacob jumped out and began to run. He had blocks to run, blocks filled with tourists, diners, children...

But at least Connor's apartment was north of the club. At least...

Jasmine was a cop; a good cop. She'd be all right. She'd think it out.

She was also emotional. She was afraid Mary had disappeared because Connor had done something horrible to her. Afraid that same horrible thing might happen to Kari...

"Hey!" a man protested.

Jacob just nudged past him and quickened his pace.

THANKS TO DEAN JENKINS, Jorge and all the other police and agents working the case, Jasmine knew where to go. Connor's room. She knew the street, the hotel complex and the number.

Naturally, it was on a side street—one that was poorly lit, for the beach. One that was a bit austere, where the rich came to stay, unburdened by the noise and ruckus of the average working-man tourist.

She ran up to the building. She could see the lobby through the plate-glass windows that surrounded the handsome interior. It was an old deco place redone—velvet upholstered chairs and a check-in reception that wasn't a counter but a desk. She could see a man with a newspaper in the lobby, watching the door.

FBI. The man watching Donald McPherson Connor? If so, he was nowhere near close enough.

Jasmine hesitated, taking a deep breath. One more time—one more try.

She pulled out her cell and dialed Kari's number. It rang once and went straight to voice mail.

She pocketed her phone and tried for a regal and nonchalant manner. She waited for the clerk to walk back into the office behind the desk.

Then she sashayed through as if she belonged there, despite her elaborate if dignified waitress uniform. She didn't know the man with the newspaper; he didn't know her. She offered him a brilliant smile and sauntered on through to the elevator.

She realized, in the elevator, that Connor had taken the penthouse; a floor all to himself. She was surprised when the elevator let her choose the top floor without any additional security.

The doors opened into a charming vestibule, rather than a hallway. It was as if she had arrived at someone's grand house. Handsome double doors led into the apartment itself.

She tried knocking, her heart beating a thousand

drums a second. It would be illegal for her just to enter. She certainly couldn't force it open.

She waited...and no one came. The door might well be unlocked in such a building—in a good neighborhood, with security in the lobby.

And if she said she entered because she thought she heard a cry...

Just as Jasmine reached for the handle, the door opened.

Connor stood there, a gun in his hand.

"Ah, Jasmine," he said. "We've been waiting for you."

AS HE RAN, Jacob envisioned every manner of horror. His breath was coming hard; his calves were burning.

He knew he had made the right choice, running. It was the weekend on the beach, cars were bumper-to-bumper. For some reason there was an element of local society who thought it was cool to drive down Collins Avenue and show off their cars, some elegant, some souped-up, some convertibles, and some...just cars. Some with music blaring, and some discreetly quiet.

He was moving far faster than the cars.

And still...

He pictured Jasmine, bursting in on Connor. And Connor, ready for her, shots blazing before she could enter the room; Jasmine shooting back, maybe even taking the man down, as well. Injuring him, maybe killing him, but then lying there in a pool of blood, dark hair streaming through it, almost blue-black in contrast to the color of blood, eyes brilliant emerald as she stared into the night, and yet…sightless.

He had to stop thinking that way. He wasn't prone to panic; he'd have never survived his past.

His phone rang; he answered it anxiously, still running. It was Dean Jenkins.

"Natasha, Ivan, and the trio have headed to the hospital. I was just escorted out of the club. It went into lockdown. I found a place behind a dumpster by the cars. They all left together in the limo."

"Thanks. But no one goes in to see Kozak. They can be herded into a waiting room. They can't be near him. They can't know he's not really poisoned."

"We've got a 'doctor' ready to talk to them. As far as they'll know, Kozak is being airlifted to a trauma center where they're fighting to save his life."

"Thanks, Jenkins."

"Anything on your end yet?"

Apparently, Jenkins couldn't hear the way that he was panting. Just one more corner…

"Almost there."

He turned the corner and saw Connor's building, grand touches of Mediterranean-style along with the fine art deco architecture.

He ran through protocol in his mind—there was no right way to burst in on the man. This was a small part of what was going on; they didn't know who had killed Josef, who had tried to kill Kozak. The operation was in a crisis situation at the moment—and he needed to keep his cover.

He ran to the front, stopped briefly for a long breath

and to gather his composure. He saw the agent with his newspaper—and the tiny dolphin tie tack that identified him. A clerk in a handsome suit sat at the desk.

There was no time; Jacob entered the lobby, headed over to the man he'd never met, and greeted him. "Henry, how are you doing?"

"Great—fine fishing today. The kids come in tomorrow. We're going to take them over to Key Biscayne to see the lighthouse and then back to the Seaquarium—let them swim with some dolphins."

"Sounds like a plan. I've done the dolphin thing myself..." Jacob watched as the clerk headed to a back room. "How long?"

"Connor—just twenty minutes or so. Kari Anderson—fifteen. And then, another woman, just a matter of minutes."

Minutes...

Jacob headed for the elevator. It only took seconds for a bullet to find its mark. But as he reached the elevator, he realized the other agent had leaped to his feet to join him.

"I'm here now," Jacob said. "If I need backup, you'll know. If I'm not down—"

"Wait, there's just something you need to hear first," the agent said.

CONNOR NEVER HAD a chance to use his weapon.

Jasmine judged her distance—and the awkward way the man was holding the gun. She ducked low and took a flying leap at him, catching his legs, toppling him.

She'd been right; he was no gunslinger himself; he

was completely inept. His gun went flying and he let out a yelp that made him sound like a wounded kitten.

She straddled him, pinning him down. "Where's Kari? What have you done with her?"

"What have I done with her?" He seemed stunned.

"You bastard, what have you done with her?"

It would be unethical, but...she was still playing a role. She'd taken him, and she meant to get the truth from him, beat it out of him if she had to. She could get away with this—one high-class escort worried about another, attacking a man...

But just as she was about to deliver a good right to his jaw, she heard her name called.

She looked up.

Kari was standing in the archway to the next room.

At the same time, she felt strong arms wrap around her waist, drawing her off of Connor. She twisted and fought and turned—

Jacob!

Jacob, stopping her, when she had the man down...

"Let me go!" she demanded furiously.

"Jasmine, Jasmine, it's all right, you don't understand!" Kari cried. She rushed over to Connor, going down on her knees and trying to help the man up.

Astonished, Jasmine turned to Jacob. "What in God's name is happening?" she demanded, wrenching free from him. "Has everyone gone mad?"

Jacob turned and closed and locked the door and then looked at her.

For one moment, she felt extreme panic. Were they

all in on it? Was Jacob a turncoat, had he somehow tricked the federal government, was this all…?

No! She believed in him, she knew him, knew this couldn't be.

"I admit, I don't fully know myself," Jacob said. "But we need to give Mr. Connor a chance to explain."

Connor was up on his feet, standing next to Kari—who was protectively holding his arm. "What is going on?" Connor asked.

"You first," Jacob told him.

"I'm just a citizen," Connor said. "Trying to…do the right thing."

Kari spoke up then, passionately. "Donald's daughter came to Miami Beach and wound up modeling with the group." She let out a long breath. "She was found dead on the beach. Drug overdose."

"I hire them to get them out," Connor whispered.

"But…but…" Jasmine began.

"Nan, my daughter, talked to me. She was frightened. She said that she couldn't forget what she had seen, and she was afraid that someone knew she knew about the cocaine, and…then she was found dead. She wasn't an addict. She didn't do drugs. I called the police—there was an investigation, and it went nowhere. The officers tried, but Nan wasn't found anywhere near the club, she'd been out with friends, she'd said she was leaving, and…they killed her. I know they killed her. And I couldn't get justice, so—"

"Donald made arrangements for me to get away—far away. Hide out, and then start over," Kari said softly. "I wanted to get ahead so badly, be rich and famous…

be loved. I did things I'm not proud of. And I couldn't see any way out. But... Donald is a savior!"

"I need some kind of proof," Jacob said. "And if this is all true, Mr. Connor, I am so sorry and, of course, so grateful, and you're a fool, as well. You're risking your own life."

"My life does not matter so much anymore," Connor said flatly. "I have proof—our airline tickets. I was taking Kari to London tonight and then on to Yorkshire, to settle her with my family there."

Jasmine stared at them all, incredulous. And then it hit her. Connor's daughter...dead.

"Mary," she murmured.

"Mary?" Connor said. "Mary Ahearn?"

Jasmine stared at him.

Connor smiled. "Lovely young woman. She tried to help me find out which one of those horrible people was responsible for Nan's death. She tried to find out what was going on."

"So, you gave her a death sentence, too," Jasmine whispered.

He shook his head, looking a bit confused but still smiling. "Mary is alive and well. She's at my estate in Yorkshire, happily working on a play she's been longing to write. Of course, she'd love to be acting, and she's very fond of British theater, so she just might want to stay on. I asked her not to contact anyone from her former life until we were sure she was safe."

Jasmine would have fallen over. She felt Jacob's strength as his arms came around her.

He was staring across the room at Connor. "We will

have to verify your information. And I hope you're telling the truth. If so, I swear to you, we will get justice for your daughter. I'm setting you up with an agent to get safely out of the country. I don't think you'll be bothered tonight—there's too much else going on right now."

"Why did you call me? Why did you hang up?" Jasmine demanded of Kari.

"My—my phone died! I figured I'd call you and let you know I was leaving as soon as possible," Kari said. "And then we were getting my things, and Donald promised he'd come back and get you out, but he thought you were safe, that Jacob might be a criminal, but he'd be watching over you and then somehow, he'd get to you and—I'm so sorry!"

"One thing, please," Connor said.

"What?" Jacob demanded.

"Who the hell are you people?" Connor asked.

Chapter Twelve

It felt odd that it had just been that afternoon that Josef Smirnoff had been lain to rest. The ceremony at the club had taken place, and Jacob had ushered Kozak out in an ambulance, pretending the man was at death's door.

While Jacob and Jasmine were at Connor's suite, Kozak had gone into the hospital—and then out another door. He had immediately been ushered out to a FBI facility out west in Miami, in a little area with scores of ranch houses built in the 1970s, heading west off the canal that bordered the Tamiami Trail all the way across the south end of the peninsula to Naples, Florida.

Agents watching the hospitals—the beach hospital where Kozak had first been taken and the county hospital with the trauma center where he'd supposedly been brought later—had kept up with Jacob; Jasmine had been in touch with the MDPD who had in turn been in touch with the Miami Beach department, and everyone was on alert in case another attempt was made on the life of their new informant.

The entire inner core of Kozak's circle had arrived at the beach hospital, only to be assured that everything was being done, but that no one could see Victor Kozak. They had left together, but now Ivan and Natasha were back at the club with only Antonovich to watch over the doors. Natasha had been a mess, so Jasmine and Jacob were told—and had to be sedated when she was told that Kozak was on the verge of death.

Jacob had received many calls from both Ivan and Natasha, but he had told them both that he also had been kicked out of the hospital for having grown too insistent on seeing a man when an intensive care crew was busy trying to save him.

It was well after midnight by the time Donald McPherson Connor and Kari Anderson had been escorted to the airport—and safely onto their plane. Jasmine had gone from being ready to rip the man's throat out to being his best friend—they'd wound up talking and talking.

Kari had told her she'd wanted to say more, but she couldn't. She'd been afraid of what Jasmine might say or do, not at all certain that Jacob wasn't on the rise through the gang—or that Jasmine wasn't already completely beneath his control.

Connor had spoken about his own grief and then about dealing with it in the most constructive way he could.

"You really took chances," Jacob had told him.

"Not so much. I wasn't in on anything. I was just a client. Not someone making money—I was someone giving them money." He paused and shrugged. "And money is something I have. But it means nothing when you don't have the ones you love to share it with."

Jacob had to admit, he was a bit in awe of the man himself. Grief and loss often destroyed the loving survivors; Connor had channeled his resources and himself into saving others.

Naturally, Jacob hadn't immediately trusted what he heard, but with the information Connor gave him, the FBI offices were able to verify his story. The man did own a huge estate in Yorkshire. In truth, he had a title. He also held dual citizenship and spent as much time in the States—recently in the pursuit of saving the lives of young women—as in Great Britain.

And so it was two in the morning when Jacob and Jasmine returned to her apartment. She didn't seem the least bit tired. She was keyed up and alive, filled with energy.

"She's all right, Jacob! Mary is fine. She's in England...and I've been so, so afraid!"

He was sitting on the sofa, wiped out. She'd been all but flying around the room. In her happiness, that flight took her to fall down on his lap, sweeping her arms around him, her smile bright and her eyes as dazzling an emerald as could ever be imagined.

Her touch removed a great deal of his own exhaustion.

"She's alive, and you have to meet her. Oh, Jacob, to think I wanted to skin that man alive, that I thought he was part of..." Her voice trailed off and she frowned.

"What?" he asked, reaching out to stroke back a long lock of her hair.

"We're no closer to the truth. Nan Connor was afraid because she was a witness to a huge cocaine deal. But we don't know who saw her, and there's no way we can find out. We're pretending that Kozak is dying, but none of the gang has risen up to try to take over."

"Jasmine, as far as I know, they wouldn't dare do so. They don't believe that Kozak is dead as of yet, and they won't dare play their cards until they do."

"Where do we go from here?"

"Everything is in motion. I don't even call the shots from here on out. I'll go out tomorrow to interrogate Kozak, but it's going to be up to men with much higher positions than mine to determine what our next steps are. Kozak was grateful just to be alive." He paused, looking at her. "That was an amazing save tonight—the poison in the vodka. How did you know?"

"When he talked about his special reserve, it occurred to me that he'd be the only one drinking it. I'd hoped I'd find out who had brought the bottle and handed it to the bartender, but the guy was from the catering company and he said the bar had been set up when he got there, with the instructions that the special reserve stuff was for Kozak and Kozak only."

"Impressive." He smiled, watching her eyes. "You are a veritable beast. I thought you were going to rip Connor's head off. We're lucky you didn't shoot. He had a gun, right? You need to slow down—you could have gotten yourself killed."

"I could see he didn't know what he was doing with the gun," Jasmine said. Then she frowned. "How did you know that he wasn't going to kill anyone?"

"The agent watching him, Special Agent Daubs, Miami Criminal Division. He'd overheard Connor and

Kari talking. And he watched them. Said he was a pretty good judge of men, and I guess he was."

"I'm glad," Jasmine said softly.

"So now, once again, we wait. Tomorrow, I'll spend some time out with Kozak. And you and Jorge and others will be on the beach, waiting, ready to move if anything does break—play your part. But don't go anywhere near the club."

"I still have my uniform."

"If they call you, let me know right away. And for now—"

"Tonight?" she asked seriously.

"Sleep would be on the agenda."

"Ah, yes, sleep."

"Perhaps some rigorous exercise to speed the process," he suggested.

"We are still playing roles," she murmured.

"Jorge did say we were method actors."

"We can always work on method," she whispered.

Jacob wondered vaguely what it was about a special woman, that her slightest whisper, the nuance in her words, her lightest touch, could awaken everything in a man. There was no one in the world anything like her, he thought.

She stood, reaching for his hand. He rose, smiling. In the bedroom, they both saw to their weapons first. They barely touched, shedding their clothing in a hurry.

He went down on the bed, patting the mattress, and for a moment, she stood, sleek and stunning as a silhouette in the pale light from the hallway. She moved with grace, coming to him, and then she was next to him, in his arms, and if anything, they were more frantic that night to touch and to tease and to taste one another. To make love.

Later, when they should have been drifting off to sleep, she rose up on an elbow, looking at him, empathy in the ever-brilliant sheen of her eyes. "Forgive me, but…"

He knew what she wanted to know. So, he told her about growing up in Miami at first and moving to New York. Falling in love with Sabrina in high school, college, the service…

"Going off to the Middle East," he said. "She was always so worried about me. And she was vibrant. Full of life. We were happy. I'd done my service and I knew I wanted to head into the FBI Academy. I was certain I'd make it. We never thought… Well, she was diagnosed, and three months later, she was gone."

"I am so, so sorry."

"It was over ten years ago now," he told her, rolling to better see her face, stroke her cheek. "But you… hmm. Can't figure how you manage to be unattached. Of course, Jorge told me that you do have a tendency to shut a guy down before he can ask you out."

"Jorge talks way too much."

He laughed softly and pulled her into his arms. "That's all right," he told her. "I'm not an easy man to shut down."

She grinned, indicating their positions. "I didn't try very hard to shut you down."

He laughed and she was in his arms again.

SHE WAS NO good at waiting. She would never make it full time in undercover work.

Jasmine actually tried to sleep after Jacob left. His phone had rung far too early, letting him know that a car was coming to take him to the safe house where Kozak was being guarded. But sleep was impossible. She made coffee, washed and dried her hair and was tempted to try to do her own nails, since she had a rare moment of downtime. She reminded herself how incredibly happy she was—how grateful.

Mary was fine, alive and well. Kari was fine, too. They'd met a man who was trying to prevent future wrongs.

Still, someone within the gang was truly cold-blooded. At least eight people were dead because of the person within who considered murder to be a stepping-stone to criminal power.

If only Jacob were there to bounce her theories off of. They worked well together. Even when they were just playing roles. But the roles had become so much more. She'd found someone who seemed to really care about her, who could be with her, for all that she was, for what she did.

These roles would come to an end. That didn't mean they had to stop seeing each other, but her life, her work, was here. And his life and work were in New York.

It was foolish to think about the future. In the middle of this, she couldn't even be certain that either of them had a future. She had faith in herself and faith in him and all their colleagues—but no one entered into law enforcement without recognizing the dangers.

Worrying about the future was not helping her keep from crawling up the walls.

She couldn't call a friend and go out. She was still undercover. And Jacob had told her not to go near the club.

She was on her third cup of coffee when she realized that she could call Jorge. She was so antsy she'd probably annoy him, but Jorge never seemed to mind. As the thought occurred to her, she felt her phone ring.

"Jorge!"

"Hey, gorgeous, whatcha doing?"

"I was about to call you. I'm waiting. Doing what I was told to do. Climbing the walls. Being such a desperate cop I'm ready to watch a marathon of *Desperate Housewives* with you."

"Well, I have a reprieve for you. I'm on my way. All sanctioned. Come out to the corner. I'll be by for you."

"Perfect. Jeans okay?"

"Jeans and sneakers. Great. See you in five minutes."

"This is cleared with Captain Lorenzo—and the FBI?"

"Yeah, we're supposed to be heading to a music venue controlled by the gang. Top groups. Acting like normal people. Waiting like the rest of the folks around us, finding out if Kozak is going to make it. Gauging their reactions."

"Okay!" Jasmine rang off and shoved her phone into her cross-body handbag. She hurried out, carefully locking her apartment, all but running by the bathers out by the pool, aware of the bright sun and the waving palms.

A car pulled over to the curb; it wasn't a car she knew, but an impressive SUV. FBI issue for work down here?

Jorge rolled down the passenger-side window. "Hop in!" he said cheerfully.

"Where did you get the car?" she asked.

"City of Miami Beach," he said. He was smiling broadly, but she frowned. Something about him didn't seem quite right.

But while she and Jorge might never have discussed their personal lives, they were solid working partners. They always had one another's back. He would die for her...

It wasn't until she was inext to the car that she realized Jorge wasn't alone in the car.

There was a man in the back, but Jasmine's focus went to the fact that he had the business edge of a serious knife against the throat of a woman he'd shoved down in the seat. The young woman was trying desperately hard not to snuffle or cry out, with that blade so close to her artery.

It was Helen Lee, the sweet and lovely young woman with whom she and Kari had shared the runway.

Helen was absolutely terrified.

The man with the knife smiled. She was not entirely surprised to see who it was.

"Welcome, Jasmine. Now, Jorge, drive. And no tricks, no running us off the road. You wouldn't want my hand to slip. You wouldn't want to see this blade slice right through Helen's throat, would you? Jorge—

drive. Now. Jasmine, smile. Please. It will keep my hand so much steadier."

Jasmine's gun was in her purse, but she couldn't reach for it then. So was her phone. She believed that the man would slit Helen's throat.

As she slid into the car, she kept her bag clutched tightly in her hands.

FROM THE OUTSIDE, it looked like any other house. It sat off 122nd Avenue and Southwest Eighth Street—the Tamiami Trail there and farther west—or Calle Ocho when you headed way back east toward downtown Miami.

Built in the 1970s, it was a ranch-style home like many of the others surrounding them. It had a large lot, but so did several other houses in the area. This house, however, had a little gazebo out front, covered with vines—a fine place for an agent to keep guard—and a large garage and a few storage sheds out back.

The living room was like any other living room. It had a sofa and some plush chairs and a stereo system and a large-screen TV. The windows were all barred—but then, so were many of the other houses in the area, a deterrent to would-be burglars.

Just like so many other houses, there were signs on the fence that warned Beware of Dogs, and the dogs were the kind for which people should be wary. Signs also warned about the house being protected by a local security company, one used by many of the other residents of the area.

There was a kitchen, usually well stocked. There was a well-appointed gym, but then again, other people had home gyms. A dining room sat between the living room and the kitchen. The house boasted four bedrooms.

One of those bedrooms had no bed.

It had a table and chairs, and it was where guests were often required to engage in conversation with those who had brought them here.

Kozak sat in one chair. Jacob sat in another. Also at the table was Dean Jenkins—the man Josef Smirnoff had first approached in fear for his life.

One other man had joined them, Carl Merrill, a prosecutor from the United States Office of the Attorney General.

"As I told Jacob—before I realized how determined my would-be murderer was—I have never killed anyone," Kozak said.

"Your actions have resulted in the deaths of many," Merrill said.

"I can give you so much," Kozak told him. "But I must have a deal. I must."

"What is that you think you can give me? We've got you, head of an organized crime gang, and enough evidence of your activities to prosecute," Merrill asked.

"Names. I can give you the names of men who look squeaky-clean, who are working with the cartels out of South America. There are bigger fish than me in Miami."

"Victor," Jacob said, "you can't even give us the name of the man who wants you dead, who wants to take over the Deco Gang. Let's see—he's been working for you. And we know he forced a lethal dose of cocaine into a young woman who was a model for you. And he's likely responsible for at least three corpses in oil drums in Broward County and three headless corpses in the Everglades."

Kozak spun on him. "I don't kill. And I don't order executions!" he said angrily. "If I knew, could a murderer have come so close, would I have been about to drink poison?"

"Deals have yet to be made, Victor. We need help now. Who locked the door to the balcony on the day that Josef Smirnoff was killed?" Jacob asked.

"Josef." Kozak sighed. "I can't go to a federal prison...not in the general population. We had reputations. There are too many men who might think me guilty of crimes I did not commit. A man in my position does not deny violent acts to others of his kind. A reputation is everything. I let mine grow as it would."

Jenkins leaned forward. "Victor, let's start here. Did you know that Smirnoff contacted me?"

"No, I did not."

"Had he been acting nervous in any way?"

Kozak appeared to think about that and slowly shook his head. His voice was husky when he spoke. "If he was afraid, he would not have shown it anyway."

"Do you believe he suspected you?" Jacob asked.

"If so, he shouldn't have."

"Was he sleeping with Natasha—were they a real couple?"

Kozak hesitated on that one. "Yes, she was...strong. And good."

"So, you inherited Natasha along with the leadership," Jacob said. "She had the key to the balcony yesterday."

"There is only one key. She had it because I would not be present."

"Do you think it is Natasha who might be trying to kill you? Would she be hard enough to have one of her girls killed—and to order the execution of those men?"

Kozak smiled. "Natasha, she is a woman. But in business...this business? Natasha serves," he said softly.

Jacob had to wonder at that.

But Kozak was convinced of the truth of his words. He shook his head. "I don't know, I really don't know. As they say, keep your friends close, but your enemies closer. I have kept my people close. I don't know how they can be hiring these killers, desperate people."

There was a knock at the door. The agent who was the house's "owner" stepped in. "Special Agent Wolff, a word."

"Now?"

"Yes, sir. Now."

Jacob politely excused himself. Outside the room, he realized the agent was anxious.

"It's a call from Captain Lorenzo, sir, MDPD. Our men on the beach were following a car out of the club, but they lost them on the causeway. I—"

He stopped talking and handed Jacob the phone.

The man on the line quickly, tersely, identified himself as Captain Mac Lorenzo.

"I don't know how she did it, but Jasmine managed to contact this number and leave her phone on. She's in a car—they're headed west somewhere. Jorge is driving, Jasmine is in the front. There's a man in back, and from what I can hear, he's taking them somewhere. It sounds as if they're headed for an execution. We've got men on it, but they keep losing them. I've already asked the Feds to hop on it as quickly as possible, but you were close to that group. I'm hoping you might know where they're being taken."

Jacob froze for a split second; he felt as if the life had been stripped out of him.

"I need the exact location those headless bodies were found," Jacob said. "Speak fast, I'm already moving. And keep the others back. If the killer feels cornered, he'll kill whoever he has close out of spite. Get me backup, but keep the backup back."

Lorenzo kept talking. Before he finished another sentence, Jacob was in a car and heading west down the Tamiami Trail.

"Not so slow that the police notice us. There's no need to risk another of the city's finest."

Hearing the voice of the man in the back, Jorge cast a quick glance toward Jasmine. His eyes were filled with agony. She knew how he felt.

A quick look in back assured her there was already a fine line of blood creating a jagged necklace along Helen Lee's throat.

Jasmine and Jorge would both fight, play for time, for the life of another, as long as they were both still breathing.

There was no way to let him know she'd gotten her

hand into her purse, and that she was pretty sure she'd hit the number one; a priority call that would hit the phone Lorenzo had just for communication with her.

But would Lorenzo know where they were going? How could he know when she didn't know?

West. They were headed west. Jorge was driving as slowly as he could reasonably manage without drawing the man's ire or suspicion. He was in no rush to bring them to their destination. They were off the beach now, across the causeway on a long, long drive that seemed to be taking them out to the Everglades.

It was a land a few of the hardiest knew well, where airboat rides could be found, where the Miccosukee kept a restaurant and reservation lands, where visitors could find out about their lives and their pasts.

A place where, no matter how many hearty souls worked and even lived, there were acres upon acres that was nothing but wetland, part of the great "river of grass," filled with water moccasins and alligators, even pythons and boas.

"To the Everglades," she said aloud, as they whipped past the Miccosukee casino.

She turned around and stared at Ivan Petrov.

"You want to kill Jorge and me. Why?"

He eyed her coldly and then smiled. "I don't believe that Kozak is dead. He's the one who brought Marensky in. You did something with his drink. Marensky called the ambulance, and now...now they do not report that Kozak is dead."

"Whatever your argument with me, why Helen?" she asked.

His smiled deepened. "She happened to be there," he said.

Ivan Petrov. They should have figured; they had looked at Kozak, at Natasha, at the goons... They would have gotten to Ivan. He was never off the list.

"I need some guarantee you're going to keep Helen alive," Jasmine said. "Then Jorge and I will do as you ask."

"You are with the government," Petrov said.

"I swear to you, I am not an FBI agent. Neither is Jorge."

"Then you are trying to take the lead, playing up to Kozak. Well, they have cold feet. The enterprise will never be what it should be under Kozak. He is a weakling—he doesn't know how to remove what festers among us. Drive, Jorge. And turn around, Miss Jasmine."

The casino was behind them. Minutes were counting down. They were coming up to Shark Valley when Petrov told Jorge to slow the car down.

He couldn't be going to Shark Valley! There were trails and bike paths, tourists and rangers all about. Unless he meant to kill anyone in his way.

They didn't turn into Shark Valley. They passed the entrance, and the Miccosukee restaurant to the right on the road.

Then suddenly, Kozak said, "Here."

Here? She knew of no road here...

"Now!" Petrov commanded.

Helen let out a scream as the knife pierced her flesh. Jorge turned.

Jacob was met by Mickey Cypress of the Miccosukee Police. The man was in his early forties, lean, bronze and no-nonsense. He'd been waiting for Jacob right outside the entrance to Shark Valley.

"You don't want to go exactly where the bodies were found," he told Jacob. "The Everglades is literally a river, and the bodies were carried until they were snagged by the mangrove roots." He had a map out on his phone and he pointed to a spot that seemed to be just beyond a canal where they stood.

Jacob glanced at the map. Suddenly, two giant male alligators went into some kind of a battle in the canal.

"Leave them alone, completely alone," Cypress told him. "There's a marshy trail we can take through here, and a small hammock. That's where I think we'll find their killing grounds. There was no road there before, but some fairly solid ground. I think they created their own way."

Cars drove up next to them. Men in suits got out—the backup.

Cypress looked at him. They were probably good agents; they just didn't look ready for a trek into the water and marshy land.

"Special Agent Wolff!" one of them called.

Jacob looked at Cypress.

"I'm with you," Cypress said. "Um, if you're trying for stealth…"

Jacob nodded and headed back to the agent calling to him. He asked him to hold their position and keep a line of contact open. He walked back to Cypress.

The local cop told him, "Trust me, I know how to

get there. I was the first on call when the bodies were found. I've been on this."

"I trust you," Jacob assured him. "We need to hurry. I got after them right away, but they still had a head start."

"Then we move."

Cypress started over a small land bridge, just feet from the male alligators defending their turf. Water came cascading over them from a massive flip of a tail.

They kept walking.

IVAN PETROV HAD his knife—and a gun on his belt. He kept the knife at Helen's throat.

Jasmine clung to her purse.

"Drop it!" Petrov commanded. His knife moved ever so slightly.

Helen gulped out a cry. Tears were streaming down her face—silent tears. She tried not to sob and stared at Jasmine—any movement would cause a great chafe of the knife against her throat. Her eyes were both imploring and hopeless.

"Go!" Petrov commanded. Jorge walked ahead; Jasmine behind him. He sheathed the knife and drew his gun.

"I don't understand, Ivan. Who were the people in the oil drums?" Jasmine asked.

"Well, I will tell you," Petrov said. "The first, his name was Terry Meyers. He thought he should manage the club—and the women. That was long ago, when Smirnoff had barely begun to settle into South Florida. Smirnoff was, in fact, surprised when Meyers failed to arrive for a meeting. The second, well, he failed to show with a payment. He made me look bad. You can't deal with people who don't deliver on goods or who don't make their payments. It's bad for business if you don't follow through. Same deal for the third loser."

"The three who weren't in the drums," she said. "They were the ones who killed Josef."

"Yes, actually, they were very good. I was sorry to see them go. But you see, they couldn't live. If they had been apprehended, well... I did hire them personally."

"You admired them so much, you beheaded them," Jasmine murmured.

Jorge glanced back at her; she was doing the right thing, keeping him talking. There were two of them. They could survive this. They had to get Helen in a safe position, and then they could rush Petrov—he couldn't shoot them both at the same time.

But they had to get Helen away from him first.

Jorge suddenly stopped, letting out a shout.

"Move!" Petrov commanded.

"There's a gator ahead in the path," Jorge said, falling back by Jasmine.

"That's fine," Petrov said, dragging Helen around and waving his gun at the small gator on the trail. "We're almost there." He fired the gun toward the gator. The creature moved off into the surrounding bracken.

There was some kind of a structure there, a broken-down shack, a remnant, Jasmine thought, from the time when various Florida hunters had come out and kept little camps.

It was now or never—Petrov had just fired the gun,

he was looking away, he was holding Helen, but the gun wasn't directly at her throat.

Jasmine didn't let out a sound; she made a silent leap for the man.

She bore him down to the ground. Helen slipped free, screaming hysterically. She began to run back in the direction from which they had come, screaming all the while.

Petrov's gun hand was flailing; in a second, the barrel would be aiming at Jasmine's face.

But Jorge was there, stomping on the man's wrist, kicking at the gun. It went flying into a gator hole, filled high with water.

But Petrov wasn't going down easily. He caught Jasmine and flipped her down to the muddy earth.

Jorge kicked his head.

Petrov had the knife on his belt now; Jasmine went for it. Seizing it from Petrov, she sliced his hand. He cried out as blood gushed.

And then, a gunshot fired. They all went still.

The knife still tightly in her grip, Jasmine turned to the sound.

Standing casually now before the rotting wood of the old shack was Natasha. She shook her head.

"Men. They are worthless, eh? They continually think they are in charge, and they have no idea. Ivan! A silly girl and these two. You have a gun, you have a knife, and they best you. What would you have done without me, Ivan?"

She shook her head again at Ivan, but then smiled at Jasmine. "Yes, you are one who knows how to manipulate a man, eh? It's the only way, until you have seized the position of real power. And then they will bow down before you, and they will become your toys, and you will command them. It's a pity you must die. It will be hard for me... Oh, maybe not so hard, because now Ivan and I will have to crawl through this wretched swamp looking for that silly Helen. If she doesn't kill herself first. Maybe it will not be so hard. I will kill your friend first, so you can watch him die, and he will not have to watch you die? How is that?"

"I should have known you were the one with ice-cold blood running in your veins—right from the beginning," Jasmine said.

Natasha shrugged. "Me? I am not so much the killer. I like others to do the killing."

"And then you kill the killers."

Natasha smiled. "Ivan killed the killers. I simply cut off their hands and their heads...and fed them to the swamp. Enough talk." She took aim.

But Natasha couldn't have known what hit her.

He came from behind. His arm came down on hers and Natasha screamed with shock and pain as she lost her grip on the gun, as she was tackled to the ground.

Jasmine stared.

Jacob was there. Impossibly, Jacob was there. He'd slipped around silently from behind the hut, and he was now reading Natasha her rights and handcuffing her, heedless of the fact that he was on her back and pressing her face into the mud.

He looked at Jasmine, his recitation breaking. He nodded toward Petrov, who was trying to turn and escape.

Jasmine turned to Petrov, but another man—never before sensed nor seen—went sliding past her.

"Not to worry. I've got that one."

Jacob yanked Natasha to her feet. He spoke into his phone. Jasmine and Jorge were still just standing there, incredulous to be alive, when men—a little ridiculously dressed in fine blue suits and leather loafers—came running through the brush.

"Got her, sir," one of them said to Jacob, taking Natasha. He was young, younger than Jasmine. A brand-new agent, she thought, but ready to do whatever was asked of him, including running through a swampy, mucky river in his office attire.

He was gone; Natasha was dragged away. And then they heard shouts; Ivan had been apprehended, as well.

"Helen—Helen Lee is running through the swamp," Jasmine called out, her voice echoing through the mangroves and pines.

One of the agents came back. "No, ma'am, we've got her. She's fine. A little scratched up and still hysterical, but…we've got her. She's going to be okay."

"Hey, I'm coming with you," Jorge said. "She knows me. I'll get her calmed down."

And then, for a moment, Jasmine and Jacob were standing there alone. A large white crane swooped in and settled down near them, seeing a fish in the shallow gator holes that surrounded them on the small hammock.

Slowly, Jasmine smiled. "Your timing is impeccable."

He let out a long soft sigh, and then he grinned. "So I've been told."

She raced across the mud and the muck that separated them and threw herself into his arms. And they indulged in one long kiss, both shaking.

"You are kick-ass," he told her.

"But not even a kick-ass can work alone," she whispered. "You saved our lives."

"Only because you were doing a good enough job saving your own life," he assured her. "Lord, help me, this may be ridiculous, but I think I love you."

"This may be more ridiculous," she said.

"What?"

"I know I love you!" she told him.

"Special Agent Wolff? Detective?" They were being summoned.

Hand in hand, they started back along the path. "Paperwork," Jacob murmured.

"And then?" she asked.

He wiped a spot of mud off her face. "Showers," he said. "Definitely showers."

She smiled and he paused just one more minute, turning her to him.

"And then," he said, blue eyes dazzling down on her, "then figuring out our lives. If that's all right with you, of course."

She rose on her toes and lightly kissed his lips.

She could have done much, much more, but others were waiting—and there were some very large predators near them. The human ones might be down, but while she wasn't afraid of the creatures here, she wasn't stupid enough to get in their way either.

She broke the kiss and looked into his clear eyes. "It's all right with me."

Epilogue

The woman hurrying toward him along the long stone path over the castle's moat was truly one of the most stunning creatures Jacob Wolff had ever seen. His initial opinion of Jasmine had never changed.

Her skin was pure bronze, as sleek and as dazzling as the deepest sunray. When she smiled at him, he could see that her eyes were light. Green, he knew, an emerald green, and a sharp contrast to her skin. She had amazing hair, long and so shimmering that it was as close to pure black as it was possible to be; so dark it almost had a glint of violet. She was long-legged, lean and yet exquisitely shaped, even in jeans, sweater, boots and a parka.

She didn't pause when she met him. She threw her arms around him and leaped up so he had to catch her, and laughed as he spun with her in the rising sunlight that did little to dispel the chill of the damp day. No one saw them.

Donald McPherson Connor's "estate" had proved to be a castle. Small, admittedly, but *a bit of an historic home*, as Donald called it, and far out in the countryside of northern England.

"Best vacation ever!" she told him, sliding down to stand.

He looked behind her. They were no longer alone.

He'd headed out for a walk on the grounds right after morning coffee; Jasmine had stayed behind to wait for Mary and Jorge—the two had been in a lengthy discussion of just how cold it might get during the day, and throwing her hands up, Jasmine had indicated he should go ahead.

His hike had been serene. The countryside seemed to stretch endlessly, beautiful rolling land with horses and sheep and cattle.

He'd had vacation time built up—you couldn't just hop off to an amusement park or the mountains or the French Riviera in the middle of work when you were deep in an undercover operation. He felt this time off was well deserved, for himself and for Jasmine. It had been impossible for them to turn down Donald Connor's suggestion that they come to visit Mary.

They had a suite in the tiny castle. No windows facing a beach, but instead an arrow slit that looked out over a stretch of land that was misty and green. They had long nights together and days with amazing friends.

Jorge and Mary caught up with them. "Off to the theater, if you're sure you don't mind the walk," she said.

Mary was as gentle and sweet a woman as Jasmine had said, wide-eyed and kind, with blond hair as long as Jasmine's raven tresses. Mary had cried when she'd come to the airport to meet them; she'd been so sorry to have frightened Jasmine, to have put her in danger. But Donald had explained that he was just an ordinary citizen—he'd needed Mary to not say a word to anyone until she was safely out of the clutches of the Deco Gang. She'd been lucky to have an up-to-date passport.

Mary told them that Natasha had instructed her they had more escort work, and the intended client was a man she had seen come and go with different suitcases. She had suspected the man was part of their drug operation. And by then she knew that the girls weren't really models, that the so-called models were being prostituted, and that she just might not be able to do all of the things expected of her. And that if they suspected that she knew too much—or anything at all—she just might wind up dead.

Jasmine explained to her over and over again that it was all right—they'd put a stop to it all, and possibly saved many more lives.

Natasha had gone through people quickly. In her mind, so it seemed, people were as disposable as silverware or linens that were no longer needed.

There was, of course, a note of sadness to it all. They could do nothing for Donald's daughter; she was gone. But while he couldn't be happy, the man was grateful and satisfied. Her killers would find justice.

"A walk is great," Jacob assured her.

"Okay, so maybe these ugly shoes are good," Jorge said, slipping an arm around Mary's shoulders. The two of them moved slightly ahead. Mary began telling Jorge about the history of the area and how old the theater they were about to attend was.

Jasmine looked up at Jacob and smiled. "It's a children's play we're seeing, you know."

"Mary wrote it—I can't wait to see it. Donald will join us there?"

"Exactly," Jasmine said.

Mary suddenly stopped. She looked back, grinning. "Hey, I was talking to Donald this morning, earlier. He thinks you guys should have your wedding here."

Jasmine stopped dead. "Mary, we're visitors here. And we haven't—" she looked at Jacob, a flush rising to her cheeks "—we haven't even…"

Talked about marriage.

They had talked about everything else. A long-distance relationship seemed like half measures. But then, what to do? Jasmine loved the people with whom she worked, and she loved Miami. Jacob understood. They were looking into a transfer for him to the Miami office.

It had only been a few weeks since they'd survived the murder attempt in the Everglades; they'd been mulling over all possibilities in the meantime. And of course, finishing the endless paperwork, the United States Attorney General, the police, evidence, witnesses and everything else that went with the end of such a complicated case.

Kozak was going into witness protection; both Ivan and Natasha would be prosecuted for the murders they had committed. Victor Kozak had given the authorities all they needed to apprehend a number of the drug smugglers in Miami Beach, and information regarding them that might lead to solving many of the cold cases on file across Greater Miami.

Antonovich, Garibaldi and Suarez had worked for Kozak, and though they had faced stiff interrogations, they hadn't actually been proved guilty of any crimes. Jacob hoped that the three would find better employment.

Petrov still had a problem believing he was going down—he'd tried to throw everything on Natasha, but in turn, Natasha had tried to throw everything on him.

The man had been a fool, Jacob had told Jasmine, when they had been alone and curled together one night. He'd underestimated the power of a woman. And, smiling, he'd assured her, "That's something I never would do."

Now, Jacob grabbed her hand, forcing her to look at him. "I don't know—the wedding here. What do you think?"

"I..." Jasmine looked at him.

Jorge let out a sound of frustration. "Oh, come on! You know there's going to be a wedding. Seriously, who else could either of you live with forever and ever, huh?"

He was right. You were very, very lucky in life when you found that one person who complemented you in every way.

Jacob looked into her eyes, so strong, so gentle, so giving... Dazzling.

He figured he could answer for both of them. "I don't really care where we get married. As long as we do. And I do need to get you all to New York. I have a friend—I've worked with him and the love of his life, and her family owns an Irish pub on Broadway. Her brother is also an actor and can score all kinds of theater tickets, Mary."

"New York—oh, I would love it! But first—a wedding in a castle. We'll let you do the honeymoon alone, and then an after-honeymoon in New York. Perfect!" Mary caught Jorge's hand and the two walked on ahead.

Jacob caught Jasmine's hand. He went down on a knee. "Detective Adair, will you marry me? In a castle, at the courthouse, Miami, New York…wherever? I cannot begin to imagine my life without you. It can be here, there or anywhere."

Jasmine came down on a knee, as well. "My dearest Special Agent Wolff, yes. Here, there, anywhere," she assured him. "I can't imagine my life ever again without you!"

He leaned forward, and they kissed. And kissed…

Until Jorge called back to them. "Hey! Time for that later. We're going to miss the play."

Laughing, Jasmine rose and pulled him to his feet. "The rest of our lives," she said.

"The rest of our lives," he agreed.

* * * * *

COMING SOON!

We really hope you enjoyed reading this book. If you're looking for more romance be sure to head to the shops when new books are available on

Thursday 23rd April

To see which titles are coming soon, please visit
millsandboon.co.uk/nextmonth

MILLS & BOON

FOUR BRAND NEW BOOKS FROM
MILLS & BOON MODERN

Indulge in desire, drama, and breathtaking romance – where passion knows no bounds!

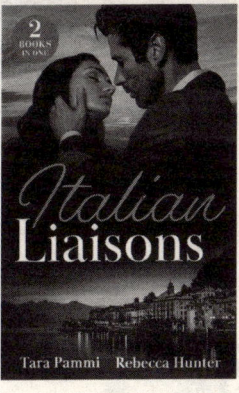

OUT NOW

Eight Modern stories published every month, find them all at:

millsandboon.co.uk

TWO BRAND NEW BOOKS FROM
Love Always

Be prepared to be swept away to incredible worldwide destinations along with our strong, relatable heroines and intensely desirable heroes.

OUT NOW

Four Love Always stories published every month, find them all at:

millsandboon.co.uk

OUT NOW!

Available at
millsandboon.co.uk

MILLS & BOON

OUT NOW!

Available at
millsandboon.co.uk

MILLS & BOON

LET'S TALK
Romance

For exclusive extracts, competitions and special offers, find us online:

- **f** MillsandBoon
- **X** @MillsandBoon
- **◉** @MillsandBoonUK
- **♪** @MillsandBoonUK

Get in touch on 01413 063 232

> For all the latest titles coming soon, visit
> millsandboon.co.uk/nextmonth

MILLS & BOON

THE HEART OF ROMANCE

A ROMANCE FOR EVERY READER

MODERN — Prepare to be swept off your feet by sophisticated, sexy and seductive heroes, in some of the world's most glamourous and romantic locations, where power and passion collide.

HISTORICAL — Escape with historical heroes from time gone by. Whether your passion is for wicked Regency Rakes, muscled Vikings or rugged Highlanders, awaken the romance of the past.

MEDICAL — Set your pulse racing with dedicated, delectable doctors in the high-pressure world of medicine, where emotions run high and passion, comfort and love are the best medicine.

Love Always — Celebrate true love with tender stories of heartfelt romance, from the rush of falling in love to the joy a new baby can bring, and a focus on the emotional heart of a relationship.

HEROES — The excitement of a gripping thriller, with intense romance at its heart. Resourceful, true-to-life women and strong, fearless men face danger and desire - a killer combination!

 — From showing up to glowing up, these characters are on the path to leading their best lives and finding romance along the way – with plenty of sizzling spice!

To see all our latest titles, please visit

millsandboon.co.uk/NewReleases

MILLS & BOON
MODERN
Power and Passion

Prepare to be swept off your feet by sophisticated, sexy and seductive heroes, in some of the world's most glamorous and romantic locations, where power and passion collide.

Eight Modern stories published every month, find them all at:

millsandboon.co.uk

MILLS & BOON
Love Always

Celebrate true love with tender stories of heartfelt romance, from the rush of falling in love to the joy a new baby can bring, and a focus on the emotional heart of a relationship.

Four Love Always stories published every month, find them all at:
millsandboon.co.uk/LoveAlways

MILLS & BOON
HEROES

At Your Service

Experience all the excitement of a gripping thriller, with an intense romance at its heart that will keep you on the edge of your seat. Resourceful, true-to-life women and strong, fearless men face danger and desire – a killer combination!

Eight Heroes stories published every month, find them all at:

millsandboon.co.uk

MILLS & BOON

HISTORICAL

Awaken the romance of the past

Indulge your fantasies of delicious Regency Rakes, fierce Viking warriors and rugged Highlanders. Be swept away into a world of intense passion, lavish settings and sumptuous details as you awaken the romance of the past.

Four Historical stories published every month, find them all at:

millsandboon.co.uk

MILLS & BOON
MEDICAL
Pulse-Racing Passion

Set your pulse racing with delectable doctors, hot-shot surgeons and fearless first resonders. Escape to a world where life and love play out against a high-pressured medical backdrop, where emotions and passion run high.

Louisa Heaton — *Best Friend to* HUSBAND?
Finding a Family NEXT DOOR

Charlotte Hawkes — *Nurse's* BABY BOMBSHELL
Zoey Gomez — *The Single Dad's* SECRET

Annie Claydon — *The GP's* SEASIDE REUNION
Kristine Lynn — *A Kiss with the* IRISH SURGEON

Six Medical stories published every month, find them all at:
millsandboon.co.uk

MILLS & BOON
A ROMANCE FOR EVERY READER

- **FREE** delivery direct to your door
- **EXCLUSIVE** offers every month
- **SAVE** up to 30% on pre-paid subscriptions

SUBSCRIBE AND SAVE

millsandboon.co.uk/Subscribe

GET YOUR ROMANCE FIX!

Get the latest romance news, exclusive author interviews, story extracts and much more!

blog.millsandboon.co.uk